MH00770946

A PRAYING MAN

A PRAYING MAN

NOT EVERY PRAYER IS MERCIFUL

HARMON SNIPES

John,

Hope you enjoy the book

Harmon

De Oppresso Liber

Deeds Publishing | Atlanta

Copyright © 2013 - Harmon Snipes

ALL RIGHTS RESERVED - No part of this book may be reproduced in any form or by any electronic or mechanical means, including information storage and retrieval systems, without permission in writing from the author, except by a reviewer who may quote a brief passage in a review.

Published by Deeds Publishing
Marietta, GA
www.deedspublishing.com

This is a work of fiction. Names, characters, places, and incidents either are products of the author's imagination or are used fictitiously. Any resemblance to actual events, locales, or persons is purely coincidental.

Library of Congress Cataloging-in-Publications Data is available on request.

ISBN 978-1-937565-56-5

Books are available in quantity for promotional or premium use. For information write:

Deeds Publishing
PO Box 682212
Marietta, GA 30068

info@deedspublishing.com.

First edition 2013

10 9 8 7 6 5 4 3 2 1

ACKNOWLEDGEMENT

Acknowledgements are tough, because in any project there are usually many to thank. So, let me start with Sue, my wife and best friend of thirty-nine years now, the local Barnes and Noble who asked me to facilitate the weekly writers group, and, of course, the aforementioned writers group who listened to, read, and commented on this book weekly for over a year. In particular, my thanks go to John Witkowski, my right hand man in the group, a true student of the craft of writing.

Then there are the people who have advised me along the way—J. D. Smith, Investigator for the Gwinnett County District Attorney's Office, whose input and advice was invaluable; Corporal Jake Smith, no relation, of the Gwinnet Police Department's Public Information Office who gave me a personal guided tour of their facilities, answering a multitude of questions; Abra Hewell Summers, who did the first edit of A Praying Man and greatly improved its content; and Jessica Jennings Naunas for her medical insight.

In life's journey it's the experiences you have and the people you meet along the way who shape you and make you who you are. Your parents, grandparents, brothers and sisters are among them. My mother may have been the hardest working, most unselfish person I ever knew. However, there is a special group I would like to thank—that would be the men of U. S. Army Special Forces with whom I served. I had the privilege of standing shoulder-to-shoulder with some of the finest soldiers who ever wore the uniform.

Now, the list wouldn't be complete without thanking my son, Rob, and daughter, Amy, who never said, "Dad, don't be silly, you can't write."

This book is dedicated to the victims of human trafficking and sex slavery. For every one that is rescued, dozens more end up dead or imprisoned in their own private hell. Many are children. There is no punishment bad enough for those involved in this crime against humanity.

CHAPTER ONE

Gwinnett County, Georgia

ANDREA CRANDALL TRIED TO SCREAM. HER ATTACKER'S HANDS were too quick. One closed onto her mouth with a piece of tape, shutting off any volume that would attract the attention of neighbors. The other hand reached behind her head, clamping down like a vise. Wide, dark menacing eyes glared from under the black ski mask. Another masked attacker appeared and helped to push her back into the house.

She covered her protruding belly with her arms, "My baby!" Her muffled voice struggled to scream through tape and the attacker's large hand. The man clamped down even harder, the pressure sending a shock of pain down her neck. Her fear filled eyes locked onto a pair that projected madness and pleasure at the same time.

Andrea kicked at her attacker while trying to protect her stomach. Her attacker's first blow found its first target, then the second....

***

Mickey Pyle stood in the darkness of the tree line. Through the den window he could see the first flicker of flames seeking the accelerant he had spread in strategic places. Some drywall, some furniture and, oh yeah, the drapes. He always liked the way flames climbed a nice set of expensive drapery.

Gasoline wasn't his normal choice. The fumes could ignite prematurely and blow you through a wall if you used too much or were careless. But, it was efficient. His personal preference was for something harder to detect, more subtle ignition-wise, and that had a slower burn rate for viewing pleasure. But the client seemed insistent, something about a message and wanting it to be fast and complete. *Whatever.*

As the flames began to illuminate the back yard, he could see the dark lump near the fence. Putting down the dog was just part of the job. People were such creatures of habit. Let the dog out before bedtime then let it back in when you go to bed. Whether out or back in, you have to turn off any alarm system.

Pyle rubbed his right eye and recoiled slightly from the touch. Shooting the woman before he threw her down the basement stairs wasn't in the plans, but that was before she tried to gouge his eyes out. He pulled out his throwaway cell to contact the client and debated the pros and cons of telling him the woman might be dead. It was a short debate. No—shit happens. Before he could make the call the kitchen erupted. He heard sirens in the distance growing louder while neighbor voices shouted. It was time to leave.

***

A half-mile from the entrance to the suburban neighborhood north of Atlanta, the smoke caught his attention. Now, Jack Crandall had a sick feeling he hadn't felt in over twenty years.

It was light gray to white and stood out against the midnight sky. Crandall had been having a relaxing drive home from his second shift as a pharmacist at the local hospital. He increased his speed and turned into the neighborhood with a slight fishtail in his dark green Nissan Pathfinder.

The houses were awash in light, inside and out. Some neighbors stood in small groups in front yards, others near the street. Crandall blew his horn, warning them as he drove past.

Blue, red and white lights that danced off the low cloud of smoke added to his anxiety. "Please God, not Andrea!" He prayed aloud.

It was your standard suburban neighborhood. A mixture of single and two-story homes, most with vinyl siding. Some had basements, some did not. Crandall's was a single-story ranch with a basement and dark gray siding. Second street on the right. Houses on his side of the street had the luxury of backing up to a stand of trees affording an extra measure of privacy.

When he made the turn his fears were realized. There were two fire trucks and a police cruiser. Beyond those he saw a paramedic truck and another police cruiser. The cacophony of lights and machine sounds greeted him and brought instant pain to his eyes and ears.

Half his house was rubble, the other half scorched and soaked. Front windows on the standing half were smashed inward. Fingers of black charred lumber reached up from the ashes as if trying to grab that standing half and drag it into the chasm the blaze had created. At least one neighbor's roof showed signs of assault from burning embers. A police officer stepped from the shadows, waving his flashlight, a reflective vest over his blue uniform.

Crandall hit his brakes, slid to a stop on the damp pavement and rolled his window down. The pungent odor of wet ashes, burnt wood and melted plastic combined with lingering smoke and diesel fumes burned his eyes, nose and throat. He leaned his head out, cleared his throat and shouted, "That's my house. My daughter-in-law was in there. Where is she?" he shouted in rapid fire succession, his eyes refusing to blink.

The officer grabbed the door, leaned in and pointed to his left with the flashlight, "Park your vehicle in front of my cruiser, please. You'll have to ask the medics about your daughter-in-law."

The officer started to turn away. Crandall grabbed his arm and took a nervous breath, "What about the baby?" he asked, with a raspy tone, just above a whisper.

"I'm sorry. You'll have to talk to the medics, sir." The officer's mouth turned down at the edges, his eyes gave a sorrowful expression. He backed away and waved Crandall to the spot in front of his patrol car.

Crandall parked and bolted from the SUV. From the officer's expression he expected the worse, but prayed he was wrong. He ran the twenty or so yards to the paramedic truck. It was a deep red with gold fire department lettering on the sides. The rear double doors were open with the inside area brightly lit. Medical equipment lined the walls and two gurneys collapsed to their shortest position sat in the middle of the truck bed. Both were empty. That vision raised his anxiety level along with his pulse, and a hundred thoughts raced through his head. Two men in navy blue uniforms stood at the rear watching the firefighters working on the remaining hot spots.

A man who looked to be in his late twenties turned toward Crandall and started to speak, but Crandall beat him to it. "That's my house. My daughter-in-law was in there. Where is she?" he repeated just as rapid fire as the first time.

The medic spoke in a calm tone, "The female was your daughter-in-law?"

"Yes. Where is she? What about the baby?" Crandall repeated, trying to regain his normal breathing.

The medic opened his mouth as if to answer then closed it without a word. Crandall started to step forward and ask again. He stopped in his tracks when he felt the pressure of a hand gripping his shoulder.

The surprise of the touch caused his entire body to tense at first then relax as he turned around. Crandall found himself looking at a man about two inches shorter than his six feet two inches. A navy blue cap with "GCPD" embroidered across the front sat upon the man's head. Though shorter, the man's shoulders were noticeably broader than Crandall's. Covering the broad shoulders was a blue windbreaker with the county police logo just over the left breast.

Crandall started to speak but was interrupted before the first word could escape his lips.

"I'm told you are Mr. Jack Crandall. I'm Detective Sergeant Paul Brennan," the man said extending his right hand. He touched the back of Crandall's upper arm and with gentle pressure guided him away. "Let's find a quieter place where we can talk."

Crandall nodded in silence.

***

The two men sat in the front seat of the unmarked white Chevy Impala. Police Radio traffic crackled through the speaker of the radio mounted under the dashboard. A robbery in progress at a convenience store just off I-85 was announced.

Brennan reached over and turned the radio off, removed his cap and tossed it on the dashboard. "Take a deep breath Mr. Crandall." He rubbed the top if his head and his well trimmed sandy brown hair. In the available light, a square jawed face with friendly, yet probing, gray blue eyes met Crandall's gaze.

Crandall looked down at his hands. They were shaking. He followed Brennan's advice, tilted his head back and let the breath out. He closed his eyes. The flashing lights intensified through the windshield while his eyes sensed strange shadows. All this combined to place him in a near hypnotic state. "Would you please tell me Andrea and the baby are okay?"

"I can't tell you that because I don't know," Brenan started. "I can tell you she was transported to the medical center in Duluth. That was the closest ER."

Crandall pressed his face in his hands. "My God, that's where I work. That must have been her ambulance I passed on the way home."

Brennan started the car. "I can tell you she was alive and semi-conscious when they left. I'll drive you there. Do you mind if we talk on the way?"

Crandall stared straight ahead, "No."

Brennan weaved his way between the county emergency vehicles, "One more thing. I can't take notes and drive, is it okay if I record our conversation?"

"Yes, I guess so," Crandall covered his mouth and coughed, still trying to shake off the effects of inhaling smoke and fumes.

Fishing a black micro cassette recorder from the center console, Brennan pressed the record button. He spoke the time, date, and the words, "Crandall Fire." Then he placed the recorder in a small receptacle between them.

"Mr. Crandall," he began, "I know this is tough but please bear with me. This fire has every indication of arson," Crandall stiffened as Brennan continued, "Do you know anyone who would want to do you, or a family member, harm?"

Crandall took in another deep breath and let it out with a deliberate slowness. His hands stopped shaking, and he stared straight ahead. "No."

CHAPTER TWO

Jack Crandall had not slept. It was just after 8:00 in the morning. Friends at the hospital offered him sofas and even empty bed space. It was no use. He did avail himself of a shower and some scrubs to replace the only set of clothes he still possessed.

He spent most of the night as a wanderer, traveling the quiet halls and locating coffee at friendly nursing stations. He did not linger, for the conversation would go places he was not ready to visit.

Andrea was in surgery. She had been found at the bottom of the basement stairs, a bullet wound in her lower back. It was concluded she was pushed down the stairs after being shot.

The first time he broke down that morning was when the doctor told him the baby did not survive. Despite all efforts, his granddaughter was in too much stress. He would never hold her, watch her take her first steps or be called Grandpa. So, he kept moving on a journey to nowhere. Whenever he stopped the tears would begin anew. The hardest part would be the phone call to his son, Mark, in Iraq. He needed to use up all his anger, to be the strong one. He spent so much time dwelling on what to say to Mark he only now realized he also needed to tell his daughter, Lisa, and Andrea's mother and father. They were divorced, but both were still close to Andrea. Mark would be the toughest. The smile on Mark's face every time he talked about becoming a father was an image permanently etched in his memory.

When Mark shipped out, three months before, Andrea came to live with Crandall because doctors had warned her of a high possibility of complications with the pregnancy. It did not occur to him the biggest complication would be his own past.

And so he walked in aimless random patterns until the P. A. system clicked overhead, a robotic female voice announced, "Jack Crandall, please report to the O. R." He felt a slight weakness in his knees accompanied by tightness in his chest as he headed toward a stairwell. He did not want to see anyone he knew in an elevator.

***

Crandall stood motionless in the shower just off the surgical suite replaying the current horror in his mind like a bad movie or some nightmare from which he could not wake. The hot water from the shower had a curious combination of both sting and comfort as it cascaded down his neck, shoulders and back, loosening tense muscles. It was the first time in over thirteen hours he felt in any way relaxed.

Dr. Eberhart, the surgeon, said Andrea was critical, but chances of survival looked good. Twenty-four to forty-eight hours would be needed to be sure. She had lost a lot of blood and her right kidney was damaged. The .32 caliber bullet had also punctured the uterus, causing a loss of amniotic fluid, but Andrea would be able to get pregnant again. This provided little comfort to Crandall.

After his shower he returned to Andrea's bedside in the Intensive Care Unit, holding her hand while he listened to the ventilator do her breathing. Other equipment and monitors buzzed, clicked and whirred in his ears. Crandall rubbed her hand, cold from the chilled IV fluids, in an attempt to warm it. Nurses he saw on a regular basis would stop by and lay a gentle hand on a shoulder, trying to provide some reassurance. There was a rollercoaster of emotions, but as time wore on anger began to dominate.

***

Detective Brennan had asked if he could come by for a follow-up later in the day. The two agreed on 4:00 PM if he was up to it. Crandall felt he would never be up to it, but understood it had to be done. So, with a fresh set of scrubs, a two hour nap, another shower and more caffeine he was ready to face the Sergeant. A patrol car picked him up at the hospital and delivered him to county police headquarters.

Brennan opened the door of the interview room and allowed Crandall to enter first. He crossed the stark room and seated himself in the gray steel chair on the opposite side of the table. Brennan sat on the front side, nearest the door. Crandall slumped in his chair. The loose fitting scrubs made him feel smaller than his muscular two-hundred-five pounds. The last time he looked into a mirror his facial color was closer to that of his gray hair, ashen. The circles under his eyes made him feel even more tired.

"I'm sorry for your loss, but I was greatly relieved to hear Andrea will recover," Brennan said as he placed his notepad, recorder and pen on the table.

With a weary voice, Crandall answered, "Thanks, but it will be touch and go for the next forty-eight or so."

"I'll keep her in my prayers."

Crandall fidgeted in his chair. "A praying detective?"

Brennan appeared a bit surprised at the response. "You find that amusing?"

"No, it's just not something you tend to associate with police work."

Brennan picked up the pen and clicked it open, "Well, I believe it helps, how about you?"

"I pray. I certainly did last night."

Brennan leaned back, "I find it helps me handle most of the crap I deal with. It's therapeutic. Anyway, I need to ask you something very important."

Crandall clasped his hands together on top of the table and stared at the wall behind Brennan, "Okay."

Crandall redirected his attention as Brennan leaned closer, "Why did you lie to me last night?"

CHAPTER THREE

MICKEY PYLE STEERED INTO THE STRIP MALL PARKING LOT. ABOUT half way down, just past the super market, he turned down the row of spaces in front of the Mail Box Store.

He pulled into the third parking space and put the Chevy Malibu rental in park. The silver Rolex Mariner he picked up two hours ago at the pawn shop was showing 4:05. Pyle liked the way this Alex Caruso guy worked. No phones except for cryptic messages like last night. No face to face contact ever. Just Corey Gibson's brother, Ed, as the go between when it was first set up, then a series of phony names, mail boxes, and throw away phones.

He stepped out of the car, closed the door and took a quick look around. Straightening his short ponytail, he put both hands in his pants pockets and walked to the store in a practiced shuffle, slumped so people would have a hard time getting his height, weight, and build correct.

Four days ago he had rented a mail box in the name of James Harrison. Inside he picked up an overnight delivery package.

Back in the car he closed the driver's side door and opened the package with his pocketknife. Inside, as promised, were $10,000 cash, a note, and a new preprogrammed phone. When he finished the note, he opened his cell phone and dialed a number.

"Corey," he said to the person who answered, "It's here as promised. Now he wants us to do the job in Nashville. When that one's over we got the Dallas thing, then the final two hundred grand—

"Yeah, I told the old bastard she was still alive the last time I saw her before I closed the door to the basement—"

"No shit, still alive? Well, she was a tough little bitch, but she didn't see our faces and we'll be long gone tomorrow. If he wants we can come back later and fix that—"

"You got it, I'll meet you at the bar in Midtown we were in last night before the job. We'll turn in the rental in the morning and head out—"

"Right, but first I need you to get on the horn and tell Leon we'll meet him and the local idiot he lined up in Nashville around noon tomorrow. They should have all the info on the target by then. See you at the bar."

As he backed out of the parking space, he made a mental note to change his hair from blond to black and switch his tinted contacts when they got to Nashville. Maybe it was time to ditch the ponytail, though he was fond of it.

***

"What do you mean?" Crandall asked, his hands still clasped as he looked across the gray steel table at Sergeant Brennan. He listened to the slight hollow echo of this own voice in the interview room. The stark off white walls and meager gray steel furniture made him feel clammy and added to his fatigue. *Not much in here to use for a weapon*, he thought for no particular reason.

Brennan looked up at the video camera mounted in the corner of the room, pointed at his eyes then made a slashing sign across his throat. He turned his attention back to Crandall, "Exactly what I said, you weren't convincing me last night, and I need to know why."

Crandall stiffened in his chair, "Which part, Sergeant?"

"Maybe all of it."

Brennan held his hand out, moving it up and down while he talked, like a father trying to get information from his uncooperative teenager. "Look, Mr. Crandall, this is what I have. The arson guys tell me there was enough gasoline in the house that an arson dog would hit from two blocks away. You're lucky the fire station was so close."

Crandall sat up straight, leaned forward and looked straight at Brennan, "Yeah, some lucky bastard I am. Look, I'm very tired Sergeant, please cut to the chase."

Brennan picked up his pen and looked at it while he rolled it between his fingers, then dropped it on his pad and looked up, "Okay, either someone with a hard on for you did it themselves or they hired a really stupid arsonist. Or maybe some idiot burglar did it. Or maybe you hired the really stupid arsonist. Gasoline is not the first choice of a pro."

Crandall slammed both fists on the table and stood, the chair sliding backwards from the abrupt movement. He could no longer hold his anger in check. "Damn it, Sergeant, I've had about two hours sleep in the last thirty-six! Somebody burned my house down, Andrea is on a ventilator in critical condition and my granddaughter is dead. On top of that I have to call my son, who's in the middle of a war zone, my daughter at Vanderbilt and Andrea's parents and tell them the great news. And you're telling me I might be a suspect in this shit? So, tell me Sergeant, do I need a lawyer or not, because no fucking body with a badge has read me my rights!"

Brennan leaned back, a crooked smile instead of surprise at the outburst on his face. "I wondered how long the stoicism would last. No, you are not a suspect at the moment. But, for now I'll keep all options open, it's my job. And, if you think you need an attorney, by all means get one. So, please have a seat."

Crandall continued to look Brennan in the eye as he lowered himself into the chair and pulled it closer to the table. In a sudden move Crandall grabbed his right forearm with his left hand.

"You okay, Mr. Crandall?" Brennan asked.

Crandall rubbed and massaged the entire length of his forearm, "Yeah, just a muscle cramp. Sorry for my outburst, but you're starting to piss me off."

"No need to apologize, I seem to have that affect on people. However, outburst aside, we still need to clear up why the hell you felt the need to lie to me. I don't want to wind up charging you with withholding evidence or obstruction. So, if someone has an ax to grind with you, you need to level with me. You weren't exactly believable when you said *no*."

Crandall looked at the ceiling and rubbed his eyes in a hopeless attempt to rid them of the pound of sand each felt like it was carrying. Just above a whisper he asked, "Do you know a man named Jerrod Wilkins?" then lowered his gaze back to meet Brennan's.

Brennan tilted his head to the right, a puzzled look on his face as he seemed to study Crandall, "Yeah. The one I know is a federal marshal, played football for Georgia Tech. Are you trying to tell me the feds burned you out?"

Crandall sat and stared. Exhaustion permeated his voice once again. "No, but I can't tell you any more until you talk to Marshal Wilkins."

Brennan placed his forearms on the table, opened his palms toward Crandall and leaned in, his forehead furrowed. With deliberation he tapped the table with the edge of his hand as he sounded each word, "Are *you* in the Witness Protection Program?"

"You'll have to talk to Wilkins."

Brennan placed both hands on the table and stood, "I'll be right back and don't touch anything. I'm going to put a call in to Marshall Wilkins."

When the door closed behind Brennan, Crandall picked up the recorder and pushed the rewind button. Nothing happened. Then he pushed play. After a few seconds he determined the tape was blank. *Well, at least he didn't record all that shit*, he thought through the fog that was his mind. He placed the recorder back on the pad.

After what seemed like an hour to Crandall, but was closer to ten minutes by the clock on the wall, Brennan opened the door to the interview room and stepped in, closing the door behind him. He walked to his chair and seated himself. "Well Mr. Crandall, Marshall Wilkins wants to meet with us tomorrow 10:00 AM, public place. You up for it?"

Crandall sighed, "Yes, but—"

Brennan held up his hand, palm toward Crandall, "No buts, I'll pick you up at 9:00. Now, you're too damn tired to drive. One of our officers will drop you off wherever you say. We'll get your vehicle back to you if you'll just give us the key. Is there anything else you want to tell me today?"

Crandall shook his head, his eyes turned down looking at the table, "No—you'll find out *everything* tomorrow."

"Just one more item. We can make the call to Andrea's parents. We have people trained for that sort of thing."

Crandall felt some measure of relief, albeit a very small one. He leaned on the table, "Thanks, that would be a big help, but one last thing. I need some things from my basement."

Brennan began picking up everything to put back in his briefcase and placed his recorder in his shirt pocket, "We'll talk about that tomorrow. It's still an active crime scene." He looked up, "Since everything down there is smoke or water damaged, I assume you're talking about your gun safe."

Crandall did not answer. A knock on the door broke the silence.

***

Brennan watched as Crandall disappeared around the corner at the end of the hall. He stepped across the hall and opened a door about one quarter of the way. Inside was a man seated in front of a console filled with recording equipment and monitors. He leaned in, "Les, did you get the audio?"

Les looked up, "Yep."

Brennan leaned against the door frame, "Bury it for now and if you breathe a word of what was said in there to anyone I'll have you transferred back to patrol." He closed the door and started down the hallway in the same direction Crandall had just gone.

***

Crandall stretched and let the sun warm his face a few seconds before he sat himself in the passenger side front seat of the patrol car. In a strange way the warm rays felt comforting. The officer closed the door and started toward the driver's side. Crandall watched the officer's progress. *I don't know what will happen tomorrow, I'm just sure I have a decision to make.*

CHAPTER FOUR

JACK CRANDALL CHECKED HIS WATCH AS HE SAT NEXT TO ANDREA'S bed in ICU, *almost ten after six.* She was off the ventilator—a good sign—but still he had not seen her conscious.

After seven hours sleep on a sofa in the office of the pharmacy director, he showered and dressed in tan Docker slacks and a navy blue golf shirt he had purchased the day before. Feeling a little more human, Crandall spent an hour navigating military channels before reaching his son's company commander. Second Lieutenant Mark Crandall was on patrol in one of the Sunni neighborhoods just outside Bagdad with three squads of Iraqi Army.

Department of Defense directives did not allow him to *break the news* to Mark directly. The C. O. and the company first sergeant would *do the deed.* A chaplain would be on hand if available. They were in short supply as of late. After that Mark would be allowed to call Crandall, but it would be several hours.

So, here he sat, holding Andrea's hand again. The rise and fall of her chest only gave him solace in that she no longer needed the respirator. One less whizzing, blinking machine to remind him she almost died.

Crandall stood, reached down and brushed Andrea's black hair from her forehead. He leaned down, kissed her cheek and whispered in her ear, "They will be found." Then he straightened and walked out of the ICU.

In the hall he turned on his cell phone to find three messages. Two from Andrea's parents saying they were on the way from Virginia. The third was Sergeant Brennan reminding him he would pick him up at 9:00.

For the first time in over thirty hours he felt the urge to eat. Before now it was going through the motions. A bite or two of a sandwich then walk away. He knew he should, but there was no appetite. Crandall made his way to the cafeteria.

Outside and now sated, he walked about the hospital campus. Near the professional building that housed the medical offices he found a stand of shade trees with a wooden bench nestled beneath their branches. A light breeze carried the smell of fresh mulch and flowers as he watched the landscapers go about their chores.

With a half hour before he was to meet Brennan, it was time to make the next dreaded call. Lisa's first class didn't start until 10:00.

"Hi, Daddy," an exuberant voice leapt from the earpiece in his phone. "I was going to call you later today. I've got some great news." The happiness in her voice brought a momentary smile to his face.

Crandall took a deep breath and closed his eyes, "That's great, Lisa, what is it?" He wanted to get it over with but his baby girl was happy about something. Whatever it was he wanted to know what made her voice light up this much. He could almost see her eyes shimmer with excitement.

"Well, I met the greatest boy last weekend. His name is David. He's so much fun to be with and he's sooo cute. He's in Naval ROTC. He wants to be on submarines. We've been out every night, but don't worry I do all my studying before he picks me up and he gets me home early. We're going for pizza and a movie tonight, it's Friday."

"Just last weekend, what do you know about him?" He trusted her, but he was still a father.

"It's okay daddy, he's my roommate's brother."

Crandall choked back tears, "Oh, Carly's brother. That's great, hon, hope to get to meet him soon."

"What, daddy, no jokes about girls should stay away from sailors?"

"Not today, hon," his voice trailed off.

"What's wrong, Daddy?"

She sounded so happy he hated to even start but...

By the time he finished Lisa was crying, "Do you need me to come home?"

"I'll let you know later, Lis, but for now stay there, have some fun with David and I'll call you tomorrow. I've got to go. I have a meeting with the police. Please be careful." Crandall closed his flip phone.

He had always felt guilty she never knew her mother. Just the stories and pictures. There had never really been a mother figure in her life, not even a grandmother. He had done it to protect her and Mark, but now he felt it had been the wrong decision. Crandall stared at the landscaping crew while the droning of their mowers and trimmers grew in volume.

At first he thought he was dreaming. It was the loudest noise he had ever heard. The concussion threw him nearly six feet through the air out of his cot, causing him to land on the hard baked ground. His head swam as if he were somewhere else, detached from reality. Distant screams of agony filled the air but were muted by the ringing in his ears. Dirt and debris fell from the sky, sounding more like rain impacting the top of the tent where he was sleeping. Pain shot through his right thigh as the heavy canvas tent teetered, groaned and gave way, collapsing onto its occupants. The center pole landed next to his head with a loud thud, missing his head by inches.

Others in the tent yelled above the din of confusion in an attempt to communicate. He struggled to his knees, looking for the closest exit through the dust and darkness under the collapsed tent. A tiny sliver of light to his left caught his attention. His mind calculated about ten feet. If they were under attack he would need his weapon, but why was a peace keeping force under attack?

With the weight of the tent and debris bearing down on his back he crawled to the edge of the canvas toward the light.

He reached the edge of the tent and it curled around his body enough for him to see out. A fine dust and smoke filled the air and choked his lungs as he tried to decide what direction the screams came from, but they seemed to come from all directions. Fear consumed him and he sucked in his breath, coughing again from the dirt that continued to fall and the faint smell of plastic explosives entered his nostrils. Just a few feet in front of him lay an arm with no body shrouded in a camouflage uniform sleeve. He needed to move, but was unsure what direction to take.

Something warm and sticky ran across his lips and chin. He looked down and saw blood drip onto the ground. He touched his nose and pulled back his hand to see blood on the tips of his fingers.

"Jack," someone called in the distance.

"Move, damn it!" He said to himself.

"Jack," the voice grew louder.

"Jack, are you OK?"

Crandall looked around. He was half way back to the hospital and had not realized he had even stood up. Next to him was one of the E. R. nurses, *Cindy*, he thought, but was unsure through the haze. "Are you OK?" She repeated, shaking his arm gently.

"Yea—uh, Cindy—yeah I'm okay." He said peering into dark, near black eyes. "Just still tired I guess. Thanks for asking."

Cindy was a full foot shorter than Jack, but had an attractive figure that even the hospital scrubs could not hide. They had dated for quite a while about two years or so back after her divorce. But, he always built a wall between himself and women. A wall he wasn't able to tear down some twenty-two years later, though he cared deeply for her.

Now a wave of shame washed over him as he emerged from his fog. He could not remember her name at first, though he remembered the spring-like scent of her shoulder length brown hair after a shower, the smoothness of her skin when he would caress her back and the soft sensual feel of her lips when they kissed. He remembered all these things and ached to hold her again. But the wall remained and would not be breached. Only an occasional trip outside the iron-gate was allowed, and when he returned, it closed and no one could follow.

"Look Jack, you need to get out of the hospital, sleep in a real bed. There's an extra bedroom at my house. You could stay there for a couple of days 'til you find a place." Her face was tense with worry.

Jack straightened up and rubbed his face and eyes. Thanks, but I'm getting a room at the Courtyard for a few days. Insurance will pay for it, and I need to be alone."

"Okay, but the offer will always be there. I won't press."

"Thanks again, but I need to go. I've got to meet the police again." Crandall said, then walked away. In his mind he could feel those dark eyes following him. If he turned around now it would only make things worse.

When he reached the side entrance Brennan was waiting, leaning on his car, "You're late."

Crandall walked to the passenger door, grabbed the handle and looked across the top of the car, "Frankly, Sergeant, I don't give a rat's ass."

CHAPTER FIVE

Sergeant Brennan turned the white unmarked Chevy Impala into the shopping center at Old Alabama and Haynes Bridge. A quick left then a right into the parking space in front of the Starbucks.

Through the glass front of the store he could see Marshall Wilkins had already arrived and was standing at the counter. He was hard to miss. Standing at least three inches over six feet, even the lines of his black pinstriped suit jacket could not hide the wide shoulders and tapered back. If one didn't know he was nearing forty, they would think he could suit up and play linebacker for Georgia Tech again like he had eighteen years before.

Brennan and Crandall both got out of the car. Brennan closed his door.

Crandall paused, took in a deep breath and let it out. He looked up at the puffy white clouds drifting past on their journey from nowhere in general to nowhere in particular. "You know Sergeant, there's a change in the air. Fall will be here tomorrow, the leaves are starting to show the first hints of turning and a cold front is headed this way. My favorite time of year."

"Crandall," Brennan spoke, shaking his head, "I'm beginning to think you're schizophrenic. You were cranky as hell when I picked you up and all the way over here you don't say a word, just stare out the window with a blank look on your face. I thought about checking your pupils to see if you were on tranqs or something. Now you're all smiles and want to talk about the weather."

"Sorry if I'm not a good travel companion."

Both men moved toward the sidewalk on their sides of the car. Brennan bounced up over the curb, a spring in his step. Crandall reached the curb, hesitated and stumbled a bit getting onto the sidewalk."

"You okay, Jack?" Brennan asked.

"Yeah, just didn't pick my feet up enough. Let's get some coffee. You're buying, right?"

The three men sat in uncomfortable brown metal chairs around a dark brown metal table outside the store and around the corner from the main entrance. The store next door was empty; the going out of business signs still hung in the window. This cut down on the foot traffic and prying ears. The occasional auto was the only thing that intruded on their conversation.

Two *tall* and one *grande* cups of coffee sat around a folder that lay in the middle of the table. The light comfortable breeze Crandall was enjoying earlier at the hospital followed him to the Johns Creek area of metro Atlanta.

Wilkins lifted his Italian Roast, sipped, sat it down and tapped the folder. "I made some copies of the general information pertaining to Mr. Crandall's entry into WitSec. It concerns one Alex Caruso."

Brennan picked up the folder and began leafing through its contents and leaned back in his chair. "Yeah, I remember him. Organized crime, drugs, prostitution, money laundering, from Memphis. He tried to open a strip club here in the county two or three years ago, so we checked him out. Not sure why he'd even try, zoning laws made it near impossible. We figured he wanted to get into direct competition with the Mexican cartels funneling drugs up the I-85 corridor. Rumor was he was already working I-40 from the Midwest into Memphis and further east. Last thing we needed was a drug turf war, so we increased our efforts against the cartel backed gangs and pushed most of them out. Caruso's guys went home, the cartels went next door. So, is that the guy?"

"Yep, that's the SOB. The Memphis guys have been trying to get him for over ten years now, but no luck, just a few low level guys who don't even know who they work for. Anyway, I was assigned to Mr. Crandall's case five years ago because the original marshal retired. As for the details, I'll let Mr. Crandall fill you in. While it had to be cleared with us first, he's now free to tell you what you need to know."

Crandall held his cup with both hands and stared at it, disinterested in the conversation between the two lawmen.

Brennan turned to Crandall, "Okay, first, do you think Alex Caruso is involved in the fire and attack on your daughter-in-law?"

Crandall glanced up from the cup, "I can't be one-hundred percent but my gut says yes."

Brennan turned on his recorder, opened his notepad and started writing. "Most people in WitSec are from the inside. So, what was your involvement with Alex Caruso?"

***

Collierville, Tennessee

Alex Caruso sat on the balcony off the master suite of his white columned mansion in Collierville, Tennessee, east of Memphis. The pump from the outdoor spa provided a steady low hum in the background. He always enjoyed the view from the second floor on the east side of the house so he could catch the morning sun. It put him on a level with the trees on his four acre estate. He was fondest of the giant hundred year old magnolia tree seventy feet from the balcony and the sweet fragrance it provided in the summer months when the air was heavy and still. It would be another eight or nine months before he could enjoy it again. Just beyond the magnolia was a stand of oak and hickory that gave him seclusion from his nearest neighbor.

Fresh from the shower, Caruso was encased in a soft white Egyptian cotton robe, the left lapel embroidered in navy blue with *AC*. He read the local paper while drinking his second cup of coffee from the fine white china cup, the top edge trimmed in platinum. A copy of the Atlanta paper lay on the glass top table next to the tray holding a carafe, a cream pitcher, a toasted English muffin, and an assortment of jellies. The paper was open to a story about a fire and shooting in the northern suburbs.

His robe was a gift from his wife, Katherine. Though he liked the robe, he had little use for her. She was down the hallway in her own suite, sleeping off another vodka hangover no doubt. Divorce was out of the question, she knew too many secrets. And, her untimely death would raise suspicions and inquiries he couldn't afford either. For now his only hope was that her liver would give out. Until then, she was useful on those occasions when one of his dummy companies hosted local charity functions. After all, appearances were important.

His biggest worry was her sister. There was no easy way to cut off contact between the two. Angela was a loud mouthed demanding bitch who could only be kept in line with the knowledge of what might happen to Katherine, or Kate as she called her.

Caruso was pleased with the job he had done rebuilding his small empire after his release from prison. The reclaiming of territory and elimination of competition, some of whom had been friends before his visit to the Federal Corrections Institute in Memphis.

It had taken several years and careful planning. This time though he was much more selective about who surrounded him. But, there was still unfinished business. A thirst for revenge had driven him for over fifteen years. The search for those who put him in prison had consumed him. One P. I. he hired had died during the quest. Last he heard it was still a cold case with the Memphis Police, and it wouldn't do for him to be inquiring into what they found.

He ran his fingers through what wispy thin graying hair that remained on his soon to be bald head. The hard bulldog frame that he once used to bully and coerce his way up the food chain had become neglected and softened, but at sixty-two he now had others to do his heavy lifting. Caruso pulled his glasses down to the tip of a nose misshapen from the effects of absorbing too many solid rights, looked at his trees and smiled. *Things are moving along nicely,* he thought while picking up his cell phone and punching in the speed dial number.

In the kitchen on the first floor, his main bodyguard, Stan Allen, answered with a mumbled, "Yeah."

"Stan, I'll be making my visit to the city tonight. Make the arrangements for the delivery around 9:00 and the usual suite."

"Sure, any special instructions for Maxson?"

Caruso thought for a second, "Tell him a more recent vintage this time."

"Okay, boss. I assume we will be leaving at six for the normal dinner reservations?"

"My usual table. Take care of it and order some more vodka for the house. She gets really pissed when it runs out. Tell Tony we'll take the Town Car." He pushed the end button, put the phone down and reached for his cup, "Mr. Crandall, your pain is just beginning," he spoke to the trees and smiled again.

Memphis

Crandall blew on his coffee, sipped, then leaned back in his chair. "Me and Caruso, well it's a long story. But, the Reader's Digest version is I was screwed up when I got out of the Marines. Beirut really messed me up. I was too proud, I guess, to admit it. Caused a lot of problems with my father. A guy I knew, Sam Greggs, got me a job doing some street muscle with Caruso, chasing pimps, strong arming dealers." Crandall took in a deep breath, sighed, then continued, "A priest friend of mine was trying to help me, set me up with my wife. They tried to talk me into leaving Caruso. I was almost convinced, then the final straw was Caruso ordered me to kill a sixteen year old who was selling in Caruso's territory. I didn't do murder, especially kids, so I tried to scare him off... Caruso had someone else do it. I walked away. Then, for kicks I guess, he had Jane killed with our newborn baby in the back seat. I wish I had just killed the bastard..." Crandall reached under the table and grabbed his twitching left arm, "But," he sighed again, looked away to gain control of his emotions, "Instead I turned state's evidence, the Feds got me into pharmacy school, and here we sit. That about covers it."

"Well, that's enough for now," Brennan said as he turned off his recorder and put away his notebook.

Crandall lifted his now empty cup and turned it around, looking at it. Without looking up he asked, "So, if that's the end, may I ask a question?"

He looked up and across the table to his right at Marshall Wilkins. "Just how in the hell did this son-of-a-bitch find me?" He sat the cup down, placed both hands on the table and leaned closer to the table. "I thought you guys were supposed to keep track of these bastards?"

Wilkins appeared surprised at the questions, and cleared his throat. Before he could answer, Crandall's cell phone ring tone interrupted. He fished it out of the holder on his belt, "It's the hospital." He answered, listened intently for about thirty seconds, "I'll be there in twenty minutes."

"Andrea is awake."

CHAPTER SIX
San Antonio, Texas

THE MAN BEHIND THE COUNTER AT THE CONVENIENCE STORE WAS bored. No customers had been in the store for almost an hour and then only some teens from the college looking for alcohol. But, it was almost midnight and his store didn't have the best of locations. Now his interest was piqued by the yellow Volkswagen Beetle that pulled into the parking lot. Even with the dim light he could see that the driver was a young woman.

He whistled and a dark haired man appeared from the back room with a bucket and a mop. The medium-sized man went to the end of the aisle that led to the counter and cash register and began mopping.

The Volkswagen came to a stop in front of the double entry doors. The young blonde girl got out of the car, entered the store and went to the cooler along the far wall that held the chilled wine and beer. She retrieved a bottle of white wine from the cooler and proceeded to the counter, brushing past the man mopping.

The man behind the counter watched her every move, taking note of how her skirt hugged her hips. He then turned his attention to her breasts where his eyes studied the way the white silky material of her blouse accented her shape. When she reached the counter and placed the bottle in front of him, he made his way to her face and hair, "May I see some ID?"

"Sure," the young girl replied, taking her purse from her shoulder. She fished it out and handed it to the man. He took a glance and smiled. More than once he had seen these fake ID's from the college students that came to his out of the way store to purchase overpriced alcohol. He glanced around at the dim lit empty parking lot, took a quick check of the lack of traffic and nodded to the man with the mop.

As the man turned to the cash register, his partner pulled out a cloth bag that had been tucked into his belt opened it and pulled it over the girl's head in a single motion. She screamed and reached both hands to her neck. She struggled and kicked, trying to break loose. The man at the cash register reached out, grabbed her arms and pulled them toward him, pinning them against the dirty counter top and her against the front of the counter. He pulled back and down, pinning her chest against the top. The man behind her pressed against her, reached around and placed his hand across her mouth to muffle her shrieks.

The one with the mop secured the bag then wrapped his free arm around the struggling girl's chest. A third man came from the back room and grabbed her legs, lifting her off the floor. The man behind the counter released his grip as the others carried her toward the back room. He lifted her car keys from her purse, calmly left the store and drove the VW to the back door.

Once back at the counter he picked up the phone behind the counter and punched in a number from memory. When the party answered, he was brief. "We have one. We'll drop it off shortly." A second call disposed of the auto. A night like this made the man more money than the store did in two months.

Nashville, Tennessee

Mickey Pyle looked up at the mirror in the motel room bath while he towel dried his now black hair. After running a brush through it, he picked up one of the green tinted contacts and placed it in his right eye, then repeated the process in his left. After finishing the job with his blow dryer, he buttoned up his shirt and opened the door as conversation from the two men waiting for him greeted his presence.

One of the men sat on a double bed. The other was in the wooden chair at the writing desk, common to most hotel rooms. He straddled the chair, resting his arms on the top of the chair back facing the man on the bed. Each had a beer in his hand.

Pyle always considered himself quite a good actor. He had spent a couple of summers doing summer stock in his earlier legitimate life where he learned the value of makeup and disguise.

On the last job his hair was blond and eyes blue. Now his hair was black and eyes a deep green. But he had kept his pony tail. He had grown quite fond of it.

The new rocker bottom black and tan shoes had lifts in them that combined with the extra thick soles to make him two inches taller than his normal five feet eleven inches. By wearing thin soled shoes and slumping he could vary his height almost four inches.

A quick stop at the local thrift store had garnered him several sets of disposable clothes for tonight and future use. He finished toweling his hair and threw the towel in the corner on the floor between the bathroom wall and the bed. Then he pulled his hair into its customary ponytail.

Corey Gibson, from his seat on the chair, took a swallow of beer, "Mick, how come we don't wear disguises?"

Pyle sat down on the corner of the bed nearest the bathroom and started combing his still damp hair, "Because they won't remember you. I make sure I'm the one the witnesses remember. I draw the attention to me, and they forget about you guys."

Pyle rubbed the thick brown stubble on his face, looked at the man seated on the bed closest to the door, "Leon, you need to get back out and hook up with Porter and keep an eye on the target. I want to finish this one tonight if we get the opportunity."

Leon Allred guzzled down the last half of the can of Budweiser, crumpled the can and tossed it toward the trash can next to the desk, missing by a foot, "Okay, Mick."

Corey Gibson chimed in, "Remember, I get to do her."

Pyle didn't really like Gibson much. He wasn't very bright in his estimation, but he was the guy who had gotten the last job from Caruso and this one. Gibson did have a special talent that was needed for this job. Leon Allred was a multiple offender from Las Vegas, a man prone to violence, with a short fuse. Pyle's native home was Albuquerque, but Vegas had served as a second home and Allred had lots of contacts there. So for now he tolerated the two of them. After this, the payday was big enough he could disappear and lay low for a couple of years.

"Yeah, I know," Pyle said, "But let's get this done so we can head for Dallas first thing tomorrow. And Leon, keep a close eye on Porter. Don't let him contact anybody. I don't want anyone looking for him when this is over."

"Got plans for him?" Allred asked.

"Yeah, he's a local. No loose ends."

CHAPTER SEVEN
Gwinnett County, Georgia

JACK CRANDALL STEPPED FROM THE HOT SHOWER AND GRABBED A towel from the rack over the toilet. Steam hung thick in the air of the small hotel bathroom. He breathed it deep into his nostrils and lungs, trying to chase away the musty stale odor of charred wood and ashes that had been his house, still damp from the fire hoses even two days later. He pushed the towel hard against his face with both hands and continued to breathe deeply in hopes the smell of the clean cotton could combine with the steam and replace the memory of the stench that was his home.

It had been a long day. The interview he didn't want to give was over. Andrea was now awake and would physically recover to near one hundred percent. Her mental state was another question that would be answered at a later time. He had spoken to Andrea's parents over the phone; since she was doing better, they were going to stop in Greenville and drive in tomorrow. It was a great relief. He was not ready to tell them their daughter almost died because of him.

Brennan had approved his retrieving some items from his basement. Other than some minor water and smoke damage, it had survived intact. There was a reason. This was not the first time his home had been severely damaged. Twelve years earlier a tornado had wreaked havoc on the neighborhood. Several homes had to be rebuilt, including his. Crandall spent several thousand dollars over the insurance settlement turning his basement into a safe-room. Brennan told him it had saved Andrea's life. The reinforced basement ceiling did not collapse when the roof caved in and the steel paneled entry door sealed so tight that water and smoke had to seek other entry points. At least he had done something right.

Dry and dressed, he picked up the rifle case, laid it on the bed, unlocked and opened it. He had scrubbed the case as best he could, but there was still a hint of smoke from the Styrofoam mold in which his Remington 700 .308 rifle rested. In a cutout just above the receiver of the rifle was his Leupold Mark 4, 14x tactical scope. The gun safe had kept the rifle, scope, and his two handguns, a .45 Sig Sauer and a 9mm Glock, free from smoke and water.

Crandall figured hotel management wouldn't be very happy if they knew about the weaponry and several hundred rounds of ammunition that was in his room. But he could not afford them being stolen from his SUV, which was why he requested a room near the rear entrance.

After he moved to the Atlanta area he had kept up his skills through some local shooting competitions and a once or twice yearly elk hunt in Colorado or Wyoming. He wondered if his local reputation had gotten to the outside and helped Caruso find him. Great care had been taken in not allowing his picture to be published, but one never knows. Crandall had always managed to miss just enough to finish no higher than third in any competition.

Some folks had questioned his slight misses after many of the shots he pulled off early on. But, he knew it was even harder to miss just enough when doing it on purpose.

He finished checking the rifle, scope, and side arms, along with the two-hundred-fifty rounds of ammunition, and stacked them in the corner near the air conditioner, which he then turned to high. The steady hum of the fan motor drowned out any noise coming from the outside. He then went to the mini-refrigerator and pulled one of the Sweetwater Porters he had picked up earlier, poured it into a sixteen ounce plastic cup, sat down on the bed and opened the photo album he had kept in the safe.

Crandall took three long swallows of the beer and flipped through the album. He paused on the third page and stared at the photo of Jane and himself on their wedding day. They stood on the steps in front of St. Mary's. He was in a three piece suit, and she was in a simple white ankle-length dress. As he stared, tears seeped from the corner of his eyes.

The young man pulled his red Chevy sedan into the parking space in front of the convenience store. Leaning over he kissed his wife. "I'll just be a minute or two." He checked his watch. It was a little after seven in the evening, and the sun had just disappeared over the horizon.

Over his shoulder he looked at their newborn daughter asleep in her carrier in the back seat and smiled. Her older brother was with his grandma and grandpa. These new parents were on their way home from the hospital. The man hopped onto the sidewalk and into the store, humming to himself. It was a new baby and a new life. He grabbed a quart of milk and some Cokes from the cooler and went to the counter. Smiling at the middle-aged lady behind the counter, he put his purchases down and reached for his wallet.

A single gunshot pierced the tranquility of the evening and the man whipped his head to the right. He froze as through the glass all he could see was the blood spattered onto the windshield of his car and the dark outline of a man standing next to the passenger side of his car. The man with the gun stared back and smiled a mocking grin, then turned and ran into the shadows.

"NOOOOO!" the man screamed as he ran out the door. His pulse pounded in his ears, his breathing short and loud, he gulped for air. Jerking open the passenger car door, he found his young wife slumped across the center armrest, her head hanging above the driver's seat, and blood dripping onto the seat from her head.

He gently pulled her from the car and sat down on the asphalt, cradling her in his arms, his shirt, arms and face now smeared with her blood. He rocked back and forth, crying and kissing her hair, now matted against her skull from the blood. It stuck to his lips as sirens wailed in the distance, growing ever louder.

Crandall's head snapped backwards as he recoiled from the images. He closed the photo album and placed it in the drawer of the night stand between the two double beds. He took another swallow of his beer then went into the bathroom and dried his eyes with some tissues. Placing both hands on the counter he leaned in and checked his red eyes in the large mirror. "You're a mess, Jack," he said to the image. It looked back at him as if to say, "What? Are you feeling sorry for yourself now?"

A knock on the door interrupted the conversation. "Be right there," Crandall said, then blew his nose and splashed water on his face. Removing the chain lock from its slot he opened the door about a foot. The smell of Chinese takeout wafted into the room.

Crandall sniffed, "Hi, Cindy," he said.

"Hello, Jack," she said holding up a white bag and a bottle of zinfandel. "May I come in?"

CHAPTER EIGHT

Memphis, Tennessee

ALEX CARUSO STARED OUT THE WINDOW OF THE BEDROOM IN THE suite on the top floor at the Gaylord Hotel. His fifteen-hundred dollar charcoal grey Armani suit hung in the closet across the room beyond the king-sized four poster bed. Next to the closet was a well-stocked wet bar. He was clothed only in the terrycloth robe provided by the hotel.

He took a deep draw on his Cuban Robusto cigar with a full 50 ring gauge, tilted his head back and let the smoke drift from his mouth in a slow defiance of gravity. After the cloud of smoke flowed from his view, he returned his gaze to the window. To the south and west he could see the Memphis-Arkansas Bridge where highways 61, 64, 70 and 79 converged and crossed the Mississippi into Arkansas. The lights from the bridge glowed with a dim orange halo while a light fog rose from the river.

His meal had been exceptional and the bottle of Sangiovese was a perfect match for the parmigiana. He looked at his watch in anticipation, 9:12. He took another draw from his cigar and placed it in the ashtray on the table next to him.

A light knock on the mahogany door to the bedroom took him from his thoughts, "Right on time," he whispered and moved toward the door.

Caruso opened the door to see his tall husky bodyguard, Stan Allen, standing next to a petite girl. "Boss," Allen said, "This is Julie, Mr. Maxson brought her over."

Caruso's eyes roved over Julie, trying to take in every curve of her body. "Come in, Julie."

The young girl entered the room with a small nudge from Allen, and then he closed the door behind her with a quiet click. Her head shifted downward and to her left at a slight angle while her long red hair fell forward, covering part of her face. She moved forward with a slow tentative shuffle and breathed in shallow, quick, nervous breaths.

Caruso put his hand on her shoulder. He could feel the tension in her body. With his free hand he touched her chin and pushed upward so he could see her face. Her skin was near alabaster. Her sad green eyes looked back at him. Julie tried to turn her head to the side, away from Caruso's gaze.

"No need to be nervous, Julie," he said as he turned her head back so he could look into her eyes again.

He tilted his head to the right as if studying her nervous expression, "Did Mr. Maxson tell you why you are here?" he asked, using his best rehearsed fatherly tone.

Julie licked her lips, then after a slight pause, answered, "He said you could help me find some work."

"Possibly." Caruso took her by the arm and directed her toward the far side of the bed facing the closet, "Have a seat and we will discuss your situation. How old are you?"

"Eighteen," Julie said, looking around the room with small jerks of her head, but not looking at Caruso.

"Now, Julie," he began as he walked toward the small wet bar, "I talked to Mr. Maxson an hour ago, please be honest with me," Caruso lied. Maxson was well aware of his requirements, but he had to hear it from the girls. It was part of the game he liked to play.

He picked up a bottle of Johnny Walker Black, poured two fingers into a cocktail glass with *GH* in frosted calligraphy on the side. He dropped two ice cubes from the bucket on the bar into the bronze liquid, turned around and leaned backward against the bar. Caruso lifted the glass to his nose and sniffed the contents, taking in the strong aroma of malt with a hint of charred oak, "Now, how old are you and where do you come from?"

"Sixteen, Birmingham"

"So, you must have run away from home, why?"

Julie looked at her hands folded in her lap and sighed, "My step-father beat me, knocked me and my mom around. I saved up enough money for a bus ticket to Memphis. I want to be a singer. Mr. Maxson said you could help me."

Caruso stirred the ice and scotch with his index finger then stuck the finger in his mouth, sucking the liquid off the tip.

"Perhaps," he said as sniffed the scotch once again, then held the glass up in front of his eyes so he could see the light dance as he swirled his cocktail, "I do have a small interest in a couple of local clubs that could use some fresh entertainment." He looked back at Julie and smiled. This was not a lie, except for the interest. He was sole owner. The clubs, though, were strip clubs whose primary source of income was drugs and prostitution. South of I-240 and west of Lamar Avenue, they were convenient to the airport for overnight travelers looking for a quick thrill. The entertainment was third-rate at best, he always admitted. Private back rooms for "connected" customers and money to the proper officials kept him informed of regular police sweeps in the area. Then there were the new rooms in the basement for his special clients and their particular taste.

Caruso started back toward the bed. As he moved closer, his robe began to work its way open and Caruso made no attempt to close it.

Gwinnett County, Georgia

Cindy entered Jack Crandall's room as Crandall closed the door behind her. His mind wished she had not come, but his heart was glad. That conflict had always been there since the day they had met. The head finally won the debate, and he broke things off. The reason he gave was so unimportant he couldn't remember what it was. He did remember it was a lie.

Cindy turned and held up the wine and Chinese food, "Well, you could at least *act* happy to see me."

"Sorry—I'm—uh just more surprised." Crandall said, his hand still holding the doorknob.

Cindy looked around the room, "I can't seem to find the dining room. Why don't you open the wine and I'll get some towels from the bathroom and set the bed."

Crandall reached out and took the bags and bottle, "But, I don't have a—"

Cindy cut him off, "There's a corkscrew in the second bag along with some sturdy paper plates, and some plastic utensils, but I remember you're pretty good with chopsticks. Shrimp fried rice and Happy Family in the other bag. Probably could have been a pretty good boy scout, huh?"

Crandall smiled, leaned over and kissed Cindy on the cheek, then moved off to the built-in dresser, set everything down and began working on the bottle of wine. Once the cork was free he started to turn around, "Could you bring—"

Cindy was standing about four feet away, holding two plastic glasses from the bathroom.

"Prepared and psychic, a deadly combination." Crandall smiled again at her in her navy blue skirt with sensible matching flats and white blouse that showed just a hint of cleavage. He found something very sensual about a woman as attractive as Cindy who went out of her way to hide it.

"Thanks, but I think I'll stick with my beer," he continued.

Cindy set the plastic glasses on the dresser, "I hope you are in the mood for dinner conversation. There's a lot I need to ask you, and tell you."

Crandall frowned for the first time and started to speak. Cindy reached up, pressed her finger against his lips and in a low voice, "It's okay, you don't have to answer anything that makes you uneasy. Besides, it's as much tell as ask."

Nashville, Tennessee

After he received the call from Leon Allred, Pyle decided this just might work out. His first drive by the pizzeria let him know this was going to be his best shot. Another day or two of delay would put them behind schedule for Dallas. As it was they were a little ahead and he wanted to keep it that way.

Six blocks from campus, the restaurant was one storefront from the corner. But, two doors further up was an abandoned clothing store with a darkened inset stoop for an entrance. Just past that was where the couple had parked their car. Being a side street was also a plus. The later the evening went, the less traffic there was with less lighting than the main drag.

The only problem was this was a low crime area of town with regular police patrols, so timing and luck had to be good.

A short stroll past the pizzeria showed seven customers as the evening was waning. It was a stereotypical pizza place complete with red checkered table cloths. On each table a chianti bottle that had suffered through multiple candles sat in a ring made of grape vine. Each corner held white statuary replicas of ancient Roman sculptures. Two of the customers were settling their bill. Fewer potential witnesses was always a good thing.

The couple of interest was seated in the far corner. They held hands across the table, smiling and talking, the remains of a half-eaten pizza pushed to the side along with glasses in which only ice remained.

He was a bit concerned about the male companion. This was not something that was reported to him a month ago. Good size, athletic looking, but not anything they couldn't handle with the proper precaution.

Pyle was dressed in the second-hand clothes, wool cap and wool overcoat complete with holes. A brown paper bag with an empty bottle and a heavy wooden cane helped to complete the look. He had even done a bit of dumpster diving for the right stench. A combination of discarded beef and spoiled vegetables were rubbed on the coat.

Could be ten minutes, could be two hours. For now, they waited.

CHAPTER NINE

Gwinnett County, Georgia

P AUL B RENNAN DROVE HIS COUNTY VEHICLE INTO THE GARAGE OF the three bedroom brick ranch style home just off Harbins Road near Dacula, Georgia. As he pressed the button on the garage door opener clipped to the sun visor, the door began its noisy descent.

He reached over and grabbed a leather valise from the passenger seat and exited the auto, recoiling slightly when he bumped his head on the car's door frame. Rubbing the spot, he walked around the back of the car, stopped, unlocked the door and entered his house. Just inside was the laundry room with a deep sink against the end wall, and through the next door lay the smallish den area. The furniture was somewhat plain and sparse. A single sofa, one recliner, one lamp. A framed photo of his mother and father taken at his father's retirement party sat on the table between the chair and sofa and provided the room's only decoration. The walls were blank, void of that *woman's touch*. It wasn't a large home, but when you lived alone it could be very big and empty at times.

Brennan put the valise down next to the recliner, went into the kitchen just off the den and retrieved a Sam Adams Boston Lager from the refrigerator. He returned to the recliner, took his sidearm off his belt, laid it on the side table and sat. He picked up the remote and turned on the flat screen TV resting on the 'some assembly required' stand across the room.

It had been another fourteen-hour day, spent working multiple cases. But, only one was on his mind at the moment. He opened the valise and pulled out a copy of the Crandall file. Here was a guy trying to do the right thing, and he gets crapped on. Wife murdered, daughter-in-law beaten and shot, the granddaughter she was carrying dead and his house burned to the ground. All from one of those guys whom Brennan had always told himself he wouldn't piss on to save their lives if they were on fire. He had never met a real life Job, but Crandall was beginning to look like one. The only real pattern was with the two adult victims, wife and daughter-in-law – it appeared Caruso hated women. But, that was just an initial impression.

Brennan sipped on the beer while some cable channel he wasn't listening to droned in the background. He flipped through the file looking for some direction to go. Thus far there was zero evidence to connect Caruso. The perp might have overdone the accelerant, but he wasn't stupid as first assumed. Nothing left behind, not even a footprint in the yard.

He leaned his head back against the chair's headrest and rubbed his tired eyes. His mind wandered. Growing up he had been very close to his father, so when he enlisted in the Army his father had told him the two most rewarding, and at the same time frustrating, jobs in the world were a soldier and a policeman. So, after six years in the Army as a Weapons Specialist with Special Forces, Brennan came to the conclusion he wanted both. He answered an ad in his hometown paper in Lockport, New York. It seems Gwinnett County Police Department was hiring and was considering candidates from all over the country. Its close proximity to the 20th Special Forces Group National Guard in Birmingham was the clincher. Three months later he was a member of both.

Brennan grew up as the son of a well respected, and well known, police officer in Lockport, a small town of just over 20,000. The Brennan clan had been part of Lockport since 1825. They were hard-working Irish immigrants that helped build the Erie Canal. Often his grandfather would take him to the canal locks and regale him with family stories of the adventures and hardships endured.

He also thought of the thing his father told him when he'd taken the job with the police force, "The hardest rule to keep is to not get personally involved." That's what led to his fourteen hour days and why the Crandall case was so hard to lay down.

There were a couple of extended breaks from his police work. One tour in Iraq and a half tour in Afghanistan. The half tour was a full one cut short by a Purple Heart, a Bronze Star with a V and the loss of a close friend.

Brennan drained the last of the beer, yawned, then closed the file, placing it and the empty bottle on the table. He rubbed his eyes again in a vain attempt to remove the gritty feeling. It was these alone times when his mind would drift. He thought of his father who died of prostate cancer less than ten years after retiring from the force. His mother was taken by a stroke just over two years later.

He also thought of his older siblings, two brothers and a sister, and how they had argued over their parents' care those last months. How they told him to butt out since he didn't live there anymore. The fallout put such a strain on their overall relationship they hardly spoke at their mother's funeral. It had been years since they had spoken. Too many years, and they were all too damn stubborn, refusing to offer an olive branch.

Then there was Annie. He thought of her and smiled. They tried to make a go of it. It had lasted for over a year, between tours. They were planning to marry. But the wounds changed things. He would have bled out right there on the ground if not for the best medics in the world. Annie became worried his day job could end worse.

Even so, her sandy blond hair, deep blue eyes and infectious laugh had always made him smile. The guys at work told him he was an idiot for letting her go. They were right.

His mental ambulation came full circle, and he returned to Crandall. This was a man who gave up everything—his family, his friends, his whole life—just to put some scum in jail and protect his children. Crandall had held his wife in his arms while she died, covered with her blood. There had been no one in his life to speak of since that night except for a son and daughter. His whole existence was built around protecting them. That was real sacrifice.

Brennan sighed, took in a deep breath and let it out slow, trying to relax. He then took his cell phone from the holder on his belt and punched in a number from memory. He stared for several seconds then pushed *send*. After three rings a voice said, "Hello."

Brennan looked up at the ceiling and responded softly, "Annie—"

Memphis, Tennessee

When Julie started begging to leave, Caruso slapped her. When she started crying he punched her. The blood on her lip excited him. The next blow heightened that excitement. He ripped at her clothes. Then the rape.

In Caruso's mind it wasn't rape. It was how things were supposed to be. He rolled off of her, lying on his back, his heavy breathing dominated the silence. Julie turned on her side, curled up and began sobbing again, her torn clothing scattered about on the floor. Caruso turned his head and looked at her in disgust. He got out of the bed and retrieved his robe from the floor where he had thrown it.

After he covered himself, he went to the door, opened it and called to Stan Allen, then he stepped through the door and closed it. The sitting room was ample size. Plush carpet in a neutral tan covered the full length of the floor. A sofa, love seat, and two chairs were arranged so each had a good view of the large television. An even larger wet bar than the one in the bedroom stood in the corner near the glass doors to the balcony that looked out on the parts of Memphis along the Mississippi.

When Allen reached his boss, Caruso said in a low voice, "Have Tony give her something to calm her down and take her back to Maxson at the club. Let him know I don't think she will work out. She just doesn't have the right talent or temperament."

Allen turned toward the love seat where Tony Oliveri was sitting and snapped his fingers. Caruso opened the door, walked past the bed with the still sobbing young girl without a glance. He went into the bathroom and turned on the shower and removed his robe as steam filled the room. *Good, at least this will drown out that goddamn crying,* he thought as he stepped in.

Gwinnett County, Georgia

Most of the dinner conversation between Cindy and Crandall moved back and forth between Andrea's recovery and the impending arrival of Mark, and Andrea's parents. He would see them first thing in the morning, but Mark was not due until late afternoon the next day.

With supper done and cleanup over, Cindy poured another glass of wine while he fetched a fresh beer from the fridge. Crandall sat back on the bed and adjusted the pillows behind his back. He was beginning to dread the next hour, for reasons other than what Cindy might suspect.

Crandall decided to start. He cleared his throat, "Cindy, I'm glad you came by and all, but I'm not sure why."

Cindy pushed her brown hair away from her face and sat on the end of the bed opposite Crandall. He looked into eyes so dark they seemed to peer into his soul.

"In some ways I'm not really sure myself." Cindy said, swirling the white wine in its cup. "Hopefully, I'm just here as a friend. But I am worried about you. I've always worried about you."

Crandall leaned forward a bit and placed his hands on his knees, "How so?"

"After my divorce, you were kind and reassuring to me. Friendly conversation over dinner, the gentle way you kissed my cheek that first night. I was pretty low, vulnerable, but you never took advantage of me. I loved it. I was falling in love with you."

"But—" Crandall started.

"No, let me finish," she paused, licked her lips and took a sip of wine. Cindy looked down at her crossed legs, "I need to finish before I come to my senses and run out of here screaming in embarrassment." She looked up, "At first, I figured it was just me. You know, the old story, falling for the first guy who was nice to me. Now that I've had some time to think about it, I *was* in love with you. In fact, I'm still in love with you. You made me laugh when I needed it. When I cried, you let me cry. You made me feel like a real woman again. You were strong, and gentle.

"After all the lies about the gambling, the drugs and the other women with Roger, you were a breath of fresh air, open, honest. I took it pretty hard when you broke it off, but you were there for me when I needed it most. You made me stronger. I want to be here for you." Cindy's eyes began to tear up.

Crandall sat up straight and placed both hands on the mattress. In a nervous voice he began. "Wow. I'm not sure what to say about all that or even where to start, but here goes.

"I was falling in love with you, too. The more I got to know you, the more I loved you. But, I had to break it off."

Cindy stared somewhat blankly, "Why, Jack? I need to know."

Crandall took a deep breath, "This is going to be hard. Remember what you said about all the lies?"

"Yes."

"That's the rub. You deserved better. You see, my whole life is a lie. Jack Crandall isn't even my real name."

Cindy sat and stared for what seemed to Crandall a very uncomfortable few seconds.

"Woo—boy!" She finally said. "I sure didn't see that one coming.

"What, did you kidnap your kids and start over somewhere else? Is your wife still out there looking for you?"

Crandall rubbed his hands together, "No, she died, but not from cancer. She was murdered by a hit man who worked for my former employer."

"Didn't see that one, either. So, you're hiding from the mob?" Cindy said with a nervous laugh.

Crandall now rubbed his sweaty palms on his jeans then picked up his beer and took three large swallows. He wiped his mouth with his sleeve. "Something like that. It's a long story."

"It's Friday, my next shift is Sunday afternoon, I've got all night."

"Okay, my real name is ..." Crandall began.

CHAPTER TEN

Nashville, Tennessee

MICKEY PYLE WAS LOOKING AROUND THE SKYLINE JUST ABOVE THE buildings. East of his location he could make out the top of the AT&T building on Commerce Street. The distinctive Batman style cowling on the top was even more *Dark Knight*-like. Shrouded in a low-hanging cloud with the light of a one quarter moon on the wane behind it cast a Halloween effect. *Perfect for a nigh time operation.*

He checked his new watch. *Almost closing time.* He signaled his men with a *tsss* and a wave of his hand.

The four men hidden in the darkened stoop of the abandoned store got to their feet. Pyle, who had been seated on the sidewalk leaning back against the storefront doing his best drunken bum impression, struggled to his feet. All just an act. You never know when someone is watching.

Pyle limped off in a direction away from the pizzeria, using his cane, placing the stoop between him and the restaurant. He stopped and positioned himself facing down the street toward the building that held his target. Leaning his shoulder against the wall, he took a swig of the cheap whiskey in the brown paper bag and swallowed. As it went down his throat, the harsh burn caused him to cough. Just one swallow would give him the right odorous quality to his breath. He knew he didn't have long to wait.

About five minutes later the door of the restaurant opened and inside lights began to dim. The last four customers walked out. One couple turned toward the main drag and disappeared around the corner while the other turned toward Pyle walking slowly, hand in hand. *Perfect*, he thought. When they reached the point he had picked out, Pyle turned the bottle up once again but spit the whiskey back and began his slow unsteady gait toward them. Her male companion was walking closest to the street.

The well-disguised derelict moved and stepped into the street. He feigned a stumble as he passed them, drawing their attention toward him while they moved closer to the storefront. He shuffled past, somewhere between eight and ten feet from where his men were hiding. Just as he had planned, his appearance, actions and odor held their attention and caused them to move closer to the store. As they passed each other, Pyle mumbled, "Evenin". The couple turned their heads in Pyle's direction. The male returned the greeting.

Pyle stopped, stood erect with a slight turn in their direction and said in a sober voice, "Lisa."

The couple stopped and turned around. That was the signal the men on the stoop were waiting for.

The three men were on top of them in an instant. Two of them grabbed Lisa; the third went for her companion. Before the assailant could strike, Lisa's friend struck. First a left to his attacker's solar plexus then a right fist found the nose and upper lip. The blood flow was immediate as a pink mist filled the air. The droplets seemed to hang suspended in the air by the dull light for a second or two before falling to the ground.

"David!" Lisa screamed as she tried to fight off her attackers.

Pyle brought his cane up so he could strike David in the head. David spun in Pyle's direction and ducked while grabbing Pyle's arm. He stood and with one smooth motion planted a kick into Pyle's midsection that sent him backward, sprawling onto the sidewalk.

David's first attacker recovered and jumped him from behind, bringing his arm around David's neck. In a judo-like move David grabbed the arm and used the attacker's momentum to flip the man. The attacker landed on the concrete on his ass and back. "Uh, shit," escaped from his lips while David kept a firm hold on the man's arm. David stood and placed a foot onto the man's shoulder. While pressing down hard with his foot he gave a quick twist and a mighty pull. The attacker screamed and a distinctive pop sounded as the shoulder's socket separated from the joint.

The other two men were having their own difficulties with Lisa but had overpowered her and were forcing her away from the fight and up the street.

Pyle regained his footing and reached into his pocket.

David turned toward Lisa and the other assailants. Pyle fired two shots from a .32 caliber automatic into David's back. As David recoiled from the bullets, Pyle rushed forward and struck him in the back of the head with his cane. David dropped to his knees and tried to rise but Pyle delivered two more heavy blows to the back and side of David's head. He fell, face-first onto the sidewalk and lay there gurgling and twitching while blood oozed onto the concrete.

"Hey!" a voice came from behind Pyle. He turned and saw a smallish man standing in front of the open door of the pizzeria. Two more shots from the pistol caused the man to duck back inside the restaurant. Pyle took off at a dead run to catch up to the men who were carrying Lisa, her mouth now sealed with duct tape.

Pyle passed the two men, reached a dark blue Taurus sedan and opened the trunk. The men placed the struggling girl into the trunk, taped her hands together behind her back then taped her feet. Pyle slammed the trunk lid closed. The attacker who went after David had struggled to his feet and reached the auto, his right arm hanging motionless at his side. Pyle motioned to Allred who entered the driver's door and started the car. Pyle instructed the injured man to sit in the back seat and told Gibson to sit with him and keep him quiet. Pyle then climbed into the passenger seat.

As soon as all doors were closed the auto sped away from the curb with the lights off. At the next cross street they turned right and disappeared into the night.

Memphis, Tennessee

Alex Caruso sat on the red and green striped sofa in the sitting room of his hotel suite in Memphis. He was enjoying another cigar and some cognac with his body guard and right-hand man, Stan Allen. His preference was a *hors d'âge* with a slight hint of baked apples in the bouquet that lingered on the pallet. But the VS provided by the hotel worked well for such a young product.

Allen had received a call from Oliveri to let him know the situation had been handled. Maxson was to make sure Julie would be cleaned up properly so that no DNA would be present and she would be properly let go.

Caruso had chosen Allen and Oliveri because of their ruthlessness. Everyone in his position needed an enforcer. He had two. Unrestrained violence was how he had worked his way to the top just over twenty-five years ago. Beatings, intimidation, and the occasional execution of rivals and turncoats made him a man to be feared. The brutal elimination of those he worked for had been the final phase. Memphis police expended minimal effort on the mysterious disappearance of a crime figure.

Once he had gained control it became important to keep people in line. He did this by violating the unwritten code that family was off limits. Once a few examples were made, it became easier to control folks.

Crandall, or whatever the hell his name was now, wanted out. The ungrateful son-of-a-bitch didn't understand the only way out was feet first. So, Caruso had to make an example of him. Allen's predecessor, Len Patrone, had followed them from the hospital. The plan was to do it in their house, but the convenience store was an opportunity for an easier kill without the chance of return fire. Crandall would have to live the rest of his life knowing his decision led to the death of his wife—and knowing that Caruso was surely coming back for him someday. But then the bastard just had to go all witness protection on him. He even convinced Sam Greggs to go along with him. Greggs had no family and had hidden away before they could get to him. Caruso had to admit, the feds made it hard to find them. One PI on his payroll had even been killed trying to do the job.

Once they were found, he had considered sending Allen after them, but he was too valuable to risk losing. Allen was, in some ways, even more brutal than himself. Truly a man to be feared.

Caruso turned to Allen, "Stan, we need to make a visit to Maxson tomorrow. If those stupid fucks that work for him can't find talent any better than that Julie, he will have to get back on the street himself. Some of our clients have been complaining. I don't like complaints, it's bad for business."

Allen nodded.

Caruso stood, "Don't tell him we're coming." He walked into the bedroom and closed the door.

Gwinnett County, Georgia

Jack Crandall lay in bed staring at the ceiling. He checked the time. It was well past midnight. Cindy now knew his entire life story. Even things the police and his priest at St. Patrick's did not know. As hard as she tried, she could not hold back the tears.

As late as it was Crandall offered the extra bed and one of his tee shirts to sleep in. When she accepted, Crandall cradled Cindy's face between his hands and kissed her gently on the cheek. He tasted the saltiness of her dried tears.

Cindy was in the bathroom changing for bed. Crandall adjusted his pillow, placed his right forearm behind his head and sighed. *Won't be much sleeping tonight.* He was tired but restless, and his mind moved from one thought to the next.

The door of the bathroom opened and the light went off. Only the light from the parking lot that seeped through the curtains and crept under the door from the hall illuminated the room, and that was minimal until his eyes adjusted.

Cindy walked between the beds and lifted Crandall's covers. He started to speak, but she put her finger to her lips with a "ssssh". Crandall moved over to make room and she slipped between the sheets. She lay on her side with her head on his chest and her arm across his stomach. Crandall rested his chin on her head and gently rubbed her upper arm.

He didn't understand what Cindy saw in him, but he was glad she saw it. And, he was too tired to question it. Crandall smiled for the first time in days, and he began to drift off.

CHAPTER ELEVEN
Nashville, Tennessee

A DARK BLUE TAURUS SEDAN TURNED INTO THE ENTRANCE OF Baptist Hospital in Nashville. The driver followed the signs toward the emergency room. A man in the passenger's seat told the driver to go past the ER entrance and around the corner of the building to a dimly lit spot he could see just ahead.

Once they rounded the corner out of sight of the ER, the man in the passenger's seat told the driver to slow down. Seeing no security personnel, he instructed a man in the back seat to open the door and dump the girl out. She landed hard on the asphalt on her side, motionless. Her head tilted toward the ground, her ear almost touching her shoulder. Once the door closed, the driver was told to drive back out to Church Street and obey all the speed limit signs.

The man in the passenger seat was not worried about the vehicle showing up on the security tape. The police, he figured, would stumble onto it by noon along with the surprise. It was just after 2:00 AM so he calculated they would be in Alabama, well on their way to Dallas, by the time it was found.

Memphis, Tennessee

Two men got out of the Dodge Minivan behind the rusted out grain warehouse on the Mississippi river just north of Memphis. It was parked three steps from the water's edge at a reinforced wall where barges once docked. They stood behind the van looking out across the river. A light breeze from the west carried the unique scent of the muddy river into the nostrils of the men.

The taller man rubbed his hands together trying to warm them. He pulled his jacket tighter and zipped it all the way up to ward off the clammy feeling of the cool moist night. "Okay, let's get this over with," he said. They opened the lift gate and pulled out a body, tied and bound from head to toe.

Carrying the body over to the edge of the wall they laid it out with its feet pointed toward the river, a foot from the edge. The two men returned to the van where each grabbed a cinder block from its rear door. They carried them over and tied both off to the feet.

The shorter man lifted the smallish body while the other struggled with the cinder blocks. They dropped the body into the thirty foot deep river. As it splashed in, there was an unexpected bob as if it was resisting the weight of the blocks. Her lifeless body turned around, staring at them with vacant eyes. Her long red hair spread gently across the water then her alabaster face disappeared into the murky brown water, pulling the hair with her.

"That was weird," the taller of the two whispered.

Gwinnett County, Georgia

The sound of his cell phone ringing was starting to irritate Jack Crandall as he began the task of clearing the fog of a deep sleep from his brain, his eyes. He tried to reach the phone with his right hand but realized he was still pinned in by Cindy who was waking at a slower rate.

Cindy sat up, and he was able to reach the phone. The blinking display told him it was just past 4:00. "Hello," he said with a yawn.

"Yes, this is Jack Crandall." He rubbed his hand through his hair and scratched the back of his head. His brow furrowed as he listened intently, "Yes, she's my daughter."

"Wait a minute, who is this?" He asked as he sat up in bed, now fully awake. "What?"

He froze, his eyes widened, he felt paralyzed, unable to even blink, "Noooo!"

Dacula, Georgia

Paul Brennan awoke. He blinked a couple of times and rubbed his eyes. With his index finger he tried to remove the remnants of the natural saline that had settled in the corner of each eye and become dried and crusty. Looking around at the dark paneling and the flashing of the television as the infomercial hocked the latest "must have" product, Brennan realized he had fallen asleep in his recliner—again.

He got up, stumbled into the kitchen and splashed some water on his face. The digital clock on the microwave read 5:17. *Well it's Saturday, a couple more hours then hit the gym,* he thought. He started out of the kitchen toward the hall leading to the master. Brennan rubbed the back of his neck, trying to work out the stiffness. He stopped, stared down the hall for a second then slapped himself on the forehead. "Holy crap! How could you be so stupid?" He spoke aloud.

He ran down the hallway into the master bedroom. Just off the bedroom he ducked into the bathroom and started the shower. While it heated up he went to his closet, pulled out some clean clothes and tossed them on the still-made bed. He went back into the bathroom, unbuttoning his shirt as he went.

***

Crandall sat on the bed drinking a cup of coffee he carried back from the breakfast area in the lobby. Cindy was dressed, sitting on the other bed facing him sipping on the coffee he brought for her. The SUV was loaded up with everything he had brought in the previous evening. He was waiting for the climate controlled storage facility around the corner to open up. There were a few things in a special box he needed to take with him.

After the phone call he told Cindy what happened. A security guard found Lisa bound and gagged lying next to a wall near the entrance of Baptist Hospital. The police officer and doctor alternately explained she had been beaten and appeared to have been tortured. Her clothes were torn and she had been cut with a very sharp instrument, most likely a knife or razor, and there had been some serious blood loss. Some of the cuts were on her back, but many were on her face and she would need reconstructive surgery. None were super deep so most of the scarring could be covered up, but her emotional state would be another question. There was no evidence of rape, but lab tests haven't come back yet.

She was awake and provided the police with as much information as she could. All the men wore ski masks except for one who was dressed as a homeless man, but she couldn't remember much about his features.

The police said for what she had been through she was holding up remarkably well. She had a strong character. Her boyfriend, David, was pronounced dead at the scene of the kidnapping.

The more Crandall talked, the angrier he became. There were no tears from him this time. Along with everything else, now people had died. Good people. A young man who had planned on serving his country had given his life to protect Lisa.

Cindy fidgeted, crossing and uncrossing her legs. She would alternate between holding her coffee cup with both hands to pulling and twirling her hair. But, she remained silent. It was as if she knew Crandall needed a good listener, a sympathetic ear. Maybe it was her training. He didn't know, but he was glad she had decided to come.

Crandall sat his cup down on the night stand, reached across and took Cindy's hands in his and looked into her eyes. "I've got to go now and I'm not sure when I'll be back. I need you to do some things for me."

Cindy nodded.

"I need you to tell Andrea's parents what happened. I know it will be tough, but I can't be there. I also need you to meet Mark at the airport. He was supposed to meet me at the USO room. Can you do that?"

Cindy nodded again, "Yes," then sniffed.

"Okay, tell Mark to get Lisa back here as soon as she can travel."

Cindy tilted her head to one side, "And just where the hell are you going and what the hell are you going to do?"

Crandall stood and picked up his blue denim jacket, slipping his arms in the sleeves. "First I'm going to see Lisa, then, all bets are off. As for what I'm going to do, I'm not sure. Whatever it is you're better off not knowing.

"Now, there may be someone watching me even now, so you stay here for at least two hours after I leave and be careful. Don't answer the phone, don't peek out the window. Just give it the two hours then leave. If you start feeling scared, contact Paul Brennan with the Gwinnett Police. He and I have butted heads a little, but he's a good guy."

Crandall pulled his 9mm from his waistband under his sweatshirt and handed it to Cindy, "It's loaded. Don't be afraid to use it. It's the same one you used when we went to the range."

He took two additional clips from his pockets, placed them in the palm of her hand and closed her fingers around them. His hands lingered, gently holding her hand between his. He looked into her eyes, but there was nothing left to say.

When Crandall released her hand Cindy laid them on the bed and stood. He pulled her close, wrapping her in his arms. The warmth of her body made him hesitant to leave. Crandall kissed her deeply. After he let her go she began to tear up again. It was his turn to touch her lips before she could speak, "I have to do this."

Crandall turned and left.

CHAPTER TWELVE
Gwinnett County, Georgia

CRANDALL SPUN THE COMBINATION LOCK DIAL ON THE SMALL storage unit rented at the Public Storage building. He opened the door and went in. Stacked along each wall of the six-by-six room were several acid free boxes that contained old family pictures, some books and clothing. He would come by every few months to dust things off and make sure everything was in good condition.

At the end of the room was a steamer trunk that once belonged to his grandmother with two boxes on top. The boxes were labeled *For Lisa*. The trunk was also for her. Things from her mother. He was saving these items for the day when he could tell them the whole ugly story. When Caruso didn't get a life sentence, Crandall made the decision to wait until Lisa got married. That may be a while now.

He fought hard to hold his anger. It was okay, but he had to be under control. He spotted what he was looking for. It wasn't hard. The olive drab wooden footlocker with the padlock turned against the wall. Several more boxes sat on top.

In less than thirty seconds Crandall had moved the boxes and turned the footlocker. He removed the padlock and lifted the lid. It was all there, what remained of it. Just a few mementos of an earlier life, one that had been replaced by a façade of an existence meant to keep his family safe.

Reaching in he pulled out the netting that made up his old ghillie suit. He had used it a few times over the years on his hunting trips out west, but only with companions who didn't ask questions. As he took inventory in his mind he spotted a small light brown box. He picked it up and looked at the label. M-13 .308 Caliber Incendiary, it read.

Hmmm, haven't thought about these in years.

It was a collection of items that he had planned to give to Mark. Unsure what he was looking for Crandall decided to take the whole box. *Sorry Mark, I know you will understand.* He relocked the box, paused, looked at his keys, *I need to go to the bank and get in and out of the hospital.*

Lawrenceville, Georgia

Brennan entered police headquarters to the usual, "Aren't you supposed to be off today?" This time the answer was a bit gruff, "Yeah, so don't bother me while I'm here."

At the desk inside his cubical he began scanning the internet news services while he attempted to contact Jack Crandall. After leaving three messages on Crandall's cell he tried the hotel. With no answer there, Brennan called the Duluth hospital. A no-show there so far.

Having no luck, Brennan decided to go to the hospital, check on Andrea and have a talk with her parents. He put on his baseball cap with GCPD on it and started gathering things to take with him, then stopped and thought for a minute. He went to the computer and looked up a phone number then dialed the Nashville Police Department.

Northwest Georgia

Crandall was on I-75 North, just past Rome, Georgia with his cruise control set to five miles per hour over the speed limit. He wanted to get to Lisa as soon as possible, but getting stopped for speeding would only impede his journey. The cell phone beeped at him again. He picked it up and checked the caller id.

"Hello, Detective," he said after deciding to answer.

"I've been trying to get hold of you for hours, where are you?"

"Well, I've been ignoring you for hours, and I'm almost to Tennessee. That bast—"

"I know, I've been talking to the Nashville police, I'm sorry."

"No need; the only ones who are going to be sorry are the fuckers who did this."

"No, Jack. I'm sorry. I should have seen this coming. I should have warned you to get Lisa back here. Caruso goes after the women. For whatever reason he either hates them or he figures that's what will hurt you the most. Probably both."

Crandall felt a wave of heat across his face and swore he could feel his blood pressure rising. "Yeah, well he figured that hurt thing right. But I'm past hurt now, and I passed pissed about five miles back.

"So, don't be so hard on yourself," Crandall said in a suddenly much calmer voice, "Caruso and the sorry excrement that work for him are the ones to blame. Look, do me a favor."

"Sure."

Crandall squinted, trying to read the road sign that was reflecting the late morning sunlight while trying to ignore the twitching in his left arm, "There's a nurse at the hospital, Cindy Fitzgerald. She's doing a few things for me, and if Caruso finds out about her she could be in danger, too. Look out for her."

"What do you mean, 'finds out about her'?"

"We dated, she can fill you in. I've got to go." Crandall put his phone on the passenger seat and rubbed the upper part of his left arm, then took the steering wheel with both hands.

Duluth, Georgia

Cindy Fitzgerald took the elevator to the fourth floor. Andrea was out of ICU and in a regular room. Cindy was dressed in blue scrubs. It was her off day, but it was easier to navigate the hospital dressed for work and using her access badge.

Two quick rights off the elevator and half way down the hall past the nurse's station on the left was Andrea's room. She knocked on the partially opened door and heard a female voice respond, "Come in."

The heavy wooden door's hinges squealed a tiny bit as Cindy pushed it open enough to step inside. Andrea was propped up in the bed, asleep. A man and woman that looked to be in their fifties stood next to the bed looking over their shoulders at her.

Cindy extended her hand and tried to smile, "You must be Andrea's parents. I'm Cindy Fitzgerald, a friend of Jack's. He asked me to stop by."

"Yes, we were wondering where Jack was. He was supposed to meet us here." Andrea's mother said in a whisper.

Looking past the couple she could see Andrea was sleeping. "Perhaps we should step outside the room where we could talk."

She was trying to hide her worry, but she knew she was failing at that task.

"Is there something wrong?" The man asked.

Cindy was unsure what to say. Instead she nodded.

***

Cindy was lost in her thoughts sitting in the corner of the cafeteria. Her back was to the door. She picked at a half eaten slice of apple pie, pushing apple slices and crust around the plate. There was the occasional dab of the eyes with her napkin. Not able to decide between coffee or milk, she had gotten both but tasted neither.

She was thirty and Jack fifty-two. As much as she loved him, she was trying to be a realist about their relationship going any further. Recent events made those chances even more remote. But, Jack needed her. ER nurses are supposed to have strong personalities to deal with the emotional swings that came with the job. This, however, was personal.

An unexpected touch on her shoulder sent a shock wave through her body. She jerked, tensed and took in a quick breath.

"I'm sorry, Cindy, didn't mean to scare you," a female voice said.

CHAPTER THIRTEEN

Duluth, Georgia

CINDY FITZGERALD SIGHED AS SHE LOOKED ACROSS THE CAFETERIA table at Jennifer Grady. Cindy had befriended Jennifer when she came to work at the hospital two years ago. It was about the same time she was dating Jack. Jennifer's short curly black hair framed her face and just touched the top of her ears. To be honest, Cindy wanted to tell Jennifer she wanted to be alone. She looked down at her half eaten pie.

"I saw Jack over at the pharmacy earlier, he seemed a little nervous, didn't want to talk. Just said he had to get some things out of his locker," Jennifer said then sipped some of her Diet Coke through a straw.

It took a second for what was said to sink in. Cindy snapped her head up, "What? Jack was here. He didn't say anything about coming here when he left me this morning." Cindy immediately wanted to withdraw that last part. Jennifer was a good nurse, Cindy reckoned, but she had an annoying habit of wanting to know everyone's business. Plus, there were the other quirks that made the gossip circuit, like the way she lingered when a patient was DOA, or Code Blue and couldn't be revived.

Jennifer leaned forward, a sly smile on her lips, "Oh, are you two back together?"

In some ways Cindy had thought Jennifer was the reason Jack had broken it off with her. She had always been flirting with him, hanging on his every word. For almost two months after she and Jack stopped dating, Cindy avoided talking to her. But, when nothing happened between them, Cindy decided she was letting all her suspicions and fears from her failed marriage and relationship cloud her judgment of other people. She decided to stop feeling sorry for herself.

But, she spoke without thinking again, "Yes—uh—maybe—I don't know. I went to see him last night. To see if I could help.

We talked almost all night. Then he got that call from Baptist in Nashville."

A look of shock came over Jennifer's face, her light brown eyes opened a little further as she slowly turned her head to each side, then leaned in and whispered, "Baptist Hospital? Is everything alright? Is Lisa okay?"

Once again Cindy's emotions shoved the words out before she could think, "No, things aren't alright." She pushed back from the table and picked up her purse from the floor. She noticed the extra weight. With everything on her mind, she had forgotten about the pistol. Now she feared the trouble it would bring if it were found out.

Cindy stood. Confusion, paranoia and fatigue were starting to consume her. She didn't understand why she felt this way. "Look, I've got to go. I have to go to the airport later so I need to get home."

Jennifer started to get up. "Can I help? Do you need me to go with you?"

"No!" Cindy blurted out. She was looking around at everyone. Something was wrong. Anxiety took control of her mind and body. Her chest tightened. The pounding of her heart made her feel like it was going to explode. *What's wrong with me?* She thought as she tried to catch her breath.

"Are you alright, Cindy?" Jennifer asked as she reached out a hand.

Cindy recoiled, "Yes, I'm fine. I just need to be alone." Cindy turned to leave. She wanted to run, but she clutched her purse close, squeezing it with both hands to keep them from shaking. The hardness of the gun inside caused even more panic. These emotions were sudden and overwhelming. She felt trapped, helpless. As she made her way toward the exit there was a sense that every set of eyes in the place was watching her. The cafeteria door seemed like a tunnel with no end. Running would only draw more attention.

Leaving the cafeteria, Cindy turned toward the hospital exit, walking as fast as she could.

"Ms. Fitzgerald."

At first, it didn't register. Then she heard it a second time.

Cindy fought the urge to run, stopped and turned around. A broad shouldered man in a blue wind breaker and a baseball cap looked at her, "Ms. Fitzgerald, I'm Detective Paul Brennan, is there somewhere we can talk?"

Memphis

The Lincoln Town Car pulled into the parking lot of the Southern Belle Gentleman's Club. The front of the club was painted in a pale blue with white clouds under which were the outlines of female figures, in black paint with parasols. Each figure had been painted in a different pose.

Above the black canopy over the double glass door was a neon sign in pink and blue announcing the name of the establishment. The first thing that pissed Caruso off was that the sign was on. They weren't due to open until 4:00 PM to welcome the rush hour avoiders and the afternoon arrivals at the airport. The second thing was the "S" was out and the "o" was blinking at a rate that would send an epileptic into a seizure.

Oliveri parked in front of the double glass doors. Both were dark tinted with gold lettering to remind you where you were and that *No One Under The Age Of 21 Admitted* "or there about" as Caruso would quip on occasion. Allen got out and opened the passenger side rear door for Caruso. "Leave the car here and come with us," Caruso told Oliveri as he exited the car. Allen unlocked the front door and the three men entered.

Caruso, Allen, and Oliveri walked past the cleaning crew scurrying about preparing for the 4:00 PM opening without a word and went down the hallway to the right of the bar, past the private entertainment rooms and entered the office without knocking. Allen entered first followed by Caruso and Oliveri.

A startled Dave Maxson dropped the remote control that was in his hand. Two men who looked like they had been up all night were sitting on a green Naugahyde sofa against the wall just past the desk. They started to get up, but Allen glanced in their direction and they resumed their previous positions without a word of protest.

"Damn it, Stan, you guys scared the shit out of me! Hi, Mr. Caruso." Maxson said and settled back into his chair behind a brown veneer desk that had the appearance it had been picked up at Goodwill for thirty dollars. Caruso didn't care much about furnishing areas the customers didn't use.

Caruso walked over to the desk and put both hands on the front edge and stared at the man with the black hair and pock-marked face, "There's going to be more than shit running out of you and your two idiots if you keep fucking up."

Maxson blinked several times and licked his lips, "What do you mean?"

"That little tramp you sent over last night. As much fun as it is, I'm getting a little tired of having to slap them around to get some cooperation. And then they just lay there whimpering like some dog I just kicked and sent to the corner of the room."

The taller of the two men began standing, "Just a minute, Mr. Caruso, she was fresh off the street and just the right ag—"

In a single swift move, Stan Allen took one step and brought up his left arm. His hand slammed into the man's throat, palm first, then the hand closed on his windpipe. Allen's strength kept the man upright when he tried to fall backwards from the impact. The more the man struggled to break free, the tighter Allen gripped. "Listen, Ed, you're not part of this conversation right now," Allen said through clinched teeth.

Oliveri stepped in front of the smaller man, cutting him off from any attempt to rise from the sofa.

Ed Gibson's face began to turn red. With his free hand Allen pulled a knife from his pocket and pressed a button. The thin stiletto blade locked into place and he brought the knife up sticking the point about a half inch inside Gibson's left nostril, nicking it just slightly.

"You ever see the movie *Chinatown*, Ed? A guy sliced open Jack Nicholson's nose from the inside. I won't be so kind. I'll cut the damn thing off from the inside out as easy as coring a fucking apple. Now sit down and shut up."

Allen shoved Gibson back onto the sofa. He landed hard, grabbed his throat, coughing and grasping for air as he leaned to the side resting on the sofa's arm. Blood trickled from the small cut onto Gibson's upper lip.

Caruso, turned and looked at the middle of the three television monitor's mounted on the wall, "Watching the security tapes from the private rooms?" He turned back, "Is this how you get your goddamn kicks?"

Maxson's eyes blinked at a machine gun pace now. "Mr. Caruso—"

Caruso pounded his fist on the desk, "Shut up and listen. I've had two guys look me up about supplying new talent for the club and the street. One from Mexico and a Somali group out of Chicago. They're not above just going out and grabbing what they need instead of waiting for all these runaways to come to them. They'll do girls and boys. So, maybe we'll just expand our client base. Give the homos cruising the bars an alternate source.

"I told the Mexicans to bring me some samples in a couple of weeks. The fucking Russians don't want to work with us. They want to control supply and distribution. Move in, take over. I want to make sure we don't lose customers. So, get the rooms finished downstairs. I'll let you know where to pick the merchandise up and where to deliver it."

Maxson nodded, "Yes sir," and ran a nervous tongue over his lips. Caruso straightened up and motioned to Allen and Oliveri. They started toward the door when Caruso stopped and turned around. "One more thing, fix that goddamn sign out front, it looks like a rundown liquor store on Summer Avenue." Then all three left the office, leaving the door open.

CHAPTER FOURTEEN
Nashville

JACK CRANDALL SAT IN A SEMI-COMFORTABLE STRAIGHT BACK CHAIR next to Lisa's bed in ICU. The chair had metal arms topped with wooden armrests. The back of the fake brown leather chair was well padded and rose several inches above his shoulders. He stared at the sonogram of his granddaughter. It was her five month picture taken a week before. Crandall had taped it to the inside door of his locker at work. Now it was all he would know of her. He touched it lightly with his fingertips. They lingered for a few seconds on the image. Crandall sighed and put it back in his shirt pocket.

Lisa had just returned from the first round of reconstructive surgery. Since she was a student, Lisa had been transferred to Vanderbilt University Medical Center. Doctors there felt surgery on the face was needed as soon as possible before the scar tissue began to build up. The back could wait.

Each time he looked at her, his control over the anger inside him weakened. Lisa's forehead, cheeks and chin were wrapped in white gauze bandages, her eyes uncovered. Her beautiful long black hair was covered with a surgical cap as she lay sleeping. The steady rhythmic peaceful breathing was of little comfort amongst the low hum and occasional beeping from the myriad of electronic devices attached to his daughter. This was a scene he had repeated too much of late.

Crandall held her hand as the fatigue from lack of sleep and anxiety began to take control of his body. He leaned his head back on the top of the chair back and closed his eyes.

When he finally found Len Patrone, the son-of-a-bitch was sitting at a bar on Lamar Avenue, a half consumed glass of beer in front of him. It was a somewhat rundown establishment, typical of an area where people came looking for cheap sex, drugs or both. The drugs were mostly peddled in the back alleys away from the light. Hookers, on the other hand, were more open in selling their wares. Entering the bar, the man looked around for potential dangers but could only see several negotiations ongoing and one man face down on a table.

Cigarette smoke hung in the air like a fog that settled just above the river, not quite touching it. As he looked around, it was plain to see the health inspectors were well paid by the owner, Alex Caruso. But he already knew that.

The thought crossed the man's mind that before tonight he would have taken little note of the condition of the place. That the floor looked and smelled like it hadn't been cleaned in months reminded him of how low he had fallen.

The door to the men's room opened and a woman dressed in a short skirt and see through blouse walked out, followed by a man in his mid forties. The woman looked in his direction with a stunned expression of recognition then slid off to the side, seeking the darkest corner of the bar and pulling her companion with her.

Patrone turned around on his bar stool and looked at the man who had just entered. He took a drag from the cigarette in his mouth and put it out in the ashtray on the bar. "Well, well," he said as he let the smoke drift out of his lungs, "Just come from the convenience store? How's the wife?" He asked as he slid off the barstool and unfolded his six foot frame tugging at his light jacket and smoothing it out.

Stopping about ten feet from Patrone, the man widened his stance slightly, his left hand on his hip, the right hand hidden behind the right hip, "Do you know why I'm here?"

"I know why you think you're here," Patrone said, giving his upper lip a quick wipe. He slowly lowered his arm to his side while sneaking his other hand inside his jacket.

The man brought up his right hand, the .45 automatic now in full view. In a measured steady voice he said, "No sudden moves, from anyone, especially you, Patrone. Easy now, both hands where I can see them, grab your crotch." He looked around briefly, "Everybody else, I got no beef with you, so just stay still right where you are."

Patrone brought both hands in front of him, "This is kind of wild west for you. I thought you were a long range shooter. One with scruples even. Sure you can handle the pressure of looking the other guy in the eye?"

"I can put my conscience aside for you. I may not be the best with a handgun, but I want the last thing for you to see is my face."

As the man peered at Patrone through his dark brown eyes, a sudden movement behind the bar caught his attention. The bartender pulled a pistol from under the bar. He quickly fired one shot at the bartender, hitting him in the upper right chest below the collar bone. Some of the women in the bar screamed. Now Patrone was moving and going for his weapon. The man turned, dropped to one knee and fired, striking Patrone in the chest. Patrone went backwards against the bar, turned sideways and fired his gun just as the man fired a second time, striking his target in the lateral side of the chest this time. Patrone's bullet found the man's left side. He fell backward onto the floor, but rolled to his right to come up in a firing position on one knee. Patrone slid down the front of the bar to a sitting position. At this close distance he knew Patrone's 9mm had made a clean exit. He was losing blood front and back.

The young man struggled to his feet holding his left hand over the entry wound, applying pressure as he walked over to Patrone and stopped. Patrone looked up, breathing rapidly, "You're better than people give you credit for." Then he coughed and blood flowed from his mouth and ran down his chin in small rivulets. He tried to lift his weapon but couldn't. Others in the bar were frozen in place.

"No, I'm not that good. You're just not as good as you think you are. There's nothing special about a man who shoots an unarmed woman in the head. You're just a coward." The man with the jet black hair raised his .45 once again and fired a single shot into the middle of Patrone's forehead.

He picked up Patrone's 9mm, removed the clip, ejected the round in the chamber and dropped the gun on the floor. Then he walked behind the bar, keeping an eye on the customers. After removing all the rounds from the bartender's weapon he looked down at the man he had just shot who returned his gaze with fear in his eyes. It was a face scarred and marked from an untreated acne problem, "Don't worry, I said I had no beef with you."

Grabbing several bar towels he stuffed them inside his shirt, front and back. Then he tucked his shirt in an attempt to hold them tight against his wounds. "I'm leaving now," he announced as he came out from behind the bar. "When I leave, call an ambulance for this guy, and tell the police I'll be at Methodist University Medical."

"Daddy," a gravelly, tired sounding female voice said.

Crandall blinked his eyes several times and turned his head to the right, "Hi, Lisa. How's my little girl?" He was still holding her hand.

Pulling a tissue from the box on her side table, Lisa turned her head toward the window, "Why did those men do this, what did we do to them?" Then she began crying uncontrollably. "David is dead!" She said through her tears.

Crandall stood and pressed the nurse call button, then began to lightly caress the top of her head not covered by bandages. "I know, baby, I know," he said in a whisper. For Crandall it was now a point of no return.

CHAPTER FIFTEEN
Lawrenceville, Georgia

AFTER HE RETURNED TO HIS DESK DETECTIVE BRENNAN REVIEWED the Crandall case and everything reported the day before and after the fire in the entire metro area. The only thing of significance was late the following afternoon when an abandoned Maxima was towed from a shopping center two miles from the Crandall house. According to the report, the registered owner was out of town, and the vehicle had to have been stolen from his house and parked at the location where it was found.

So, here he was walking around the white Nissan Maxima on the towing company lot looking for what, he didn't know. But, that's the way these things worked; you looked and picked. Then you tried to make sense from whatever you found.

After a cursory exam of the outside of the vehicle he donned his latex gloves and popped the trunk. Nothing unusual there. Then he moved to the inside. First the back seat, then the front, a meticulous slow search to not disturb anything that might need further processing.

In the glove compartment he found an assortment of lottery tickets, expired insurance cards, a pen and several crumpled pieces of paper. Brennan unfolded each one with extreme care. Nothing. Then he checked between the seats and the center console. Wedged next to the passenger seat was another piece of paper, a purchase receipt dated the morning after the fire from a pawn shop on Beaver Ruin Road. *Maybe now we have a starting point*, he thought as he read the date/time stamp over and over.

Smoothing out the receipt Brennan placed it in a Ziploc Evidence Bag. Five more minutes revealed nothing of note. He checked the time on his cell phone. *I've got time to get over there.*

He instructed personnel at the wrecker service's office not to let anyone touch the vehicle until further notice, including the owner.

Dallas, Texas

The Citation Mustang landed at Dallas / Fort Worth International Airport just after 5:00 PM and taxied up to the terminal in the southwest quadrant reserved for private business aircraft. Mickey Pyle stared out the small portal window at all the ground crews and baggage handlers scurrying about in a ballet of organized chaos. "Ants got nothing on these guys," he mumbled to no one in particular. His two fellow passengers were waking from their two and a half hour nap during the flight from Birmingham to Dallas.

The call had come out of left field. Caruso decided the Dallas problem needed fixing sooner. A chartered jet would be waiting for them at the Birmingham airport and a rental car was reserved in Dallas under the name of Edward Noonan, his current alias.

The local he hired to keep an eye on the target would be waiting at the hotel. He hoped he was better than the one in Nashville. That guy had let some college punk beat the shit out of him. Though he did have to admit, the college punk had some skills. Not good enough to dodge a bullet though.

The plane came to a stop. Pyle unbuckled and looked over his shoulder, "Grab your jocks guys, we got a lot to do. Everything's been moved up at least twenty-four hours."

Gwinnett County, Georgia

It was your standard small pawn shop. An assortment of jewelry, watches, electronics and weaponry were organized in sections. A security camera mounted in each corner provided full coverage of the sales floor, but not of the type that showed much detail on faces. A short man in his early sixties stood behind the counter. Brennan quickly flashed his ID and followed with a quick explanation of his visit. Then he placed the receipt on the counter, "I'm trying to ID a man who purchased something in your store. Did you process this sale?" Brennan tapped the receipt with his index finger.

As he studied the receipt, the man rubbed his left ear between his thumb and forefinger, "No, that would have been Kenny, maybe Bill. But from the time stamp on it, I can show you our security tape. It should give pretty clear detail on the guy's face."

Brennan looked around at the cameras, "Well, Mr. Tanner, these cameras don't seem to be angled right for the face." He returned his gaze to Tanner.

Tanner chuckled slightly. "Those are mainly for show. They just show movement. Helps us catch any shoplifters. They also make folks look where we want them to look. Folks trying to hide won't look directly at 'em. That's why we have the high quality cameras hidden. You're looking at one right now just over my shoulder.

"You see, I got burned a few years back. Long story. So we had a security expert come in and set us up. The good stuff is all digitized on DVD's. That way we can keep a year's worth. Ain't hi-def, but it's pretty good."

Brennan was unsure if he was barking up the right tree, but he at least knew he was about to see a car thief—except that car thieves aren't prone to dropping by a pawn shop in the vehicle and buying Rolex watches with cash.

"I'm impressed, Mr. Tanner. I'll need to take it with me. We'll send you a copy in a couple of days, but I need to hold onto the original for a bit."

"Okay, if you'll jus' follow me to the back we'll pull it up on the monitor and make sure we get the right date and time."

Ten minutes later Brennan was driving away from the pawn shop headed to the department with the receipt, DVD, and a photo of the watch. A name on the receipt would have been nice, but no such luck. If Dick Clancy was still there he would have him freeze the frame with the perp's face and ship it off to the FBI to run through their facial recognition software. Since the perp was wearing driving gloves, he doubted there would be any fingerprint evidence. He made a quick mental note to include the fact that this case could involve Alex Caruso. Maybe that would speed things up. The guy didn't look like your typical grand theft auto suspect.

Police departments across the country had been alerted about the two assaults and the suspicion that they were related. Maybe now he would have a face for a proper Be On the Lookout or BOLO. If the FBI came through he might just have a name to go on the BOLO. His mind kept coming back to the image of the man on the DVD. Something about the guy was nagging at him.

It was right there, how he looked, how he carried himself. Then it hit him and he knew he would be studying the video a lot closer in the morning, but he had to get Clancy or one of his techs working on this right away.

Nashville

It was hard talking to Lisa's doctors. But the news was as good as could be expected. If her recovery went well, she could leave the hospital in time to attend David's funeral. Mark would come up and go with her, he would have to. Then Mark would take her back to Georgia. Crandall had other plans.

The update on Andrea wasn't as good. Something was interfering with her kidney function. They weren't sure if it was physiological or pharmacological. More tests were ordered for today.

Dr. Chung, Lisa's surgeon, recommended a friend who was Chief of Reconstructive Surgery at Emory Hospital in Atlanta. Dr. Simmons could take care of the remaining procedures, he said. Crandall figured he would be back by then. The next step would be the hardest thing he had ever done in his life. He was going to leave his little girl when she needed him most. Caruso would be expecting him to stay with her. Crandall could not let him win, not this time. Caruso had gotten away with it the last time when a corrupt judge threw out much of the testimony on conspiracy to murder.

Lisa was out of recovery and in a surgical room now. Crandall slowly opened the door while he searched for the words to explain it all. They just weren't there. How do you tell your baby girl your whole life and hers is a lie? Or that she is lying in this hospital bed covered with bandages and David was killed because of the father she looked to for protection?

What he would not tell her was that the police found the Taurus sedan used in the abduction. She didn't need to know the trunk in which she had been imprisoned held a body when they found it. The man's blood type matched the blood on David's knuckles leading police to believe it was the attacker David had fought off. With a stab wound in the chest and his throat cut, the guy either bled to death or drowned on his own blood. Either way, not a pretty way to die. Crandall had no sympathy.

He felt a modicum of relief when he saw her sleeping. He would wait until morning. Crandall was feeling like a man on death row who had just received a stay of execution. A temporary reprieve, but welcomed nonetheless.

With his confession postponed, Crandall poured a glass of water from the pitcher on the night stand, removed a prescription bottle from his pocket and tapped out an oblong white pill. After swallowing the pill, he sat. Crandall retrieved the sonogram photo from his shirt pocket, leaned back and simply stared at the image.

Dacula, Georgia

Cindy poured the last of the zinfandel she had taken home from the hotel into a long stemmed wine glass, sat on the sofa in her living room, and placed the glass on the flowered coaster on the oak end table. She shivered and zipped up her heavy red sweatshirt even though the temperature in the house was quite comfortable. A nervous, fretful sigh escaped her lips while she wadded and un-wadded a napkin with unconscious repetition. *What the hell have I gotten myself into?* The worst part now was she didn't know if she loved Jack or if it was just sympathy because of his situation. *Self doubt now?* She asked herself.

After she picked up Mark at the airport, she insisted he stay with her rather than a hotel. Self preservation might have been her motivation. Having a paratrooper in the house did give her some comfort. Jack had demanded it. And after everything he told her it took very little convincing on her part.

Mark was at the hospital now and would be back in a few hours. The one thing he insisted on was a rental car. For some strange reason, there were not a lot of the questions she assumed were coming. It was as if he knew, or suspected, the truth about his father's past and connected it to the last few days' events.

She brushed away a few renegade strands of her long hair and took several sips of wine. Its effect eased her tension, but not her anxiety. Detective Brennan had given her his personal cell number after he told her of his conversation with Jack.

After a quick look at her watch, she decided to shower and dress for bed before Mark returned. As she stood she heard a noise outside, slight though it was. With slow deliberateness she made her way to the window, lifted a slat on the blinds and peered between the small opening. Outside was the dark outline of what she thought was an SUV in front of her house, its headlights off. There was a shadowy figure sitting in the driver's seat while exhaust fumes floated from the tail pipe in the cool night air.

From where she was standing the light switch next to the front door was only two feet away. With her free hand Cindy turned on the porch light while continuing to look out the window, afraid to even blink. The car slowly pulled away, headlights off. The house across the street was dark, no one home yet.

Cindy sucked in a quick breath, hurried down the hallway to the panel of her security system and turned on the alarm. Then she returned to the living room and this time sat in an overstuffed easy chair facing the door. She removed the 9mm from her purse on the side table, chambered a round as Jack had trained her, and laid the weapon on the table.

Leaning back, resting her head on the top of the chair back, Cindy rubbed her eyes then ran both hands through her hair, brushing it back from around her face. She leaned forward, rested her elbows on her thighs, then placed her face in her hands and tried to stop shaking. In a nervous whisper she asked herself, "What the hell have I gotten myself into?"

CHAPTER SIXTEEN
Nashville

FOR THE BETTER PART OF THE LAST TWO DECADES, JACK CRANDALL had been looking forward to the day he could tell his children about his and their pasts. He thought by making a full break with their past was the best way to protect them. But, in a cruel twist of fate, that history was why he was looking down at his daughter while she lay in a hospital bed, her dark blue eyes looking back at him between layers of white gauze. She had gotten his hair, but her mother's beautiful eyes. An early morning sun lit the room through the east facing windows, while shadows did a slow creep back toward the window as the sun rose.

"It's okay, Daddy," Lisa said quietly as tears soaked into the bandages on her cheeks. "It's not your fault. You did what you thought was best for Mark and me.

"Mark used to tell me he remembered Mama a little bit. Said she was even prettier than the pictures you showed us."

Jack breathed heavily and rubbed Lisa's hand as he held it between his. "She was, baby—she was. She saved my life, but I couldn't save hers. She died in my arms. I thought we were finally safe. That Caruso had stopped looking for me. I was wrong, I'm sorry. I'm sorry for you and Andrea. I'm sorry about David. But, he won't stop. That's why I have to leave for a little while."

"Please don't, let the police do this. I don't want to lose you, too," Lisa said between sobs.

Crandall tried to force a smile, but his eyes remained sad, "You won't. You're the reason I'll be coming back. But I have to make sure he can't hurt you or Andrea anymore."

"What about Mark?"

"Caruso's too much of a coward to go after someone like your brother. Besides, he has duties and responsibilities now. It's my job now to see he's free to do them.

"If I don't do this, Caruso wins. And you will have to live in fear the rest of your life. Even if I'm dead, he wouldn't stop. He's a cruel sadistic bastard. He loves to hurt people and cause pain. He's like a rabid animal. I've seen it."

Lisa tried to sit up, "Promise me you'll come back."

Crandall leaned over the railing on her hospital bed and wrapped his arms around his baby girl, holding her tight and rocking her back and forth with the slightest of movements. He kissed her on the top of her head, a tear ran down his cheek onto her matted hair, "I promise baby girl—I promise."

Lawrenceville, Georgia

Paul Brennan was back at his desk, poring over the file again. He was now convinced he found the perp. The BOLO with a description, but no name, had gone out before midnight. The one common thread was the ponytail. Hair color was different, height was a bit different and only Andrea remembered eye color. But, Andrea distinctly remembered a blond ponytail. Lisa could only give a rough description of the face, but the black ponytail stood out. Height and weight were close enough for him, even though the height estimates were four inches apart.

In his career he had come across very few coincidences. A guy with a blond ponytail attacks Andrea, the next day a guy with a blond ponytail shows up at a pawn shop in a stolen vehicle. Two days later some punk with a black ponytail puts Lisa in the hospital and kills her boyfriend. The guy likes to change his appearance, but criminals are many times creatures of habit. Those habits tend to get them caught.

Who, if anyone else, might be on his list? He leaned back in his chair and stared at the wall for almost a full minute and rolled that question back and forth in his mind. Brennan opened the desk drawer and pulled out the business card for Jerrod Wilkins, U. S. Marshall. He was about to dial Wilkins' number when his own cell began to buzz and vibrate.

***

It was right at two hundred miles from Nashville to Memphis. Three and a half hours of steady driving on I-40, Crandall figured. There was an urge to set a new land speed record getting there, but he suppressed it. He wasn't even sure where he was going first. There was the place he wanted to go. Hell, he wasn't sure if he would be welcomed. Most likely the house had new owners anyway.

Before he got on the highway, he needed to make another call. The first one that morning had been to Cindy and Mark. Andrea was doing better but would be in the hospital a few more days; her kidney still wasn't functioning the way the doctors wanted.

Cindy was upset with him for not telling her he was going by the hospital before he'd left Georgia. For the most part he was honest with her. There was some medication he needed, but some things she was better off not knowing. He promised he would call in a day or so. Until then Mark would be there when she was home and at the hospital when she was at work until he left for Nashville.

Now he sat in his SUV in the hospital parking garage and pulled a card from his wallet and punched in a number printed on it. While the other phone rang, the hate and anger began to well up again. It came and went like an ocean tide on the Maine coast.

"Sergeant Brennan, this is Jack Crandall. I just wanted you to know I won't be back for several days, maybe a week or two," he said after Brennan answered.

"Where are you going?" Brennan asked.

Crandall contemplated telling him the truth as he stared through the windshield at the other cars in the garage. For a second he thought about the people in those cars visiting family and friends in the hospital. More feelings of guilt crept into his psyche. Was he deserting family members again? Was he making the right decision? Did he really have much choice?

His thoughts returned to Brennan's question and telling him the truth about where he was and even going so far as to what he was planning to do, "That's not important. While I'm gone please keep in touch with Mark and Cindy." Crandall figured if Brennan was worth his salt as a detective he'd figure it out soon enough.

"It is important, Jack, don't do anything stupid. I understand how you are feeling."

Jack clinched his teeth and griped the steering wheel, "My feelings have nothing to do with it. I just have some business to take care of."

"Right, Jack, I know your history, your real name. I know what business you're thinking about. Look, just stay with Lisa and come back when she can travel. We've had a break in the case. I think I have a photo of the guy who did this. I'm just waiting to hear back from the FBI on an ID. We've got a BOLO on him nationwide."

Crandall sat in silence for a few seconds trying to decide whether Brennan was lying just to get him back to Atlanta. *Nope, not his style.* His jaw was so tight he felt it would break, "Maybe it's just best you keep that picture to yourself and not let me see it."

"I'm not sure I understand."

Crandall was on the verge of snapping, knowing there was now a face to hate, "Well, if I get my hands on the fucker, he better be a praying man."

"What's that mean?"

"It means I'm going to send him straight to hell!"

Crandall pressed the end button on his cell phone. He opened the battery case and removed the battery, replaced the cover and put both phone and battery in the console compartment between the seats. He looked at his hands. They were not shaking. He rubbed his upper left arm, then starting his vehicle, Crandall backed out of his parking place.

Lawrenceville, Georgia

Brennan had pressed the callback button on his phone several times, but each time it went directly into Crandall's voicemail. Laying the phone down, he leaned forward, elbows on the desk and rubbed the bridge of his nose, "Shit!"

He tried several more callbacks, no answers. Then Brennan gave a quick call to the tech guys to see if they could locate and track Crandall's cell phone. It really didn't matter. He knew Crandall was going to Memphis. He leaned back in his chair for a moment then sat up. A few mouse clicks and he pulled up the directory he was looking for.

CHAPTER SEVENTEEN

THINGS WERE BUSY IN THE ER. CINDY HAD JUST ARRIVED FOR THE noon shift and there were already two auto accident victims with fairly minor injuries, a fractured arm from falling out of a tree, one potential heart attack, and a few patients running fevers. On her way in from the parking lot she provided assistance to a couple. The wife was passing a kidney stone and had severe pain and nausea. They weren't a Level One Trauma Center, so this was pretty standard fare.

But, if this was a sign, it would be a busier than normal shift for a Sunday. It became a double edged sword. She felt for the folks who needed the emergency room, but it would help keep her mind off things. Jennifer Grady came by to let her know she was working on the fourth floor. She would be able to keep her updated on Andrea's progress. Doctors were trying to figure out the irregular functioning of her kidneys.

Cindy walked out of the room where the kidney stone patient was trying to relax. All the rooms were arranged in a rectangle around two counters where nurses did most of their paperwork. The two counters were located at each end of the rectangle. Between the counters was a glass walled area where patient monitoring equipment maintained status of the most critical patients. Refrigerators for IV fluids stood next to tall ovens used for heating blankets to warm patients.

Cindy removed one of the blankets from the oven, held it close and absorbed its comfort as she returned to the patient's room. She made the patient as comfortable as possible then returned to the nurse's station to update patient charts.

A radio blared at the other end of the rectangle near the ambulance entrance. Paramedics were on their way with a patient who was in cardiac arrest. Every available staff member dropped what they were doing and rushed to the entrance.

Lawrencville

"This is Detective Harris, Major Crimes Unit, how may I help you?" The voice on the other end of the telephone connection said.

"Detective Paul Brennan here, Gwinnett County PD in Georgia, I need to pass some information along to you, and maybe ask a favor," Brennan said as he checked his watch. He was supposed to meet Annie for a late lunch at three. He still had an hour and a half.

"As always detective, the favor depends on the information. And of course the information comes first."

"Well, the two are related. You have a guy there, one Alex Caruso, I believe?"

"Yeah, I've been trying to put that bastard away for years. Can't get anybody to flip on him and he always seems to know when we're going to show up. Personally I think he has a couple of folks high up in administration, too. But, nobody will listen to me on that one. We need more than your gut feeling they keep telling me. But, you don't want to hear about my problems, what is it you want to tell me about this whack-job?"

"I think there's a guy on his way to Memphis right now who plans to kill Caruso," Brennan said with as much conviction as he could muster.

"You think?" Harris asked.

Brennan laughed lightly into the phone, "Okay, my gut is telling me that. He wouldn't tell me for sure."

"You talked to the guy?"

"Yes." Brennan picked up an ink pen from the desk and began clicking the point in and out while he talked.

"Okay, Paul, you said your name was Paul right?"

"Yes, Paul Brennan."

"Just wanted to make sure I wrote it down right. Okay, Paul, as much as I want to bring this child raping, murdering bastard to justice, I wouldn't mind pissing on his grave either. So, why are you providing me with this little tidbit?"

A man approached Brennan's desk and dropped a piece of paper off. He dropped the pen, picked it up and read it over quickly while he swiveled his chair sideways, *Crandall's cell is off and un-locatable for now. Last known location Nashville, Tennessee*, it read.

Brennan put the note in the file, "Deserved or not, if he does kill Caruso it will be murder. The guy doesn't deserve to go to jail, and I don't want to put out an area wide BOLO on him."

"Well, most people who want Caruso dead are either cops or scum like Caruso. I assume your guy isn't a cop, so what makes him so damn special?" Harris asked with a hint of sarcasm in his voice.

Brennan turned around to his desk, dropped the paper on it and leaned forward. "How much time you got?"

"If it will get me two inches closer to nailing Caruso, I got all damn day."

Nashville

The cruise control was set for seventy-five mph. Crandall sipped on a cup of coffee from a travel mug he picked up at Starbucks. Two hours, maybe three. No need in calling ahead of time, as the number had been changed about fifteen years ago and was unlisted. But, he didn't know where else to go for now. St. Mary's maybe, but who was the priest there now?

Hell, what does it matter when the bottom line is you really have nothing more to lose? Crandall pressed the accelerator, moved to the left lane, and passed the tractor trailer.

CHAPTER EIGHTEEN
Memphis

THE HOUSE WAS JUST AS HE REMEMBERED; EVEN THE COLOR WAS the same. It was a craftsman-style home with charcoal-grey siding and contrasting white trim. The front porch was lined with white square posts topped with a white railing.

The name on the mailbox was the same, but the oak tree in the front yard was bigger than he remembered. Well, it had been over twenty years. The slow drive past the home allowed him to admire the immaculate flower beds on each side of the steps. Dwarf azaleas sat alternating between perfectly trimmed rose bushes.

No one seemed to be home, so he made a u-turn at the end of the street and pulled into the third driveway on the right. The rutted gravel drive went the length of the house to the single detached garage in the back yard. In the very rear of the yard was the white wooden work shed.

Crandall stopped the car. After knocking on the back door, he was relieved to find no one home. As fast as he could Crandall unloaded the boxes from the rear and placed them in the shed. Then he locked the door with a padlock he found on the work bench inside the shed. Back inside his vehicle, he gripped the steering wheel and took several deep breaths to relax, then backed out of the driveway and headed for Methodist University Hospital parking garage.

Dallas

The house in the suburban neighborhood twenty miles south of downtown Dallas was smaller than Mickey Pyle had expected. His observations confirmed the local guy's description was accurate. The entire neighborhood was crammed with these small houses. Much closer together than he liked.

It made the job harder. Not impossible, just harder. Sound carried better at night, so the distance was important. Houses this small didn't contain noises very well either. Brick also made it a bit harder to burn. He would have to set a few ignition sources in the attic to make sure it collapsed downward, bringing the outside walls inward.

After this job he would be able to kick back for about six months or so. His first stop would be the old miner's shack outside Albuquerque. It belonged to his grandfather. The old guy spent his last dime on it, thinking it was full of silver. Died penniless. Assault, murder, and arson definitely paid better.

Over the last few years he had made the shack livable, but he would have to lay in some stores if he decided to ride out the winter there. It could be isolated, even more so when the snows came, but it beat the hell out of prison, and law enforcement types didn't come knocking in that part of the world. It was his personal *Hole in the Wall.*

Six blocks from the hotel he pulled into the parking lot of a pawn shop he passed earlier. *Might as well see if they have anything interesting.*

Dacula, Georgia

A ghostly figure stared back at Paul Brennan from behind the fog on the bathroom mirror. Steam hung in the air from his just-finished shower and added to the vision. It reminded him of how tired he was. In his younger days he had survived Camp Mackall at Fort Bragg.

Two Weeks in Hell they called it now. The physical part was extreme, the mental even more so. A large part of those first two weeks included sleep deprivation. Four hours sleep a night might have been a good night. To him, that was worse than the physical part. The extreme fatigue seeped into every muscle and fiber of your body. It fogged your mind thicker than the mist flowing across the moors in a 1930s horror movie.

The course was designed to break you down psychologically and push your physical limits to the max. It started hard and got harder by the hour.

Of the two-hundred-fifty-four candidates that started the selection course, sixteen voluntarily dropped out in the first three hours during log drills. Many others were seen puking their guts out. Bathroom breaks were not allowed, so you just pissed down your leg.

During *Land Navigation* you had to go from point A to B to C... through the woods in a specified time limit using only a map and a compass while laden with full gear. At night. Wherever you had to be and what you did next was posted on the bulletin board. Things changed on a moment's notice to see how you would adapt.

The second week they called *Team Week*. Things could become catastrophic. Those who couldn't work well as a team would be weeded out. When you felt you couldn't take one more step, you didn't want to let your team members down, so you found a way. When you lost a member of the team, you had to keep going without them. There was no substitute sitting on the bench to come in and help carry the load.

With about thirty hours remaining in the two weeks you were greeted with a twenty mile march in full combat gear and seventy-five pound rucksacks. After two weeks of true hell, many would drop out here. So close, yet so far.

Of the one-hundred-eighteen that finished the two weeks, just over one hundred actually were selected. Then there was another year or more of training before you got your beret. As best he could estimate, probably only fifty to sixty of the original group made it all the way. He was one of those few.

It was that experience more than anything that got him through Afghanistan after he was wounded twice in the leg. Dave Balfour, the team medic, had patched him up on the field, but he had lost a lot of blood. Dave hooked him to a plasma IV then put him on the medevac chopper. But, it was touch and go as he willed himself to take just one more breath. Dave refused to give him morphine. It would suppress his already labored breathing further.

But that was then. Eight hours sleep in the last forty-eight and he was close to exhaustion. Lunch went well. He and Annie had a very good time. More laughs than discussion of bad memories. A dinner date on Thursday was on the calendar. But for now Chinese takeout, a beer, and bed. *Oh-dark-thirty* came early.

From the nightstand in the bedroom came the pulsating beeps of the ringtone he had assigned to his lieutenant.

CHAPTER NINETEEN
Memphis

IT WAS A NICE COMFORTABLE EASY CHAIR WITH MATCHING OTTOMAN in a brown western-style plaid. A leather sofa on his right backed up to a window that looked out on the neighbor's side yard and house. Against the far wall on top of a short glass front cabinet was a tube type television that appeared to be between ten and fifteen years old. No cable outlets, which explained the antenna mounted to the chimney. There was a digital converter box next to the TV, so Crandall assumed it was watched on occasion. Against the wall to his left beyond the arched entry to the room was a secretary cabinet with glass doors that contained several bottles of liquor.

Crandall sat in the dark waiting. He wondered if he was right. He knew the man was still alive, and his name was on the mailbox. Like it or not, he was about to find out. Circumstances dictated he didn't like it.

A car had turned into the driveway and made its way to the back before stopping, Crandall presumed, just in front of the single car detached garage. Crandall heard the squeak of old rusted hinges on the rear screen door followed by the opening and closing of the inner door. Then the soft fall of footsteps on the hardwood floors coming through the kitchen. Much softer than he expected from leather soled shoes. *Does he know I'm here?*

The revolver appeared through the entry way first, and turned in his direction as the man behind it made slow deliberate moves. Crandall felt it best he remain motionless.

A man in his seventies, about Crandall's height, looked him in the eyes. The solid silver hair stood out in the dim light. A curious expression replaced the initial tension in his face. "Well, I'll be damned. Look what the cat dragged in. What's it been eighteen, nineteen years?" the man said as he lowered his revolver.

Crandall looked up from the chair, "Twenty-one."

"Time flies I guess." The man turned to walk toward the secretary cabinet.

"You don't seem happy to see me?"

"Aw, you know; bad penny and all that," the man said then cleared his throat, "I was wondering who the hell put that padlock on the shed. Whatever you're hiding in there you're going to have to cut the damn lock off, I lost the key years ago.

"So, how've you been Theodore, or do you prefer your new name?" He lowered the desk shelf of the secretary and laid the revolver on it.

Crandall shifted in the chair and switched on the lamp sitting on the table between the chair and sofa, "I've been better. I prefer Ted, or Jack."

"Sorry *Theodore Patrick Reardon*, but your mother and I gave you that name. Besides, it was good enough for your grandfather," Crandall's father said while opening the door of the cabinet.

"You know you really should get an alarm system, Dad."

Reardon gave a slight turn and looked over his shoulder, "What, for this shack?" he said almost with a laugh then shook his head and grinned as he returned his attention to the liquor cabinet.

"I was thinking more for self protection. At least you should lock the back door." Crandall shifted his weight in the chair.

A soft chuckle escaped the older man's lips, "That's what my three-fifty-seven is for. I figure I drop some bastard who breaks in and the others will leave me alone."

"You still carry I see."

"Never stopped. Plus I work at a casino. You'd be surprised how many idiots think you always have a lot of money on you because of that. You still a long-barrel guy?" The man said as he took out a bottle from the middle shelf and a glass from the top, unscrewed the cap and poured.

"You do what you are best at," Crandall sighed nervously, "Look, I need a favor."

The older man turned around and faced Crandall, glass in hand. "What, no dinner, no movie, not even a kiss on the cheek, just leap into bed. Hell, you could at least buy me a drink for old time's sake."

"You have one in your hand. Single malt?"

"Oh, yeah," Reardon looked down at his glass then held it out and smiled, "two fingers neat, *Glenlivet* twelve years old, but hell you know that. It's the only vice I got left, except for black coffee that could strip paint and high fat foods. Even quit smoking ten years ago. Doc says I'm a walking time bomb."

"I don't have much time. Will you help me?"

Reardon sighed, turned his head and gazed out the window, his shoulders slumped. He looked down at the glass he now held with both hands. After a few seconds of nervous silence he returned his eyes to his son. "You know" Reardon sighed again, "Your mom miscarried twice before you were born and once after. So you were all we had until you married Janie. Then she was killed. You take our grandkids and disappear into some damnable government program. Broke your mother's heart. She's in a nursing home now and hasn't a clue as to who I am most of the time. You waltz back in and start asking for goddamn favors," his voice rising at the end.

Reardon took a quick sip from his glass and moved his lips and cheeks around like he was chewing on the liquid, then let out a quick breath through his nostrils and swallowed.

Crandall leaned back in the chair and ran both hands back and forth through his hair, looked at the ceiling, then back at his father, "Oh boy—I guess I deserved every bit of that."

"You're damned right you deserved it. Can't your Marshall friends help you?" Reardon stared out the window again and worked his jaw and cheeks up and down, tension growing on his face.

Crandall tightened his lips and bowed his head for a second then looked back at his father, "Not in this. Look, there's nothing I can do to make up for all that, but the bottom line is I need some help and you are the only one I've got left to turn to. Will you help me?"

"Depends," the words escaped through tightened jaws and lips. "You here after Caruso?" Reardon asked as he walked across the room and sat on the sofa, the rushing sound of air being forced from between and below the cushions seemed to deflate the room.

That question caught Crandall a little off guard. But, it did leave him a little curious as to why his father would so quickly arrive at that conclusion, even though it was a logical one.

"Yes." He answered, realizing his father's interrogation skills were as sharp as ever. First the guilt trip, then the inquisition. His shoulders were tense; his neck felt it could snap at any moment.

The leather sofa creaked a bit as the man shifted his weight and leaned against the arm of the sofa while he took another sip of his scotch, "He's been out of prison for a while, so why do you want him?" Reardon asked in a more matter of fact tone.

"He's trying to settle some old scores."

"And you're one of them. So, how'd he find you?"

Crandall rubbed his hand back and forth through his hair again, an old nervous habit, leaned forward and put his elbows on his thighs then clasped his hands. "Don't know yet. I have my suspicions, but he did and this time I'm going to end it. He's going after the people I love."

"Sounds like him, you still in WitSec?"

"So far."

"Well, you gonna tell me what happened or do I have to guess?"

Crandall licked his lips with nervous determination and began...

Reardon sat in silence as his son gave the full ugly details. Crandall stopped or slowed on those occasions where his emotions tried to take over. The silence on the part of his audience was nothing new. It was his way when you finally opened up. He would process everything and then ask specific questions.

"It's funny," Crandall continued, nearing the end, "I had to learn how easy it is to kill in order to learn how precious life is. Nine months to bring a life into this world and it can be gone in less than a second. Now I hand out medicine for people desperately trying to hang on just one more day.

"And, now I'll never know what it's like to hold my grandchildren," he sighed, "Poetic justice, I guess, after what I did to you and mom." Crandall paused for a second, took a deep breath and continued, "Did you know you can go to a doctor and get an abortion at five months, but if someone causes injury that kills the baby at five months they can be charged with murder, infanticide?" Crandall fell silent, letting the question be an invitation to his father to speak.

Reardon spoke with little emotion. "Welcome to real life. It doesn't always make sense. So, just what is it you want from me?"

"I need a place to stay and some help in finding Caruso and who he sent to burn me out."

Reardon took a sip of his scotch, paused and swirled the liquid in the glass, looked away then looked back at Crandall, "Tall order. Are you asking me to be an accessory to murder?'

Crandall sat back and rubbed his face with both hands, then shook his head. In a tired voice answered, "Don't know. Maybe. I guess. I'm not sure yet."

"Have to think about that one. So what's your plan, just walk up to him and put a bullet between his eyes like you did Patrone or try for a headshot from three-hundred meters?"

"Haven't finished working out the details."

Reardon sat his glass on the table and leaned forward, "Look, Ted, I've got no problem with Caruso taking one to the head, the bastard should have been fed to a wood chipper years ago. But, maybe I have some ideas, if you're willing to listen."

"Do I have a choice?" Crandall asked as he licked his lips, his nerves still showing.

"Not if you want my help. Can I get you a beer, scotch or something else to drink?"

"A beer would be nice, thanks." Crandall began to relax a bit; maybe this was a peace offering.

His father started to stand, "By the way, that's my chair. Move your ass to the sofa."

Crandall smiled, nodded, then looked around the room. In the light, he noticed the picture next to the TV, "Dad, what is that?" He asked, pointing at the TV.

"That," Reardon said as he walked past headed toward the kitchen, "Is a picture of you, Mark, and Lisa at Lisa's high school graduation."

CHAPTER TWENTY
Memphis

Four men sat in the large corner booth in the rear of Antonio's Ristorante. Two booths on each side were cleared except for Tony Oliveri who remained on vigil in the booth nearest the kitchen door. Waiters scurried about knowing to keep their distance unless signaled by Oliveri. Caruso preferred being near the kitchen. The traffic in and out masked most conversation, plus many other patrons preferred to be away from the kitchen which made it easier to keep people away.

Eric, his regular waiter, was Antonio's nephew. Always attentive, he made sure the wine never ran dry. He remained alert at all times for the signal from Oliveri. His reward was always a full day's worth of tips and free admission to the *Southern Bell.* Caruso considered it a small price for excellent service. He and Antonio had been childhood friends, both graduating from Catholic High. They had even shared the same love interest, Kate Whitlock. Caruso won out, but they remained friendly.

In the booth two bottles of chardonnay sat next to a plate of calamari. Alex Caruso popped a piece of the calamari in his mouth and sipped on his wine. He put his glass down, dabbed his lips with his napkin and placed it back on his lap. Leaning forward, he placed his elbows on the table and turned his attention to the dark haired man in his late forties sitting next to him. "So, Mr. Aguilar, you say you get some of your merchandise by recruiting, just how does that work?"

Eduardo Aguilar smiled, his dark eyes and white teeth stood out in contrast to each other. He looked at his body guard on his right, then back to Caruso. "Alex—uh—may I call you Alex?"

"Yes."

"Good, it makes things much friendlier." Aguilar said in a calm, slightly accented voice. "Well, Alex, in certain areas of Mexico, offering someone a better life can have many, many advantages.

There is a level of security, too. In Ciudad Juarez and some other areas we use *feminicidios* as a recruiting tool."

"My Spanish isn't quite as good as your English, what does that mean?" Caruso asked as he picked up his glass. Stan Allen, on his left, sat in silence watching the two men across the table.

"I guess the English word would be *feminicide*, if there is one. In the past few years there have been a lot of murders in Juarez. Thousands. About five thousand of those have been young women. Most under twenty years of age. So, you see they are scared. Many will look to us as a way of surviving. We promise them jobs and bring them to San Antonio. I have some friends in the medical field who check them out then we deliver them to our clients. It works well if you have the right recruiters."

"Recruiters?" Caruso asked. He was now very intrigued, "And who might they be?"

A quite short laugh escaped Aguilar's lips with a short bob of his head, then a smile. He reached for some calamari, "My wife and her sister. Let's just say they have become accustomed to a particular life style that my business provides and the drug trade in Mexico has fallen into a state of civil war."

Caruso shared the man's smile and laugh, "I would like to meet a woman who takes such an interest in her husband's work."

"I'm afraid she doesn't travel much outside Mexico. I handle things north of the border. Perhaps you can pay us a visit sometime."

Caruso leaned back against the red leather back of the booth's seat and sipped on his wine, "Perhaps. Do you ever sample your product?"

Another smile, "What prudent businessman doesn't?" Aguilar took a slight pause. "So, for $100,000 I can provide you with five girls. Two will be taken to your hotel room. The other three your men will take to your club early that evening. If you are satisfied I can bring you some replacements every few months and you can move the girls to any of your other establishments or sell them, it's up to you. But the cost will be higher. This is my introductory price. 20,000 apiece is a bargain for such quality."

"What about the age of the girls."

"We don't deal with birth certificates, and we don't ask."

Caruso raised his eyebrows, "Virgins?" He wondered what it would be like to *break in* a virgin.

"If our medical people find a virgin, we send them overseas. I can get 500,000 plus expenses for one depending on her attractiveness and the client. Sometimes more."

"I'm impressed. You do know you have competition for my business?"

Another laugh. "Of course. This is a competitive field. I also know you have dropped the Somalis and are talking to the Russians from New York. The Somalis are pissed about it, but that is nature. I offer quality and price. The Russians get theirs after they have been used up in Europe or from local crack houses. Kidnappings, runaways, hooking them on drugs, these are techniques for all of us. I like to be more particular."

"The Russians are out. They don't want to partner, they want to take over. How do you keep them in line? Keep them from running away if they aren't locked up all the time?"

"It's no trade secret. The same way you do. There is a penalty upon their families. What many of mine don't know is sometimes the penalty is already carried out. Fathers in Mexico can be very protective of their little girls. Just like they are up here. Sometimes they must be eliminated."

"What about an American like I asked?"

"We have acquired a young blonde from Texas. This has pushed back our delivery schedule a couple of days. But, she should be worth the wait."

"I'll be the judge. Make sure the American is with the ones brought to the hotel." Caruso picked up his glass and tilted it toward Aguilar in a mock toast, "If the quality is what you say, we will be interested in a future relationship. My clients are as particular as I am."

Memphis

Reardon gave his son a beer then retrieved two manila envelopes packed with papers and photos, plus a shoebox with recordings. He told Crandall just to read the contents of the envelopes then ask any questions. Information about the picture would wait until morning. What he was about to see was more important.

Crandall made his way through the first envelope and was starting on the second, "So, how long have you been working on this and how many people know?" They had moved to the kitchen table, a beer to his left, leafing through the ream of paper and photos. In the shoebox to his right sat audio recordings.

"Only four people in Memphis, not including me. There is a lawyer in a small town I won't reveal who has all the originals. I send them to him after I make copies." Reardon sipped on his second glass of scotch.

Crandall ran his fingers through his hair again, "Do the police know?"

"One," Reardon said then cleared his throat, "And, he's taking a career ending risk letting this go on. There's an ongoing FBI investigation into Caruso, but there always has been. This is almost two years worth of work."

Crandall laid the ledger sheet he was looking at down, "Who are you working with?"

"Primarily, Angela Whitlock, Caruso's sister-in-law. We hooked up at the casino. She looked me up. I was dealing blackjack and she slipped me a note. We had a couple of coffees but haven't spoken face to face in quite a while. We use burn phones, but mostly dead drops to communicate. She would have made a hell of a spy. But, if Caruso finds out, her sister Kate is dead. That's what he holds over her head. So, she wants him put away for good."

"How's she getting her information?"

Reardon squinted with his eyes as if trying to decide whether to say, then with some hesitation in his voice, "She went out with a guy named Dave Maxson at first. She convinced him she was in love with him, but he got cold feet. Didn't want his wife or Caruso to find out. But, that was our foot in the door. Got a ton of information to get us started. It's a very fine line she's walking if Caruso finds out what's going on. I think you might know Maxson."

This brought a wry laugh from Crandall. "Oh yeah, I know him. Not one of my favorite memories. That's probably him in a bunch of photos at the strip club. His name is all over some of these documents. Who's the cop?"

"Not going to tell you. I only talk to him every month or so. And, he's seen very little of this. I'll give him the whole packet when it's finished. The lawyer knows to contact him if anything natural, or unnatural, happens to me or Angela. The photos were taken by me with a telephoto lens except for the ones inside the club. The guy who did those is kind of a sneaky little techno nerd, but doesn't look like one. I've only met him once, but Angela says I can trust him, so I do."

Crandall picked up his beer, drained the last two swallows then sat it back down. "Well, I guess twenty-two years as an Army intelligence officer came in handy."

"Yeah," his father said, "Now I've got a question for you. Just where the hell is your car? I know you didn't walk here from Nashville."

"It's in the parking garage at Methodist Hospital. I figure it can stay there two days before I need to move it. I didn't want to drive it around with out-of-state plates. We had an abandoned car where I work for probably a week. Folks are sometimes there for three, four days. Plus their family. How long until this is finished?"

"Basically it's done. Almost two years of work. I'm just organizing and verifying. Only have one more thing I'm trying to find out. We may be closing in on Caruso's inside man."

"Inside man?"

Reardon tapped the stack of photos with his finger, "In all this, and in the recordings, there is a hint of someone, maybe more than one. No names. But they have local inside information. My police connection has suspected it for quite a while, but has had trouble finding out just who. There seems to have been more vague references to them lately in some of the recordings."

"How'd you get the recordings?"

"Most came from a single person. Same guy who did the inside pictures, but I'm not going to tell you who, not right now anyway. When the time is right. Claims he's tapping into some video stuff the last couple of weeks. That person's life is on the line and has been for over a year now. Suffice it to say he sees Caruso on a regular basis. I've probably told you more than I should have."

Crandall looked around the room. It was the same as he remembered. Even down to the wooden table with the folding leafs he was sitting at. The vinyl table cloth with the old newspaper ads seemed somewhat new. He breathed deep to take it all in, and it even smelled the same. Then he turned to his father, "I still want him dead. None of this will guarantee a death sentence, and even if it did he would stay on death row for years."

"It also includes most of his inner circle. Over a dozen people will wind up in prison. Why don't you sleep on it and we'll talk. Now you need some rest. I think in the morning you should go to Saint Mary's. Have a talk with Father Wisniewski. He was a great comfort to me and your mother when you left, and now again with her medical problems."

"Jozef's still there?"

CHAPTER TWENTY-ONE

Lawrenceville, Georgia

"Listen to me on this, Paul. You're doing it *again*," Lieutenant McMichael said from behind the desk in his office. A Mr. Coffee sat in the middle of a small credenza against the wall behind the lieutenant. Brennan sat in a straight-back wooden chair in front of the desk. Behind him was the closed door. Outside the door a hallway led to a cubical farm squad room. This was a private meeting.

Brennan leaned forward in his chair, "You're going to have to be more specific, Terry, what exactly is it that I'm doing again?"

"Getting personally involved. You are becoming obsessed with the Crandall thing. Just like you did in the Walton case," McMichael leaned back in his swivel chair and clasped his hands in front of him.

Brennan shook his head, "No, not personally *involved*. Personally *pissed*. Cathy Walton was eight months pregnant. Her *boyfriend* beat her to death then dumped her body into the trunk of a car and set it on fire. How do I not get pissed? Not just her, but the baby was near full term. The bastard killed his own son, whose only crime was to be conceived."

"Damn it, you almost shot the guy in cold blood when he gave up. I don't want shit like that happening again."

"There wasn't anything cold about it. That piece of debris deserved to die slow and painful. What I was thinking of doing was actually pretty damn humane if you ask me. Would'uv saved the taxpayers a hell of a lot of money, too." Brennan paused and took a deep breath, "Look, in spite of what people think, I wouldn't have shot him, but I sure as hell wanted to. He was too much of a coward to make a stand."

"Be that as it may, you are stretching yourself pretty thin on the Crandall thing. You got guys jumping through hoops here at all hours. There are other cases to work on."

Brennan leaned forward, "Well, be *that* as it may, some bastard is running all over the southeast beating up pregnant women, killing babies, dogs, and ROTC students and cutting up young twenty-two year old women. How the hell do I not get personally involved? I need to find this guy before Crandall does. Crandall doesn't deserve to go to jail."

"How do you know that? He worked for Caruso once."

Brennan placed both hands on the front of the desk, "I've gotten to know the man. He's a decent guy. A Jarhead. Almost got his ass blown up in Lebanon in '83. Lost several good friends. It messed him up for a while, and he couldn't hold a job when he got out. A street buddy got him on with Caruso. All he did was do some street muscle and collect money. Then Caruso wanted him to kill a competing pusher. A sixteen year old, for Christ's sake. Crandall couldn't do it, tried to get out. Caruso had the kid killed anyway, then went after Crandall's family, had his wife killed. So, Crandall fought back, then went into WitSec.

"Now, Terry, tell me how I don't get personally involved," Brennan pushed back in his chair and folded his arms across his chest.

McMichael sat silent for a few seconds and started to speak just as Brennan's cell phone began sounding. He looked at the number, "It's the hospital."

After answering he listened intently, a few "uh huh's" later he pressed the end button. "I've got to go, it's about Crandall. I'll do my best to stay detached, but you're going to have to tell me how you got those lieutenant bars and never got personally involved."

McMichael said nothing.

"That's what I thought." Brennan continued, his voice much calmer, "Look, I know you're just doing your job. But, a wiser man than me once told me the worst— and the best— thing you can do is get personally involved in a case."

"And who was that?"

Brennan stood, "My father."

"Good advice, just try and find some balance," McMichael said.

Brennan nodded, turned and left the office, headed toward the parking lot.

Memphis

"Yeah, Dad, you're right. You could strip paint with this. Just how old is this percolator? Looks like the same one you had when I left," Crandall said, pouring his second cup.

"Yes, it is. If you don't like it why did you go back for seconds? Damn thing still works," Reardon answered as he pulled a chair away from the table and sat down.

Crandall sat across from him, "Didn't say I didn't like it. Just said you were right."

"I'm going to get some burn phones and send two to Cindy. But, I need transportation."

Reardon sipped his coffee and gestured over his right shoulder toward the back yard, "Your mother's truck is in the garage. Hasn't been driven in a while. I crank it two or three times a week. She spent so much of my money and her time at the nursery I felt she needed a truck. Wasn't about to put all those rose bushes in the back of a '64 rag top Caddy."

Crandall picked up his cup with both hands and blew across the top of the steaming coffee, "Now, how about that picture."

"The short story is I got it from Mark. I hooked up with him his junior year in ROTC at North Georgia College. Made him promise not to tell you. Not because I was mad at you, just one less thing for you to worry about. He's a great kid and if you get pissed with him then we're done here."

Crandall was stunned, "But how—"

Reardon held up his hand, "Long story. Besides, it just may be one of those things you're better off not knowing."

Crandall sighed, looked around the kitchen again, "I may be the reason Caruso found us. A little over a year ago I snuck up here to see Mom. The Feds told me about her condition. I didn't want you to know. It would have put you in danger. I have a strong suspicion I was spotted. For the first ten to fifteen minutes she didn't know who I was, even when I told her. Then just all of a sudden she called me Ted. Kept asking me how Janie was. Wanted to know if Lisa was walking yet."

Reardon reached out and put his hand on his son's shoulder, "I figured you were the mysterious good looking stranger they told me about. First I thought they were kidding. Then they said he looked like we were related."

There was a few seconds of silence. Both men looked into each other's eyes. Reardon broke the quiet reflection, "So, I guess we've both been sneaking around behind each other's back. Now, what about the other things you were going to sleep on?"

Crandall became pensive and began searching for the right words, "I'll go by and see the Father, haven't done confession in a few months. But, I still want Caruso dead," Crandall took a deep breath. Through clenched teeth he continued, "I want that slimy piece of shit dead and buried *before me*."

Reardon looked at his son with furrowed brow, "What does that mean?"

Duluth, Georgia

Brennan was sitting in the office of Fred Thurber, MD when Dr. Thurber opened the door and entered. Brennan stood from the leather sofa set across from a six foot mahogany desk. Behind the desk was a wall of books and publications which lined the built in shelves. The dark paneled wall to the left of the desk was filled with diplomas, awards, and certificates. The two men shook hands and exchanged greetings, and then the doctor took his place behind the desk.

Brennan noted it was the second time in three hours he was on the receiving side of a desk, though the chair he was about to sit in was much more comfortable than Lieutenant McMichael's.

The earlier call was from the pharmacy director. It seems there were some shortages in certain drugs. Chief among them were digitalis and the medicinal cocaine. According to their computer records, Jack Crandall's security code was the last one used to access those particular items in the narcotics cabinet. There was also the question of the medication he picked up. The pharmacist informed Brennan he would have to discuss that particular item with Crandall's doctor. So, here he sat.

"Dr. Thurber, you are Jack Crandall's neurologist. Correct?" Brennan began as he sat down, notepad and pen in hand.

"Yes, but I'm afraid I can't tell you about any treatments he may be undergoing," Thurber said as he adjusted himself in his chair.

"Well, I'm hoping to appeal to you as a friend of his. I'm told the two of you target shoot on occasion."

"Oh, yes," the doctor grinned a bit, "He's quite good."

"No doubt. But, he's left town. I'm sure you are aware of his recent troubles. And, he's apparently stolen some drugs from the hospital."

"What's this got to do with me?"

Brennan scribbled a note in his pad, "Well, there's the question of his medication. The pharmacist insisted I talk to you about it."

"That's all well and good officer, but—"

Brennan slammed his hand on the desk, "Yes I know. Privileged information. But, I'm trying to keep the man from going to jail. He's on the hunt to kill someone, maybe several people. I need all the damn information I can get to stop him if I can. So, let's cut to the chase, are you going to help me or not? As a friend, not as his doctor!"

Thurber thought for a moment then picked up his phone and asked his assistant to bring him Crandall's file.

After hanging up he looked at Brennan and sighed, "Sounds like you are also becoming a friend, officer. The drug in question is called riluzole. Are you familiar with it.?"

Brennan continued to lean forward, both hands now on the desk, his voice still irritated, "No, not at all."

Dr. Thurber shifted his weight nervously, "It's for the treatment of Amyotrophic Lateral Sclerosis."

Brennan almost dropped his pad and pen, "You mean—"

Thurber cut him off, "ALS. Jack Crandall—my friend—is dying. A very slow tortuous death. He's probably got only two years left. You may have noticed a twitch or him acting like he has a muscle cramp. Primarily on his left side."

Brennan nodded, "Yes, a couple of times."

"He will have episodes. Sometimes a day or two apart, sometimes hours. It's in the early stages and he's still very high-functioning. The medicine is helping there, but after a while the only thing it will do is keep him out of a wheel chair a little longer. It attacks the nerve cells in the brain and spinal cord. All his muscles will begin to atrophy. Eventually everything will shut down, even his breathing. In the end, about all he will be able to do is blink, maybe move a couple of the small jaw muscles. We don't fully understand the mechanism for this yet. Oh, everything will shut down *except* the cognizant portions of the brain. He'll be fully aware of what is happening to him."

For one of the very few times in his life, Paul Brennan found himself speechless.

CHAPTER TWENTY-TWO

Memphis

WITH THE BURN PHONES PURCHASED AND SHIPPED, CRANDALL entered the church. After he told his father about his ALS, there had been a long period of nervous silence. It was followed by a strange conversation about getting the job done while it was still light and sins of the father that left Crandall with the feeling his father was keeping a secret. He felt it better to not press for the moment. There were enough family secrets on the table for now.

The vestibule of St. Mary's Catholic Church was anything but ornate. It was fairly small. The white floor tiles were highly polished ceramic, not marble. On the wall to the left side of the double doors leading into the nave hung a large Crucifix; on the right was the Virgin Mother for whom the church was named. To her right was a plain white door behind which a narrow staircase led to the balcony that looked out over the nave. Little had changed since the days he hung out in that balcony over thirty-five years before.

Crandall entered the main part of the church through the open doors and paused. In Memphis, St. Mary's was one of the few remaining neighborhood churches with enough membership to conduct regular masses. Most practitioners had migrated to the larger facilities. At the end of the aisle between the pews was the altar. Just to the left and back of the altar stood the chancel and old choir box. All as he remembered. To the right, in front of the altar steps, on top of a table sat a display of candles arranged in three rows of about ten each. It appeared eight of them were flickering. The second and third rows of candles were tiered to be higher than the one in front of each.

To the left, in the second row of pews, two priests knelt in prayer. Crandall crossed himself and moved quietly as possible down the carpeted aisle. He looked around at the light streaming through the arched stain glass windows. Each piece of glass was cut, colored and assembled to depict different events in the history of the Church of Rome, including the Crucifixion. There was even one depicting the

Knights Templar. Memories of his wedding day began to flood his mind. Every day he longed for that feeling to return.

Two rows behind the priests, Crandall halted and waited in silence. He heard a quiet, "In the name of the Father, and of the Son and the Holy Spirit, Amen" while the priests blessed themselves. Crandall cleared his throat, but in quiet reverence for where he stood. With a querying pitch in his voice asked, "*Ojciec* Wiz?"

One of the men turned to look in Crandall's direction, the other lifted his head and without turning around said, "Only one person ever called me Father Wiz in Polish." The priest stood, made a slight gentle turn then stepped into the aisle. He was a man of medium height and build. There was little to distinguish him in a crowd except for his clerical garb and collar. His lean face with its square jaw gave the appearance of a man who maintained a good level of fitness throughout the years, despite the thinning hairline. Gray-green eyes sparkled as a smile came over his face, "It is you, Ted. It's good to see you again, old friend. I had almost given up hope."

"It's good to see you too, Joe. It's been too long." Crandall moved forward and the two best friends from high school embraced.

After they separated, Father Jozef Wisniewski turned to the younger priest, "Father Espinoza, I'd like you to meet my best friend, Ted Reardon. We played some football and generally tried to stay out of trouble in high school." A toothy grin contrasted with the light mist in his eyes.

When the two men had shaken hands and exchanged greetings, Wisniewski said, "I spoke to your father a couple of days ago. He didn't mention you coming to town. So, what brings you back to St. Mary's after all these years?"

Crandall glanced over at Father Espinoza then back to his friend, "It's a little complicated."

Without looking at Espinoza, Wisniewski's face took on a more serious expression, "Juan, could you give us a few moments?"

Dallas

"Okay, we're going to do this thing tonight then get the hell out of Dodge," Mickey Pyle told his crew as they sat around his hotel room in Dallas. "Bobby here," he said pointing to the man sitting in the straight back chair in front of the motel room desk, "is going to keep an eye on Sam Greggs and let us know when he is on his way home. He works from ten to seven cleaning at the local mall. Then he goes to a bar half way home looking for cheap booze and cheaper hookers. It's a pretty regular routine, four to five nights a week. It's a wonder the guy's not dead from AIDS."

Bobby Hancock, Pyle's local *spy*, interrupted, "Why don't we just take the guy out in the parking lot of the bar instead of breaking into his house? That would be simpler."

Pyle considered using locals only for information. In the long run though, he would include them in the operation to keep tabs on them. He preferred working with the more submissive types. Didn't want them thinking for themselves. Made life easier for him. Under normal conditions they would be given menial tasks. His bottom line was he had little patience for them when it came to planning, "Look Hancock, if you don't want to get the rest of your money you can walk now." In reality Pyle would never let him just walk away. "When I was in the Green Berets we learned to follow orders. That's what I expect you to do."

"You were a Green Beret?" Hancock asked, with a measure of surprise in his voice, "What did you do?"

Pyle's statement got the intended response and show of respect from Hancock, "A lot of secret stuff. Had to kill a bunch of people. You just do what you're told and let me make the decisions. Now, depending on when he leaves the bar, we will either be waiting in his house or we wait until he gets home then go in after he's settled into bed. There are no signs of a security system so that will make things easier. We'll set the delay for the burn for twenty minutes to give us plenty of time to get a few miles away. Any questions?"

"What if he brings a hooker home?" Corey Gibson asked.

"She picked the wrong john."

Duluth, Georgia

A cool breeze wafted across the hospital campus in Duluth. The sun was out, though there was a chill in the air. Fall temperatures had arrived a little early this year, if only for a few days, according to the local TV weather personalities. Cindy Fitzgerald sat on a bench wrapped in a heavy blue wool sweater that covered her beige scrubs top. She blew her nose with the handkerchief Paul Brennan had given her. He rubbed her back with a gentle touch and waited in silence while she finished.

After his talk with Dr. Thurber he returned to the hospital to find out if Cindy was aware of Crandall's ALS. They had walked out to the bench to avoid prying ears and eyes. It took several probing questions without revealing the exact nature of his query before Cindy broke down. She cried on his shoulder for several minutes and explained that Jack had told her the night before he left town. He had asked her not to tell anyone, including Mark. For her it had been a huge burden and now the dam broke. All of her pent up emotions spilled out. She no longer felt alone. Brennan needed to return to the station and try and make sense of it all. He promised not to tell Mark. For the time being.

The news was not all bad. Andrea's liver and kidney functions seemed to level off, but they needed to see significant improvement before she could go home. Before leaving, Cindy thanked him for all his effort and kissed him on the cheek, and then they shared a long embrace.

He inhaled the clean fragrance of her hair and realized during all his time in Afghanistan and Iraq that was one of the things he missed most. The clean sent of a woman's freshly shampooed hair, the soft touch of her lips, the gentle pressure of her arms as they encircled him. It was a world where women covered their hair and public embraces were frowned upon. You were not allowed to comfort a widow or a mother who lost a child murdered by the Taliban. He thought of Amed and his mother. It had made him jaded, even more hardened against cowards who would hurt women and children or hide behind them. It was how his father raised him.

Though Brennan rarely told anyone involved in an investigation where he lived, he let Cindy know their homes were less than five miles apart near Dacula. He hoped it would give her some feeling of security. He was also pissed at Crandall for placing this burden on her.

Memphis

Alex Caruso sat behind the sparse desk in the main office of the *Southern Bell*. Dave Maxson sat on the green sofa against the opposite wall. The one decorative item in the office was a display cabinet to the right of the entry door. It was a large display case with a collection of statuary that represented fertility symbols from different cultures throughout the world. Most were representative of the female form. Many others were on display in the different private party rooms and were changed out weekly.

Caruso conducted a meeting to prepare the club for the *new* arrivals and to take care of some old business. He explained to Maxson that his assistants would make the transfer of custody at The Lamar Lounge. Two of the girls, the blonde American and the youngest, would be delivered to his hotel room. The other three were to be brought to the club for *orientation*. Maxson was also to make sure the girls' dormitory rooms in the basement were finished and secure for occupation.

He turned to Allen, "Stan, I need you to go to Georgia and tie up the loose ends while Crandall is in Nashville. Get with your source down there, get the daughter-in-law taken care of and you take out the girlfriend."

Allen was leaning against the wall next to the sofa, his arms crossed, his voice nonchalant, "What about the son?"

"If he shows his face, kill him. I don't give a damn. Otherwise let him wallow in the misery with his father. When you get back, take care of his old man. You fuck with me, you lose your family. Besides, I never did like that sneaky shit anyway. Take that bouncer, Big Moby, with you."

Allen pushed himself away from the wall with a bit of surprise in his voice, "Will Moby? He's big as a house. Why do I need him?"

Caruso let out a sly chuckle, "You need backup. The young Crandall is in town and the cop could be trouble. From some of his press clippings, he can be a bit of a hothead. Some sort of war hero."

Through a crooked half smile Allen retorted, "That cop ain't squat. I'll cut his balls off."

"Yeah, you do that, if you see him. But take Moby with you. Use him for a shield if they start shooting, or drop him in a river on the way back, I don't give a shit which. Just leave tonight and take care of it. Tony can handle things here."

After they left and he was alone, Maxson waited ten minutes to make sure no one would be returning. He pulled open the left-hand drawer of the desk, picked up one of the several remotes, pointed to a near imperceptible spot on the wall next to the light switch and pushed the stop button. Then he left the office and entered the janitorial closet next door. Maxson opened a panel door that looked like a breaker box and punched the eject button on the front of a DVD recorder. He cradled the DVD of the meeting in his hands, smiled and in a quiet whisper said, "Thank you, Eric."

CHAPTER TWENTY-THREE
Memphis

BETWEEN HIS STUDIES AND HIS JOB AT HIS UNCLE'S RESTAURANT, Eric Benedetto had not taken the time to check his video downloads from The Southern Belle in several days. When Dave Maxson asked him to install the recording equipment for his office, he was prepared. He knew the request was coming. Maxson had been querying his skills in this area. So, he said no the first two times. Then he reluctantly agreed.

It was all off-the-shelf-stuff. A COP CS25PA Snake Cam with a built-in microphone that fed a DVD recorder controlled by remote. What Maxson didn't know was a Dell laptop was also recording everything. Benedetto tied it into the clubs internet connection. From a simple desktop in his bedroom he set up a utility app that monitored the laptop 24/7 across the internet. When a video file was available, the program would automatically download the file then delete it from the laptop.

He sat down in front of his twenty-one inch LCD screen with a can of Red Bull and toggled the screen, mouse and keyboard to the computer hidden in his closet. The first thing he noticed was there were several new files. He went to the closet and popped in a clean DVD and began copying and reviewing the files. The first one was innocuous enough, Maxson getting his kicks *auditioning* a potential dancer for the main room. The second video file almost caused him to knock his Red Bull off the table.

Benedetto snatched up his phone and dialed the number he had memorized. "Hello, Ms. Whitlock. Uh—" he stuttered, swallowed hard and cleared his throat—"I have a delivery for you, the purple ones you ordered. Will you be at your home in forty-five minutes?"

"Yes, the purple ones. Forty-five minutes will be fine," a female voice replied.

"Thank you," he replied then hung up.

It was a prearranged signal. He wanted to say more, but the only words he could come up with were, "Holy crap!" After sitting for a moment he considered calling in sick to work but Uncle Antonio needed him. He did know he would have difficulty sleeping when he returned home after work. When he got in on this, the man he called Pops had warned him it might be a good idea if he didn't know what he was recording.

Memphis

John Reardon drove his Caddy down Chancy Street past a row of upscale townhomes. Several of the homes displayed seasonal wreaths behind the glass storm doors. Fall earth tones encircled brass door knockers. He had been here many times, but never stopped, never went inside and never came from the same direction twice in a row. Sometimes in a taxi, on rare occasions with a friend and even rarer occasions in Margaret's truck. Today though, he was in his prize Caddy with the top down, wearing his Kangol Herringbone Ivy cap and military style aviator sun glasses. Just another hip senior citizen out for a ride in the cool weather. This was his favorite time of the year, something he always shared with his son. The cryptic wrong number he received a short time ago set him on his ride.

At the end of the street he halted at the stop sign where the street ended and made a "T" with Muir Street. Looking left first, then right, he glanced at the corner window in the end unit. A deep purple vase filled with dark red roses sat on a round wooden table atop an artfully crafted doily, drapes pulled aside. The drapes were always open during the daytime, but the vase would alternate between clear, red and purple while the flowers ran the gamut its genus had to offer. This combination had special meaning. Reardon flipped on his left turn signal and pulled away from the stop sign in a direction opposite to his eventual destination.

Memphis

Jozef Wisniewski and Ted Reardon had known each other since the age of fourteen when Reardon's family moved into the neighborhood. Wisniewski was the youngest of seven siblings and the only one born in the United States. His father had fought with the Polish Underground in World War II against the Nazi occupation. After a decade under the thumb of the Soviet Union, the family escaped into West Germany, eventually arriving in New York and making their way to Memphis. Wisniewski's father found work as a sanitation worker and when he rose to a supervisor position they moved into the house two doors down from where the Reardons would eventually settle.

John Reardon moved his family to Memphis, his home town, before his scheduled retirement from a career as an Army intelligence officer. He had one more tour to make in Vietnam, so he decided it was time to find permanence. The constant moving had been hard on the family. A young wife and a single child.

The Wisniewskis took great pride in welcoming new families to the neighborhood. Both families being Catholic made it easier. Ted and Jozef became fast friends, playing football, baseball, and even double dating to the proms. Ted always liked to call his friend Wiz.

Their senior year, Jozef announced he was going to seminary to become a priest. While most of their classmates would always want to know why he would do such a thing, Ted went to Jozef's mother to find out how to say *Father* in Polish. From that day on he would kid him by calling him, "Ojciec Wiz".

When Ted came home from the Marines he was troubled, confused, and angry. Father Wisniewski tried to help, but he rejected all the offers of assistance, until Janie came along. It was the happiest he had been since high school. With much effort, Janie and the good Father got Ted to leave Caruso.

Father Wisniewski had performed their wedding ceremony. He had even introduced the two of them. She worked at the Catholic orphanage where she had grown up and met Jozef who was coaching the baseball team.

Now, here the two friends were decades later, getting to know each other again.

"You look fit," Crandall said to his friend, his hands on the Father's shoulders. "Do you still practice?"

"I still study, yes. The Archbishop even allowed me to build a small dojo in the basement. I have a few students from the parish. They can't afford professional lessons."

"So, fighting Father Dunne lives," Crandall quipped with a smile.

"No. Fighting Father Dudziak, I'm Polish remember." Wisniewski smiled back, "How about you?"

"Off and on. I never fully stopped after you whipped my butt then drug me to that gym on Benton with Mr. Ito."

Wisniewski gave a gentle shake to his friend's shoulders, "Good, now quit changing the subject. What brings you back to Memphis after all these years?"

Crandall's face took on a serious look, "I've got troubles."

"Mmm, something you need to confess?"

"In a way, yes. Dad said I should talk to you."

"Would you like the standard confessional booth? Or, we could sit right here in the pews. We're a little more informal these days."

"That would work," Crandall said, and motioned to the nearest pew.

After both men sat, Crandall licked his lips and began, "It's been, uh, five months since my last confession."

Wisniewski touched Crandall's hand, "I'm glad you are still in the church. Please continue."

Crandall cleared his throat, "Bless me Father for I am about to sin."

Wisniewski looked his friend in the eye, "You're just full of surprises today, Ted. I'm afraid we didn't cover preemptive absolution in seminary. Perhaps you should explain."

Lawrenceville, Georgia

Sweat poured down Paul Brennan's face as he hit the heavy bag with two more body shots then grabbed it with both hands and planted a hard knee in what would be a lower abdomen or testicular area of a man, depending on his opponent's height. He had just finished twenty minutes on the wrestling mat with Pete Williams, a young patrolman and former Georgia state wrestling finalist. They worked out together on a regular basis. Brennan was a pretty fair high school wrestler, but he had never bested Williams, though he was getting closer.

Being shorter, he had taken to attacking the thigh area, trying to wrap up both legs and dropping Williams to the mat to take away his opponents leverage advantage. Williams's specialty was the counter and always seemed to be able to reverse himself out.

Today Brennan almost got a pin before Williams was finally able to hook one of his arms and turn him.

After a short rest he went to the heavy bag. Practicing mixed martial arts he felt gave him more tools for the situations he might encounter on the job or in combat. It was a late lunch workout on his way back to his desk and he was nearing the end when he heard his cell phone howl from his bag against the wall.

Unable to get to the phone in time, he listened to the voice message, "Paul, Dick Clancy here. Got a reply from the FBI. The fellow's name is Michael James Pyle. Goes by Mickey. History of assault, burglary, even a little arson thrown in for good measure. So, he fits the profile. Likes to hang out in Vegas. No known connection to Caruso, but he claims to have been a Green Beret. FBI is still checking with Department of Defense on that one but nothing back yet. I've put their response in an envelope on your desk. There's a last known address with it."

Brennan pushed the number to save the message. He thought for a minute then pulled up a number in Birmingham from his address book, pushed the dial button, and waited. After four rings he got an answer.

"Sergeant Major, Paul Brennan here," he said, breathing deep while wiping sweat from his eyes with a towel. "Good to talk to you also, but I need a favor."

After a short pause to allow the Sergeant Major to respond, he continued, "I need one of your connections at the Pentagon to circumvent the normal channels and check a name for me. Email me the results when you get it. Guy claims to be SF and I need to know for sure—

"Arson, murder and maybe a few other things—

"Yeah, I know we have our bad apples, but something about his MO doesn't work for me. His name is Michael James Pyle—"

CHAPTER TWENTY-FOUR
Memphis

THE PRIESTHOOD MUST REQUIRE ONE TO BE A GOOD LISTENER, Crandall thought as he went through the narration of his life the past week or so. *Or so*, because he had, literally, lost track of all time. When he finished, the good father sat back, stroked his chin in quiet reflection and shifted his weight a bit in the pew. "I am truly sorry for your loss and the injury to your family, Ted. Your ALS saddens me greatly. While it's understandable you would want revenge, I'm not sure a hundred Rosaries or even a Novena would bring you the solace you may be seeking—"

Crandall cut his friend off, his voice full of rage, "Solace is the furthermost thing on my mind, Wiz. Whether he pulled the trigger or not, the bastard killed my wife, my granddaughter, Lisa's boy friend, and who knows how many other people. Lisa and Andrea are in the hospital, and I'm dying. I'm way past solace. Call it revenge if you want. I've tried it the legal way and here I sit. This time it ends."

Wisniewski sat back against the pew, fingered the cross hanging about his neck then turned to Crandall, "Your father didn't tell you *everything* about his current little operation. This time the priest confesses to the parishioner."

Crandall slipped into semi-stunned silence as the priest began.

"Your father does not know all the players in this plot to bring down Caruso. I'm the only one who knows *everyone*.

"Close to five years ago Angela Whitlock came to see me. She had heard that Caruso had a private detective looking for you and that he was getting close. She wanted to get you a warning somehow. Even gave me the name of the PI. I didn't have a clue on how to get you a message. So, I passed the information along to John. Seemed the proper thing to do, except instead of going to the marshals he paid a visit to the PI himself. Turns out this guy was looking up almost everyone Caruso had a beef with.

"At the time your mother's dementia was beginning to show. John had become enraged at God, the Feds, everyone. So he went to see the guy to convince him to not turn anything over to Caruso. He came back to see me that night, visibly shaken, upset. I took him home and stayed with him and Margret the whole night. In the morning he was a changed man. It was about a year later he got in contact with Mark."

"What happened that night?" Crandall asked still shocked at the events being revealed.

"You will have to ask you father. I was not with him, and this is not something you should hear second hand. But I will tell you that knowing Mark was a great comfort to him.

"Angela and I stayed in contact, but a little over two years ago she paid me another visit. Said she wanted to bring Caruso down. I should have just said no, but I arranged the first meeting between her and John by sending her to the casino. From there, for everything that was needed, they came to me and I found someone who hated Caruso as much as they did. What I did not do was tell them all of my go betweens."

"But, how did you know all these people?" Crandall asked.

"A priest hears many confessions."

Crandall started to speak, only to have Wisniewski hold up his hand as a stop signal, "You see, the few times my father would talk about the war he would never talk about glory or battle, only evil. He always told us, 'evil should never win.' Alex Caruso is evil. The bottom line is I have become the enabler in all this." Wisniewski clasped his hands and sighed, "Not good if the Archbishop finds out."

Father Wisniewski reached out and grasped his friend's hands and looked him in the eyes. In a soft yet emotional voice he continued, "Ted, I won't pretend to tell you what to do. But this is what I believe. God sets us on a path with many choices; however, *we* do the choosing. Our paths have merged again after all these years. I'm not sure if God has a plan for each of us as many believe, but maybe he has brought us together again for a reason. Which direction we travel from here will be of our own choosing. I think both of us already know what direction that is. When this is over I will probably be defrocked, and maybe excommunicated. Your fate is sealed. You and I have reached the point where neither of us will turn back. I am in too deep, and you have nothing to lose."

Lawrenceville, Georgia

"First of all, Paul, the answer is no. You can't go to Memphis. Now before you get your butt all up on your shoulders you're the one who said I was only doing my job. So, I'm still doing my job," Lieutenant McMichael said to Paul Brennan across his desk again. He opened the right-hand drawer of his desk and pulled out two manila folders.

Brennan wasn't happy about being summoned to McMichael's office twice in one day. When he saw the note on his desk he was wishing the heavy bag was hanging close by. He fidgeted in the chair.

McMichael opened the folder on top, "I took the liberty of going over the marshal's file on Crandall and the psychological profile on you after you were wounded in Afghanistan. You gave us a copy of that voluntarily."

"Yeah, and you still sent me to the department shrink. So, am I still fit for duty? Or do you want my gun?" Brennan asked as he stared at the wall behind McMichael, his mind on other things.

McMichael looked up, "I'll let that pass for now. What I'm trying to understand is why this case has you all tied up in knots. And, I think I know."

"You mean besides trying to find a killer and keep a good guy out of jail?"

McMichael closed the folder and clasped his hands together on top of his desk, "Yes, you identify with the guy."

"Enlighten me."

"Okay, I will. On your team in Afghanistan, what position did you fill?"

Brennan sat motionless but boiled underneath, "Weapons Specialist."

"And team sniper, correct?"

"Yes—so?"

"I'll get to that. When your team was in that village in the Helmand Province west of Kandahar, you befriended a fifteen-year-old boy. What happened to him?"

"His name is Amed—do we have to cover this?" Brennan stopped staring and began to fidget again.

"Yes."

"A goddamn Taliban cut his throat because he thought the kid was feeding us intel."

"Did you see this?"

Brennan shifted in the chair, "Is this a cross examination, do I have to be sworn in?"

"Yes and no. Just answer, please."

Brennan leaned forward and narrowed his eyes, "Yes I saw it. The asshole was using him as a shield. Knife to his throat. I begged him to let the kid go. He basically cut Amed's throat out and dumped him on the ground. We couldn't save him."

"What did you do?"

Brennan looked at the ceiling and sighed, "I emptied a thirty round magazine in the fucker's chest. I tried my best to cut him in two."

"One of the guy's friends shot you in the leg. Two rounds I believe. Hit the femoral artery and you almost bled to death."

"So, the rest of the team sent that guy and five more of his buddies to hell after that. But I didn't almost bleed to death. I lost a lot of blood, but I had a damn good medic."

McMichael leaned back in his chair, "That's not what the report said."

Brennan was becoming irritated, "I was there, the shrink who wrote the report wasn't. You see Terry, that's one of the things Special Forces does. We go to godforsaken villages and live for months with people who two days earlier wanted to kill us. Then we try and get them to trust us and teach them how to fight back. We were making headway, Amed trusted us. How do you face a mother after that? We were supposed to protect him, save him. Now where are we going with this?"

McMichael tapped the papers in the open folder with his hand, "You and Crandall, both snipers, both have survivor's guilt, you both feel responsible for a teenager's death, he lost his grandchild before it was born and you wanted to kill a guy who killed his own unborn child."

Brennan took on a sarcastic tone and gripped the arms of the chair as tight as he could, "Good work; I didn't know you were a psychologist."

McMichael leaned forward, "Master's Degree. But, I find police work more to my liking."

Brennan shifted his face from one of a mild sneer to one of surprise, "Didn't know that, Terry, but you left off one thing."

"What's that?"

"Crandall is dying, and I don't want him to die in prison!"

McMichael's face now took on a look of surprise.

Brennan returned to his desk and opened his email program. There was an email from Sergeant Major Norris. Quick work, Sergeant Major, he thought. It opened up on his flat panel screen and he read. "Interesting," he said under his breath, then opened the attachment and read it.

CHAPTER TWENTY-FIVE

Dallas

A SLIGHT BREEZE BLEW THE EXHALED CIGARETTE SMOKE BACK INTO Sam Greggs's face as he stood on the loading dock outside the maintenance section of South Side Mall in Dallas. He cleared his throat and spat in the direction of the trash dumpsters on the ground off the dock, missing wildly.

Sucking in another lung full of tobacco smoke, he scratched the two-day growth on his cheek and exhaled the smoke through his nose without removing the cigarette from his mouth. Silently he cursed Alex Caruso, but not as much as he did Ted Reardon and the federal marshals who handled his file in the Witness Protection Program. He should have never listened to Reardon. He probably would have been Caruso's top lieutenant by now, ready to take over when the time was right.

It had been five years since he dropped out of the program and took his real name back after they refused to intervene on an assault charge that cost him ninety days in county. He figured if Caruso was going to find him, he would have done it long before now.

They wouldn't give him any more money or relocate him again. Besides, that bitch deserved it. The feds owed him more. After all it was his testimony that really put Caruso away more so than Reardon's. "Non-admissible," the judge had said about Reardon's testimony on the conspiracy to murder charges. Then they let the bastard stay in the program.

Ahhh, he didn't need them anyway. All he had to do was find the right scam to run. The best were going after old folks. They would fall for almost anything. He may have drifted from job to job since leaving the program, but that was about to change. He'd show them all.

Greggs threw his cigarette on the dock, stepped on it and ground it into the concrete with the sole of his work boot. He reached into the breast pocket of his coveralls, pulled out the pack of cigarettes, tapped another one out, stuck it between his lips and lit it. A quick glance at his watch told him his break was over five minutes ago. *Who gives a rip!*

Memphis

As the sun set and the skies over Memphis darkened, the pushers and hookers of Lamar Avenue began to scurry about beneath the soft amber glow of street lights like nocturnal insects stirring from their daytime slumber; each seeking the territory they hoped would bring them the day's remuneration. As in nature, the best territories are claimed and fought over by brute force. A male grizzly retains his hunting grounds only as long as he can keep the younger bears at bay.

Jack Crandall wore his favorite flannel red plaid shirt and jeans. A nondescript dark blue baseball cap on his head with the edges of the bill curved downward partially hid his face and eyes. The lightweight navy blue jacket concealed the .45 in his belt.

It occurred to Crandall that not much had changed along Lamar Avenue as he drove past the bars, lounges, and dives that dotted both sides of the street. Different lettering on the glass windows, different color paint, but the whole street was just as dirty. He was in his mother's silver Toyota pickup truck, complete with matching camper shell, window down, cruising.

Garrison's, where he confronted Patrone, had long since become The Lamar Lounge. His assumption was that it remained the center of Caruso's operations on the street. Other than a fresh coat of paint and a new neon sign, it looked the same. It was prime real estate for drugs and prostitution.

When trouble started, a paperwork shuffle began, a name changed, and local politicians would announce they had closed another den of iniquity. Most times these interruptions lasted a couple of weeks and were considered a cost of doing business. But in time, the epicenter would return here.

Darkened alleys also served as retail locations where members of both genders would ply their trades and sell their commodities. These are the ones who have fallen to the lower levels of the local food chain. Women no longer young enough, or pretty enough, to merit a room with a bed were now pimped and reduced to a mattress behind the nearest dumpster. Pushers who had been caught and served their time now return to the street hawking their product, hoping the next customer wasn't a narc.

When Crandall was an enforcer here, Caruso owned three of the establishments in the area. Considering the man's rise since then, the number had to be at least double. If trouble reared its head at one location, you would just move next door or across the street. Efficient logistics. Regulars knew the drill and plan B was only a few doors away.

At the end of the red light district Crandall turned left, drove two blocks and made a U turn. Retracing his route he made his way back down Lamar, making mental notes of who congregated where and paying particular attention to The Lamar Lounge. This was where the delivery would be made.

Having made his reconnaissance, Crandall made a right turn. After three blocks he decided no one was following him. He then made two left turns and headed for home, taking a circuitous route in case he was wrong.

Dallas

Mickey Pyle came out of The Bunker Bar and Grill, a local joint south of Dallas with a not-so-family-oriented reputation. Mostly it was a cinderblock structure with a brown coat of paint on the front. It was large enough so as to not give the fire marshal a heart attack, yet dark enough to keep one's identity secret from across the room. It sold three types of beer and hard liquor by the drink. Limited, but enough to satisfy its clientele. The menu was barely adequate to earn the *Grill* part of the name. It wasn't very hard for one to see the health inspector rarely came by.

Pyle slapped at a mosquito nibbling on his neck as he walked to the recently stolen Chevy Malibu and got in on the front passenger side. "I made arrangements for a girl to get him out of there soon. She's not supposed to tell him I sent her over. Told her he was my uncle and it was my birthday present to him, but she can't mention it's his birthday."

Corey Gibson drove, "How you gonna' keep her quiet?"

"I told her if she got him out of there in the next ten minutes I'd give her an extra hundred when I come over in the morning. We need to get him home so things can settle down before we go in."

The front door of the bar opened as Pyle finished. Greggs came out, a slight unsteadiness to his gait. A woman with a very unnatural red color to her hair walked next to him, arm-in-arm. She laughed and tapped Greggs on the arm with her free hand as they walked to his car.

"Follow them, but not too close. We'll wait until a while after midnight before we go in. It'll be quieter then."

"Why so long?" Gibson asked as he started the car.

"Let him have one last ride," Pyle said. He signaled to the dark blue minivan holding the two other men. After allowing Greggs to exit the parking lot, the two vehicles fell in behind him, maintaining a safe distance. After all, they knew where he was going. *Enjoy this one; she'll be your last.*

CHAPTER TWENTY-SIX

Memphis

THE LATENESS OF THE DAY ONLY ADDED TO THE FATIGUE AND tension of the last few. Jack Crandall and John Reardon found themselves at the kitchen table again. Crandall sat with his beer, a Sam Adams Cream Stout he found at the local package store, and Reardon nursed his nightly cocktail. Crandall had swapped his jeans and flannel shirt for a tee shirt and shorts. Due to the amount of recordings they had to cover, Crandall decided he would wait until morning to ask his father about the PI.

Spread out before them was a collection of DVD's, audio CD's, and a laptop, one of Reardon's few capitulations to the twenty first century. Reardon would have reviewed the whole lot by now, but he had to fill in at the casino. Seems one of the regular blackjack dealers couldn't make it in. He stalled them off long enough to make the pickup at the drop site. Reardon remained in his card dealer's garb, complete with black vest, though he allowed it to be unbuttoned and hang loose on his shoulders.

The DVD's were something new for him to review as the recording equipment had only been in place for two months. The audio CD's had been collected over the last eighteen or so months during Caruso's regular visits to Antonio's. These were the last three visits. As was his custom, Reardon reviewed the audio first. He was still new to video espionage. Audio had been around for decades and he had used it quite a bit in the service.

"So, now the son-of-a-bitch is expanding into the sex slave trade. Five girls, who knows how young," Reardon said as he clicked the audio program closed on the laptop.

"Do we have enough to bring his organization down with this? You've been on it for two years," Crandall asked as he sipped on his beer.

"I want it concrete, no wiggle room. I need to see if I can be at that meeting he mentioned tomorrow. I don't know who he's meeting, but it sounded important," Reardon responded as he picked up the DVD labeled *Important – Watch First.*

Crandall said nothing, deep in thought as he watched his father slip the DVD into the drive. The auto-play feature opened up the program and the black and white video flickered to life on the screen. Reardon stood, arched his back, stretched his arms, picked up his scotch and returned his gaze to the computer screen. He rubbed his nose as if trying to calm an itch, then took a sip. The quality of the picture and audio wasn't the best, but both were clear enough.

Maxson was sitting behind his desk at The Southern Belle, sliding the right drawer closed. Ed Gibson and his smaller assistant, Fred Hartley, stood up from the sofa, a surprised look on their collective faces. At the bottom of the screen a woman, then a man, came into view. From the back Reardon recognized the man as Tony Oliveri, while he identified the players to his son. He had seen that small bald spot on the crown of Oliveri's head many times in photos. The dark sport coat was also a regular clothing item. The woman he had never seen before but he had not seen her face, just the long hair. Neither was sure of the hair color, but both agreed it was something other than blonde or brunette. Red perhaps? Oliveri pushed the woman ahead of him in a rough controlling manner, holding the back of her upper left arm with his left hand.

He said something unintelligible and pointed at a chair in the corner. Gibson and Hartley brought the gray metal chair with lightly padded seat, backrest, and arms to the center of the room. Oliveri forced her to sit in the chair. From her physical movements she appeared to be quite drunk or heavily drugged, swayed a bit and seemed to have a hard time keeping her balance. She looked around, a blank gaze of confusion on her face.

Crandall's brow furrowed, "She can't be more than fifteen or sixteen, and her skin, so pale."

"Caruso likes the young ones. The younger, the better. Makes me want to puke," Reardon added.

Oliveri barked an order and Gibson and Hartley grabbed the girl's shoulders and arms to keep her from getting out of the chair. From the inside pocket of his coat, Oliveri pulled a medium-sized clear plastic bag with a heavy drawstring in its opening. He opened it as the girl began to struggle against her human restraints. Oliveri jerked it over her head and drew the drawstring tight around her neck. The young girl began to flail about. She kicked out and tried to get out of the chair, but was pushed back down by Gibson and Hartley. There was an attempted scream. Gibson put his knee on the girls forearm to keep it pinned to the chair arm and placed his free hand across her mouth, pressing the bag tight against her face. Over the next few minutes, the girl's violent contortions and muffled screams began to lessen as her movements slowed, then came to a halt. Oliveri kept the bag in place a full five minutes to insure the job was complete.

Oliveri removed the bag, folded it neatly, and placed it back into the inside coat pocket. From his back pocket he pulled a white handkerchief, wiped his hands, and dabbed his lips. He pulled her head backward, looked down at her lifeless face with its open blank eyes, then turned his attention to Maxson, "Now, clean her up and dump her. Make sure there's no chance the boss's DNA can be found on her. He's not real happy at the moment." Oliveri turned and walked out of the office. Maxson, in a composed steady motion, opened the drawer on his right, reached his hand in, and the screen went blank.

Reardon stopped the video program. Like watching a train wreck, neither could take their eyes off what had unfolded on the screen.

Crandall pushed his chair back from the table, stood and walked to the sink. Placing both hands on the edge, he leaned forward and stared out the window into the black moonless night. His eyes fell on the darkened house next door. The family there slept safely, securely. Crandall fought back tears of anger while his left shoulder and upper arm began to spasm. A small drop escaped from the corner of his eye. It made its way down the side of his nose, paused in the crease above the opening of his nostril then continued across his upper lip. He clenched his teeth, balled his right hand into a fist and slammed it into the counter next to the sink. The impact rattled dishes in the cabinets. He turned to his father, his hand still in a fist, "I don't care anymore. I'm going to kill every single one of those fuckers. I'll leave tonight. Give me a few days. Tell the police I stole the truck. You and Wiz don't need to be a part of this."

Reardon gulped down the last of his scotch, wiped his lips nervously with his sleeve and placed the glass on the table. It only took two steps to cover the distance to his son. He gripped both of Crandall's shoulders. Crandall could feel his father's right hand begin to squeeze and relax in a massaging motion on his twitching muscles, "I just got you back, Ted, I don't want to see you die in prison," he said, his eyes just as red and moist, his voice shaky.

Steadying up his voice, Crandall took a deep breath and accented every word, "Dad, where and when I die no longer matters."

Reardon pulled his son into his arms in a gentle embrace, patting Crandall's upper back. "It's time—time to end it, but we have to get the girls out first." he whispered. With that the two men decided to leave the remaining disk until later. The potential of something else just as horrific on the next one was too much to handle at the moment. Without a word between them they both retired to the living room. Reardon poured a new measure of scotch into his glass. This time Crandall joined him, knowing it would be several hours before sleep would come.

Dallas

Three dark-clad men hooded with ski masks approached the back door of the small single story three-bedroom home. Even well after midnight it was still a bit warm. South Dallas had been left out of the cool front that passed through the Atlanta area when Pyle was there. The hum of air conditioning condenser units filled the warm, moist night air, including the one at Greggs's house, about ten feet from the back door.

Pyle stepped up onto the short concrete slab stoop. The door had nine panes of glass framed into it, each piece about six inches wide and ten inches long. Pyle pressed several strips of duct tape against the pane closest to the door knob. He then held a folded hand towel against the back of the tape. With a ball peen hammer he tapped around the edges of the towel, cushioning the sound. He increased his effort just enough with each blow until the glass started to crack. Once he had enough of a hole in the glass he used a screwdriver and pulled the glass pane toward him, removing most of the glass, leaving enough room to reach the doorknob without cutting himself.

Once open the four men crept into the tiny utility room and entered the kitchen to their left. Several days worth of old pizza and takeout boxes were scattered about the counter, with dishes piled in the sink. They left the kitchen and entered the main living area, going down the hallway that led to a bath on the left and the two bedrooms on the right. At the end of the hall was the master bedroom. The silence coming from the other side of the door led Pyle to believe the room's occupants were asleep. On his signal the men burst in. The room was small enough for Pyle to reach the startled woman and get his hand over her mouth before she could scream. He slammed her head back into the wood veneer headboard attached to the Hollywood frame bed.

Greggs aroused a little slower, "What the—" he tried to say but was hit on the side of his head before he could finish. Pyle explained it was a robbery and if they cooperated everything would be okay.

After covering their mouths with duct tape and binding their hands, Pyle folded a pillow around his .32 caliber pocket gun and with a quick move placed it against the woman's head and pulled the trigger. The woman slumped over toward Greggs. Pyle reached behind her head and pushed her upper torso forward, folding her at the waist.

He repositioned himself so he could look Greggs in his wide unblinking eyes. Pyle loved to see the look of fear in people's faces. He listened to the deep breathing, the attempts to form words and screams through the wide strip of tape. Picking up a pillow that had fallen on the floor, he folded it around the pistol again. Greggs tried to roll out of the bed but was pushed back in place by Pyle's minions. He smiled, "Alex Caruso sent me," he said, then pushed the pillow against his victim's face, forcing the back of his head against the cheap headboard. With the muffled report of the pistol Greggs's body stiffened, then went limp. Pyle pulled the pillow away and admired his handy work, including the blood pattern on the headboard behind the man's head. Gravity took control as the body tilted toward the middle of the bed. In a slow slide, it continued, only to be stopped by the body of his female companion. Light smoke rose from the two pillows and a slight acrid burnt odor mingled with the smell of ignited gunpowder.

Pyle told Bobby Hancock, his local spy, to call Corey Gibson and have him pick them up out front. As Hancock pressed the end button on his phone, Pyle pressed the still-folded pillow to the back of Hancock's head and pulled the trigger. Hancock dropped to the floor but appeared to still be breathing. Pyle pressed the pillow against Hancock's head and pulled the trigger twice. *No loose ends*, he thought. He would love to stay and see the fire, but these houses were too close together and there were no woods to hide in this time. Besides, New Mexico was calling. With luck, they would be at the small gorge near the *El Malpais* in the Badlands by nightfall.

CHAPTER TWENTY-SEVEN

Memphis

WHAT STARTED OUT AS A MORNING RITUAL HAD CHANGED SINCE they viewed the video the previous evening. Both men were silent while seated across from each other at the kitchen table. They stared at their cups while the aroma of fresh, strong, coffee hung in the air. Rain rolled down the glass panes on the window above the sink. It was a gentle rain, falling just hard enough to echo down the aluminum pipe connected to the vent fan over the stove. The tense quiet was first broken by Crandall. He told his dad what Father Wisniewski had passed onto him about the night with the private investigator.

At first Reardon refused to talk about it, but Crandall persisted, "No more secrets, Dad. We've come too far the last couple of days and there's still a long way to go."

Reardon relented and exhaled with a deep sigh, "So much for priestly confidentiality. It was my first confession in years," he began, running his finger around the lip of his cup while he stared at the black liquid. "I was going to convince the guy to turn over his files on you—even if I had to kill him. I was that mad." He looked up at Crandall.

"Did you?" Crandall asked when their eyes locked.

"I wish it were that simple. Yes, he was killed that night, no it wasn't me. The man was dead when I got there. The place was a mess, files everywhere. Ellison, the PI, was sitting in his chair staring out the window behind his desk. I spoke, he didn't answer, so I spun the chair around. He just flopped over, his eyes wide, that blank death stare. Best I could tell, his neck was broken. His head just hung at an ugly angle, like a chicken on your grandfather's farm after he rung its neck. And his pants were all wet. Sometimes you lose control when you die like that. Anyway, it scared the hell out of me."

"Why is that?"

Reardon looked over at the window, little rivulets of water made their way down the individual panes of glass. Without looking back he answered, "Because I didn't know if whoever did it was still around. I wiped off everything I touched and tried to find your file. No luck. I ran when I heard some sirens in the distance."

Crandall thought for a second, processing what he just heard, then asked, "So, what about you and Wiz?"

Reardon turned back to his son, picked up his cup and blew on the hot liquid. After a sip, he turned sideways toward the window and placed his arm over the back of the chair, "I went back to the church and asked the Father to come stay with your mother and me, in case whoever did it saw me. Killing a man by breaking his neck is not easy like in the movies. I knew some men in the Army who could do it. And, you don't always die instantly either. It can take several seconds to a minute for the brain to die."

Crandall knew all this, but allowed his father to continue. When he was on a roll it was best to not interrupt. He would get to the answer.

"Jozef stayed with us all night. We talked about everything. I was angry at God for taking you away, for your mother's dementia, for Caruso still breathing. I hadn't been to Mass in years, even though Jozef visited us regularly. I guess you could say I had my epiphany that night. I've only missed two weeks since. The strangest part is two days later a package arrived with your file in it. That's how I found out how to get in touch with Mark."

Crandall wrapped both hands around the warm mug and stared at the steam rising from it, "Why didn't you go to the police?"

"Your name would have come up. They would have been curious about why I was there."

"Did they ever find the guy?"

"No, it's a cold case."

A shiver went up Crandall's spine, he pushed hard against the back of the chair in reaction to it, "So, there's another vigilante minded guy out there."

"Seems so," Reardon replied, his voice showing the fatigue of a short fitful night's sleep.

Crandall ran his hand back and forth through his hair and wondered if their paths would cross. More important, where had he been in the last five years? Maybe he wasn't after Caruso, but why did he take Caruso's files? Too many questions for now.

Memphis

Alex Caruso was enjoying his breakfast in the sitting area of his bedroom suite when Tony Oliveri entered the room with a letter in his hand. Stan Allen was on his way to Georgia, so Oliveri now functioned as Caruso's primary bodyguard, assisted by Turk Jackson, one of Caruso's enforcers on Lamar Avenue and part-time bouncer at The Southern Belle.

"Boss," Oliveri began, "We got this letter this morning. I think you need to take a look at it. Some guy says you are being spied on."

Caruso reached out his hand to take the letter, "Who in the hell writes letters anymore? Besides, I'm always being spied on. Wonder what this idiot thinks makes him so special."

Caruso picked up his glasses from the table, put them on and read. When he finished, he looked out at his trees then handed the paper back to Oliveri, "Call this clown and set up a meeting here in one hour. Find out what he wants for this information. Let him know he better have solid proof and names. I don't like being jerked around. Send Turk to pick him up and tell him to make sure he's not followed back here."

He picked up his coffee cup and looked at the rain drops running down the glass in the French doors leading to the balcony. *When are people going to learn not to screw with me?*

Memphis

The prepaid cell phone buzzed, vibrated and beeped as it lay on the kitchen table in John Reardon's home. He walked over, picked it up and looked at the display. Then he yawned and pushed the answer button, "Hello."

"Uh—hello—this is Cindy Fitzgerald. I'm trying to reach Jack Crandall." A nervous voice said in the earpiece.

Reardon allowed himself a slight smile, "Cindy, nice to hear your voice. This is John Reardon, I'm Ted— uh— I mean Jack's father. He probably didn't mention he was coming to see me."

"No, no he didn't. Is he available?"

"Not at the moment, he's gone to see a friend. How's Andrea?" Reardon figured a query about Andrea might help her loosen up and let her know she could trust him. From the silence on the other end of the connection he assumed his attempt was unsuccessful.

There was a short sigh then, "Well, that's kind of why I wanted to speak to Jack."

"It's okay," he tried to reassure her.

"Jack told me everything. Mark is staying at your house. He should be on his way soon to get Lisa. Jack really is seeing a friend. You can tell Mark hi for me, we've been sneaking around behind Jack's back and seeing each other for a few years now."

A pregnant pause filled the air, "Well, okay. Mark left this morning for Nashville. He'll be back in two days with Lisa. Andrea's kidney and liver functions keep going up and down. They improved some yesterday so he felt it was safe to go. Her parents are still here."

"That's great news. I'll have him call you when he gets home. Did he remind you in his note to keep these phones a secret? I'm the one who suggested he use them," Reardon said as he pulled a chair back from the table and sat down.

"Yes, but why all the sneaking around spy stuff?"

Reardon switched the phone to his *good* ear, "Jack will have to explain. He really appreciates all you've done for him. But, that's about all I can say, except I look forward to meeting you when we get to Georgia."

"That's great, when will that be?"

"I'm not sure at the moment, a few days, maybe a week."

"Good, please have Jack call me."

"I will, nice talking to you, Cindy."

Reardon hung the phone up, laid it on the table. He stared out the window. The light rain had abated for the time being, but a gray dreary overcast remained with a promise of more showers. *Yeah, maybe a week, if we live through this.*

Memphis

Turk Jackson was driving Dominik Voloshin back to his apartment. Voloshin worked with Eric Benedetto at Antonio's. He had just explained to Alex Caruso how he observed Benedetto removing what appeared to be recordings from a hidden CD recorder in the kitchen. After checking it, Voloshin saw a wire going through the wall. On the other side of the wall was the booth occupied by Caruso most of the time.

Tony Oliveri sat at the table in the sitting area of Caruso's bedroom. Caruso was in the process of choosing which slacks he would be wearing that day. He had a secret meeting with a local politician in two hours. He chose a pair of tan Brioni slacks to go with the light blue Oxford shirt he had laid out on the bed.

"Pick Benedetto up tomorrow when he leaves for work. Take him to the club. The basement rooms there are soundproof. You know which one to use. Find out what he knows, then dispose of him. Take this Voloshin kid also."

Oliveri busied himself cleaning under his fingernails with his pocket knife, "Why?" He asked without looking up.

Caruso laid the slacks on the bed and smoothed them out, "You can use him as an example if you wish. He seems to think this information is worth ten grand. He could talk to the police. He seems a little too nosey about what I do. Like they say in Chicago, he can swim with the fishes. Besides, he might be hooked up with the Russians. If he is, we need to let them know this is my town."

CHAPTER TWENTY-EIGHT

The church's green Dodge minivan pulled into a parking space near the entrance of Saint Bernadette's Nursing and Convalescence Home. Small puddles of rainwater dotted the asphalt landscape around the vehicle.

"When you said you wanted me to go with you to see someone I didn't think you meant mom," Crandall said as he stared through the steady beat of the wipers.

"Your mother is a patient here and we can see her if you like, but I really wanted you to see my sister, Krystyna," Wisniewski replied, offering an umbrella to his friend.

Crandall held his hand up, shaking it back and forth in a declining manner, "Wiz, it's been a really long time since I've seen her, but couldn't we do this some other time?

Wisniewski placed the umbrella back under the seat, "Trust me on this, Ted."

"Does she work here?"

"No," Wisniewski sighed, "She's a patient also."

The two men exited the vehicle in silence and made their way to the entry door. There were three steps to climb that ended on a large tiled porch. Some of the patients were sitting under the cover watching their approach, smiling as they passed. Father Wisniewski stopped to greet each one. A large statue of Christ stood atop the porch roof in front of the second floor windows, his arms thrust down and spread at the waist. The palms of his hands faced outward, welcoming all who enter. A smaller statue of Saint Bernadette stood beside the entry door.

After brushing off the rain droplets, they entered the building. Crandall began to remember the layout as the odor of hospital antiseptic invaded his nostrils – a rectangular building, built around an open courtyard in the middle. The administrative offices were opposite the entry behind glass panels that reminded him of their high school's office. To their right were the meeting rooms, recreation area, and dining hall. Left were patient rooms, treatment rooms, and rehab facilities. The second floor was all patient rooms. His mother's room was almost directly overhead with a view of the parking lot. He wondered if she saw them arrive. If she would recognize him.

A young blonde in dark blue scrubs passed by in a rush, her rubber soled shoes squeaking against the polished floor. She came to a sudden stop, smiled and offered her hand, "Father Joe, nice to see you again. You should have called."

"And you Sister Mary Alice. I will next time." Wisniewski replied with a smile of his own and an ever so slight bow at the waist as he took her hand.

Crandall stopped and stared as the young woman resumed her journey and hurried off down the hall, "She's a Nun?"

Father Wisniewski enjoyed a light laugh, shook his head and patted Crandall on the shoulder, "We don't discriminate against the attractive. She's also a registered nurse." He answered, "Father Joe is her greeting for me. It's a little more familial. We normally try to have coffee when I drop by, but it appears she is busy today. And, I didn't call ahead. Krystyna's room is this way." He pointed to his left and led his friend down the hall.

Krystyna sat in her brown leather recliner, a gift from her younger brother, staring out the window. When Father Wisniewski would take her hand and speak to her she would smile then turn her gaze back to the window. She did have a smile and a nod of recognition for Crandall. Her shoulder length hair was no longer black as Crandall remembered her. Instead, it was mostly silver with streaks of her former color, yet nicely styled. A well pressed cotton dress with bright yellow sunflowers made a striking contrast to her silence. The eyes were still a beautiful dark blue, but for the most part were empty and lifeless. Scars on each cheek and across her forehead remained as visible signs of whatever hell she had endured.

The recliner rested on a round braided area rug while her hospital bed was made and covered by a blue and white quilted comforter with matching pillow shams. All the walls were adorned with a collage of photos of her family including one of Father Wisniewski and Crandall. Two proud seventeen year olds in their high school football uniforms. On the dresser in a 5X7 frame was a picture of her four year old grandson.

Crandall's immediate realization was, like his mother, Krystyna was not a patient, but a resident. She was a prisoner locked away in some private cell within her mind.

"She's been like this for about nine years now. She recognizes people, but is mute and shows very little emotion beyond a smile and an occasional squeeze of the hand," Wisniewski said to Crandall after they returned to the hallway. The Father leaned against the doorway. It seemed he needed it as much for emotional support as physical, as his voice cracked somewhat. "Darrel, her grandson, will sit in her lap. She will hug him, and smile, but will not speak. There's no physical reason for her being mute."

"What caused it? Is it related to the scars on her face?" Crandall asked as he stared through the door at the back of the recliner. Without thinking he placed his right hand on his friend's shoulder in a small attempt to provide comfort like his father had done to him the previous night.

"It's somewhat complicated," Wisniewski said looking at Crandall, "Perhaps over coffee in the dining hall? Then we will visit your mother."

"You know that, most likely, she won't know us." Crandall added.

"But, we will know her." Wisniewski answered.

Crandall offered a tired smile of agreement and nodded.

Memphis

John Reardon sat on a bench outside the *Graceland* exhibit where Elvis' *Lisa Marie*, his private jet, sat on public display. The steady gentle rain had halted in South Memphis and the sun was now out. A cool breeze helped clear the sidewalks of shallow puddles and rustled the leaves in the large oak tree that shaded the bench. The leaves were beginning to take on their red and gold hues for fall.

He turned up the collar of his jacket to protect the back of his neck against the chill while he waited. Just up Elvis Presley Boulevard, tourists lined up to purchase their tickets for the different exhibits that lined the street. RV's entered and left the park across from *Graceland*.

When he got the call from Detective Park Harris saying they needed to meet, it caught Reardon off guard. He hoped he wouldn't be asking to turn over all the collected evidence. Wishful thinking for the most part, he figured. It had been ongoing for almost two years.

Looking to his north toward the lines of tourists, he saw Harris paying a peanut vendor then turn in his direction. This was a man definitely unsuited to undercover work as he would stand out in any crowd. It's hard not to notice a tall dark skinned Asian looking man well over two-hundred-twenty pounds with a shaved head. As Harris explained in their first meeting, his mother was from Korea and his father was a six-foot, six-inch black Tech Sergeant in the Air Force, stationed at Osan Air Force Base. As he put it, his face was Asian like his mom, but was built like his dad. It did come in handy though, he would say. He could many times intimidate perps, extracting confessions by just staring at them. To date no judge had thrown out one of those confessions based on coercion by looking. His mom's maiden name was Park so that became his first name.

Harris strolled up, both hands in the pockets of his black overcoat and sat down. A thin black tie that appeared too small for his stature hung from the collar of his white shirt. The knot was loosened and hung with a slight twist to one side. From one of his pockets he produced a small brown paper bag containing the roasted peanuts he purchased. He opened it and offered some to Reardon, who politely refused.

The detective shelled one and popped the peanuts in his mouth. He stared straight ahead while chewing, "So, how long has your son been in town?"

It was not the question Reardon was expecting. He steadied his voice, "What makes you think he's in town?"

Harris laughed, "Look, don't try to blow smoke up a redneck Korean's ass. This morning we towed a green SUV from Methodist. Ran the plates and it just so happens to belong to one Jack Crandall aka Ted Reardon. I know that because I had a very interesting conversation with a Detective Brennan in Georgia a couple of days ago. So far I've kept that conversation to myself." He pulled another peanut from the bag, "Ah, a triple," he said, shelled it then tossed them into his mouth."

Reardon leaned back, sitting upright on the bench, "I don't know where he is at the moment."

Harris continued to enjoy his peanuts, "Unless you have a GPS locator on him I would assume that. It wasn't my question. Look we need to wrap this thing up and if your son is here to leave dead bodies all over my town I'm not going to be very happy. Too many innocent people can get hurt."

Reardon spread both arms across the top of the bench, "Yeah, well a lot of innocent people have already been hurt and killed. A lot of them close to me."

"That's the only reason I've cut you some slack. I got another call from Brennan this morning before he went into court. He told me Ted was dying. Is that true?"

Always direct and to the point, Reardon thought. He sighed, brought his hands together and clasped them. He blew on them to warm them from the chilled air, "Yes. ALS."

"Bad shit. You've got forty-eight hours. After that I'm gonna have to ask you to bring him in with all the evidence you have."

"Fair enough," Reardon answered.

Reardon swallowed hard, "Any more on the P.I. who worked for Caruso that turned up dead?" Reardon had always felt he was the primary suspect, though he had nothing to do with it. He even suspected Harris was going along with his plan in hopes he would slip up.

"No, not unless you got something you want to tell me."

Reardon wasn't sure he would tell even if he did know something more. Whoever killed the guy had dropped a shitload of information on his porch.

"Well, it's still cold. It's not easy to break a man's neck like that." Harris handed the bag of peanuts to Reardon, "Here, feed that squirrel over by the trash can, and give me five minutes before you leave." The detective stood and brushed the peanut shells and skins off his coat. "Be sure and clean up, don't want you to get cited for littering. And give my best to the good Father." He placed both hands in his coat pockets and strolled back toward the north, whistling.

Memphis

All the tables in the dining hall were round, seating six to eight at each with dark blue table cloths. Different varieties of flowers sat in the middle of each table. To make the large room more festive, a mural adorned two of the walls. One of Elvis, the early years, and Graceland, the other of the Memphis Belle paddlewheel steamboat on the Mississippi. A third wall was reserved for a large bulletin board, and room for local artists to display some of their works.

Crandall and Wisniewski chose a table in the back corner away from the main entrance and the five to ten folks milling about between scheduled meals. Wisniewski decided on a glass of iced tea instead of coffee, while Crandall stayed with coffee but it was mostly a hand warmer after three cups of his father's extra strength paint remover.

"After her divorce and her kids finished college, Krystyna started working at the halfway house for runaways and women. She was quite familiar with Caruso's operations on Lamar Avenue. One night a girl came to her after being on Lamar for several months. A few days later one of Caruso's enforcers showed up to bring her back. Evidently the young woman was a fairly good source of income. Normally they don't get to us until they are used up," Father Wisniewski began his tale.

"How young?" Crandall asked.

"If I remember correctly, about seventeen."

Crandall sighed, mostly from disgust, "There's your reason. It's that special affinity for any girl with the word *teen* in their age."

Wisniewski added some artificial sweetener to his tea and stirred, "So I've heard. Well, Krystyna got between the two and confronted the guy. Word is it got pretty heated and the guy left, but with a threat. That night when she was leaving she was evidently abducted when she went to get in her car."

Crandall furrowed his forehead and squinted, "Evidently?"

The priest took a deep breath, "There were no witnesses. One of the volunteers noticed her car in the parking lot roughly an hour and a half later. After an all night search turned up nothing, a homeless guy found her in an alley beaten and cut up. Her eyes were swollen shut, hair all matted with blood, left for dead. Another hour and she would have been. She spent three weeks in the hospital and hasn't spoken since. The doctors call it a conversion disorder, selective mutism due to trauma. Normally it's a situational thing. But, Krystyna chooses to not speak at all. There's no physical reason for it. It's kind of like PTSD."

"I'm familiar with the term. We've seen patients at the hospital who were paralyzed for no apparent reason. Severe trauma can really mess your mind up. Now, your reason for this visit?"

Father Wisniewski clasped his hands together, interweaving his fingers almost as in prayer, put them on the table and leaned forward. In a low voice laced with anger, "So you would know I have a stake in this also.

"Publically I have to tow the company line. No death penalty, no vengeance. But, late at night alone in my apartment in the rectory, I pray for Caruso to die a hideous death. Everything he touches withers and dies. He, and those around him, embody evil as much as Hitler or Stalin or bin Laden. Maybe not on the same scale, but how do you assign degrees to his type of malevolence?"

"I used to be one of those around him."

"Yes," Wisniewski paused and cocked his head to one side. He turned his eyes down, reached out and gave a few gentle pats to his friend's wrist before pulling his hand back, "But you were in your own private hell at the time. You have served your penance and you, too, have suffered mightily at his hands."

"True, maybe. Mostly it was the people I cared about who suffered. Did they get the guy who cut Krystyna?"

"No. But it would make no difference with me in this if they had. Caruso is the head of the snake. Did you change your opinion of him after Patrone?"

The more they talked, the more Crandall seethed. This time Crandall leaned forward, his own voice low and emotional, "Not in the least. But, I have seen those scars before, on Lisa's face. Did they come up with a name?"

"The young girl did identify the enforcer who came to take her back. Some of his photos were shown to Krystyna. She withdrew, curled up in a corner, but never spoke or nodded. He disappeared and hasn't been seen since."

Under the table, Crandall's left leg began twitching as if convulsing from electric shocks. He grabbed it with his left hand

and slapped the table with an open hand that startled his friend a bit, "Wiz, I want a damn name, I don't know how much time I have left!"

Wisniewski glared at his friend, "Corey Gibson. His brother is Ed Gibson, and I'm not just a middle man any longer."

Crandall bent forward and grimaced, grabbing his leg with both hands, "Sorry, Wiz."

The Father's scowl dissolved into a look of concern, "Ted, are you okay?"

CHAPTER TWENTY-NINE
Location Unknown

ALL THE YOUNG WOMAN COULD TELL IN THE DARKNESS WAS THE truck had made a few sharp turns, and after a very slow drive that lasted a minute or two it came to a sudden stop. The action caused her to bounce the back of her head off the front wall of the darkened cargo area. She sat on the dirty mattress in the bed of the large delivery truck. There were sixteen girls crammed into the truck. She knew because she must have counted them over one hundred times since they left San Antonio.

With no air conditioning and only the cracks around the rear roll up door for ventilation and light, the interior had become hot and dark. Between ninety and one hundred degrees she assumed, maybe higher at some points. A heavy rain storm earlier had cooled things down a little as it pelted the metal sides and roof with a deafening sound. The temperature, however, was on the rise again.

Amid the heat of the cramped space, body odor had mingled with fumes from the two small chemical toilets near the door. She may have smelled something more putrid in her lifetime but could not remember. The thin mattresses against the walls provided the only comfort and protection from the splinters in the rough wooden truck bed.

Every time she attempted to talk to the other girls, she was met with silence. The only exception was two girls who spoke very broken English. What she understood was they were afraid for their lives. Guards would threaten them when they were caught talking. They had become scared to whisper, even when the guards were not around. So, she sat in silence, a silence that threatened her sanity.

Reaching up, she felt the skin on her face, sticky from dried sweat and dirt, and then her hair, now flat against her scalp and with a slight oily coating. The crease behind her ear had become crusty where the dirt mixed with perspiration. The itch may have been the worse part.

Between counting her companions and trying to sleep she spent most of her time praying to be rescued from this nightmare. Sleep came in fifteen to twenty minute segments at best she estimated. Each bump in the road or sudden turn would awaken her. Then there was the wondering about what lay ahead, or worse, did anyone miss her yet. She assumed this was the human trafficking she had heard about. Except, she always figured it was over-exaggerated or would happen to someone else. After all, she didn't go to *those* parts of town. At least that was what she thought—until three days ago.

Hers was the only car in the parking area at the all-night convenience store on the way home from her job at the mall. Four days away from work and no class at school before 11:00. She just wanted a bottle of wine and to relax a little before bed. Why did she let Jeff make her that fake ID? She just wanted to go home, stand in a hot shower for an hour and be nineteen again.

Tears flowed again and she was wiping her eyes and nose on the sleeve of her tattered white silk blouse when she heard the metal clacking of someone unlocking the rear door. A loud rush of noise from the door rollers was followed by bright light and cool air flooding her prison. She held up her hand to shield her eyes from the blinding intensity and squinted. Through the haze of light she could make out two men she had not seen before. They were pointing rifles of some sort into the truck, speaking Spanish and waving their arms. The other girls began to stand, helping each other up and started toward the opening. She struggled to her feet and joined the herd.

Duluth, Georgia

With her shift at the hospital having ended a little over an hour ago, Jennifer Grady had just stepped out of the shower and toweled off. She walked from the bathroom to the kitchen with her freshly shampooed hair still wet and hanging right below her ears. Right before she reached the kitchen the doorbell of her apartment rang. She tightened the tie on her red terrycloth robe around her waist, walked to the door and looked through the peephole.

A smile spread across her face as she opened the door. Before her stood a tall, broad shouldered man in a gray tee shirt with a light, tan colored jacket. His green eyes smiled back at her, "Hi, Jenny. Long time, no see."

"Yes, it has been," she replied and stepped aside so he could enter. After Stan Allen entered, Jennifer threw the door shut, pulled the tie around her waist loose and leaped into Allen's arms. When he caught her she wrapped her naked legs around him as her robe fell open. Grasping him behind his neck, Jennifer kissed him with a deep kiss of long lost lovers reunited. Her breasts pressed against the cotton tee shirt as her left thigh rubbed against the shoulder holster under the jacket, "Ooo, is that a gun, or are you just glad to see me?" She laughed and threw her head back, shaking her wet hair loose.

Allen smiled, and ran his hands up under her robe, grabbing the cheeks of her shapely butt, "Both, but Will Moby is still outside in the car."

Jennifer smiled a crooked wicked smile, "Can he wait thirty or forty minutes?"

"I'll tell him to come back in an hour."

Location Unknown

She had been asleep for about an hour this time as she woke with a start. The dark blue van with no windows in the rear area had stopped moving and the engine had gone silent. With no seats in the van she and the now four other girls were sharing a mattress again. These were a little thicker and much cleaner.

The side door slid open. One of the men who had taken them from the big delivery truck was standing with a rifle propped on his hip, gesturing with his free hand and barking orders in Spanish. The other girls began filing out of the van into some sort of garage. Through the open door she could see two other cars and a workbench with some tools lying about. As she stepped out of the van the young woman wobbled and tried to gain her balance. The man with the rifle pushed her forward.

In a fit of rage she whirled, slapped the man and screamed, "Leave me alone!" With an angry look he drew back a fist and started to hit her in the face then changed and landed a punch to her stomach. As her breath left her, she collapsed to the floor. The man spat at her while one of the other girls stepped to the young girl's side and covered her with her own body. For her efforts the one trying to protect her received a blow from the butt of the man's rifle on her shoulder. He barked some more orders the young girl didn't understand.

Her protector helped her up; she looked into the dark sad eyes that gazed back at her from a beautiful light brown face. There were streaks of tears through the light coating of dirt. "Thank you," the blonde girl managed to say between gasping for air.

"No talk," her protector replied and guided her forward toward a door as she held her stomach and tried to regain her breath. Where the door led, she was afraid to think.

West Memphis, Arkansas

John Reardon almost didn't get to West Memphis in time. Meeting with Harris had thrown him behind schedule. Dumping his Caddy for a Ford Focus rental took a little time also. But after circling the block a few times, he was able to settle into a parking spot in front of a dress shop with a reasonable view. Wiping the nervous sweat from his forehead he put his Ivy Cap back on then blew his nose in the handkerchief while he checked his surroundings. Now it was a quick inspection of his old 35mm Minolta SRT 201 with 70-200mm zoom. *Thirty years and still taking great pictures.* Passersby seemed to take little note of the old guy waiting for his wife to come out of the shop, checking his watch every thirty seconds or so. He positioned his mirrors so he could get a reasonable check of his environment in two to three seconds.

In less than five minutes he took his first photo of Caruso and Oliveri. Who Caruso might be meeting, he had no idea. From the recording it sounded important. It was a week old and had he gotten it a day later there would be no way of knowing in time. He made a mental note to talk to Eric about checking these things nightly. Caruso was due for his next visit to Antonio's tomorrow if Reardon understood the recordings.

He knew about this small, very upscale, clothing store on West Broadway Avenue. It was dotted with these types of shops mixed in with the occasional sidewalk café and coffee shop. Caruso owned this particular shop. Reardon figured he laundered some of his money through here since it seemed to be operated as a legitimate business. No trafficking of any sort, and it was out of Memphis' jurisdiction.

Plus Caruso had visited many times in the past, though nothing fruitful came from those outings, just a few shopping bags and such with legitimate purchases, he presumed. There was no way to bug the place without him finding out. He wasn't sure, but Reardon had a feeling this meeting would be different. Maybe it was just the tone in his voice and the mention of future *happenings*.

It wasn't easy, but Reardon had developed a method of aiming and snapping pictures with the 35mm SLR and its long lens without being too conspicuous. The 125 ASA film should allow for quality enlargements if necessary. About ten more minutes and a new customer approached the door. He took a peek through the lens.

"I'll be damned," he mumbled to himself as he snapped off four quick photos, "this cannot be a coincidence. Clothes shopping on the same day and time, same location!" Just up the street another customer strolled up and entered. A few more pics.

Reardon sat the camera on the passenger seat and began scribbling names, dates, times, and locations in his notebook. Hell, he even made some notations about the cool temperatures and wind conditions. One thing for sure, these guys were above his pay grade. From here on it would, in fact, be in Harris' purview. After rewinding the film, he popped it out of the camera. Once sealed in an envelope he placed it in the inside pocket of his jacket and then got out and locked the car.

Being as discreet as possible he put the camera in the trunk and decided to stroll down the block for a better vantage point. Reardon tried not to look as he walked down the sidewalk across the street. It took him in direct line of sight with the display window. Deciding between the two coffee shops on the street, he chose the one cattycornered across the street from the store entrance with outside seating. It was on the corner and provided the best views. Reardon bought a coffee, a paper and picked out a table near the sidewalk. Most patrons stayed inside out of the cool blustery conditions. *Wimps*, he thought, *try a Korean winter*

CHAPTER THIRTY

Duluth, Georgia

The smell of ginger and garlic wafted through Jennifer Grady's apartment. Still robed, she sat on her sofa and ate from the white waxed cardboard containers of Chinese takeout. Allen had finished and sat on the opposite end of the sofa, working to remove the food bits with a toothpick. Moby sat in the easy chair in front of the window by the entry door and started his second container of lo mien.

"Like I said before, Caruso sent us down here to tie up some loose ends while Crandall is out of town. He wants you to finish up with the daughter-in-law. Can you do that?" Allen asked as he placed the toothpick in the ashtray on the coffee table, picked up a pack of cigarettes and tapped one out.

"Of course," she said with the slightest of giggles, "I've been spiking her meds to keep them from sending her home. I started again yesterday morning after my off days. Her husband is not in town and the parents don't get there until around noon. I can disappear in the confusion, then you and me can go have some fun."

Allen lit the cigarette and stood. He took a drag and blew the smoke in the air, "Yeah, well don't hang around too long. I know how you like the look on a dead body's face."

"Yes," she smiled and placed her fingers on her lips, "They look so peaceful." She stared into space for a few seconds then went back to her eating.

"Not when somebody puts a bullet in their head. Will and I have to take care of the girlfriend when she gets home tomorrow."

Jennifer looked up from the container of food, "Why two of you? It's not like she's some kind of bad ass."

Allen took another drag and rolled his eyes a bit, "Backup. Is this cop going to be a problem?"

Jennifer laughed again and put her food on the table, "No. Jack being out of town seems to have him on hold for now. I talked to some of the patrol cops that come in. This Brennan guy has a reputation of having a short fuse with perps. Gets him in trouble with the brass, so they say. But the uniforms seem to like him."

Allen put out his cigarette in the ash tray. The scent of singed wood from the toothpick rose with the fading smoke, "Good, if he shows, bad luck for him."

"Well, I have some things to help you get into her house. Several months ago Cindy went on vacation, I fed her cat. She gave me the codes to open her garage and to turn off her alarm system. The damn cat died a few weeks later." Jennifer smiled and licked the remnants of the Chinese food from her lips. Allen returned the smile and gestured toward the bedroom.

West Memphis, Arkansas

Reardon looked up from his paper. Across the street, Tony Oliveri was standing outside the clothing shop. He stepped to the curb, looked both ways, then started across the street. His current direction was taking him straight toward the coffee shop. Reardon looked back at his folded newspaper and snuck his right hand inside the left flap of his sport jacket, touching the handle of his Smith and Wesson .357. He eased it out of the holster clipped to his belt.

Oliveri walked up and stopped in front of the table. There were five other tables on this side of the café, all solid black aluminum. The chairs were a matching color, made of iron, with lattice work seats. Green umbrellas adorned each table.

"So, it is you, Reardon," Oliveri said as he leaned over and placed both hands on the table.

Reardon laid the paper down with his left hand and shifted in his chair. As he looked up he repositioned his right hand under the table, "As I live and breathe, Tony Oliveri. It's been what, six months, a year now?" Reardon was remembering the one time he slipped up and was caught taking pictures. He got roughed up a little, and they took the film, but he had been extra careful since.

"How's your boss," he continued. "What's his name—oh yeah, Caruso? Better yet, get any Rogaine for that little skull cap you got working? I hear the stuff makes your dick limp." Reardon grinned, knowing his coffee and nicotine stained teeth showing through his very gray whiskers would piss off the immaculate anal retentive Oliveri even more.

"Don't be a smart ass," Oliveri countered under his breath.

"Who me? I'm a wise ass—" he grinned even bigger—"smart asses are much younger. You know, with age comes wisdom and all that happy horse shit."

"What are you doing here?"

"Drinking coffee and reading the paper," he slid the paper across the table, "Want to ask me some questions on current events?"

Oliveri leaned closer. "You were told to stay away," he said through clinched teeth.

Reardon laughed, "We live in the same town, there's a reasonable chance we will cross paths once in a while. Maybe you could just send me his weekly itinerary; I'll know where not to hang out."

Oliveri straightened up, tapped his jacket where his gun was holstered, then opened it just enough for Reardon to see it. "Don't push me, old man!"

Reardon laughed and pulled his chair closer, "Here, outside in public." His tone and expression took on a sudden seriousness, "Bold, especially for a cockroach like you. I figured you only scurried across the kitchen floor at night."

Oliveri slipped his hand inside his jacket, "Don't tempt me, asshole."

Reardon shifted his right hand under the table, "I wish you would try, my .357 will go through the table and you before you can get your little 9mm out from under your coat. Depending on my aim I might just turn you into a eunuch. Most likely break my wrist at this angle, but hell, it might be worth it."

Oliveri moved his hand further inside his coat, "Nice bluff old man, won't work."

"Feel free to call my bluff. It's double action, won't even have to cock it. Nickel plated. Want to see it? How 'bout a demo?"

Oliveri's face took on a shade of white as if all the blood drained from it at once. He stammered a bit then regained his composure, "You better watch your back." He slowly backed away before turning and retracing his steps across the street.

Reardon put his pistol back in the holster. Pulling his hand out, he could not control its shaking. "Phew," he said out loud as he exhaled. The shortness of his breath made him wonder if he even took a breath in the last three minutes. Taking a look around, he noticed no one was close enough to see what just transpired. *That was real damn stupid*, he thought while waiting for his heart rate to return to normal.

Dacula, Georgia

Paul Brennan sat back in his recliner. His mood wasn't the best in the world. Most of the day was wasted in court. After he was called to the witness stand, his testimony was suspended when the judge called for an adjournment until the next morning at 10:00 AM. It was a textbook assault case, one that should have been pleaded. But, the perp's family had money, so they had a seven-hundred-fifty-dollar-an-hour attorney who used every trick in the book to stall and twist the facts.

Brennan never understood. It seems every once in a while, you run across some asshole who thinks just because they have money and daddy has connections, they can do whatever they want. In this case it wasn't going to work.

He opened his notebook on the Crandall case and found the phone number he was looking for. After entering it into the address book in his cell phone he called it. Following the fourth ring the voicemail kicked in, "Hi Cindy, Paul Brennan here. If you know how to get in touch with Jack please let me know. He has turned off his cell, so I have no way of reaching him directly. I have some important information about the man who set the fire and attacked Andrea. We may have an ID on him. I need to let Jack know. It's very important I reach him. I'm worried he will do something rash and possibly get hurt. Call me if you have any way of getting in touch with him. You should still have my number."

After hanging up, he punched in Annie's number.

Memphis

The conversation with Cindy on the burn phones had been a pleasant one for the most part. Andrea was doing better. Lisa would be back in Georgia in a couple of days. He told Cindy he would return in a few days or so, once he cleared up some unfinished business. When pressed, he would not elaborate just what that unfinished business was. That was the sticky part of the conversation. When her regular cell phone went off in the next room she said she would let the voice mail pick up.

In spite of Cindy's concern for his general welfare, Crandall was becoming more and more comfortable with what he was about to do and feeling less guilty each passing hour. That last part was a long time coming. He had found peace with what he was planning to do.

While he sat at the kitchen table, facing the back door of the house, Crandall had removed several items from the chest that accompanied him on the trip. To his left, lined up on the table, were several vials and bottles of different drugs, along with a few hypodermic needles taken from the pharmacy prior to his departure. To his right, in a neat row, were five clips of .45 caliber ammunition, ten rounds each.

He had just finished cleaning and reassembling his Sig Sauer P220 Combat TB and was screwing the Gemtech suppressor onto the threaded barrel when the back door opened and his father entered, carrying a bag. According to the printing on the bag, Reardon had just come from the one hour photo counter at the local drugstore. "Hi, Dad." Crandall said.

Reardon stopped and looked at his son with a frown, then tossed the bag onto the table. As he pulled out the chair he responded, pointing at the suppressor, "You know those things are illegal in some states."

Crandall finished attaching the suppressor, inserted a clip, and checked the weight and balance. He pulled back the slide and let it move forward, loading a round into the chamber while he responded, "Are they illegal in Tennessee?"

"Don't know. I don't use 'um."

Crandall popped the clip out and ejected the round from the chamber. "Nah, don't bother. Worst case is they'll add five years to my sentence." He said, with just a hint of sarcasm in his voice, then, "What's in the bag?"

"Some pictures my detective friend is going to love," Reardon answered as he pushed the bag across the table, "Take a look."

"I've seen enough, Dad," Crandall smiled and continued, "I'll leave that wrap up to you."

Reardon flashed a self-satisfied smile, "No, you need to see these. I've identified Caruson's inside source. Get this—they are father and son, and pretty high up in the food chain"

Crandall sat back in his chair, "Okay, after I finish with this."

"Sounds good, so, what about all those drugs and shit?" Reardon asked.

Crandall laughed and shook his head, "Seemed like a good idea when I borrowed them from the hospital. I figured I would inject Caruso with enough Digitalis and cocaine to make his heart explode and watch him suffer. But, I've changed my mind. Just one more mark on my rap sheet. Who knows, it might still come in handy. Don't really know why I took the anesthetic, but I think I've come up with a use for it. I'll explain that later. Right now I'm tired."

"Okay, but you need to know, I got spotted today," Reardon replied. "Oliveri. We had words and I threatened to blow his nuts off. I think Oliveri basically painted a target on my back."

"Well," Crandall started, amusement in his voice, "We'll just have to make sure he doesn't get the chance to follow through. Besides, you just gave me something to think about. Let's clean up and get to bed."

Reardon nodded in agreement and pushed back from the table, "Cocktail?"

Crandall smiled and nodded.

Collierville, Tennessee

Oliveri held the door of the Lincoln Town Car open while Caruso exited the vehicle in his four car garage. As he stood, Caruso placed both hands on the top of the door, "Tony, if Eric Benedetto is somehow working with Reardon, I want the old bastard in the river tomorrow night."

A sneer showed on Oliveri's face, "With pleasure, boss."

CHAPTER THIRTY-ONE

Duluth, Georgia

STAN ALLEN LIT HIS CIGARETTE THEN LAID THE LIGHTER ON THE nightstand next to the bed. A long drag filled his lungs. He scanned the bedroom of the furnished apartment Caruso had been paying for the last two years. The clock next to him showed just 4:17 AM. He pulled the small roll of tobacco from between his lips, inspected the glowing tip then exhaled the smoke through his nose. Jennifer Grady lay next to him, in deep sleep. She lay on her side while the bed covers draped across her just above the cheeks of her lovely backside. He stared at her naked back, the smoothness of her skin. Allen put out his right hand and in the air he traced the curve of her side from just below the shoulder to where her waist fell into the lower back.

They met five years ago in a bar. She picked him up. After several dates Jennifer confessed an obsession with death. The looks of serenity on faces of the newly departed were of particular fascination. She also took pleasure in watching them expire. Then there was the confession. At several of the hospitals she worked across the country, she had assisted in accelerating the process for maybe a dozen or so patients. Allen wondered, since sending her to spy on Crandall, if the tally had increased.

He recalled all this as he drew in more smoke. Then he took note of the healthy glow of her sun browned body. With summer's recent end there were no signs of tan-lines. Visions of her lying naked in the sun flooded his thoughts and filled him with mixed feelings. He put out the cigarette and placed a gentle hand on her shoulder. Jennifer stirred and rolled in his direction, blinking the sleep from her eyes. She reached up, interlaced her fingers behind his neck, smiled and pulled him down to her. Allen returned her smile. *You will be the hardest part of the job, my love*, he thought as their lips touched.

Location Unknown

The young blonde girl ran the brush through her hair again and again. Time for her was lost, only the rising and setting of the sun to mark its passage. What day of the week it was, she could not say. The bristles felt good against her scalp. It was the only thing she could use the word good about in days. What little sleep she had came in fragments, and only when she could fight it no longer. She did not wish to sleep, for it was filled with nightmares.

Their room had no windows and just the single door. It was furnished with two folding metal chairs and three mattresses. *The mattresses!* Always the same. Same feel, same smell. At least the toilets were not in the room with them. The walls were a blank stark white with several small holes in random spots. All electrical outlets were covered. A single bulb in the ceiling fixture provided the only light. Its switch, located somewhere on the outside of the room, was turned off and on at random times. Someone was always outside the door, armed, or so they were told. There was no reason to doubt them.

Upon entering the door from the garage yesterday, they were greeted by a woman who spoke Spanish and English. This woman made it clear that if you did not cooperate, members of your family would die. In her case, the woman repeated the home address from her driver's license and said someone had already checked it out.

After that she was handed some soap and shampoo. They were herded to an open, tiled, shower with several shower heads. When she objected to showering in front of the guards, the dark haired woman with the cold black eyes told her she needed to get used to men watching her. It was her protector who intervened again, pulling her away before she was struck by the woman.

The shower had a strong stale odor mixed with the scent of bleach and ammonia. She tried her best to not touch the black splotches growing in cracks and crevices. Leering eyes of her captors made her tremble with shame. Water cascaded across her face, but it could not hide her tears, her sobbing or her shaking. Nor could it make her feel clean. She wondered if she would ever feel clean again.

Taking away all their clothes, including underwear, the girls were each given one pair of pajama pants and a white tee shirt. Herded to another room, they were forced to watch a video. A girl with long dark straight hair was stripped naked, tied up and beaten with a baseball bat. When she could no longer move, her tormentors doused her broken body with gasoline and set her on fire. A high-volume level insured they heard each scream, each strike of the bat, every laugh, every insult, and every spit from her torturers. Guards stood behind those who could not watch and forced their heads toward the screen. At the end, the cold-eyed woman said, "This will happen to you if you do not do what we say."

With her mind back in this present hell, she put down the brush and looked at her protector. Pointing at one of the other girls, one who seemed much younger, she said, "Sister?" Her protector nodded and whispered, "Si, hermana." Touching the sister on her shoulder she said, "Carmela," then pointed to herself and again whispered, "Ramona".

The young girl put her finger on her own chest and whispered, "Elsa".

Ramona pointed at Carmela, herself, then the door and pressed her finger to her lips. Elsa nodded.

Memphis

At a small kitchen in the rectory, Father Wisniewski was enjoying a plate of scrambled eggs and wheat toast with his morning orange juice and coffee. Father Espinoza and he were catching the news show. The morning hosts, relaxing on a sofa, were switching to a reporter from their San Antonio affiliate.

A female reporter was standing in front of an apartment complex. A slight breeze blew a few strands of reddish brown hair across her face, "Nineteen year old Elsa Franklin is missing. According to police the student at the University of Texas at San Antonio has not been seen since she left her part-time job at the mall four days ago. She lives alone in the off-campus complex behind me. Her parents, who reside in Houston, became concerned when Elsa did not return repeated phone calls, and contacted local police."

A picture of a young blonde woman standing in front of a car appeared on the screen as the reporter continued reading from her notepad, "According to the police, there is no sign she made it home from her part-time job, and they are still looking for her yellow

2006 Volkswagen Beetle. Police are refusing to comment, other than it is a missing person's case at this time. Anyone knowing the whereabouts of Elsa Franklin is asked to contact the San Antonio police immediately at—"

"It's sad," Wisniewski said to Father Espinoza, "All these young beautiful girls. They disappear, only to be found dead or not found at all. As a priest I would like just once to be able to do something other than just comfort the family."

Father Espinoza nodded as he leaned on the table with his elbows. "That would be nice, but we are also restricted by church policy. When I was in Guatemala, near the Mexican border, kidnappings were very common. They still are. Started mostly with political types, police chiefs that tried to stand up to the cartels. Then it became women and young children, mostly young females. For the slavers, I guess."

Espinoza pulled his reading glasses down to the tip of his nose, looked over them at Wisniewski and held his fork up, shaking it with each word, "I found it harder to comfort families of those who disappeared than those who died. I prayed to just once be able to tell a mother or father their child had been found alive. *That* would be nice."

"Yes," Wisniewski said looking past Espinoza at the cabinet on the wall behind him, "That would be nice indeed. How much would you like to do that?"

Lawrenceville, Georgia

Paul Brennan prepared to enter the courtroom while other folks went up and down the halls in seeming random patterns at the *Justice Center* in Lawrenceville, Georgia. His mind was elsewhere and not on his impending testimony. There was the question why Cindy had not returned his call. And, why Crandall had not turned up in Memphis even though the police found his SUV. Were the Memphis Police sandbagging him? Harris seemed like a straight shooter. Something was going on, and he couldn't put his finger on it. There must be more to it than Crandall hunting for Caruso, but Harris wouldn't disclose anything. Brennan blamed himself for part of it. He didn't want to issue the standard BOLO, so Harris agreed to put word out on the street discreetly.

Amid all that, there was the upcoming evening. He was also looking forward to his dinner with Annie, though he was a little puzzled why she insisted on meeting at the restaurant instead of him picking her up.

If things went well here, maybe he could go by the hospital after he got out of court. He put his game face on and opened the ornate wooden doors of the courtroom.

Duluth, Georgia

The ding of the bell shook Cindy from her thoughts as the elevator stopped on the fourth floor. She was two hours early for her shift so she could take a nice long visit with Andrea.

"Hi, Lenny," she greeted the male nurse behind the counter when she arrived at the nurses' station, "How's our favorite patient?"

"It's Len," he replied with a look of disappointment. "I stopped being Lenny when I was eleven. If it were anyone but you, I'd be pissed," he smiled.

"I know," Cindy replied, "I just like to yank your chain, and don't call me Cynthia to get me back. So, how's Andrea?"

A frown interrupted his banter, "I'm afraid her liver function took off again. Lab results came back this morning. We've notified Dr. Levinson. He should be here soon."

"What?" Cindy asked then continued, "Can I see her chart."

Len looked up and down the hall, then over his shoulder at the two nurses in the room behind the counter, "Here, but I didn't show it to you." He plucked the chart from the stand and laid it on the counter.

Cindy read the top page then flipped back several pages, scanning all the blood tests. They were like a roller coaster. A thought popped into her mind. With a shake of her head she dismissed it. It returned, stronger. She shook her head. It refused to go away. Two nurses shared a laugh behind Len in a glass enclosed room. Cindy looked up and down the hall.

Panic began to set in as the thought repeated itself again and again. *Shit*, she thought and slapped her hand on the desk. The two nurses stopped laughing and looked out at her through the glass. Cindy leaned forward. She calmed down and under her breath she asked, "Is Jenny Grady here?"

A look of mild surprise was replaced with a sly smile, "Yeah and you should see her. I think she had a real good time last night. She forgot her bra this morning. The male patients—"

"Where is she?" Cindy interrupted, continuing to scan the hallway.

"She's with Andrea. Visits with her pretty often. Why?"

Cindy didn't answer but snapped her attention back to Len, "What's her rotation?"

"Just got back yesterday from her days off, why?"

Cindy leaned forward and in a low voice ordered, "Call security and be quiet about it. Send them to Andrea's room, and you guys stay here," she said nodding her head toward the two nurses. "And, get Dr. Nguyen up here from ER stat with a crash cart."

"Why?"

She glared, "Just fucking do it, Len!"

Cindy left the nurse's station on a dead run.

CHAPTER THIRTY-TWO

CINDY FITZGERALD SHOVED THE HEAVY WOODEN DOOR OF THE private room open. It banged against the doorstop beside the small chest of drawers on which sat an assortment of flowers in vases of all sizes. To her left, about eight feet inside the room, was the bed. Andrea appeared to be sleeping. Next to the bed, in front of her, was the bed table with the breakfast tray still on it. The metal plate cover was off to the side. A standard plastic water pitcher wrapped in Styrofoam sat next to it. Against the wall were a nightstand and a visitor's chair.

Sunlight from the window provided the only illumination. On the opposite side of the bed was the IV hanger. In the corner sat another visitor's chair. Beside the IV hanger stood Jennifer Grady, a hypodermic needle in her hand and a stunned expression on her face.

"What the hell have you done?" Cindy demanded, breathing hard. She stared at Jennifer with rage-filled eyes. Cindy continued, moving forward, not taking her eyes off Jennifer until she reached Andrea's bedside and stopped.

Jennifer appeared frozen at first. She stammered a bit, "I—uh—was just—giving her something to help her sleep. What is wrong with you?" She dropped the needle into the trashcan beside her.

Cindy's jaw tightened, she could barely form her words. "It's not on her damn chart."

Jennifer put both hands on her hips, "Listen, bitch, you need to leave before you get hurt."

Cindy grabbed the metal plate cover from the tray and let it fly across the bed. Jennifer ducked and screamed, "Get out of here!" The cover bounced off her shoulder and clanged onto the hard tiled floor.

While Jennifer crouched, Cindy raced around the foot of the bed with water pitcher in hand. Before Jennifer could stand erect again, Cindy launched the pitcher. Another duck, the pitcher hit the wall behind her target and ejected water in all directions.

A moan came from the direction of the bed. Cindy turned her head to look. Before she could come back to her opponent, she found her throat in Jennifer's grasp. She grabbed Jennifer's wrist in an attempt to break her grip. Cindy pushed away as Jennifer's hold loosened. Her momentum took her backwards. Cindy stepped in one of the puddles from the pitcher and slipped. Her feet went out from under her as she fought to keep her balance. Cindy fell to the floor. First her butt impacted the floor hard, then her back and shoulders. Her head bounced against the floor as the cold water soaked through the back of her scrubs, sending a mild shock through her body.

With Cindy dazed, Jennifer leaped on her, sitting astride her waist like she was riding a horse. Cindy reached up, but her arms were knocked aside. Jennifer slapped her across the face then punched and scratched her on the cheek when she turned her head. Jennifer grabbed Cindy's hair and slammed her head against the floor again.

Her head now swimming with pain and dizziness, Cindy managed to get her arms inside Jennifer's. She reached up and grabbed her foe's breasts through the scrub top and dug her fingernails in as hard as she could. Jennifer screamed with pain and tried to wrench Cindy's hands away. The more Jennifer pulled, the deeper she dug her fingernails in. With a mighty effort she turned to her left, pulling as hard as she could on Jennifer's breasts.

When her adversary landed and twisted away onto her back, Cindy released her grip. She rolled back a little and saw the metal plate cover just to her right lying upside down. On her left she sensed Jennifer trying to recover and come after her again. With great effort Cindy stretched out her body toward the cover, inching it closer with her finger tips. When it was close enough, she grabbed it by the rim and rolled to her left. Cindy brought the plate cover up and swung with all her strength while Jennifer took hold of her hair and yanked. She caught her target aside the head. Jennifer let go of Cindy's hair and collapsed to the floor on her back, grabbing the side of her head then tried to push up on her elbows.

Now Cindy scrambled onto her knees. She pulled back her arm and brought the metal weapon down again as hard as she could. The edge caught Jennifer's nose flush. Blood spurt from underneath the plate cover and Jennifer collapsed again.

"I trusted you bitch, did you kill my cat, too?" Cindy screamed in Jennifer's face as she delivered a second blow that landed flush on the face. Jennifer raised her arms into a defensive position. Cindy pulled her arm back for one more strike. A strong hand grasped her wrist and a deep voice shouted, "Stop!"

Cindy went limp and let the plate cover drop. It first hit Jennifer then rolled off and resounded on the floor, then again when it tipped over and settled on its side. Another hand grasped Cindy's arm and helped her to her feet. She gulped air into her lungs. Her chest felt tight, like it would not allow her lungs to expand. She looked down at Jennifer, now moaning, with her arms crossed on her chest, blood from her nose oozing down her cheek. Jennifer rolled onto her side and whimpered, "She's crazy," through sobs and moans. Cindy heard Dr. Nguyen shout from somewhere behind her, "Out of my way, people!"

Two uniformed security guards escorted Cindy and Jennifer out the door and down the hallway. Cindy heard Dr. Nguyen shout orders. Then she heard "Epinephrine!" Cindy's knees buckled.

Memphis

Eric Benedetto checked his watch while he finished packing his gym bag. He had time for a quick workout before going to the restaurant. Both were walking distance away, and the cool weather made it more enjoyable. A side pocket held his black shoes. Neatly folded in the bottom of the large flat bottom bag were his black slacks, matching vest, belt, underwear and socks. A copy of his master's thesis resided in a separate pocket to work on during his break at the restaurant. Two plus pages of notes needed to be entered when he returned home to his small one bedroom apartment. The end of the tunnel lay in sight.

His apartment was half of the second floor in an old house in an older section of downtown Memphis. This house had been converted to four apartments well before he was born, but he liked old houses. It was close enough to work so he could walk, and being convenient to what social life he enjoyed when not studying, was a huge plus. Once he had his Master of Science degree in Information Technology, he looked forward to working in computer security and forensics—with the FBI if they would have him. The application had already been submitted. His experience in gathering data on Alex Caruso only heightened his interest in the area. He was still a few weeks away from that day and had to admit it wasn't easy being patient.

Benedetto threw his gym bag strap onto his shoulder, left his apartment, and hurried down the old wooden stairs to the first floor. He knew the pitch of each squeak in every step like an old friend after going up and down them the last three years. When he reached the bottom of the stairs, Benedetto turned, looked back, and smiled. Before long he would be leaving his friends to begin the next phase of his life. For now though, Simon would be meeting him out front and then off to the gym.

He opened the front door and stepped out onto the wide wooden covered porch that ran the length of the house's front. To the right of the wide gray concrete steps, just a few feet from the railing, were the branches of an old giant oak tree. He started down the steps. Just to his right, initially hidden by the tree, were two men leaning against a black sedan. He recognized Tony Oliveri. The other he knew as Turk Jackson, sometimes security at Caruso's club.

Benedetto slowed his pace down the steps and looked in their direction. It felt like the hair on the back of his neck stood up when he recalled the video of two days ago. Something wasn't right. He looked up and down the street, praying Simon was nearby. A couple walking away from them about a half block up was the only thing in view.

Oliveri motioned for him to come over, "Hi, Mr. Oliveri," he said as he approached, "What brings you over here?"

Oliveri opened the rear driver's side door, "You do, get in."

Benedetto stopped about four feet away, "I'm just on my way to the gym, can this wait until later?"

"No, I'm afraid not," Oliveri opened his jacket for emphasis.

Benedetto glanced up the street. He thought he saw his friend turn the corner from two blocks up. At that distance he could not be sure. Turk Jackson stepped behind him and grasped his shoulders. Benedetto dropped his bag and tried to twist away. Jackson hit him across the back of his head with some kind of hard object. His legs became unsteady. Jackson half carried half pushed him toward the open car door, shoving him into the back seat. Benedetto fell over onto his side, dazed and groaning. His bag landed on top of him. Oliveri shoved his legs aside and sat down. One door closed and the vehicle shook as another door opened. Someone sat down and the door closed. He thought he felt and heard the engine start. Everything was spinning. It sounded like Oliveri who said, "Okay, let's go get this Voloshin guy."

Dominik? A very confused thought entered Benedetto's head, then things went black.

Location Unknown

Elsa and the other girls were sitting around, talking in low whispers. She had been trying to communicate with Ramona. It was slow, but she managed to learn the sisters were from Ciudad Juarez. Ramona was eighteen, Carmela fourteen. Both were kidnapped after a nice woman promised them some work.

The door opened with a suddenness that startled the room occupants. Cold Eyes, the name Elsa gave to the woman, stood at the door. She motioned a man with several paper bags into the room. An armed guard remained behind her. Bagman, she decided to name him, handed each girl one of his bags. The last two he gave to Elsa and Carmela.

When they dumped the bags out, three of the girls had plain white blouses, panties, a black cotton skirt, and black or brown pumps. Almost like a uniform. She and Carmela had short black leather skirts, a see through blouse with strategically located pockets, a thong, and black spike heels. Each girl had a tube of red lipstick. Bagman smiled at the girls. Elsa picked up her clothing issue and threw it at Bagman's feet. He kicked them back at her, stepped over, gripped a handful of hair, jerked her head back and raised his fist.

"Armando, no en la cara!" Cold Eyes shouted.

Bagman shoved Elsa backward with the bottom of his foot. She landed on her back. He picked up her clothes and dumped them on top of her.

Cold Eyes instructed them in both languages to get dressed and put on their lipstick. They would be leaving in thirty minutes. She would be back before long to check on them.

When the door closed, the girls helped Elsa sit up. She was able to ask Ramona what Cold Eyes had said to Bagman.

"No face." Ramona said and touched the side of Elsa's face with a fist.

Carmela looked at the skimpy clothes. Her body convulsed with uncontrollable sobs.

CHAPTER THIRTY-THREE

Duluth, Georgia

CINDY SAT IN A WOODEN STRAIGHT-BACK CHAIR INSIDE THE hospital security office across from ER patient check in. The blinds that covered the window looking out into the waiting area were closed for privacy.

She checked her face in the compact mirror from her purse. The right side of her face was bruised and sore with a slight puffiness. A gauze bandage and antiseptic covered the scratches. Cindy laid the small mirror down on the desk, picked up a chemical ice pack and placed it against the back of her head where a small butterfly bandage pinched together a wound. She could still detect the slight iodine odor from the butadiene applied to her scalp.

Officer Pete Williams occupied the desk chair to her right, taking down the last of her statement. The metal framed chair squeaked with each shift of his weight. After a few more questions, Cindy leaned back in a slow deliberate motion to prevent the shock of pain from her bruises, stared at the ceiling, and blew air from her lungs. Her shoulders slumped.

The door opened and another officer handed Williams a piece of paper then left, closing the door behind him. Williams read it and whistled. "Dr. Nguyen sent word. Ms. Crandall is stable and in dialysis now. He thinks she will be okay, but won't know for sure for about two hours. They still have to determine how much kidney or liver damage may have occurred. He wants to thank you for your quick actions."

Cindy's shoulders slumped, she breathed out a heavy sigh, "Thank God!"

Williams looked over at his notes, "As for Ms. Grady, you said you fought?"

Cindy leaned forward, placed the ice pack in her lap and sighed, "Yes, I've already covered all that."

He looked back at the paper the other officer handed him, "Well, it says here she has a broken nose, black eye, chipped tooth, split lip and her breasts are a deep purple and green. No sign of a concussion though. Doc says he normally only sees this in an auto accident." Williams placed the paper in his notebook and looked back at Cindy smiling, "That's some fight."

Cindy put the ice pack back on her head, "Well, three older brothers taught me if I had to fight, fight dirty. Besides—take a look—I'm not doing so good myself."

The door opened again, two officers stood on each side of Jennifer Grady. The officer who opened the door spoke, "Okay, Pete, the Doc has cleared her so we're going to transport Ms. Grady."

Williams looked up and waved them on, "Thanks guys, I'll finish up here and brief Brennan when he's available."

Cindy glanced up at Jennifer. Her hair was still unkempt, blood dried on the front of her scrubs, and some purple discoloration had begun to show around her eye.

Jennifer glared, "You'll get yours, bitch," she slurred through swollen lips.

The officer closed the door as they led Jennifer away, then they heard her scream, "You'll get yours!" Cindy imagined what the patients and their families were thinking.

She turned back to Officer Williams with a puzzled furrowed brow, "What does she mean by that?"

Williams returned her look with a reassuring smile, "Threats of revenge from these types is usually empty blustering. Take precautions and call 911 if you feel the least bit in danger." He looked down at his note book, "Weird, that one."

"Yeah," Cindy answered, "I think she has necromania. Seems obsessed with all things dead. People, animals, doesn't matter. Used to talk about the look on dead people's faces. Weird doesn't begin—" Cindy flopped against the back of the chair, her bruised shoulders smacked against its hardness, "Ouch!"

Location Unknown

Elsa, Ramona, Carmela, and the other girls were cleaned, dressed and inspected by Cold Eyes. They were now pushed, prodded, and cajoled back into the blue van. For the first time, Elsa noticed the name on the side of the vehicle, Thompson Brother's Garage. Cold

Eyes informed them once again that death, like the one on the video, would be the punishment for anyone trying to escape.

Bagman drove, for which Elsa was glad. He had a hideous odor to his breath and didn't seem to understand the relationship between soap and water. There was another in the passenger seat and one in the back with the girls. Both were armed. When the door closed, the man in the back blindfolded each of the girls. He was much gentler than Bagman or Cold Eyes.

Elsa and Ramona had worked out a way to communicate through the language barrier. Keeping as quiet as possible they taught each other some of the other's language. Just a word here and there; however, it began to make things easier. The small amount of English Ramona already knew simplified the process. Some added hand signs improved things further. The other two girls were from Mexico City and were both teenagers. They were kidnapped off the street almost a month before.

Huddled in the darkness of their blindfolds the group leaned in unison as the van backed out of the garage. One of the girls began whispering, "El Señor es mi Pastor." As she continued Elsa recognized the rhythmic patterns of *The 23rd Psalm*. She clasped her hands together and bowed her head.

Memphis

"You know, if we get stopped, we'll definitely spend the night in jail," Crandall said. He was doing a mental inventory as he packed the medium-sized duffel. Sedatives, digitalis, cocaine, hypodermics, first aid kit, several rolls of surgical tape, latex gloves, smelling salts, spare jacket, shirt, cap, and extra ammunition. *Overkill*, he thought. He checked a burn phone—plenty of battery. Switching it to vibrate, Crandall placed it in one outside pocket and his regular cell with battery taped to the outside in the opposite one. He walked to the kitchen door leading to the back porch and placed the bag on the floor.

"Are you sure you want to go through with this?" his father said from behind him.

Crandall stood straight and turned toward his father who stood in the entryway between the kitchen and living area. Crandall slapped his hands together dusting them off. "Yes. What about you?"

Reardon leaned against the frame of the entryway, rubbed the three-day growth on his cheek and shrugged, "Eh, somebody's got to cover your ass. Seriously though, I've done a lot of thinking since you showed up. I think about that young girl in the video. If I had finished up this mess earlier she might still be alive, Andrea would be pregnant, you and I would be sharing a reunion drink with Mark, and then there's Lisa and David."

"You're not to blame for this." Crandall responded as he walked to the sink. His left leg twitched a bit. He took the medicine bottle from his pocket, opened it and tapped out a riluzole. A little self-reprimand was in order. He forgot to take his morning dose. Why the ALS only affected his left side for now was a mystery to him. He was right-handed and used his pistol with the right, but preferred shooting from the left side with a rifle.

He stared at the pill and continued, "If I'd taken out Caruso before going to the feds back then we wouldn't be having this conversation. I should never have gotten Sam Greggs involved either." Crandall sighed and took a glass from the dish drainer on the counter.

"We all have our crosses to bear I guess," his father replied with a solemn tone.

"I wonder whatever became of Greggs. He always had such big plans. All I ever wanted was safe and normal." Crandall said while he filled the glass halfway with water, drank it down with the pill, then turned around.

"What's normal anymore?" Reardon asked, the melancholy lingered in his voice.

Crandall answered with a gentle shake of his head, realizing the question was rhetorical.

After a short glum silence, Reardon continued, "As much as anything I think about those five girls that piece of shit is selling to Caruso. They sounded like it was a used car sale. I'd love to have that Eduardo Aguilar in my sights. Then again, I wonder if we're the right people to do this. Is revenge the right thing?"

Crandall let out a light laugh, shook his head and smiled for the first time today, "It's not revenge any longer, Dad. Not for me.

It's self-redemption, recovery for the last twenty plus years and to answer a prayer."

Reardon's face assumed a surprised expression. He cocked his head to one side as if trying to see his son in a better light, "Well, I didn't know you were a praying man."

Crandall shuffled his feet a bit, put his hands on the edge of the sink and leaned back against it, a sheepish grin on his face, "My best friend is a priest, what choice do I have? Besides, you said every time the cops show up its like Caruso knows they're coming."

"True enough. But I think I finally have the answer for that puzzle." His father walked over to him and for the first time in over twenty years, Crandall was the recipient of a hug from his father. There were no words passed. Only a silent rediscovered mutual respect.

As they released their embrace, Crandall's father placed both hands on Crandall's shoulders. Reardon's eyes and mouth downturned, "If we get though this, whatever time we have left I want to be there for all of it. I think it would help your mother more than any therapies they are doing. Being a family again, that's my prayer."

"Well, we'll just have to get through it. But for now, there are five scared young girls out there. I'm sure they've been praying, too. I know there are probably hundreds, maybe thousands just like them that we can't help. I also know helping five is better than helping zero."

Reardon smiled and nodded. "Maybe this will be a good start. After you," he said, and motioned toward the door.

Crandall put his .45 in his holster under his oversized Dickies hooded camouflage canvas shirt jacket he picked up from Wal-Mart. The grease and dirt stains were added. The suppressor hung out the bottom of the holster but remained hidden. He checked it for comfort. His Wrangler cargo jeans provided more capacity with the extra pockets. The Ozark Trail hiking boots were light enough they wouldn't slow him down.

From the corner of the table he picked up the non-descript well-worn blue baseball cap, donned and adjusted it, then scratched an itch on his chin. His own three-day growth was showing significant areas of gray, but wasn't solid yet like his father's. After checking his belt to make sure his Puma Whitetail folding knife was secured in its sheath, he lifted the duffel and walked out of the house. It was a hunting trip, except this time the game was human. Something he hadn't hunted in a long, long time.

CHAPTER THIRTY-FOUR

Lawrenceville, Georgia

At long last, Paul Brennan was out of court. About halfway through his time on the stand, he figured out the perp's lawyer was trying to bring out his infamous temper. Over the years he had learned to not get sucked in by the ploy. The therapist had told him his temper was related to PTSD. He wasn't so sure about that. What he was sure of was if you try to hurt people smaller or weaker than you, or who can't defend themselves, it pissed him off.

He made his way through the back streets, crossed Highway 316 and turned into the parking lot at 770 Hi Hope Road. Brennan pulled into the personnel parking lot on the north-side, parked and entered the side door of the Gwinnett Police Department.

Once inside, he took an elevator to the second floor. The door opened to a cubical farm that was the detective bureau and made the trip to his little semi-private corner of the law enforcement world. Almost simultaneous to his arrival, Ginger Wiley showed up bearing a piece of paper.

He pulled out his chair, "What 'ya got, Ginger? I'm under a time crunch. I've got to follow up with Pete Williams on the incident over at the hospital, voice messages to follow-up on, and I've got a hot date."

Ginger laid the paper on the desk and tapped it with the tip of a well manicured forefinger, "Got this hit through ViCAP. A house fire in a Dallas suburb, three victims shot. I contacted police there, and the preliminary ME report is at least one vic was shot with a thirty-two caliber. I've sent our preliminary ballistics from GBI for comparison. In light of this I'm trying to push them for the final. Thirty-two's are not your standard criminal weapon. They usually go for something sexier. Plus a fire here and Dallas. Us, Nashville, now Dallas, all .32's. Think we got a serial?"

Brennan slowed his descent into the chair and stared at the paper, "Serial for hire maybe. Anybody ID the bodies yet?"

"Only thing they could tell me at present was the owner was one Sam Greggs. He cannot be located. They are trying to obtain dentals for an ID. Right now they only *assume* he is one of the bodies."

"Son-of-a-bitch!" Brennan exclaimed and picked up the paper, "I know that name. This is connected. I guarantee it."

Ginger came around the desk and looked over Brennan's shoulder, "How do you know that?"

"He's in the U. S. Marshall's report on Crandall. They went into WitSec for the same case. Get me your contact info for Dallas."

"Back in a sec," Ginger said as she left.

A check of his voice messages showed only two of note. Williams' message saying he had wrapped up at the hospital, and one from Cindy saying she would be checking on Andrea and would call him later. No mention of his message from yesterday made him wonder if she had heard it yet.

"I've got to get in touch with Crandall," he mumbled as the Dallas contact info landed atop his desk.

Memphis

Crandall and Reardon sat on the sidewalk, their backs against the wall of the establishment next to The Lamar Lounge. Instead of the Wal-Mart outfit Crandall chose, Reardon went with well worn jeans, a tattered gray sweatshirt, his yard shoes, a black wool cap, and his near forty year old Army field jacket with the name tag removed.

Between the two buildings ran an alleyway large enough to drive a good sized truck down. Behind the buildings was another alleyway. Trucks making deliveries and emptying the dumpsters would maneuver through this maze several times a week. The occasional rat would make an appearance after sundown. Crandall had already seen one at the dumpster just past the rear door of the lounge when he made his first reconnaissance.

The father and son passed a Jack Daniels bottle in a paper bag back and forth. It was filled with strong brewed tea for proper color. Reardon took a swallow, feinted the harshness of the drink, then passed it back, "You look like hell," he said to Crandall.

Crandall tipped the bottle at Reardon in a toasting motion and smiled, "Like father, like son," then he took a swallow.

"I got one question though," Reardon said, looking across the street at a man negotiating a transaction with one of the early arriving hookers. In a darkened alley, a few feet away from the temporary lovers, he could see an ongoing drug deal, "What's with the smelling salts?"

"Trade secret, but if you must know," Crandall replied and took another swallow, "I was watching an NFL football game, and this punter came out on the field. When the rest of the team was setting up to snap the ball he took his spot and broke some capsule and waved it under his nose."

Reardon snatched the bottle from his son, "Smelling salts?"

"Yeah, then he proceeds to kick the ball over sixty yards."

Reardon thought for a second, "You know, I think I've seen the guy. So, what's that got to do with you?"

"I started doing it during shooting competitions. Don't know if it was the reason, but there were some days I had to miss on purpose."

Reardon turned his vision to Crandall and cocked his head to one side, "No shit. I hope you have a pocket full then." He turned his attention back to the negotiations across the street.

"Here comes trouble," Crandall said and pointed up the street. Father Wisniewski was approaching them. Wisniewski stopped in front of the father and son derelicts.

"I thought you were going to stay with the vehicles," Crandall said, looking up at Wisniewski.

"Father Espinoza can watch a pickup and a mini-van. Besides you need someone who speaks Spanish."

"And you do?" Crandall inquired.

Wisniewski put out his right arm and leaned against the wall, looking down at the two men, "I've spent the better part of four years sharing living quarters with a guy named Espinoza from Guatemala. As part of the arrangement we spend two days a week talking only Spanish."

"Well," Reardon said, took a swallow and continued, "You stand out like a sore thumb with that collar. What's your cover?"

"Saving souls." He waved his arm with a flourish, sweeping from one end of the street to the other, "'*On hearing this, Jesus said unto them, it is not the healthy who need a physician, but the sick. I have not come to call the righteous, but sinners.'* Jesus wandered the countryside seeking the sinners, downtrodden and sick. They did not seek him out. This is not my first visit to Lamar."

"Okay," Reardon replied smiling, "But, how did you get your compadre to join our little gang?"

"I lied," Wisniewski answered straight-faced.

Reardon handed the bottle over to Crandall and pointed a wagging finger at the priest, "You, my young friend, are a walking contradiction."

Wisniewski laughed, "Tell me something I don't know. My inner conflicts are too numerous."

Crandall looked up, "When you get the girls back to the church are you going to hide them in the catacombs?"

"No, the dojo. I don't think they want to be locked up. They've been prisoners for a while. They'll need to trust us. The catacombs would only scare them again."

"And just what the hell are the catacombs? Is there something you're not telling me?" Reardon asked.

"No, Dad. The catacombs is that bomb shelter they built in the basement of the church back in the early sixties. Wiz and I used to goof off down there when Father Jerrod was the priest. Steel door, no windows, and an air vent. The Ham Radio was pretty neat though. Anyway, that was Father Jerrod's nickname for it. What then, Wiz?"

"When time permits we'll take them to a Salvation Army safe-house over in Lebanon, Tennessee. They are set up to help girls like this, and others who are victims of human trafficking and sex slavery. No questions, no judgment, medical checkups, counseling, then get them back home if they have one to go to. They have a network that specializes in reuniting families in situations like this."

Wisniewski glanced up and down the sidewalk, "I'm spending too much time trying to save you guys. I'll just walk up the street a ways and keep my eyes opened." Father Wisniewski winked, then turned and strolled up the sidewalk as Crandall sent him away with an exaggerated dismissive wave of his hand. People who saw him coming would rapidly disappear inside the different storefronts, like Wisniewski carried the plague.

Crandall turned to his dad, "There's some irony for you. Lebanon almost took my sanity when I found Jack Crandall's arm that day. He and I were a two man team, and he was the best friend I had in the Corps. I was supposed to be in that bed, but I made him go sleep inside in a bed and I took the cot in the tent. Now, Lebanon may be part of my salvation. Just this one is on the opposite side of the ocean."

Reardon held up the bottle in the bag in a toasting manner, "Here's to Jack." He took a swallow and passed the bottle to his son.

Crandall took the fake whiskey, held it up toasting the air and stared off into space, a quiet tone in his voice, "Yeah," he paused and swallowed hard, a tear made its way down his right cheek, "Here's to Jack."

Wisniewski had made it about fifty feet away when a dark blue Cadillac sedan slowed and turned down the alley.

"There goes someone who doesn't want to be seen," Reardon commented.

Crandall snapped back to the present, "Why is that?"

"Would you drive a new caddy down that rat infested hole? Not me. Give me some more of that swill. I'll need to go pee soon, and I can check things out."

"No, I'll check things out. I don't want anyone recognizing you."

"Hell, I'll still have to pee."

Memphis

Armando Reyes turned the corner onto Lamar. He was following the directions exactly. The girls in the back of the blue van were mumbling and whispering. Armando glanced to the rear of the van and screamed, "Silencio!" Then he spotted the Lamar Lounge up ahead on his left. After the blue Cadillac ahead had turned down the alley he spotted two winos sitting on the sidewalk to the left of the alley opening. As the van drew closer, he rolled the driver's window down. Making the turn into the alley he slowed the vehicle, spat toward the winos and shouted, "Borrachos," then accelerated down the alley, laughing and waving his arm out the window, his middle finger extended.

CHAPTER THIRTY-FIVE

Lawrenceville, Georgia

WHEN BRENNAN ARRIVED AT SPERATA ON THE SQUARE, HE WAS about fifteen minutes late. Annie was already seated at a table at one of the front windows. He was wearing his best navy blue pinstripe, a holdover from court. Sperata was one of his favorite restaurants. Upscale enough for a special evening out, casual enough for a drop-by after work.

He kissed Annie on the cheek, apologized for his tardiness, took his seat and glanced out the window. Annie was dressed in a short peach jacket and matching skirt and a white blouse with a small ruffled collar. The sidewalk along Coogan Street was busy with the late afternoon crowd looking for food, entertainment, or both. A few cars passed by, the drivers scouting for a parking space. Across the street a photographer took pictures of the Historic Courthouse.

The server arrived almost immediately. Brennan ordered a Diet Coke. The flickering light from the candle danced off the glass of white wine Annie was nursing.

"Rough day?" Brennan inquired.

"Yes," she answered, looking at the glass while she ran her finger around the rim. Her blue eyes glistened a bit with moisture.

Before he could ask what was troubling her, his cell phone began to vibrate. His mood became deflated. It changed a little when the caller ID showed *Cindy Fitzgerald*.

"I have to take this," he said.

"Of course," Annie replied with a sigh. She wrapped her fingers around the stem of her glass and turned her gaze toward the window. Her mouth turned down at the corners.

The conversation lasted just a couple of minutes. After he made sure Cindy was feeling better, she admitted she just heard his phone message. It didn't take very long for him to convince her it was urgent he contact Crandall. She promised to call back and leave the number in his voice mail. Then she needed to call him herself and tell him about Andrea. She was out of danger, for now.

Brennan put his phone away, leaned forward and whispered, "So, what's bothering you?"

Annie brushed her sandy blond hair back behind her ear with her fingers and cleared her throat. "I had a lot of fun at lunch the other day." She paused and took a sip of wine.

"But," he interjected for her.

"Yes—" she took a slight pause and swallowed—"but, I did a lot of thinking and I know it won't work between us. Not because of you. I'm just not strong enough to be the wife of a cop, especially a cop-soldier." Tears began to form in the corner of her eyes. She wiped her eyes with her napkin and continued, "I'm not strong enough, and I can't be so selfish to ask you to give up something you love."

"I love *you*, Annie." Brennan said as he stared into her eyes and slid his hand across the table toward hers.

Annie pulled back slightly, "You do now. But, what about when you hate your job and it's all because of me? That would be worse. I'm sorry, Paul. I don't think we should see each other anymore."

Brennan had no response. He felt his face and ears flush with a slight warmth and imagined how he must look. A tense silence hung in the air as Annie left the table and walked out of the restaurant. He stared out the window. She walked by, holding a tissue to her eyes. He continued to watch. She turned the corner and disappeared from his view and his life. After a few minutes of mindless staring, he laid a twenty dollar bill on the table and left.

Brennan wandered across the street, found a shady spot and sat down on the courthouse steps, numb. A multitude of questions whirled through his mind. He wondered if he had made the right decisions in life. Couples walked up and down the sidewalk smiling, laughing, some hand in hand.

He didn't want to be a hero. To him none of the things he had done were heroic. They were just part of the job. All he ever wanted to do was make a difference. Some difference he made in Amed's life. Andrea almost died today. What was it about men like he and Crandall? You just try and do the right thing and life keeps hitting you in the gut.

His phone vibrated again. It was Cindy. He let it go to voice mail as he promised. *She made a difference today, a hell of a difference,* he thought. "Well, no point in feeling sorry for yourself," he mumbled. Brennan put his phone away and stood.

Memphis

When the blue van had turned down the alleyway, it took everything Crandall could muster to stop his father from going after the driver who spit on them. They were too close to the end to blow it on some meaningless punk.

Things were becoming active. A short time after the blue van entered the side alley and disappeared into the back, a white van followed. Reardon, now calmer after being targeted by the Spitter, explained the white van was the key. It belonged to the club. Gibson and Hartley had used it many times to transport the girls to the hotel.

However, Caruso's Town Car had joined them. It parked on the curb in front of the lounge. This was out of the regular routine. The positive was Oliveri wasn't in the car to ID anyone. Reardon recognized Turk Jackson, but not the man with him. "Oliveri must be at the hotel with Caruso. I don't know why these guys are here," he told Crandall and Wisniewski, who had rejoined them.

"There are too many folks here, we need a diversion, a blocking action," Wisniewski said.

"What are you talking about?" Crandall asked, looking up.

"I'll go down the alley and check things out. Let me have your knife." He grinned.

"Why?"

"I just may need to inspect some tire tread to see if they're safe enough for the road."

"No, that's too dangerous. What if they see you?" Crandall grumbled as he got to his feet.

"I'm just a priest looking for derelicts like you who might accept my help instead of arguing with me. Besides, somebody needs to keep an eye on that Town Car. I don't like it being here."

Crandall looked up and down the street. They were beginning to attract attention. Two new bums would always be looked at with some suspicion. The positive was Father Wisniewski's presence had pushed most of the activity across the street.

It seemed a slow night, but it was early. A few customers disappeared with their acquisitions into bars that dotted the street. Some vanished into the lounge. Each one eyed the derelicts sharing a bottle, but none questioned them. They were all on to the evening's pleasure, addiction, or labor.

Once he was sure no one was watching, Crandall handed over his knife with the order, "Now hand me that cell phone. That thing goes off at the wrong time you're dead," he followed with the obligatory, "Be careful," instructions. Wisniewski slipped the knife into his pocket, patted his friend on the back then blessed himself and set off down the alley.

***

The alleys were left over from a time when deliveries and garbage removal were always done out of sight. A maze of alleyways dotted the older sections of town. Three or four storefronts would be joined together. An alley would separate those businesses from three or four more joined together to make the block. One long wider alley would run the length of the block, behind the establishments. This alley was shared by businesses that faced the next street over. The longer alleys carried the delivery and garbage collection trucks.

Father Wisniewski reached the end of the smaller passage without incident. He peered around the corner. The white van sat empty. In front of it was the blue one, then the Cadillac. About ten or so feet beyond the Cadillac was a dumpster. It was positioned at an odd angle that blocked a vehicle's passage.

A man faced the dumpster relieving himself. The man was on the opposite side of the three vehicles beyond the Cadillac. Wisniewski licked his lips, removed the knife from his pocket and slowly opened the three and a half inch blade. It locked into place with a light click that echoed like a small explosion to his nervous ears.

He wiped the sweat from his brow, took a deep breath and ducked down behind the white van. With slow steady movements Wisniewski moved in deliberate steps to the tire on the rear driver's side of the blue van. He wanted to be involved but underestimated his nerves. Both hands shook as he placed the tip of the knife against the sidewall of the tire. He twisted it back and forth, drilling a hole into the tire. Air escaped. He shoved the blade in, twisting to make the hole bigger. A quiet hiss came from the hole as the tire flattened.

He folded the blade back into the handle then crept forward and peeked through the driver's door window. The man pulled back the door of the dumpster and peered inside. Wisniewski stole a quick look inside the vehicle. The keys were in the ignition. The Priest stretched his arm inside and pulled them from the switch while keeping his eyes on the man who was now leaning the top half of his body through the dumpster door. The smell of urine drifted through the air.

With the keys and knife secured in his pocket, he ducked down again. Wisniewski blessed himself twice as he leaned against the side panel of the van. Then he heard loud voices from inside. A female voice shouted, then another one. From the other side of the vehicles a male voice said, "Qué?"

He looked under the van. The man was walking back from the dumpster. While squatting, Wisniewski duck-walked backward as quietly as possible. He stepped in a puddle of water in a small pothole. When he pulled his foot out the water rippled and sloshed over the edge of the hole. Wisniewski fought the urge to run and backed into the space between the two vans. He could see a wet footprint just behind the pothole.

Wisniewski peered under the vehicle and watched the man's progress in front of the unit, and around the side. He approached the still rippling water and footprint. Just then a large rat ran in front of the man and through the water. He jumped backwards. The rat now under the van looked in Wisniewski's direction with black beady eyes, squealed and ran toward him. He held his breath as the rat ran across his foot then turned and ran back into the open. The man shouted something in Spanish the priest couldn't quite make out, took three long strides and disappeared into the back door of the lounge.

When the door slammed shut, the Father stood. He started at a quiet trot, then a run. When he rounded the corner of the building and could see the street, he was moving faster than he had in years.

CHAPTER THIRTY-SIX
Memphis

In the sparse back office of the Lamar Lounge, Elsa and the other four young girls sat in fear and confusion. They were crowded onto a sofa covered in some sort of blue-gray corduroy material. The back and seat cushions had small rips in several places and were dotted with different sized stains. Above the sofa hung the only wall decoration, a painting of a dead tree on a bright orange background. A gray metal desk near the far wall faced the girls. Behind it were a single chair and small safe. On top of the desk sat a calculator, pad of paper, and a pencil holder with an assortment of writing utensils. No telephone, desk lamp, or computer were in sight. An overhead light held a bare bulb with no cover. It reminded her of the room she was held captive in, except with some furnishings. The dark wood paneled walls were cracked and worn. A lack of windows created a tomb-like feeling, despite the noise from others in the room discussing which girls went where, as if they were cattle.

Elsa crossed her arms over her chest, trying to hide from leering eyes. Ramona held tightly to her sister. The other girls sat motionless with blank empty stares. Multiple conversations carried on in low volumes led Elsa to believe this small group would be divided further. She heard something about a "hotel" and "the club", but was unsure who would go where.

The one who called himself Jackson shook hands with a man named Aguilar. The two men who came with them in the van stood by the door holding their rifles. Bagman remained outside with the vehicles. Two others, who were with Aguilar when they arrived, leaned against the back wall, unspeaking, observing things. Two others Jackson called Gibson and Hartley, whispered to each other, laughed and pointed at the sofa.

Jackson and his silent partner approached the sofa. They reached down and grasped Elsa and Carmela by the arms, pulling them up in a rough, quick move. Elsa snatched free. Jackson grabbed her arm and clamped down hard, "Watch it, slut. You do that with the boss you'll wind up in the river."

Elsa and Carmela were steered toward the door of the office by Jackson and his partner. They had been pushed only a few feet when Ramona screamed, "Carmela, mi hermana!"

Elsa jerked away again and turned toward her new friend. "Ramona!" She cried out. Jackson slapped her in the back of the head, but she kept going and rushed to Ramona who was being held by one of Aguilar's men. Elsa took Ramona by the shoulders and said, "I'll take care of her. We will find you." Tears and sobs consumed both as they embraced. Jackson and the other man jerked them apart.

"Touching," Jackson sneered, then, "Shut the fuck up and get moving."

"Let's go, Carson," he said to his partner.

Yanking them about, Jackson and Carson guided them through the door and down a narrow hallway toward the bar area. The back door opened then slammed closed. Jackson turned toward the sound. Elsa looked over her shoulder. It was Bagman. Jackson pulled a pistol and waved it at him. Bagman backed up and retreated through the door.

They continued to the bar that had the odor of stale alcohol and a few other things she had never smelled before. Elsa felt the eyes of everyone in the bar on them. She fought the urge to scream. As they neared the door, she reached over and took Carmela's hand in hers.

Memphis

Crandall peeked around the corner from his sitting position. Wisniewski was coming toward him full-tilt. When he reached the sidewalk after running up the alley he moved to his right and leaned his butt against the side of the building. He gulped in air and placed both hands on his knees. His chest heaved while he fought to regain control of his breathing. Sweat beads formed on his forehead.

"Wiz, are you okay?" Crandall asked after scrambling to his feet.

Through gulps of air he answered, "I'll—be—alright. Don't ever—let me do—anything like that again."

As his breathing approached normal, he explained the voices he had heard, exchanged Crandall's knife for his phone and showed the keys, "That should slow them down a little."

The door of the Lamar Lounge opened. All three men turned their attention to the four people emerging. Turk Jackson and the other man were guiding two young women dressed in short leather looking skirts and spike heels toward the Town Car. The women were holding hands. The taller of the two girls looked in their direction. Her blond hair swayed as she walked. The blonde's sad eyes seemed to beg for help. Reardon grasped Wisniewski's and Crandall's arms, tugging backward.

The two girls were pushed into the back seat, followed by Jackson. The other man got behind the wheel. He started the car and drove off.

Father Wisniewski raised his hand and touched his collar. With a sad voice he said, "I am a failure."

Reardon gave his friend a surprised look, "What do you mean?"

"Elsa Franklin. It was on the news this morning. That's Elsa Franklin! She went missing in San Antonio several days ago. They're taking her to the hotel to feed that monster. I should have done something. We've got to go after her."

Crandall took control of Wisniewski's arms and got into his face, "I will, I promise. But, we've got three more girls in there. We've got to find out if they are going to be in that van when it comes out."

"Then I'm going with you to the hotel."

Crandall placed both hands on his friend's shoulders and looked into his sorrowful eyes, "No. Someone needs to stay with the other girls. They need you, too. You're the only one I know who can truly protect them."

Glancing around, Crandall noticed many of the druggies and hookers on the opposite sidewalk were beginning to pay attention to the goings on. There were also a few people on their side of the street who were inching closer after earlier giving them a wide berth. He lowered his voice, "I promise I'll get her out."

"What if you can't?"

"Then I'll be dead." Crandall answered, he took a deep breath and let it out, "But, I'll need you and Dad to continue the fight. Put this fiend away."

"Get ready. Somebody just cranked up back there." Reardon got everyone's attention. "Get your needle ready quick."

Crandall pulled the first aid kit from his cargo side pocket. He flipped open the small hard plastic case, removed a prepared hypodermic from inside and put the case back. Then he took a spot on what would be the driver's side, his father on the other, his pistol at the ready. Father Wisniewski took his place behind Reardon.

Dacula, Georgia

The parking lot at *Fatso's Sports Bar & Grill* was around three quarters full when Brennan pulled into the last open spot on the curb. As he exited the county Impala, he scanned the lot out of habit. What he was looking for he wasn't sure. His mind was still on his now second breakup with Annie. He did see two out of town plates, one from Alabama, one from Tennessee. *Fatso's* was his fall hangout. It was reasonable driving distance to his house and carried all the NFL games on Sundays. It also helped to be on a first name basis with Nick, the regular bartender.

He shrugged his shoulders, stepped back from the vehicle and shoved the door of the car closed with his foot. "That was real mature," he admonished himself under his breath. Brennan made his way to the door. Once inside, he went straight to the bar and took the fourth stool from the end. This position allowed him to see what was behind him in the mirror. Another old habit.

"Hi, Paul," Nick said, wiping up the glass ring left by the previous customer and placing a coaster over the spot. "The usual?"

"Yeah," Brennan replied, adjusting to the stool and straightening his suit jacket.

"You're a little overdressed for us aren't you?" Nick asked.

"Long day." He paused and stared at his reflection. A few gray hairs were forming at the temple along with a few new wrinkles, "How long have I been coming here?" He asked while pondering his reflection.

"Let me think. I've been here five years, you were already a regular."

"Then you remember Annie."

"Yeah."

"She just broke up with me *again*."

Nick looked up and smiled, "Ah, drowning our sorrows, we get that a lot here. I'll be right back with the Feeling Sorry for Ourselves Special," Nick replied as he wiped down to the end of the bar.

Brennan watched Nick make his way down the bar and glanced out the window. He could see his county car. He dropped his chin, shook his head then waved at Nick, "Make it a Diet Coke, no ice. I'll drown my sorrows when I get home. Any games on tonight?"

Dacula, Georgia

For a day where she did no work, it had been long, tiring and painful. Cindy took two extra strength aspirin, deciding against the prescription pain reliever. The silence in the house was almost overwhelming after the day's events. She eased herself onto the sofa, placed her purse on the oval cherry wood coffee table with glass inlaid top and picked up the TV remote.

She paid no attention to what show was in progress when the screen flashed to life. The background noise made it a little easier to relax. She thought about what Officer Williams said, then remembered the 9mm was in the drawer of her nightstand. She got up and went to set her alarm.

CHAPTER THIRTY-SEVEN
Memphis

THE SUN WAS GONE FOR THE DAY. THE WARMTH IT PROVIDED disappeared with its glow. Just a small amount of light from the waning moon shone between passing clouds. A streetlight in the middle of the block, dim lights from windows and over doors provided what luminosity remained. Dark shadows formed odd angles up and down the alley. A chill in the air made Crandall pull the hood of his jacket over his head. He broke open a smelling salts capsule, passed it under his nose, breathed it in and shook his head, then peeked around the corner of the brick storefront.

The white Ford van was about halfway up the alley as it made its way toward the street. Splashing water from tires going through puddles and the hum of the engine broke the quiet of the moment. In the darkness it was hard to make out the front seat occupants, but it appeared Gibson was driving, Hartley in the passenger seat, both with elbows sticking out windows, resting on the door. As they closed the distance, Crandall heard laughing from within the van.

There were two unknowns. Were the girls in the van and was there a third sorry bastard in the van with them? The latter was the least of his worries. Everything they knew about these two indicated they always worked alone. If the girls were there, their safety now became his greatest concern.

When he went off in the Marine Corps, his father passed along some advice learned from an Army colonel in the fifties. When you're out of ammunition or in a tight situation, your mind is a weapon that never runs out of ammo. Use it. That weapon was working overtime. Something didn't seem right with the plan. His eyes darted back and forth to the van, his father, and Wiz. He stuffed the hypodermic needle into his jacket, trying not to stick himself. Then he snatched his .45 from the holster, signaled his compatriots, and hid his pistol behind his back, "Follow my lead!"

As the vehicle grew closer he took a breath, stepped out into the alley opening and gestured for the others to join him. When all three stepped into the open, Gibson slammed on the brakes, stopping some ten to twelve feet from them. He leaned his head out the window, "Get the hell out of the way!" Gibson waved his hand and arm in a frantic pattern like he was trying to part the Red Sea with one arm. Hartley bent over; he seemed to reach for something.

Crandall shifted sideways as if complying. He brought his suppressed .45 from his back, extended his arms and raised it to shoulder level. He spoke with a forceful but calm voice, "Turn the engine off. Tell your friend to freeze or I'll blow your fucking head off! No sudden moves!"

Reardon raised his revolver, taking the two handed position. Father Wisniewski stood just off Reardon's shoulder.

With the engine off Crandall started a slow walk toward Gibson, "With your right hand, take the keys from the ignition and keep your left arm out the window. You start the engine, I pull the trigger."

Gibson complied, Hartley sat frozen, his arms in the air. Reardon approached on the passenger's side of the vehicle.

Crandall opened the door and checked the rear of the van, "They're here," he said over his shoulder. He jerked Gibson out, snatched the keys, placing them in his jeans pocket then pushed Gibson face down onto the grime of the wet stone alley pavement. Crandall squat down, settling his knee in Gibson's back, and holstered his pistol. He removed the needle from his pocket, grabbed the man by his hair, and pulled his head back. "Don't move, don't speak." He pushed the needle into the trapezius muscle under his collar and pressed the plunger, forcing the milky propofol into Gibson's body.

Gibson jerked, "Shit, that hurts."

"Glad to hear it," Crandall replied, putting the needle away.

He helped Gibson to his feet and pulled his prisoner's arm up behind his back, "You're going to go to sleep for a few hours, now get in the back and keep your mouth shut." He pushed Gibson through the open door.

On the other side of the van his father had already taken over the passenger seat. Hartley was sitting on the bed of the van just in front of the girls who were shaking, their heads moving in all directions as if trying to see what was happening through their blindfolds. They were bound and gagged.

Crandall waved at his friend, "Wiz, get in here and make with your Spanish magic."

Wisniewski squeezed himself between Crandall and the door, leaned inside the opening and shouted, "Soy el Padre Wisniewski, nos vamos a llevar a la Iglesia de Santa María." He repeated it louder, then entered the vehicle.

Crandall looked toward the street where one of his fellow derelicts stood on the sidewalk staring. They needed to move before a crowd gathered. He reached his hand inside his jacket and waved the guy away. The man backed down the sidewalk. As Wisniewski started to climb over the driver's seat, a loud voice came from down the alley. He stopped and stuck his head out. They saw the spitter running up toward them shouting. He carried no weapons.

"Get in the back, I'll take care of him," Crandall slapped his friend on the shoulder.

Crandall turned and started walking toward the man. When the spitter got close, he launched a right fist. Crandall blocked it. With a sweep move, he took the man to the ground, pinning him with one knee in his opponent's midsection while the other secured an arm to the ground and placed his left hand over his mouth. Ignoring the flailing free arm of his opponent, with a practiced move from decades of hunting, he removed the knife from its sheath, snapped the knife opened and locked the blade in place with one hand. In a single continuous motion, Crandall plunged the knife into the spitter's chest half way up, aiming for the right lung. As the blade found its mark, the man's eyes opened wide. He gasped. Crandall covered his mouth before he could scream.

"Next time you spit, it will be your own blood," Crandall said through clinched teeth. He wasn't sure if the man understood. But, he didn't care.

Running back to the van, he pulled the keys from his pocket and jumped in.

His father asked, "What did you do to him?"

"He'll need medical attention, but considering his associates I doubt he'll get it," Crandall answered while starting the engine.

He pulled forward, clearing the sidewalk, turned left onto the street and accelerated. Looking back over his shoulder, Father Wisniewski was removing the bonds and blindfolds from the girls and was speaking to the one who appeared to be the oldest. She was crying and quite animated. Gibson was almost out and Hartley had the expression of a scared puppy. *So far, so good*, he thought as he concentrated on his driving.

"Why don't you put Hartley to sleep, too," Reardon asked his son.

"I'm going to need some info about the hotel, and I only have so much of the stuff," Crandall said as he accelerated down the street.

Traffic was light. Still, he had to make a quick maneuver around a slower moving sedan before returning to the right hand lane. Four blocks down, the tires screeched as Crandall made a quick right turn through a light changing from yellow to red, throwing the passengers in the rear off balance. There were a few squeals from the girls, Hartley said, "Shit," but said no more in protest. A quick look and he saw there were no injuries. Gibson had fallen over from his sitting position and his head rested on the wheel well. Reardon was not buckled in, but remained facing backwards, his S&W magnum trained on Hartley, gripping the seat with his free hand.

At the next intersection Crandall shouted, "Hold on," and made another fast right turn. Tires squealed, bodies thumped against the walls of the van with a hollow echo. A few of the girls squeaked and gasped. He was doubling back to where they had parked.

In the middle of the next block they turned into an empty abandoned lot frequented by homeless. The chill of the night had most seeking warmer refuge. Three had braved the weather and deposited their meager belongings in the premium spots out of the wind. One was engaged in a conversation with Father Espinoza.

Crandall brought the van to an abrupt stop next to the church minivan. Throwing the door open, he leapt out and ran to the rear. Father Espinoza had broken off his dialogue and met him. Without a word they opened the rear doors and began helping three frightened young girls onto the ground and freedom.

Wisniewski got to his feet. In a stooped position he stuck his head out and grabbed the top of one of the double doors for balance.

With an agitated tone he said, "The oldest is named Ramona. One of the other girls we saw leaving with Jackson is her sister. They're taking a fourteen year old to that bastard." Everyone froze and just looked at each other with stunned expressions.

At that moment Father Wisniewski's cell phone went off. He jumped to the ground and answered it while the girls were hustled to the church vehicle. "What?" He asked, then he followed with, "No, no, I'll call you right back." He placed the phone back into the holder then grabbed Crandall by his shoulder, "Ted, that was Antonio. A friend told him two men forced Eric Benedetto into the back of a car. Looks like Caruso's men snatched him."

Crandall looked at his surroundings. His eyes moved back and forth, searching as he turned his head, looking for an answer. At last he fixed his eyes onto the inside of the van. His father still held his position guarding Hartley. "Close the doors and give me two minutes," he said, climbing back into the bed of the vehicle.

He crawled up beside Hartley as the doors closed. Grabbing one of the gags used on the girls he tied the man's hands together. Hartley started to protest. Crandall slapped him across the face and looked at his father, still holding his sidearm on their prisoner. "Leave us alone," he said, and turned back to Hartley.

Reardon slipped out of the van and closed the door. Crandall removed his knife and opened it, the blood on the steel blade that had yet to dry remained on the steel blade, fresh from its last use. He held the knife up so Hartley could see the blood, took a handful of his shirt and placed the edge of the blade against the man's neck. Hartley whimpered and sucked in a gulp of air. "Where did they take Eric Benedetto?" Crandall asked and pricked the skin with the tip of the blade.

CHAPTER THIRTY-EIGHT
Memphis

ONE THING CRANDALL LEARNED IN HIS DAYS ON THE STREET working for Caruso was few criminals are willing to take a bullet for the leader, very damn few. Or, a knife to the throat. Hartley tried to play the tough guy. But Crandall waved the bloody knife blade in his face then informed him his lifeless body lying in a pool of blood might put Gibson in a more cooperative mood. Hartley decided to provide everything asked of him. He became a treasure trove of information. The only question now—would he be in time to help Eric Benedetto?

The dropping temperatures combined with rising humidity and a light fog greeted Crandall as he turned into the near full parking lot of The Southern Belle. His headlights reflected off the water droplets that floated on the light breeze not quite touching the pavement. While he weaved his way between rows of cars, Crandall had to be careful to avoid the handful of patrons wandering about in various states of inebriation. At the front door a limousine service dispensed several customers, two of whom were accompanied by expensive looking arm candy.

When he reached the secluded rear of the club, the tires creaked a bit on some loose sand and gravel. Crandall eased the white van to a quiet stop next to a black Crown Vic near the back door. A check of nearby buildings revealed no windows with a view of the club's backdoors. The outside atmosphere carried a heavy base beat from muted dance music that forced its way through the concrete and cinderblock walls. Lighting on the rear of the club was off. After viewing the video of the young girl's execution he understood why. One thing he could not comprehend was what a young girl like her could have done to deserve such a fate. Still, what reasons did Caruso ever need?

There were two sets of doors. One was a single door with an electronic cipher lock and the other a set of double doors with no visible way to open them from the outside. In the darkness he could make out "Ring Bell For Deliveries" painted in red over the double doors.

Hartley assured him the same code opened all locks in the back of the building and he could get to *the room* in the basement without encountering security. Caruso did not want some activities that occurred in that area of the club recorded. Crandall, in turn, assured Hartley if anything he said proved false, he would not live to stand trial or see another sunrise, "Depending on my mood." Hartley and Gibson should be locked in the catacombs by now and would remain there until his return.

A heated discussion had ensued trying to convince everyone to go to the church and allow him to go after Eric alone. Father Espinoza was not happy when he discovered he had been deceived. He became agitated and argued with Wisniewski. Crandall intervened to remind them the safety of all the girls was paramount and they were running out of time.

If Eric Benedetto was still alive, he would have to accompany him to the hotel. There was also the potential that Caruso could be alerted. Things were becoming more complicated. They were supposed to snatch all five girls at once then go to the hotel to take care of Caruso. It was something every military man knew, every mission runs like clockwork until it's launched.

After a quick inspection of his surroundings, Crandall slipped out of the van. Another smelling salts capsule, then he closed off the right nostril with an index finger, blowing hard through the open one to clear his sinus. The procedure was repeated on the left. A whiff of rotting garbage replaced the ammonia from the capsule.

Pistol in hand, Crandall made his way through the shadows to the back door. His head on a swivel, eyes darting, he checked anything that moved or might do so. Taking in slow breaths he tried to control his heart rate while checking the air for abnormal odors. His ears were now attentive to every footfall, each scurrying rodent.

The cipher lock was similar to ones at the hospital. He punched in the five digit code. The green light came on followed by a low beep and moving metal parts. Crandall gave a gentle turn to the handle and a slight push on the door. It opened. First an inch, then a foot. Muted dance music jumped several decibels. The air vibrated with the shock wave of each beat. He checked his surroundings once more then slipped inside, silent as the mist that drifted through the cold night. Little by little, the heavy steel door settled into place, finishing with a quiet click.

Memphis

One hand rested on his hip, the other gestured wildly through the air, "I'm sorry I lied to you, but it was you who wished you could just once call a mother or father and tell them their child was alive and safe," Father Wisniewski said to Espinoza. The two priests argued just outside the door of the small basement gym Wisniewski used as his dojo. It was across an open space from the catacombs that housed a still sleeping Gibson and a nervous, shaking Hartley. The steel doors were closed and secured with two padlocks and a deadbolt. Two large columns in the open area supported the church floor above.

Espinoza pointed his finger at Wisniewski, "That does not mean I wanted to become a vigilante to do so. And do not try to use my words to justify what you did."

"I'm not. But if I hadn't lied to you about tonight you wouldn't have helped, and these girls need you more than me now. John will be back soon with the supplies and clothes. I need to go up to the nave and wait for him."

"That was just one lie," Espinoza said while he pounded a fist against an open palm. "Now I find out you've been involved in this—this espionage—or whatever you want to call it." He put his finger in Wisniewski's chest, "You told me we were going to receive five girls who escaped from the slavers. Do you realize how many lives may be in danger now?"

"Yes! And I said 'rescued'. If things had gone as planned that would have been the truth." Wisniewski held out both hands, trying to reach his friend and colleague.

Espinoza backed away, "Well, things did not go as planned. Two years you have been keeping this from me. You do realize you will be defrocked?"

"No, I won't!" Wisniewski shouted, then lowered his voice. He turned away, unable to face the man he had deceived. His shoulders slumped. His head first tilted forward, then back up, "I've already written my letter resigning from the priesthood. I'd like you to just give me forty-eight hours then you can take it to the Monsignor yourself." He turned back and faced Father Espinoza, "I've absolved you of all blame and detailed the lies I told you."

Espinoza folded his arms over his chest, "What about excommunication, or jail?"

"I hope not," Wisniewski took a deep breath. He could no longer keep it in. In a quieter voice he continued, "I was hoping for a Catholic wedding—here—in Saint Mary's."

Memphis

Eduardo Aguilar was pissed. Three girls stolen and he had only received half his payment. He could either return to Mexico, or find the girls and get the rest of his money.

Armando Reyes had stumbled into the office of the lounge, bleeding, coughing up blood and babbling incessantly about the borrachos who hijacked the van with the girls. When they questioned people hanging around on the sidewalk an addict said one of the guys looked like a preacher. As the crack-head put it, he spoke Spanish and said something about one of Columbus' ships, the *Santa Maria*.

Aguilar figured out the preacher must be a priest and the ship was Saint Mary's church. But it was the beginning of his problems. The van's keys were missing and a tire had been slashed, so he took out his anger on Reyes, kicking and beating the wounded man senseless. It took four men to move the dumpster enough to free the Cadillac from the alley. They were almost an hour behind the thieves, and if you steal from a thief, you must pay a price. These would pay a heavy one, even if they truly were men of the cloth.

Aguilar stared out the window of the car as the older houses of the neighborhood flashed by. The blaring horn of an oncoming truck broke Aguilar's concentration. His driver had run a stop sign, "Watch what the hell you are doing! Moron!"

Five minutes later the driver made a left turn into the parking lot of Saint Mary's and parked. Getting out of the car, they saw nothing suspicious. He felt comfortable since Caruso had assured him he would know of police activities. When pressed, Caruso would only reply, "Friends in high places."

Aguilar and his two companions approached the front doors of the church. The man on his right drew his weapon.

CHAPTER THIRTY-NINE

Memphis

CRANDALL CLOSED THE DOOR WITH A SLIGHT CLICK. He was visualizing the club layout Hartley had provided. A hallway ran between ten and fifteen feet to his left then made a sharp right. That hall led past the private party rooms to the main area of the club. Faint flashing colored lights reflected off the walls of the back halls. Poster sized photographs of women in various stages of undress and provocative poses hung on the walls every few feet. The deep bass beat felt the same for each piece of music. To his right, a short distance past the double doors, was the entry for the club office. Another door on the left wall led to the basement. Both the office and basement entry points were secured with identical cipher locks.

He put in the code on the basement door lock and heard the same beeps and metallic clicks from earlier. Now he hoped no one was in the open area of this dungeon while he pushed the door with silent, measured deliberation. Slipping in, he closed the door with the same unhurried motion.

Once inside, he knelt on one knee, his left hand on the rail of the stairway landing, the .45 at the ready, muscles coiled and prepared to spring. His left hand began to twitch a bit. Several deep breaths helped to calm it. Four steps down to his left was a second landing that cleared the walls of the main floor. The stairs turned to the right into the open area of the basement. Crandall knelt again and made a careful visual sweep of the area while his eyes adjusted to the dim light. Again things were clear.

To his far right in the corner sat most of the mechanical and electrical equipment that hummed and clicked. Somewhere out of sight a large fan was droning, and he could feel the slight movement of air against his face. As his eyes adjusted, Crandall made out several small puddles shimmering and reflecting available light. Against the far wall were doors to three rooms. All three had the identical locks. According to Hartley two of the rooms were prepared and waiting for the girls. The third, middle, room was reserved for Oliveri's or Allen's interrogations and other entertainment options. It seems Caruso and a few close friends were into sadomasochism along with his other perversions. All three were soundproofed, and Caruso didn't want the girls sharing a wall. A fourth steel door to the left of the others led to the area of the basement under the main entertainment. That area was primary storage for the club. A service elevator in that area moved needed items to the main floor.

Crandall crept down the fifteen steps and across the open space. His eyes darted back and forth while he processed his surroundings. He made it to the middle door without disturbing anything. From the room layout Hartley had provided he went over his first move in his mind. He wiped his brow then rubbed his hand against his jacket, drying it off. A quick flick of the tongue moistened his lips while he loosened up his hand. The twitching had slowed for now. As fast as he could, Crandall punched in the five digits. The sounds made by the lock seemed to reverberate throughout the basement. He pushed down on the handle, shoved the door open, stooped to provide the smallest target possible and moved left as he entered, bringing his weapon to a firing position.

Memphis

Father Wisniewski was in the nave going through his evening prayers while he waited for John Reardon's return. It should only be another thirty to forty minutes. He was in his favorite third pew, kneeling, praying for some nature of forgiveness, however small, even miniscule. He and Angela Whitlock had not planned on falling in love. She was a striking, beautiful, sensuous woman five years his junior. They were first drawn together by a mutual hatred for Alex Caruso. The dinners and secret meetings evolved into something neither expected.

So many of his vows had been broken these past two years, they were near uncountable. When she would cry on his shoulder over the plight of her sister, Kate, he would hold her and comfort her with light caresses of her long brown hair, so soft to the touch, such a pleasing delicate scent. Kate was as much a prisoner of Caruso's as those girls would have been. Her only escape had been to crawl into a bottle.

He remembered with vivid detail the night it happened. Angela was crying. He went to pull her close, to offer comfort, but his hand was drawn elsewhere. He gently lifted her chin and stared into her moist eyes. The deep emerald green took on a sad glow from the tears. With his other arm, he pulled her to him. As their bodies touched, he kissed her. Angela folded into his arms and surrendered to the moment. Not since his decision to enter the seminary had he kissed a woman this way. But, this was different. At that moment he decided to leave the priesthood if she would have him. This was the secret that was hardest to keep. A small slip of the tongue was all it would take, all it did take. Though he longed and ached to lie beside her through the night, his vow of celibacy was one of the few vows he had not broken. And, if he had, it would not be his worst sin.

The doors of the church creaked open behind him. Wisniewski blessed himself, stood and turned. Three men entered. A shorter man flanked by two taller, more menacing types. The one on the left held a handgun. His right arm at his side, bent at the elbow, the weapon pointed at Wisniewski.

"May I help you?" Wisniewski asked, stepping into the aisle as the three approached. "If it's money you want, we have none."

The man in the middle wore a dark brown sport coat over an open neck white dress shirt with new jeans. His build was unremarkable, which gave reason to why the others accompanied him. The dark eyes, hair and brown skin that matched his companions told the Father what he needed to know, but he had to at least demonstrate some innocence, even if it were false.

"You disappoint me, Padre." The man in the middle began. "I have come for the girls. If you give them to me, we will leave you in peace."

Wisniewski folded his arms behind him, crossing his hands in the small of his back and walked toward the men, "I'm afraid you have me at a disadvantage. I don't know what you're talking about."

The three stopped about half way as Father Wisniewski continued to close the distance. The shorter man shook his head and smirked, "More disappointment, you should be afraid." He raised his right hand, "Alejo."

The larger of the two men stepped forward, his weapon drawn. He was at least four inches taller than Wisniewski and maybe fifty pounds heavier. The man approached Wisniewski, aiming his pistol as the center of the Father's chest.

"Careful, that may go off," Wisniewski said, his voice calm and steady. He made a slight rocking motion heal to toe with his feet, keeping his knees in flex while he weighed his options.

"It does not have to," the leader said, "All you have to do is cooperate."

When Alejo reached Wisniewski he went to grasp the priest's upper arm. With catlike quickness, Wisniewski slid to his right away from the handgun and threw a forearm block into the elbow of the man's extended arm, throwing him slightly off balance. Wisniewski lifted the foot closest to Alejo. The surprised gunman tried to follow him with the muzzle of his weapon. Bringing his knee waist high, Wisniewski delivered a blow with his foot to the side of Alejo's knee. A scream of agony echoed through the empty church as the big man's knee buckled and snapped then he crumpled to the floor. Alejo's right hand flinched and fired a round into the floor.

Another kick launched at Alejo's gun hand sent the weapon flying. It rebounded off the side of the closest pew, landing back in the aisle behind Alejo. Then Wisniewski sent one more kick to the side of Alejo's head.

The other big man went after Wisniewski with a bull rush as Alejo finished collapsing. He decided on a right cross. The Father ducked and delivered a hard blow to his new attacker's diaphragm, driving air from the man's lungs. Grabbing the free arm and using his attacker's momentum, Wisniewski hip tossed him into the side of a pew on the opposite side.

"Enough," the leader shouted.

Father Wisniewski looked up. The leader was holding Alejo's discarded fire arm. Wisniewski just smiled as he stood erect.

"I will not get so close. Now get the girls or I will—"

"Go ahead, Eduardo. Give me an excuse." Reardon's voice boomed from behind Eduardo Aguilar. Aguilar did not move, but kept the gun trained on Wisniewski. "Give me just one tiny reason, and I'll put a fucking hole in you big enough to drive that caddy through." Reardon pulled the hammer back on his pistol.

Aguilar made no move, "if you pull the trigger, the Padre dies."

"Maybe so, but you'll still be dead. And, I'm pretty sure I can take at least one of your asshole friends. It's up to them to decide which one."

Aguilar made a slow turn. When he saw the .357 Smith & Wesson Magnum pointed at his chest he dropped the gun. "Such language for church. How do you know me?"

"I recognized your weasely voice, and if I go to hell for what I've said in church then you'll have to put up with me for eternity. So I suggest you pray for my soul. Pray real, real hard."

Wisniewski's last attacker shifted and grabbed the arm of a pew.

Reardon glanced in that direction, "Eduardo, if either of your guys break wind without permission you get the first bullet. Understand?"

Aguilar nodded. "Jozef," Reardon flicked his head in the direction of the gun lying at Aguilar's feet, "Pick up the gun and check them for weapons. If they resist show 'em just how good you really are."

Aguilar smiled and began to bend at the knees, "An old man like you—I don't think you are the killing kind."

"Then by all means, try me. We'll find out who shakes hands with the devil first."

Memphis

Crandall burst into the room moving sideways and to his left. In a half squat he pressed his back against the wall for balance, his finger on the trigger. Oliveri was wiping his hands with a towel. He stood in direct line of fire facing two men shackled against the wall to his right. Their mouths were covered with wide gray tape. One had Oliveri's clear plastic bag over his head, tied off. With no jacket on, Oliveri's pistol was clearly visible on his belt. The surprised Oliveri dropped the towel, turned toward Crandall and reached for his weapon. Crandall fired.

CHAPTER FORTY
Memphis

CRANDALL'S SHOT WENT A LITTLE HIGH. THE ROUND STRUCK Oliveri's clavicle just to the right of the neck. It passed through the bone and cut a deep gash through the shoulder area on its way to the back wall as Oliveri shrieked. One inch higher, he would have missed, he might be dead. The extra half second may have been all Oliveri needed. It was a lucky miss.

Crandall watched with some amusement at the spasmodic movements when Oliveri tried to pull his pistol. But, every move of his right arm resulted in extreme pain and the 9mm automatic landed on the floor. *That's why you learn to shoot with either hand.*

"No one move!" Crandall shouted as he stood. The door closed with a metallic clunk. Dave Maxson stood frozen in front of one of the prisoners. The one with the bag over his head looked lifeless, his eyes opened with a slight bulge.

Oliveri dropped to his knees and tried to reach his pistol with his left hand.

"Do you really want to do that?" Crandall asked, this time taking careful aim.

Oliveri looked up, breathing hard, his right arm limp at his side, a tight grimace on his face, "Who—the hell—are you?" He asked between painful gasps.

Crandall moved forward and kicked Oliveri's pistol out of the way, "Why don't you ask Dave? I put a bullet in his shoulder once."

"Reardon," Maxson gasped, "Holy shit! You're supposed to be—"

"Home, taking care of my family, letting the police handle it," Crandall interrupted. "The situation's changed. The police are looking for me now. I see you still have a face that looks like five miles of bad road."

"Shit," Oliveri sneered, "Look at you. You're so damn nervous your hand is shaking."

"Not the one holding the gun." Crandall replied, his mind and voice now calm.

Crandall's eyes swept the room as he moved slowly and deliberately to his left, seeking a better position. Behind him to the right of the door were a large bathroom sink and towel rack. In the corner past the sink stood a six foot tall cabinet. His mind shuddered at what it might contain. Beside the sink was an outdoor faucet with a hose attached to it. At the base of the far wall was an industrial sized drain. The floor had the slightest slope in that direction. To his left were a couple of portable chairs. An assortment of whips, chains, collars and leashes hung from the far wall. It had all the appearances of a medieval torture chamber. *Caruso, you're one sick son-of-a-bitch.* He thought while working out his strategy.

Two men were shackled with short chains, hands and feet, to the right wall. Their hands were in manacles about shoulder height. A third set between the two hung empty. One of the men stared wide eyed. He remained silent behind the tape. His face had a red tint to it. One eye was already showing discoloration. Some fresh blood trickled from a swollen nose. The other man, in the set left of center, hung limp in his chains, his knees buckled. The plastic bag over his head looked like the same one from the video. It was tied tight around the neck. The face inside had dried blood around the lips and on the chin. His finger tips were a deep red, covered with blood. The front of his shirt was soaked in crimson. On the floor at his feet were whole blood stained fingernails and a few teeth scattered about.

"The dead one better not be Eric Benedetto," Crandall said. "Take the tape off that guy." He pointed with his left hand. The shaking had begun to subside again, "You, Oliveri, back against the wall, stay on your knees." Oliveri moved backwards in slow deliberate movements while Maxson removed the tape from the prisoner's mouth.

With the tape off, the prisoner gulped in some air, "I'm Eric Benedetto. You must be John Reardon's son. Nice to meet you."

"We're not clear yet kid, don't relax. Maxson, unlock him. Slow, no sudden moves."

"Hey, I'm bleeding here!" Oliveri shouted, still on his knees against the back wall.

"Shut up, or you'll be dead there," Crandall replied with a quick glare.

The manacles were unlocked from around Benedetto's wrist and ankles. The chain around his waist fell against the wall with a clanking thud. It bounced a few times against the wall from its anchor point before settling down. Benedetto stared at Maxson while he rubbed his wrist. Anger and hate filled his eyes. He started to speak.

"Don't say anything, Eric," Crandall cut him off. "The two of you lock num-nuts over there in the ones they just let you out of."

"Hey what the fu—," Oliveri started to protest.

Crandall fired a shot into the back wall just to Oliveri's left. Oliveri pressed his back against the wall and grimaced. A painful scream escaped his mouth.

"I told you to shut up; I'm not going to say it again." He motioned with a wave of the pistol. "Put him in the chains."

Oliveri winced, moaned and let out several near screams of pain as he was lifted and placed into the shackles. "I hope you're fucking happy," he said between grimaces.

"As a clam. Don't go anywhere, I've got a few questions for you," Crandall replied, but did not smile. "Now, Maxson—you're next— into the middle ones." He motioned again with his pistol toward the chains. The barrel extension created by the suppressor acted as a pointer.

"Look, just take Eric and leave. You don't have to—" Maxson began in protest.

"This is not a goddamn debate!" Crandall shouted at him. "I know this room is soundproofed and I've got eight more rounds and four more magazines. Now, shut up the both of you, and listen." Crandall took a deep breath, moved two steps closer, and aimed the gun squarely at Maxson's chest from about four feet away. "Last time I saw you I said I didn't have a beef with you. This time I do and I'm on a tight schedule. So, if you want to be alive when the police find you in a day or two, I suggest you do as you're told. If you cooperate I won't kill you, but, I've got about one nerve left if you care to step on it. ASSUME THE DAMN POSITION!"

Maxson said nothing. He swallowed hard and moved against the wall, holding his hands up. Without saying anything Benedetto locked the manacles on wrists and ankles, then the chain around Maxson's waist.

"Eric, put all the keys in your pocket, pick up the pistol, and go stand by the door," Crandall ordered.

Benedetto moved out of the way as Crandall holstered his weapon and removed the bag from around the other man's head, "He a friend of yours?"

"Not really," Benedetto answered. "Name's Voloshin. Seems his uncle is big in the Russian Mafia. He came down here to find out as much info on Caruso as possible. He was going to turn me over to get closer after he discovered I was bugging conversations at the restaurant. He couldn't stop talking once Oliveri got him going. It's all on video. Before I left for work today I activated all the cameras Dave had me install and recorded everything direct to my home server. I—I almost recorded my own death." Benedetto swallowed hard and leaned against the wall.

Maxson's lower jaw dropped open in surprise. Crandall shot him a look and he closed his mouth.

"Eric, you just wait there, keep quiet and catch your breath." Crandall pressed two fingers against Voloshin's carotid artery after he removed the bag. "No pulse. He's dead." He folded the bag and placed it in his back pocket. Crandall lifted the man's hands and inspected them. All the fingernails were missing.

"So, what'd you use, a penknife and regular pliers, they work pretty good? Or did you just go with thin needle nose?" Crandall asked, looking at Oliveri.

"Fuck you," Oliveri answered.

Crandall removed his pistol from his holster, stepped in front of Oliveri and held it by his side. "So tough guy, you like smothering and choking defenseless young girls who piss off your boss?"

"What the fuck are you talking about?" Oliveri answered, trying to hold his head up.

Crandall grabbed the wounded shoulder and squeezed as hard as he could. Oliveri screamed.

Crandall wiped the blood from his hand on Mason's shirt and raised the weapon, pointing it at Oliveri's chest. "I saw the video. Young girl, probably red hair, fair skin. How old was she, sixteen, seventeen? That pervert you work for likes 'em young." Crandall pulled the bag from his pocket and rubbed it in Oliveri's face. Pressing hard he moved the man's face back and forth. Then he stopped and got nose to nose, "You like the smell of death asshole? Want me to put it over *your* head so you can see what it's like? Now, how old was she? What was her name?"

"I don't remember her name. She was fifteen I think." Oliveri began to sob. His head hung forward, chin almost touching the top of his chest, "She said eighteen, but her id said fifteen when Gibson and Hartley took it off her body."

Crandall folded the bag up, placed it back in his hip pocket and stepped back, "Yeah, eighteen would have made it much more tolerable. I bet you guys had a real good laugh over that. Just wanted you to know why." He raised the weapon from his side.

Oliveri's head shot up, "Wait— you—you said you weren't going to kill us."

"No, I said I wasn't going to kill him," Crandall flicked his head in the direction of Maxson then brought his gaze back to eye contact with Oliveri.

Oliveri shouted, "NO! NOOO!"

Crandall backed away about five feet further and pulled the trigger. The bullet went through Oliveri's chest. The second round was also in the chest, then one in the face for good measure. Some of the blood spatter landed on his jacket and Maxson's face. He gasped when it hit. Oliveri's head hung loose and flopped from side to side before coming to a stop. Red liquid dripped from his face. The brighter new mingled with Voloshin's older, darker drying blood on the floor.

"That was way more humane than what you did to that girl, you son-of-a-bitch," Crandall said then moved to Maxson.

"How do I find Corey Gibson? Before you answer, remember I said 'if you cooperate'. Your buddy Hartley was smart enough to tell me what I needed to know about this place. He's still breathing."

Maxson began to show panic, "I—I don't know. He works with some guy named Mickey Pyle now. They stay out west somewhere. His brother Ed knows where they go. He's the one that found them for Caruso. I swear to God, I don't know anything else!"

Crandall placed the barrel of the weapon against Maxson's temple. Maxson closed his eyes tight, he shook, "Please, I swear to God," he begged. Crandall leaned forward and whispered in the man's ear, "Know what, I believe you." He grabbed a roll of the tape off one of the chairs, tore off a strip and placed it over Maxson's mouth and patted him on the cheek, "Enjoy your company. They're not much on conversation."

He turned to Benedetto, who was standing by the door with a shocked expression on his face.

"Let's go," Crandall said.

"I— uh—I need my bag." Benedetto stammered pointing to the gym bag lying by one of the chairs.

"Then grab the damn thing and let's go."

They were able to make it back into the darkness outside without incident. The loud music still hung in the air. Crandall scanned their surroundings. Nothing moving. He prodded the slow moving Benedetto along. When they reached the back of the Crown Vic, Benedetto stopped, dropped his bag, and bent over, grabbing his knees. First he gagged, then heaved, then vomited—twice.

"You okay, kid?" Crandall asked, his eyes still checking each corner, each shadow.

"I'd never seen—anyone—killed before." He sucked in some air, "Now—I've seen three in the last two days," he said, still bent over taking deep breaths. Moisture rose from his head in the cold air like smoke from a chimney.

"The night's still young," Crandall said without emotion. His words hung in the air as his breath turned to mist with each word, then faded away. "Go get in the van."

Benedetto gulped in one last swallow of air, wiped sweat from his forehead and mouth with his sleeve, picked up his bag, and stood. "Where are we going?"

"To kill Caruso."

CHAPTER FORTY-ONE

Dacula, Georgia

THE DARK FORD TAURUS MOVED SLOWLY DOWN THE STREET. STARS and a near new moon had long since replaced the sun in the sky. Daylight was becoming shorter at an accelerated pace this time of year.

When Stan Allen reached the fourth house from the corner, he slowed even more and crept pass. It was a modest two story *Dunwoody Box* as some locals called it. The garage door was closed, but from the street he could see the digital garage opener Jenny told him about. One light was on downstairs, one up. In the room on the bottom floor the light brightened and darkened, flickering in differing shades and colors. *She's watching TV.*

When Jennifer Grady called him after her arrest, he had to lie to her about someone coming to see her in the morning. She kept raving about "scratching that bitch's eyes out." At least she didn't say anything to indicate what was about to happen. And, that was also a problem.

Once this Fitzgerald woman was dead, it wouldn't take more than five minutes for the cops to connect the dots. He planned to be out of the state by morning, with or without Moby. He didn't want to bring the fat slob along anyway. The guy may be six-four, but he had to be three-hundred-fifty pounds if he was an ounce. He sweat like a pig and smelled worse. Maybe he could dump him in the woods somewhere. He would think about it. They needed another hour for things to quiet down some more. He sped up, made a U-turn at the next street, and drove back by the house. A shadow moved across the downstairs window. First the flashing from the TV stopped then the room went dark. He would check back sooner.

Memphis

Crandall was relieved the clerk at the upscale wine shop didn't question the man dressed like this week's dumpster diver trying to find a bottle of *MD 20/20*, or his companion who appeared to have just walked away from a bar fight. This was especially true when he paid two-hundred-fifty dollars cash for a *Salon 1995*. For Crandall, upscale alcoholic beverages ran between seven and ten dollars a six pack.

In a sometimes heated disagreement, Benedetto convinced him the expensive champagne would get them into the room. Simply busting in could cause greater harm to the girls. Seeing one girl die at their hands was too much. If Crandall wasn't going to turn this over to the police, Benedetto told him he wasn't going to ride it out in the safety of the van.

He would dress in the waiter's garb he carried in the bag, and present the bottle as compliments of the hotel. Crandall preferred Benedetto wait in the van, but this was as good a plan as any, and he reminded Benedetto of the danger several times. The light tan jacket Crandall had packed away for this part of the evening should get him through the hotel lobby without much notice.

They were about three blocks from the hotel looking for a parking space to avoid garage security cameras. Finding one with enough room, Crandall pulled to the curb and double checked for "No Parking" signage.

As he started to get out of the vehicle Benedetto asked, "By the way did you get word to your folks in Georgia?"

Crandall stopped halfway out the door of the van. He sat back down and snapped his body around looking at Benedetto, "What are you talking about?"

"Didn't you go over all the stuff I dropped?" Benedetto asked with shock in his voice. "John always reviews everything."

"Shit! We stopped after the girl's video. Too damn much in that one. What did we miss?"

Benedetto reached over and grabbed Crandall's arm, "Caruso said something about sending Stan Allen and some other guy to Georgia to tie up loose ends. The daughter-in-law and some girlfriend."

Crandall's face went pale, "Where are those burn phones?"

Dacula, Georgia

Not wanting to be alone was something new the past year for Paul Brennan. There were times after Afghanistan all he wanted to do at night was sit in silence and stare at the wall. He would relive Amed's death. The other stuff didn't seem to bother him. Not even the seventeen men he stared down through his scope at a thousand yards or more. He never lost a minute's sleep over them, during or since, and didn't replay their faces in his dreams like some. It was war. It's just that Amed was different. He was just a kid who only wanted to help his family and people. It was a rare find in a country where they were still fighting five hundred year old tribal feuds.

All Brennan wanted to do was help him. He was never overly idealistic. They flew planes into buildings and killed three thousand people. Bad guys were just that—bad guys, and you didn't hurt kids. There were very few shades of gray from his viewpoint. Until he met Jack Crandall, that is. There were a few gray areas around the edges in Crandall's vendetta. It didn't make it right, or legal. They were a lot alike, he and Crandall. Brennan wondered what would tip him over the edge. Then he realized he had been there. With Amed.

But, even now being in *Fatso's* watching the last quarter of a college football game involving two teams he cared nothing about while nursing a Diet Coke, no ice, was preferable to his empty house. Through the ramblings of a cluttered mind a thought forced its way to the surface, and he picked up his phone.

On the fourth ring a sleepy voice answered.

"Hi, Ginger. It's Paul Brennan. I know it's late, but did you get that background on Jennifer Grady I asked you to rush?"

"Okay, it's on my desk. But, I'm not at the office and I need to know if you remember where she worked before coming to Gwinnett?"

He took out his note book from his coat that hung on the back of his stool and a pen from his shirt pocket, "Okay, you said she moved around a lot. Where?"

Crandall wrote and repeated while Ginger searched her memory, "Salt Lake, Oklahoma City, Little Rock, Memp—wait, was that her last stop before us?"

Laying his pen down he looked in the mirror and listened intently, "You're sure?" He asked, still deep in thought.

After a short pause to allow Ginger to reply, "Just something in Pete Williams's report."

Brennan smiled for the first time that evening, "In the morning check all those hospitals for mysterious deaths while she was there. You're the best, Ginger. If you weren't married I'd be first in line."

Well, at least you're over your one man pity party, Brennan thought as he put his phone back in its holder. He laid two twenties on the bar, "Thanks, Nick."

Crandall snatched his coat from the stool back and headed for the restroom at a rapid pace. He pulled his phone out again and looked up a number. After four rings the voice mail kicked in.

Dacula, Georgia

Cindy Fitzgerald woke with a snort and a bit of a jerk, finding herself still in a sitting position. She blinked and rubbed her eyes then wiped the dribble from her chin. The TV was still droning on about some fish named vacuum cleaner.

She turned it off and climbed the stairs to the master bedroom over the garage. Reaching the master bath, Cindy decided a hot bath would sooth her sore muscles and started the water. Disrobing, she eased herself into the steaming water and leaned back. When the water reached the level she was seeking, she stretched out a leg. Spreading her toes she grasped the faucet knobs and turned off first the cold, then the hot, laid her head back and closed her eyes. She soaked a wash cloth in the water, wrung it out and laid it over her face. Cindy took in a deep breath and warm moist air soothed the lining of her nostrils. She felt the tension leave her body. *The first guy I fell for was a liar and an addict, the second is dying and I've been beat all to hell and back. What else is going to happen to me?* The cell phone on her night stand began to beep and vibrate, interrupting her thoughts. *I'll check when I get out*, she thought. Cindy succumbed to the damp warmth and fatigue.

Memphis

While the dinner wasn't as pleasing to his palate as Antonio's, the hotel dining room did provide a more elegant atmosphere. Caruso would have to think up something special for his old friend, Antonio. Perhaps an unexpected grease-fire after closing would be in order.

Carson had accompanied Caruso at dinner. He hated to eat alone. The girls were safely under the guard of Turk Jackson in the bedroom of the suite.

Once the later than usual dinner was over Caruso dismissed Carson for the evening and told him to take a cab home or to whatever destination he had in mind. Then he made his way through the main lobby past the fountain and into the elevator, pressing the button for the top floor. The door closed and he began his ascent. He checked his image in the decorative mirrors lining the walls then removed a comb from the pocket of his Navy blazer. Once he straightened what remained of his gray hair, he buttoned his jacket and tugged on the collar of his white turtleneck.

The elevator's bell interrupted his self-admiration, and the door opened to the top floor. He was the only occupant on the floor. He made a special arrangement with the hotel on these slow nights. The room directly below his would also be empty. Tonight would be a unique experience for him, to sample the first two of the five young ladies he would keep around for his personal pleasure and the pleasure of his associates. That's why he requested Commissioner James Blackmon to join him in the room. It would not do well for them to be seen enjoying a meal in public, but this would be behind closed doors.

Blackmon was a low class bastard, but he and his son in the DA's office were handy tools to have around. He was evidence that an expensive suit and haircut could only hide so much. With such types an occasional sharing of the talent could lower expenses. In a month or two he would move the girls to Lamar or upstairs to the club then train a new shipment.

Caruso stopped in front of his room door. He would miss this place and its opulence. But, ground would be broken soon on his new weekend place outside West Memphis. If things went well

with this sample, new arrivals could be expected monthly. The best
would be sent to West Memphis.

He slipped in his room cardkey and turned the handle. As
the door opened, he saw Commissioner Blackmon seated on the
loveseat, "Is Turk in with the girls?"

A distinguished looking man in his late fifties holding a glass
of brandy answered, "Yes, he said I was to wait for you, that you
wanted to handle the introductions. And, what is my name to be
this evening?" He stood, threw back the remaining brandy and
placed the glass on the coffee table. A crooked smile on his face, "I
hear they are quite lovely."

My god, a disgusted Caruso thought as he closed the door, *brandy
is for savoring, it's not to be swigged down like some distilled corn swill.*
He managed a smile anyway, "Allow me to check on the evening's
entertainment." Caruso made a short walk to the bedroom door.
He turned the ornate gold doorknob, opened the door and looked
in. This time the smile was genuine.

CHAPTER FORTY-TWO

Dacula

The lights in the downstairs portion of the house were off, only what looked like a table lamp shone upstairs. Allen and Moby cut their headlights and pulled to the curb. Lights in surrounding houses were dark except for external porch lights and one dimmed security light with a motion detector. A lone dog barked in the distance.

With a relaxed gait the two men walked up the driveway to the garage door opener attached to the frame of the door. Allen checked the number Jennifer Grady had provided and punched it in. The door began to open. Inside there was only the one car, the Toyota Jennifer told him Cindy drove. Reaching the entry door, Allen found it locked. He fished his pocket knife out, jimmied the bolt back and opened the door. The alarm began a rhythmic beep. Just to the right of the door was the alarm. This time Allen entered a separate alarm code from Jennifer. The alarm went silent. Moving away from the door, Moby entered behind him and closed the door. Both men drew their weapons.

They moved to their right through an opening into the kitchen. A short hallway to their right led to the foyer and the stairs to the second story. Allen motioned for Moby to check the upstairs while he checked the first floor.

Moby crept down the hall, paused to listen, looked up the stairs then made his way up the steps, a slight creak under his weight.

***

What the hell? Cindy woke with a start, snatched the washcloth from her face and sat up. Water sloshed about, some spilling out of the tub onto the floor. *That sounded like the garage door!* She struggled out of the tub and wrapped up in her heavy terrycloth robe without drying off. Mark Crandall was not supposed to be back from Nashville until tomorrow. She had talked to him earlier.

She rushed to the nightstand and pulled open the drawer, removing the Glock 9mm. She almost dropped it, but managed to take it off safety and check for a round in the chamber. Then she picked up her phone, *One Missed Call*, showed on the display. On the list it showed *Paul Brennan*. She pressed the call button. Cindy gulped in air: it felt like her heart stopped. Her alarm was beeping. Her heart rate began to increase.

Dacula, Georgia

When his phone went off Paul Brennan had just sat down in his vehicle. "Cindy," he said instead of the traditional hello. There was panic in her voice, "There's someone in the house," she said in a high pitched whisper while trying to breathe. "They know my codes and turned the alarm off. Mark isn't coming back until tomorrow."

"Hide somewhere and stay quiet, I'm on my way. I'll call it in. I know your address."

Brennan started the car and grabbed his radio mike. He put the vehicle in reverse, backed out of the parking space, snatched the gear shift into drive, and pressed the accelerator. Tires squealed and small bits of gravel bounced off parked vehicles. As he pulled onto Auburn Road without slowing down, he pressed the key on the mike, "Dispatch this is badge two-eighteen, we have an intruder at 2715 Laurelwood, Dacula. I am en route; send a car and paramedics."

When the dispatcher acknowledged his request, the mike landed on the passenger seat. He reached for the blue light on his dashboard and pressed the accelerator.

***

When she looked around the room, Cindy began to panic. Her anxiety rose higher. Whoever was in her house knew the codes to garage and alarm. Her options were limited. Under the bed she felt she would be trapped, unable to move. The only choice left was her closet. She ran to it, opened the louvered bi-fold doors, pushed the hanging clothes aside and closed the doors. Cindy sat on the floor, shoving her shoes out of the way and drawing her knees up under her chin. The pistol was held tight in her right hand while she rocked forward and back in an unsuccessful attempt to settle her nerves and slow down the heart that was pounding in her chest.

Light filtered through the louvered doors and her eyes adjusted, bringing some clarity to her surroundings. Heavy footsteps entered the room. She caught her breath as a shadow passed to her right and moved toward the bathroom door. Cindy clinched her jaw to keep from screaming. Her skin, still warm from the hot bath, was surrounded by her heavy robe. She began to sweat and shake from nerves. The shadow turned and made a retreat from the bathroom. It stooped and disappeared for a moment beside the bed then reappeared.

The shadowy figure then made a slow move toward the closet. Cindy's heart beat even faster as the shadow grew in size. She brought the 9mm up to her knees and grasped it with both hands. Her mind raced, trying to remember what Jack had told her and what she practiced at the range. The shadow stopped at the closet door. As the door opened she gasped at the dark outline towering over her. The light behind him outlined his massive frame. Her eyes locked on the pistol in his hand.

First he laughed. Just a light chuckle, then spoke, "Now little lady, you don't want to hurt anyone. Put the gun down and come with me."

For some unexplained reason Cindy stopped shaking, she took a deep breath and spoke calmly, "Fuck you," then pulled the trigger four times.

All four bullets entered the large man's chest, and his gun hand dropped to his side, releasing the firearm. It bounced heavily on the floor. Like a tree toppled by a lumberjack he began a slow forward fall. He continued with increasing speed, landing atop Cindy with a near crushing impact. First she screamed. Then she began to struggle against the dead weight of the body. When she finally freed herself and stood, she felt something sticky and warm. She looked down. Her robe had come open and her chest and naked abdomen were smeared with the man's blood. With shaking hands she closed and tied the robe, but her hands and robe were also soiled in red. She turned her hands over and stared at her red streaked palms. Tears flowed as she wiped her hands on her robe, but all the blood would not come off. Cindy ran from the room and down the stairs, sobbing and wheezing.

At the bottom of the stairs she turned and continued toward the living room. As soon as she entered the room a hand closed over her mouth and jerked her off balance. She felt a body press up against her. An attempt to scream was muffled by a strong hand. Cindy began to struggle to free herself when she felt a sharp point against her neck and heard a deep voice in her ear, "Don't move."

CHAPTER FORTY-THREE

Dacula, Georgia

PAUL BRENNAN TURNED HIS BLUE LIGHT OFF WHEN HE TURNED onto Laurelwood. When he saw the vehicle parked in front of Cindy's house he cut his headlights and moved as stealthy as possible up behind it. *Damn,* he thought, *that's the same car I saw at Fatso's with the Tennessee plates.*

He exited the car and pulled his Glock Model 21 .45 caliber, crouched and ran toward the driveway. Brennan disappeared into the shadows cast by the trees and made his way up the grass along the side of the driveway. Whoever was in there didn't bother to close the garage door. He heard four quick gunshots, "Shit!"

Inside the garage he reached the door to the house. It was unlocked. He took a quick look over his shoulder to check his surroundings. Lights came on in homes across the street. He was torn between busting in and going slow and easy. He chose quiet and eased it open. As silent as a ghost passing through a wall he crossed the threshold into the house. To his left was the den area. On his immediate right was the entryway to a small kitchen. Beyond that lay the dining room. If he figured correctly, just off to the right of the dining area was the living room. Footsteps reverberated through the walls, then stopped. Someone had run down the stairs. There was heavy frightened sobbing. At that instant he heard a female voice gasp and a male voice say, "Don't move." It came from the living room, *she's still alive.*

The first rule of a sniper is to not be seen or heard. Always move with caution. He crept through the entryway into the kitchen, moving slow and deliberate, the way they were trained at Fort Benning and Fort Bragg. Brennan paused and peeked down the short hallway. A dim light shone through the glass panes around the front door from the porch light. He could hear the sounds of a couple's heavy breathing with occasional high-pitched muffled moans.

Brennan picked up the pace a little, being very careful with every footfall on the tile floor as he made his way through the kitchen to the dining room entrance. Pausing, he stole a look through the entryway to the dining area. No more than three or four feet away was the entrance to the living room. The dining table and chairs to his left were not an obstacle. Neutral beige carpet covered the floor in both rooms. The male voice continued, "It sounded like you took care of my partner. Good. I see he bled all over you. Even better. If I do this right it will just be a fight between the two of you and you both lose. Too bad, you seem to have a nice body under there. But, I'm short on time."

Brennan's pulse was steady, but his anger and nerves were not. He took in a breath, closed his eyes and let it out. He snapped his eyes open and went for the living room. As he broke the entryway he pivoted toward the foyer and raised his weapon. Cindy was directly in the line of fire, twelve maybe fourteen feet away. A tall muscular man covered her mouth with his left hand and held a knife to the side of her neck with his right. His side arm was on his right hip. "Police, let her go!" He edged forward. Even though the light from the porch was dim, his eyes had adjusted and he could make out each person's features.

The man looked at Brennan first with surprise, then with a laugh, "Well, if it isn't Mr. War Hero himself. I recognize you from your pictures. You know, all I have to do is just push hard enough and she'll bleed out in five or so minutes."

Images of Amed flashed through Brennan's head. "Backup is on the way, you won't make it out." He took a step closer while he talked.

The man glared at him, "Stop right there." Then he smiled, "Tell you what, put the gun down and we'll negotiate the terms of my surrender."

Brennan was determined this would not happen to him again. He needed a plan, and options. It was now that he first looked at Cindy. Unable to speak, she managed muffled cries of fear. Her eyes were so wide it seemed impossible for her to blink. In the struggle her robe had opened a bit and he could see the blood smeared on her skin. She returned the look, pleading with her eyes. Brennan conceded, "Alright—alright, I'll put it down, just don't hurt her."

"That's a good boy. Put it down and kick it away. If you're carrying a backup and go for it, she dies." He pressed the tip of the knife against her neck ever so slightly.

Brennan kicked the weapon toward the glass topped coffee table. The man relaxed the knife a little and shifted his grip. Brennan looked at Cindy and made a slight biting motion with his mouth. She blinked then pushed her head back against the man's shoulder. Her mouth came free and she bit down on her captor's hand.

The man screamed and drew the knife back. Brennan lunged. He stretched out with his left hand and grabbed at the blade. As his fingers closed around the stiletto he grimaced and pushed back against the hilt of the knife. The blade sliced into his fingers and palm while the man continued to apply pressure toward Cindy's neck. Cindy bit down again and the man released her. Brennan continued his attack with a palm strike to the chin that pushed the thug backwards. The man crashed against the wall, but his shoulder caught the corner of a window frame. Brennan now grabbed the man's wrist with his free hand and slammed it against the window, cracking the pane. The assailant hit Brennan on the side of his head with a fist as the detective continued to smash the knife hand against the window. With each blow against the window the glass crinkled and finally broke, cutting the back of the larger man's hand. The attacker released the knife but the blade remained in Brennan's bloody hand. He heard sirens in the distance and let go of the knife. It hit the floor with a loud metallic thud.

Brennan ducked a punch from the taller man. He wrapped his arms around the man's thighs, pulled him tight against his shoulder and lifted him from the floor with a loud grunt. The man began to beat him on the back and head, blow after blow as he carried the man toward the sofa and coffee table and away from Cindy. The sirens grew louder—multiple vehicles.

Brennan was breathing hard as he stopped short of the table, shifted his face to the center of the man's chest, reared backward and with a loud growl brought his opponent forward and down on top of the table. He held tight with all his might like a linebacker wrapping up a running back and slamming him to the turf. In a violent explosion from the pressure of the two bodies the wooden table snapped and collapsed while the glass top shattered into thousands of pieces.

Both men continued to the floor, landing atop the debris. The man screamed in pain at the impact. Splinters, chunks of wood, and glass settled onto the carpet. They rolled hard to Brennan's right. He felt a sharp pain in his side and winced. Then they rolled back to his left and settled. Brennan pulled his arms from under his opponent across shards of broken glass and sharp pieces of wood. Both sleeves were cut and torn. Blood seeped through the material. He climbed on top of the man who tried to push him away. Brennan hit him hard on the jaw with his semi-good right fist, "So, you like picking on women!" He drew his fist back and hit him again, harder, "I guess you bastards didn't count on one that would fight back!" He was pulling his fist back a third time when he heard Cindy yell, "Paul!"

Brennan looked over. Cindy held her hand against her neck where blood flowed between her fingers in spurts, down her arm and dripped from her elbow soaking into the carpet and spreading outward in a reddish brown circle. Brennan struggled to his feet. The man appeared semiconscious. Brennan kicked him in the head. He retrieved his sidearm, removed the man's pistol, tossed it well out of reach and turned to Cindy.

Her voice pleaded, "Get a towel."

"Not enough time!" He ripped off his shirt, pulled his thick white cotton undershirt over his head. He winced from the movement then folded it into a square bandage as he strode to where she sat, leaning against a wall. Even the undershirt was torn and had blood on it but no embedded glass. "Where are those damn medics?"

Brennan pulled her away from the wall and squeezed between it and her. He leaned her back against his bare chest, and pressed the makeshift bandage against her wound as hard as he could to stem the flow. It wasn't big, but it pierced the artery, and she was losing blood too fast.

The sirens that had reached a deafening level came to a sudden silence. Flashing blue lights appeared through the cracked and broken window, taking his attention, then the red and white of the Fire Department. He looked down. Some of Cindy's blood trickled down his hand and mingled with his own. He laid his pistol on the floor and gently stroked her hair with his cut hand. Her hair soaked up blood from his mangled hand. He whispered in her ear, "Stay with me. It's almost over."

The man lying on the floor across the room started to move. Brennan picked up his weapon with his wounded hand and took a shaky aim at the man's head. With much effort he was able to insert his finger inside the trigger guard.

Before he could squeeze the trigger the front door burst open, almost torn from its hinges. "Police," the lead officer announced, his weapon drawn and aimed at Brennan.

"Detective Paul Brennan badge two-eighteen! Cuff that bastard now or I swear I'll put a bullet in his head! Where the hell are the medics?" Brennan barked without taking his eyes off the perpetrator.

The first officer went to cuff the perp while the second knelt at Brennan's side, "They're coming up the drive now. You know the drill, we had to secure the scene first." He pressed against the makeshift bandage to add some more pressure. Brennan's gun hand flopped to the floor. He made known his condition with a loud painful groan, feeling the totality of the pain for the first time. Exhaustion filled his voice, "There may be another body in the house somewhere." He leaned his cheek against Cindy's head.

She was crying, her voice becoming weak. Three paramedics rushed through the door with two kits and a gurney. One went to Brennan's position and took over for the officer. Another started toward the unconscious man.

Brennan looked up, "Hey! Leave that asshole alone and get her out of here now, don't waste time with me or him!"

"But—" one of the medics began.

"Don't argue with me. Call in another unit and get her out of here, she can't wait. I'm not losing another one." Brennan released his hold as the paramedic began to apply a clean bandage. He started caressing her hair again with his free hand. Both medics commenced their well rehearsed, coordinated move of the patient. His surroundings were a little out of focus. Just before they lifted her from Brenan he gave her a gentle kiss on the head and whispered again, "Don't leave me." As the pressure of her weight left him he leaned his head back against the wall. While two medics left with Cindy on the stretcher the third began working on Brennan. His body went limp. Just before everything went black he heard the medic say, "Oh crap, get that second unit here stat!"

CHAPTER FORTY-FOUR

Memphis

ALEX CARUSO OPENED THE DOOR TO THE BEDROOM OF THE LUXURY suite and stepped in. It felt as much like home as his house did. Yes, he would miss it. But things change, as was hotel management. Samuel was retiring. He was paid well to look the other way.

On the right near the panoramic windows was the king size bed. In the sitting area were two arm chairs on each side of an oval table topped with a Tiffany reading lamp. All the furniture was solid mahogany, Queen Ann. First class. The best part was the occupants of the chairs. He smiled. Aguilar had delivered as promised.

Turk Jackson had seated himself on the edge of the bed. The two girls were bound with leather wrist and ankle straps. Each had a ball gag in their mouth with a strap that buckled behind their head. The ankle straps were connected to the chair legs, while the wrist straps were connected to restrict arm movement. Restraints on their upper arms were attached to the chair-back. He was impressed with the style of dress chosen by his supplier. Leather had become a favorite as he grew older. The girls could not have been more different. A light skinned, blonde with blue eyes and freckles and a young brown skinned, black haired, black eyed beauty. *The spice of life, as they say.*

The younger one had a look of fear on her face. A little fear was healthy, made them more cooperative. The blonde was different. Though her expressions were similar, it was the eyes that told the story. She looked defiant, even angry. He would see if Blackmon could handle the fiery type. Besides, he had had his share of blondes but never a young Latino, *I wonder if she's a virgin who slipped through.* He turned back to the open door. "James, it appears things are ready, would you like a scotch before we begin?"

There was a nod and a smile from Blackmon. Caruso instructed Jackson to wait in the living area of the suite.

Memphis

Just down a small hall off the lobby of the hotel was the public restroom. Jack Crandall busied himself by washing his hands. He had changed to the cleaner tan jacket that still hid his Sig Sauer. Crandall looked in the mirror, "Would you hurry up in there? I can only go back and forth to the urinal so often."

"Almost done," Benedetto's voice came from the handicapped stall.

The door squeaked open and Benedetto stepped out, "Okay, I think I'm ready." He was dressed in his server outfit with black vest, white shirt, and string bowtie.

Crandall cocked his head from side to side, inspecting his new partner, "Yeah, I do believe you'll pass. The guys here wear the red vests, but I think it will work. Come here and turn around."

Benedetto turned around, "I've worked some catered events here, so several of the folks know me. We should be okay."

Crandall reached around to his own back and pulled Oliveri's 9mm from his waistband under the jacket, put it in Benedetto's waistband and pulled the back of the vest over it. "It bulges a little, just walk in front of me. You remember what I showed you?"

Benedetto turned around, "Yeah, but—"

Crandall jerked on the front of his vest, testing the looseness, "No buts! An hour ago these guys had you chained to a wall next to a dead Russian. They were planning on you joining him. I hope you don't have to use it. But, if you do, don't hesitate. It just might be my ass you're saving."

Benedetto sighed and cast his eyes downward, "I—I don't know how to thank you for coming after me."

Crandall put a now calm left hand on Benedetto's shoulder, "Like I said, we're not out of the woods yet, but you put your butt on the line for my father and a few other people; I was paying *you* back." He looked around, "Now, let's get out of here before someone else comes in. Walk in front of me, carry the champagne naturally, I'll carry the bag. Straight to the elevator. Got it?"

Benedetto swallowed hard and nodded, his dark eyes blinked at a rapid pace.

Crandall gave an ever so slight nod, "You're nervous, that's good. Let's go."

Memphis

Pure animal rage coursed through Elsa Franklin's mind when she saw Caruso. The one they called Turk directed her and Carmela to call him *Mr. Caruso*. The ball gag made it almost impossible to utter protest. Each time she did, saliva would flow down her chin, which seemed to amuse Turk to no end.

After Turk left the room another man entered, taller than Caruso, with more and darker hair. They exchanged some small talk, something about "zoning". Caruso poured each a drink and they toasted the upcoming evening's pleasures. The longer they talked, the angrier Elsa became. *Just get it over with, you bastards!*

"Well, if I remember correctly, you are partial to blondes." Caruso said to the other man while he swirled his drink.

The taller man glanced in her direction, "You know me well, Alex. She seems a bit spirited."

"Then I would suggest you leave the bridle in." They both shared a laugh.

I'm not some damned farm animal, she thought growing angrier, grunting, almost growling.

Caruso finished his drink and placed his glass back on the bar. He walked over and removed Carmela's ankle restraints first, then Elsa's. He left the straps that bound their wrists together in place with the gags. Caruso turned to the other man, "She's all yours." Then he looked Elsa in the eye, "I strongly suggest you cooperate. My friend in the other room is not very gentle when dealing with my problems."

Elsa said nothing, but returned his stare with a glare of defiance. He lifted Carmela to her feet. She looked at Elsa, fear in her eyes. Elsa just nodded. While he led Carmela to the bed the other man slipped off his loafers, walked over and pulled a resistant Elsa to her feet. He turned her so that she was facing the bed and positioned himself behind her. He touched her shoulders and began to massage, and she recoiled in disgust.

The man jerked her back against him, grabbed her around the waist and ground his crotch against her buttocks. He whispered in her ear, "If I'm not happy, he's not happy. If he's not happy you will most decidedly not be happy." He slipped his hand under her blouse. Elsa tensed, she wanted to vomit.

Caruso laid Carmela on the bed and stripped to his boxer shorts and climbed onto the bed. He then started pulling Carmela's leather skirt down. Carmela whimpered through the gag, but offered no resistance.

Elsa began to relax and the man loosened his grip. She even moaned as best she could. He whispered, "That's more like it."

Caruso tossed Carmela's skirt onto the floor. Carmela began to cry, sobbing and almost choking. She pulled her hands up toward her chest. Caruso began to cuss Carmela as he straddled her, "Look, you little Mexican bitch—"

Elsa lifted her foot and rubbed the man's leg with the inside of her calf. "Now you're catching on," he said as he nuzzled her ear.

Then with a sudden move she brought her spiked heel down on top of his shoeless foot. She struck so hard the heel pierced the skin, releasing a small flow of blood. He screamed, "Shit," and released his grip. The man reached to grab her again, tearing at her blouse. The two top buttons popped off. She spun and reached out with her bound hands and scratched and pushed hard against his eyes. The man screeched again and grabbed his face. Elsa pushed him away. He caught his injured foot on a leg of the chair as he hopped backward, cussed again, and fell to the floor.

Elsa then ripped at the ball gag as she ran to Carmela's side, freeing it from her mouth. She reached the bed and began to pound Caruso's back with her bound hands, now clinched in fists, as he was trying to get off the bed, "Leave her alone you son-of-a-bitch!" She screamed and continued to pound while Caruso turned and blocked her blows. He reached in, grabbed her blouse, and yanked her off balance. The remaining buttons popped and some material tore off into his hand. She fell against the bed. While Elsa tried to regain her footing, Caruso stood on the floor and grasped her throat. She gasped for air as she felt the pressure of his fingers close about her throat, closing off her windpipe. She tried to fight back, kicking and grabbing at Caruso's arm. He pushed down harder, pressing her into the mattress and comforter covering the bed. Caruso drew back a fist with his free hand. A maniacal smile spread across his face, "You asked for this bitch, and I'm going to enjoy giving it to you." The door knob rattled, Caruso snapped in that direction with his fist ready to strike.

CHAPTER FORTY-FIVE

Memphis

WHEN THE ELEVATOR DOORS OPENED ON THE TOP FLOOR CRANDALL breathed a sigh of relief. *No one in the hallway.* When Caruso made these little trips, someone in management made sure this floor was empty, along a couple of the rooms directly below his suite. Crandall wondered how much it was costing the piece of shit to keep his pedophilia a closely guarded secret. Maybe it was the barter system. In the end it was irrelevant to Crandall. Caruso may have only raped them and someone else pulled the trigger or strangled them, either way he was guilty of both. So was Oliveri, Allen, Maxson or anyone who worked for the bastard. He wanted to kill them all.

They stepped from the elevator onto the blue and red swirled carpet. Along each wall were an assortment of prints depicting the blues, jazz, and rock heritage of the city. The solid blue wallpaper was a perfect match for the blue in the carpet. One could only imagine what went on behind the solid mahogany doors. He looked at the first few door numbers. Crandall concluded Caruso's suite was the fourth one on the left. It would face the bridge across the river into Arkansas.

As he and Benedetto made a cautious approach down the hallway, the total silence was both nerve-racking and comforting. Crandall wasn't sure which emotion was the more dominate.

They reached the room. The door opened from left to right inward. Crandall took his position on the left side of the door his back against the wall, weapon drawn and ready. He dropped the bag to the floor next to him. Benedetto centered himself in front of the door. Crandall nodded. Benedetto knocked.

Crandall readied his mind and body. After Benedetto knocked he took a couple of steps back. Several seconds passed before a gruff voice came from inside the room, "Who is it?"

Benedetto held up the bottle; label out, toward the peephole partially hiding his face, "Room service, compliments of management. An excellent *Salon 1995*."

From inside the room there was some muffled movement, the door handle began to move. Benedetto lowered the bottle and held it by the neck with one hand. Crandall dropped his gun hand to his side. He flexed his knees, flattened against the wall and moved his left hand away from his body, turning his palm toward the floor and opening his thumb until it formed a ninety degree angle to his fingers.

As the man inside pulled the door open, Benedetto stepped backward, clearing the space in front of the door. Crandall sprung with his knees bringing him up, his left hand spinning around the door frame. He caught his target directly on the Adam's apple between his thumb and forefinger. The edge of his hand drove the Adam's apple back into the man's throat, cutting off his voice. Crandall turned his hand and grabbed the throat, squeezed, and pulled the man out of the room and onto the floor. He lifted his gun hand and brought the side of the pistol down on the base of the man's skull. His target went limp. Crandall gave a quick survey of the inside of the room, looked at Benedetto and whispered, "Lucky—they usually don't go out that easy. Help me get him inside and be quiet about it." Crandall wiped sweat from his brow and released a sigh of relief.

Crandall grabbed the gym bag and the two of them carried the man inside the front room of the suite, laying him in front of the loveseat. Crandall dropped to his knees, unzipped the bag and looked inside. "Damn," Crandall whispered, "I left the cable ties and tape in the van." He looked around the room and pointed toward the sofa end tables, "Get me those lamps."

Benedetto scurried to the sofa and returned with both lamps. Crandall took them and ripped the cords from the base. He tied the unconscious man's hands behind his back then tied his feet. Their prisoner started to moan. Crandall pointed to the man's feet, "Give me his socks." Benedetto said nothing. He pulled the shoes off, then the socks, and handed them to Crandall. Crandall pulled the man's mouth open and stuffed both socks inside. The man on the floor shook his head and tried to cough. A groggy mumble escaped his mouth.

Crandall snapped his head toward the bedroom door as several loud painful shouts came from beyond it. A second or two later a female voice screamed, "Leave her alone!"

Without looking back, Crandall rose and pulled his gun, "Stay out of sight. I don't want them to know you are here, but get that gun ready and disarm this SOB."

As he approached the door he could hear the muffled sounds of a struggle. He tried the door handle, turning it back and forth several times. It was locked. Crandall backed up a step and delivered a kick to the door just to the side of the knob. It flew open, bending the metal door frame. He stepped through the opening, his weapon ready.

What he saw first was Caruso on the other side of the bed holding the young blonde he saw in front of the Lamar Lounge by the throat with his fist raised ready to punch, "Do it and you're a dead man!"

Caruso looked at him with a wide eyed expression, his mouth open, but he said nothing.

"Let—her—go—now!" Crandall took careful aim.

Caruso released his grip. The young girl rolled over, slipped off the bed and dropped to her knees, gasping for breath and coughing. She tried to pull her blouse closed with one hand while rubbing her neck with the other.

Crandall began scanning the room. A young dark haired girl lay on the bed unmoving, but breathing, her hands clutched across her chest. She looked naked from the waist down. Crandall's rage began to swell. He started to press his finger against the trigger then noticed a man bent over in a chair holding his foot in a bloody sock with one hand. The man stared at Crandall. Light streaks of blood covered both cheeks with some under the eyes and across the bridge of his nose. "If your friend comes after me, you die first then him," he said to Caruso.

"I believe you, Ted, or is it Jack now?" Caruso said as he backed away.

"Freeze!" Crandall warned. Caruso stopped.

"Now, go over and sit next to your friend." Crandall motioned with the pistol.

"What?"

"Share the chair or sit on his lap, I don't give a rat's ass which one. Just do it!"

After Caruso squeezed next to his friend, Crandall moved in the direction of the blonde without taking his eyes off Caruso. In a softer comforting tone he asked, "Are you Elsa Franklin?"

Elsa cinched her blouse tight around her, a raspy "Yes" escaped her lips, then uncontrollable sobbing followed. He went to her, shifted his weapon to his left hand and put his right hand on Elsa's shoulder. She struggled to her feet and buried her face into his shoulder as the tears continued. He heard crying over his shoulder, released his hold on Elsa, and whispered in her ear, "Go to her." Caruso started to get out of the chair. Crandall straightened his left arm, the muzzle of the pistol pointed at Caruso's chest, "I really—really—wish you would."

Lawrenceville, Georgia

The hard bump shook Brennan awake. He blinked several times in an attempt to adjust his eyes to the bright lights overhead. There was a muffled distant sound of a siren. He felt a sensation of movement along with a slight back and forth rocking motion. With a slight turn of his head to the right he saw an IV bag swaying. He started to move then realized he was restrained. His feet were elevated. The sudden realization came over him. He was in an ambulance. Brennan looked straight up and made out the fuzzy outline of a face surrounded by lights then he recognized the dark blue uniform blouse of a county paramedic.

"Glad you're back with us, Detective. Don't move and don't speak, we're pulling into the ER at Gwinnett Medical. You went into shock. We stopped the bleeding, but you lost a good bit. You've got a jagged piece of wood jammed in your side. We don't know how far in it goes. Right now it's sticking out about an inch. Once they get you stable you'll probably need surgery. You know the drill so don't give them any gruff. Your friend is already here, they'll update you. How in the hell did you not know that was in you?"

Brennan took a breath and sighed, the overall weakness was evident in his voice, "I don't know. What about the perp and where's my phone?" He looked around as best he could.

"He's in a separate ambulance under guard. Last I heard they think he has a broken jaw and is missing two or three teeth. Your phone is in a bag, it will go into the emergency room with you. Now, be quiet, we're there." The paramedic began prepping the IV and gurney for exit.

The ambulance came to a stop then began backing up. Loud beeping tones pierced the walls of the vehicle. It stopped again. Someone Brennan could not see jerked the doors open and the gurney began moving toward the opening. The foot of the gurney tilted down and Brennan saw the sliding glass doors of the ER. The two men on the outside locked the legs of the stretcher in place, pulled it out then locked the legs at the head. All the men began moving in unison at a fast practiced pace. As they passed through the opening all Brennan noticed was the ceiling tiles and bright florescent lights. He closed his eyes.

CHAPTER FORTY-SIX
Memphis

JACK CRANDALL CLOSED THE BEDROOM DOOR AND WEDGED THE vanity chair under the knob to keep the door closed. When he kicked it open, the frame had bent. After Elsa regained control of her emotions, her hands were free enough to unbuckle and remove the restraints from Carmela who returned the favor. Crandall had them cover up with Caruso's and Blackmon's shirts. Every button on Elsa's blouse was missing.

He made Caruso stay in the arm chair. The girls were more than happy to use the restraints from their imprisonment on both Caruso and Blackmon. Blackmon was secured with the ankle and wrist bonds and the ball gag. Caruso was strapped to the chair, but without the gag. Crandall then used torn bed sheets to tie Blackmon in the fetal position on the lush burgundy pile carpet. He assumed it was to hide food, wine and other stains. Crandall wondered if they had blood in mind when they chose the color.

Crandall now turned his attention to Caruso. He picked up the other gag from the floor, turned it over several times in his hands, looked at Caruso and allowed himself a quiet laugh.

"Hmm, so this is how you get your kicks now? Just ruining people's lives isn't enough?" Crandall asked as he walked toward the man he had been hunting.

Caruso seemed to have calmed himself and answered with a smirk, "What's it to you?"

Crandall tapped Caruso on the side of the cheek with a smile and a smirk of his own, "Ah, confident. Well, let's see how it goes. I have just a few questions I need answered." Crandall removed the Sig Sauer from his holster and tapped the suppressor in his left hand.

Caruso leaned his head back and shook it. His comb over hung off the left side, several strands hung below his jaw line, "That's supposed to scare me?"

"Let's review the situation. You're strapped to a chair. You're in your boxers. Commissioner Blackmon is hogtied on the floor. My father has some nice photos of you and him in West Memphis. Your bodyguard is unconscious and tied up. You also like to beat up young girls who don't want to have sex with you." He waved the gun in front of Caruso's face and smiled, "Oh—yeah—I've got the gun." Crandall bent forward, his nose almost touching Caruso's. He glared, "To be honest, I don't care if you're scared or not." Then he straightened up.

Crandall followed Caruso's head movement as he looked toward the nightstand beside the bed, the digital clock showing just after midnight. Caruso sighed, then looked back at Crandall and smiled, "You know that thing doesn't make them silent."

"It does a good enough job when you are the only one on the floor and the room below you is empty. I've done my homework and I'd like to thank management for being so accommodating. Now, let's get down to business. It seems you are expecting company," Crandall stated with no emotion in his voice. He reached into his back pocket and removed the plastic bag he took from Oliveri, shook it open while slapping Caruso's face several times with it, "Recognize this? Oh, by the way, Eric Benedetto is alive and well. I'm afraid the cavalry isn't coming."

Jack Crandall straightened the shade on the lamp sitting atop the reading table next to the chair then walked over, grabbed the other Queen Ann arm chair and began dragging it toward Caruso's. On the way he passed Blackmon lying on the floor, bound and gagged like a hog his grandfather was ready to slaughter and butcher. Blackmon was whimpering, trying to breathe through his nose. The ball gag caused excess saliva that drooled out of his mouth and created a dark spot where it soaked into the carpet. Crandall paused, released his grip on the chair and kicked the man in the back, aiming for the kidney. "Shut up," he said then continued moving the chair. He positioned it in front of Caruso with about two feet of open space between the two and sat.

Crandall rolled his weapon over in his hands. He looked at it and wondered how he had become the animal he was now. All he wanted was for the world to leave him alone, to have what time remained spent in the company of his family and to hold his granddaughter while his body still cooperated. That was gone now. But he also wondered if it was about protecting his family or more about himself, about the hand he had been dealt. Either way, he reasoned, Caruso deserved much worse than what was about to befall him.

He cocked his head to one side, stared into Caruso's eyes and sighed. There was no emotion toward the man any longer. No hate, no despise, no loathing, not even pity. He could garner no more sentiment toward this piece of human debris than a cockroach to be stepped on and scraped from the bottom of his shoe. He glanced back down at his pistol.

Caruso jerked forward, "Say something!"

Crandall looked up, no change in his expression, his voice steady and quiet. "What was her name?"

Caruso's face froze, his mouth fell open, "What?"

"The beautiful fifteen year old girl with the red hair that you raped and Tony Oliveri executed with the plastic bag. He said he remembered you saying her name but he couldn't remember so I left his body hanging in your little secret room next to Voloshin and Maxson."

"I don't—" Caruso began.

Before he could finish Crandall hit him aside the head with the side of the pistol. Caruso yelped in pain. His ear turned bright red and blood trickled from it. Crandall remained calm, "Wrong answer. Now, what was her name?" Crandall added calmly.

"I can't—"

"Let me jog your memory." Crandall placed the muzzle of his weapon against Caruso's kneecap. "Three—two—one." He jerked the pistol to the side and pulled the trigger. A round buried itself in the carpet and floor.

A muted squeal came from Blackmon. Caruso jerked and let out a short shriek, "Okay—okay," he said grimacing while sweat beads formed on his forehead, "Her name was Julie."

"You're sure?" Crandall said, raising the pistol again.

Caruso turned his head to the side, panting, "Yes—yes", he gasped and looked back at Crandall, "I'm sure. Why the fuck do you care?"

"Because she deserves to be remembered," Crandall said as he stood and moved behind Caruso who twisted his head back and forth trying to see.

"What are you doing?"

Without a response Crandall laid his weapon on the table and lifted the gag, forcing it into the mouth of a struggling Caruso. Grunts and groans came from the man's mouth as the gag tightened around the back of his head. Crandall pulled it as tight as it would go then forced it one more notch and hoped Caruso didn't pass out before he was finished.

Gag in place, Crandall retrieved his pistol and resumed his position in his chair facing Caruso. He held the weapon in front of Caruso's face, "Do you know what the kinetic energy of a .45 caliber two-hundred-thirty grain bullet can do?" Caruso tried to speak through the gag. He rocked back and forth straining to break free, "No?" Crandall answered for him. He leaned forward, grabbed the back of the chair and whispered, "Why it can literally tear certain body parts off and at this range I don't think I'll miss." He pressed the muzzle into Caruso's crotch.

Caruso began hyperventilating through the gag. He stiffened and strained against his bindings. An arm of the chair began to loosen. Caruso squealed and grunted as he worked the chair-arm back and forth. Sweat rolled into his eyes. Clear mucus escaped from his nostril followed by a light red as blood mixed with it.

Crandall gripped Caruso's chin and steadied the man's flailing head so he could look directly into the wide reddening eyes, "This one – is for Julie." He squeezed the trigger.

Lawrenceville, Georgia

The room was cold. The table was cold. All manner of people in green or blue gowns, masks, and skull caps covering their heads buzzed around like bees in a hive. An electronic monitor beeped in rhythm with his heart. The blood pressure cup on his left arm clicked, hummed and hissed as it inflated then deflated. He felt a little groggy from the medication intended to relax him. His mouth was dry. He'd had nothing to drink since being admitted to the ER. For now Brennan was covered with only a sheet. Beneath it he wore only a hospital gown. He shivered. The location of the wound dictated emergency surgery.

"It's alright, Mr. Brennan," the nurse hovering closest to him said. She looked down at him from behind the surgical mask and plastic shield that attached to her head like a clear welder's mask. The vision made her glasses seem redundant. "You'll be asleep in a minute," she continued in her best bedside manner. He was too tired to speak, but only glanced down at his right arm. Shards of glass shone, reflecting the bright light. Not one, but two IV's had been started. For now his left hand was useless. It had been stitched, wrapped in heavy bandages and immobilized with a splint.

It wasn't the cold that bothered him so much. It was the embarrassment. Brennan knew that as soon as he was out the sheet and gown would come off. Then he would be catheterized and cut on. A large portion of his body would be set upon with scalpels, clamps, tweezers and all types of medical torture devices he didn't know the names of. Tubes would be shoved up his private parts. For that procedure he was glad he was going to be asleep.

It was a little sketchy, but through the fog he remembered being told Cindy would be okay—physically. The medics managed to contain the bleeding en route. Once it was sealed, her main requirement was whole blood and rest. The man who attacked her was missing three teeth. Only two were reported found at the scene. He was awaiting x-rays.

"Mr. Brennan," the nurse interrupted his thoughts. As he focused on her, she inserted a hypodermic needle in the Y-Site of the IV tube and began to push the plunger, "You're going to go to sl—"

CHAPTER FORTY-SEVEN
Memphis

JOHN REARDON WATCHED THROUGH THE OPEN WINDOW AS THE buckle on the seatbelt snapped into place. Crandall checked the breathing of the still sleeping Ed Gibson. He reached across Gibson's lap, grasped the handle and laid the seatback into a more reclining position. Crandall straightened and secured his own seatbelt on the driver's seat of his mother's silver pickup. All five girls were now safe in the basement of the church. Benedetto and Father Espinoza were watching things. Once the girls were inside he grabbed Gibson and carried him to the truck. Reardon followed with Father Wisniewski. Crandall had said almost nothing.

Crandall turned to his father standing outside the truck grasping the door through the open window. Reardon glanced back at Father Wisniewski who stood several feet away in the fog and dark, silent and unmoving. The drifting mist surrounded the priest and gave him the look of an apparition rising from the swamp. Reardon returned his gaze to his son.

It had been a long night and Reardon was tired all over, feeling his age. The fatigue even invaded his voice, "It's time to end it, Ted. We've got enough to collapse his whole empire. Hartley's not just singing, he's tap dancing to avoid the death penalty. A jury sees that video, it's all over."

Crandall gave a gentle touch to his father's hand, "It's not over for me. There's still bastards free who killed my grandbaby and put Andrea in the hospital. They killed David and slashed Lisa and Krystyna." He reached up and gave his father a light touch on the cheek, "It's okay, Dad, I'm just doing what I've always done best—hunt—and kill."

Crandall looked straight ahead through the windshield. "I've only got a few hours until the sun is up. When it is, call your detective friend and tell him to go to the Gaylord Hotel, the old grain warehouse, and have them pick up the prisoners."

"But—"

"No," Crandall cut his father off, "I have to do this."

Reardon reached into his inside jacket pocket. His hand returned with a small silver crucifix and medal on a beaded necklace, "Here, this is your mother's rosary. I carry it for good luck and to remember how she was, not how she is. You need it more than I do now. She got the Saint Michael the day you left for boot camp."

Crandall paused and looked at the medal, fingering the intricate carving that depicted the Patron Saint of Warriors, his angel's wings fully extended, sword raised with his foot on the chest of a conquered minion of Satan. He sighed, "Thank you. Tell Mom I love her." After a few seconds he looked past Reardon at Wisniewski, "Wiz, your prayer was answered."

Reardon turned at the waist moving his head and shoulders to get a better look at the priest. Wisniewski said nothing, but acknowledged the statement with a slow sad nod of his head.

Crandall hung the rosary around the rearview mirror and started the truck. Reardon backed away and his son drove into the thick haze that swirled about the truck, swallowing vehicle and driver. He turned to Wisniewski, "What did he mean by that?"

"I take no solace in it, but I told him that privately I prayed for Caruso to die a hideous death," Wisniewski answered.

"I'm sorry, Jozef." Reardon said, his fatigued voice sighed and broke, "I brought Ted in on this. I may have created a monster."

With a shake of his head the priest disagreed, "No John, you are not Doctor Frankenstein. Alex Caruso created the beast when Jane was killed. But, it was Caruso's pursuit of the monster that unleashed its wrath. And...," Wisniewski breathed deep, his shoulder rose then fell as he exhaled a sigh, "in the end, the creature consumed its creator and those around him." Wisniewski motioned Reardon closer with his hand, "Come—let's go. I need to pray God will forgive me for letting Ted leave."

Reardon put his arm around Wisniewski's shoulders and the two men started toward the church, supporting each other. Reardon looked at the church door, the mist in his eyes mingled with the mist hanging in the air, "Let's pray he returns also."

Memphis

The fog was growing thicker as Memphis moved closer to the sunrise that would burn it away. When he stopped the truck by the entrance to the abandoned grain warehouse, the headlights could barely penetrate the murky soup. Ahead in the haze stood a creosote light pole that no longer worked. Crandall opened the door of the truck, but only the sound of lapping water and the smell of The Big Muddy told him the water was near. Just a mile across the river were the lights of West Memphis, but even those could not break through the fog.

He stood outside the vehicle taking it all in. His mind replayed the last days' events like a bad movie. Julie's video, Oliveri hanging on the wall, Caruso still sitting upright, fear and pain in his eyes when the trigger was pulled that last time. Then there was Hartley and Gibson in the van, laughing and joking like the girls in the back were nothing more than sacks of flour to sustain Caruso's appetite. If not for Jane, he may have become one of them. Who knows, maybe in some ways, he was.

Crandall took in a long breath sucking the moisture laden air into his lungs. It felt soothing, cleansing. This was a fitting end to the night. The fog had crept in gently on the cool evening breeze, but would leave with the sun, taking with it what remained of his soul.

There was still much to do and Gibson was starting to stir from his slumber. Crandall went to the back of the truck and pulled out his bag and a flashlight. He had stopped by his father's house and loaded up all his equipment, since he had no plans to return. When this was over he would be leaving for wherever the journey would take him. His destination depended on the man in the passenger's seat.

Crandall dropped the bag on the ground, kicked the door open and shined the light inside. Some of the mist had slithered through the broken windows. Evidence of the rats and mice that were living off any remaining grain was scattered about. He also checked about for nocturnal reptiles that fed on the rodents. There weren't as many spider webs as he had thought. But enough were in place that he could imagine hundreds of eyes would be watching the proceedings. Musty mildew-like odors attacked from all angles.

Satisfied, he returned to the truck and pulled a groggy, limp Ed Gibson from the passenger seat. He lifted the man over his shoulders in a fireman's carry and entered the building. Ten feet inside, Crandall turned so he could face the door and deposited Gibson on the concrete floor. A small cloud of dust rose and drifted away. The shuffling of his feet on the floor echoed through the cavernous building. He retrieved his bag and knelt beside Gibson, dropping the bag next to him. From the bag he filled two syringes, one with digitalis, the other with a mixture of digitalis and medicinal cocaine. With his knife he cut Gibson's shirt sleeve up to the shoulder, revealing the whole arm.

Crandall did not have a heavy rubber tourniquet so he snatched Gibson's shoe laces and tied one tightly around the left bicep. The vein in the bend of Gibson's elbow showed itself nice and blue with a few needle tracks. *Huh, a user.*

He took the syringe of digitalis and emptied it into the vein. Gibson was still groaning and recoiled slightly from the needle as he came out of his stupor. Crandall broke a smelling salts capsule and waved it under Gibson's nose. He woke with a start, shaking his head and shouting, brushing Crandall's arm away with his flailing right arm. Crandall waved the capsule under his own nose and tossed it away.

He placed his hand on Gibson's chest and held him down, "Good, you're awake. We haven't much time. We're at the old grain warehouse. Where did you dump the body?" He knew the answer from Hartley. But his father always told him the first rule of interrogation is to ask a question you already know the answer to. He also knew there was more than one body. This was their primary graveyard.

"I don't, uh—know wh—what you're talking about." Gibson struggled with the words as he became more alert.

"Okay, let's go over this again. We don't—no, wait. *You* don't have much time. That pin prick you felt. Well, in about five minutes your heart will explode unless I give you the antidote." Crandall grabbed the other syringe and held it up. He gave a slight push to the plunger for affect and a few drops rolled down the needle.

Gibson licked his lips and sucked in a deep breath through his nose, "Screw you, you're lying."

Crandall watched as small sweat beads formed around Gibson's hairline. Some mixed with the dust that settled on his forehead creating darker brown spots. "Suit yourself, but you licked your lips because your mouth is dry. You sucked in air because you feel a little short of breath. And, you're starting to sweat."

Gibson pursed his lips and swallowed hard.

Crandall smiled, "Feeling a little nauseous are we? Well, in a few seconds your heart is going to feel like it is coming through your chest. You're going to need almost all of this," he held up the needle and squirted a small stream through the needle, "So, take your time. You've now got about four minutes. Where did you dump the body of the young girl last week?"

"Over by the light pole, now give me the stuff," Gibson was fully awake, his body shaking.

"Just one more and if I don't like the answer I squirt more into the air. I keep doing that until I get the answer I want." Crandall continued to hold the syringe straight up. "How do I find your brother Corey?"

"What? I don't know, man."

Crandall squirted a small stream of liquid from the needle onto Gibson's face for affect. "No, Hartley says you do. Says you've been there. He hangs out with some guy named Mickey Pyle. Used to be a Green Beret according to Hartley. So far everything he's told me is right. You're running out of time and antidote."

"Alright, alright," Gibson clamped his jaw shut, stretched his neck and swallowed with difficulty. He gulped air through his mouth again. "West of Albuquerque in something they call the Badlands up in some canyon. Down route one-seventeen. I don't know exactly, but there's an old guy. Runs a backpacker's store on route one-seventeen. He delivers stuff. He'll know. That's all I know, now give me the stuff!"

"You know the name of the store?"

"No—no!"

Crandall grabbed Gibson's right hand and slapped the syringe in it and stood, "I guess you've earned this. Do it yourself. I see you know how."

"You bastard!" Gibson grunted. He struggled to a sitting position. Though his hand was shaking he found the vein and pushed all the liquid into his bloodstream.

Crandall laughed.

"What's so damn funny?" Gibson wanted to know, his shoulders and chest heaved as he breathed through his mouth.

Crandall squat down next to the shaking man. He smiled, reached out and patted Gibson on the shoulder, then tapped the side of his own head with his forefinger, "This is funny. You'll like this. I have to apologize. I said antidote, but I meant anecdote. So here's an amusing little tale for you. I've got somewhere around two years, give or take, to think about my death. You just doubled up on that shit I put in you. You've got about thirty seconds. Use it wisely."

Crandall stopped smiling, grabbed his bag, stood, and walked toward the door. The syringe whizzed past his head and hit the wall.

Gibson screamed. His body sounded with a solid thud as it collapsed onto the floor.

"Damn," Crandall said as he passed through the door, "Wrong again. That was only about fifteen seconds."

***

Crandall finished carving *Julie* into the makeshift cross as the first small rays of sunrise began penetrating the fog. He cobbled together enough string along with Gibson's shoelaces to attach the cross to the creosote light pole. With his mother's rosary beads in hand he knelt before the cross, kissed the crucifix and bowed his head and prayed. Once finished, he started to rise, stopped and looked down at the beads. After a few seconds he was able to remove the Saint Michael medallion and put it in his pocket.

Crandall hung the crucifix over the homemade cross and straightened the beads so the cross hung down the middle. "I don't know if you are Catholic or not Julie, or what kind of personal hell brought you to this place. But, I believe mom would approve." He stood, crossed his hands in front of him. He felt a Bible verse would be appropriate though he knew very few by heart. So, he recited his favorite Old Testament passage, "'May the Lord bless you and keep you. May the Lord make his face to shine upon you, and be gracious unto you. May the Lord lift up his countenance upon you—and give you peace.' Rest in peace, Julie."

CHAPTER FORTY-EIGHT

Memphis

AFTER THE HOTEL MANAGER OPENED THE DOOR TO THE SUITE HE stood back. Detective Park Harris told the female detective, two uniforms, and the manager to wait in the hall. His large frame filled most of the door as he entered, his weapon drawn and wearing latex gloves. When he saw what appeared to be power cords from lamps scattered on the floor, along with the lamps and end tables out of place, he motioned Detective Shelia Lamb into the room. He instructed her to photograph everything, but not touch.

The bedroom door was slightly ajar. The door and bent frame showed definite forced entry from the outer room. Something or someone from the other room was grunting. After the photo of the damage was taken he motioned Shelia back, eased the door open and stepped in. "Jesus H Christ," he mumbled while he put his sidearm away. Against the outer wall City Commissioner Harold Blackmon lay bound and gagged, eyes begging for help. Straight ahead sat Alex Caruso. Cursory impression was at least four wounds, blood from head to knees down the shins onto the carpet and a plastic bag over his head. A point of curiosity was the hole in the front of the bag with blood spatter inside the bag. It was hard to see through the blood, but the mouth appeared agape. A trail of additional blood spatter on the carpet behind the chair pointed at the far wall where he saw a bullet hole.

"Shelia, get in here!"

Shelia Lamb stepped through the opening. Tall and lithe in appearance, her detective's shield hung about her neck on a cotton lanyard framed by a dark blue jacket worn over a light blue blouse neatly tucked into her comfortable jeans. Her small camera was carried in a white latex encased hand. She brushed her short black hair back with her free hand and whistled followed by, "Jesus Christ!"

"Exactly my sentiments," Harris replied. "Get several pictures of the commissioner but don't untie or whatever until I get back. I'll only be a minute."

He went back to the men waiting in the hall. After telling the hotel's morning manager to remain in his office and available, he emphasized that nothing was to be leaked to staff or press and all security tapes were to be secured.

After a few seconds the manager was out of earshot. Harris turned to the two uniformed patrolmen and barked out instructions, "Gus, I want you to stay here in the hall. Anyone gets off the elevator or comes out of the stairwell that you don't know, detain 'em. Don't let them off the floor or allow them to use any phones. Jay, I want you to go over to the DA's office. Discretely tell Assistant DA Harold Blackmon Junior his presence is required here at the hotel, but don't tell him why. If he balks, remind him that requested and required have two different meanings and he should have learned that in law school. If he still resists, cuff 'im. I'll get word to DA Wilson so don't take any crap. Put him in the back seat, I don't want him jumping out. Blue light it, but no siren. Get moving."

"Park," Shelia shouted from the bedroom, "I think the commissioner is cussing us out through the gag and he smells like he pissed himself."

Harris pulled out his cell phone, "Tell him to shut up, he's part of a crime scene. I'll be in there in a minute and let him loose. Put an outline of some sort where he's layin'. I've got to call the captain."

On the third ring the captain picked up, "Hi, Cap. Well, my source was correct. I need you to do a few things for me."

He started walking back to the bedroom as he listened.

"Yeah, as the proverbial doornail. First, get the morticians and evidence nerds over here. Second, we're going to need a couple of uniforms out to the old Agraco grain warehouse to secure it. And, we need a warrant for the Southern Belle ASAP. Also send a wagon to Saint Mary's. Have a couple of SWAT guys ride shotgun and tell them to wait until I get there and nobody leaves. I'll be ready for the press in about two hours. We won't be able to keep a lid on this one after the ME and crime scene folks get here. Oh yeah, see if you can get the Collierville Police to pick up Caruso's wife and bring her over here ASAP. I don't want her hearing rumors in the news before we talk to her."

Harris stopped in the doorway and stared at Caruso, nodding his head at the person on the other end of the phone call, "My best guess is this. Shot through each kneecap, then shot his penis off. After that a plastic bag was pulled over his head. Looks like the muzzle was stuffed in his mouth through the bag then the kill shot. Not sure about the sequence on the first three. This guy really wanted to inflict some pain first. And a lot of fear."

Harris paused a few seconds then laughed, "Not me, Cap. I'm sure the collection of detached appendages falls under the purview of the ME's office."

Harris put a pinky finger in his open ear canal and shook it back and forth satisfying an itch, "I agree, let's hope we don't get some turf war started when this hits the street. Plus, we've got a vigilante out there and, as much as some folks might admire his handy work, we need to reel his ass in before an innocent gets hurt. I'll keep you posted."

More grunting came from Commissioner Blackmon as he hung up, "Hold your water commissioner, I'm on my way and *you* got some '*splainin* to do."

Memphis

At Saint Bernadette's many of the residents were gathered in the recreation room waiting for *The Price is Right* to come on. Sister Mary Alice was talking to ninety-seven year old Al Connelly, the home's oldest resident. He was explaining to her that if he was just ten years younger he would take her dancing.

At the top of the hour dramatic music escaped from the TV's speakers and the local station announced breaking news. The studio news anchor handed off the report and the screen shifted to a reporter on the scene in front of *The Gaylord Hotel*. The young nun turned her attention toward the TV.

"Details are sketchy," the male reporter began, "But, police are reporting the body of alleged crime boss Alex Caruso was discovered in a suite on the top floor of the Gaylord Hotel this morning. Detective Park Harris would not comment at this time as to the cause of death or rumors about a second person found in the room alive, only that the body was positively identified as Alex Caruso. We will provide more details as they become available.

"Repeating—"

A scratchy voice drifted from the back of the room in what sounded like a loud whisper, "Alex Caruso is dead!"

Sister Mary Alice looked behind her and the person spoke again, their voice cracking and shaking, "Alex Caruso is dead!" A murmur of voices flowed across the room as heads turned. It was Krystyna Wisniewski.

Stunned at first, Mary Alice froze. Then the sister ran to the door and shouted down the hall, "Call Father Wisniewski and tell him to get over here immediately!"

She went to Krystyna who continued to stare at the TV, rocking forward and back with her hands clasped in front over her mouth, tears rolling down her cheeks.

CHAPTER FORTY-NINE

Off I-40 in Arkansas

IT WAS SEVERAL HOURS FROM MEMPHIS AND FIVE HOURS SLEEP later. Crandall sat in the cab of the truck. He stared through the bug spattered windshield at the other campers. Crandall had stopped at a campground off I-40 he used many times over the years on his hunting trips out west. It provided everything from hookups for motor homes to spaces for tents. The big thing was it had showers. He slept in the back of the truck under the camper shell, which reminded him he owed his father a sleeping bag and air mattress. His had been destroyed in the fire.

It had been the fitful sleep of a restless mind full of dreams he either did not remember or chose not to remember. Though he was no longer sleepy, he was not rested. Perhaps that would come tomorrow. For now he needed to be on the move. The sooner the better. Too long in one place and he would be discovered. Then Pyle and Gibson would escape justice.

The phone call just concluded with his father had filled him with many emotions. But, strangely, none of them were guilt. He guessed that came with the loss of one's conscience. Some things had happened in Georgia that could have been prevented had he been more diligent in the review of everything. None of that would have changed his actions once he saw Julie's execution. These men did not deserve to sit in prison the rest of their lives. They had earned their place in hell, and he would reward them. His name might legally be Jack Crandall, but Ted Reardon had been awakened.

First he had to square some things. He picked up his cell phone and placed the battery back in, looked up a number in his address book and pressed call.

Lawrenceville, Georgia

He had great respect for the medical profession. He was alive now because of it. But Paul Brennan had to figure he was one of the worst patients ever inflicted on these poor nurses. Three hours in surgery, another three in ICU. Now he was in his room not wanting to take his medication and wanting to know when he could go home. He was told it would be two more days—maybe. It depended on whether he developed any infections or they missed any glass or wood. His left hand might require an additional surgery. If the tendon they reattached healed properly he would be okay. Otherwise they would have to do some additional work on it. The recent phone calls didn't make him feel any better either.

The last round of medication had made him a little groggy so it took a couple of rings before he realized his cell phone was trying to get his attention. He picked it up. The caller ID said, "Jack Crandall".

Brennan sighed. He could answer or just ignore it. If he chose the latter, he knew he wouldn't sleep even with the meds. With the former the problem would be controlling his anger. He pressed the button and held it to his ear, "Hello, Jack."

"Hi, Paul, I just talked to my father."

"What a coincidence. I talked to him about thirty minutes ago. And, I just got off the phone with Detective Harris in Memphis. Seems you've been busy." Well, at least the meds didn't take away his sarcasm.

A tired voice responded, "I couldn't take it anymore. They were killing and raping kids. Fourteen and fifteen year old girls. These kids should be planning their prom night, not being forced to do the bidding of some perverted bastard then flushed away like toilet paper. You know my history. I was just kidding myself all those years I thought I was helping people."

Brennan sighed again and lay his head back on the pillow, "You were. But, you need to come home now so I can help you."

"It's too late for me."

Brennan tried to rub his forehead with his free hand. The splint and bandages reminded him that was a bad idea, he cussed under his breath. "We have a lead on the guy who burned you out and a last known address. We'll bring him in. Infanticide is a death penalty offense in Georgia."

The fatigue in Crandall's voice seemed to fade away, "What, and have him wait a couple of years to go to trial then spend—what— ten to twenty years on death row? I'll most likely be dead before he even stands trial. Worse yet, he cops a plea. No, I want to see Mickey Pyle's corpse."

Crandall was becoming more agitated, something Brennan didn't want to deal with at the moment. Though something Crandall said did grab his attention. "How do you know his name?"

"I have my methods. I don't think you would understand."

For the first time Brennan was becoming irritated, "It's not my job to understand, but I do. More than you know."

"And how is that?"

Maybe it was the drugs or maybe he was just tired of keeping stuff to himself but Brennan let go. "I've looked through a scope and sent a round down range. I've killed seventeen men with no emotion. I didn't lose a minute of sleep on any of them. But, I held a young Afghani boy in my arms while he bled to death. His crime was being friendly with Americans. A young kid just starting his life and those fuckers cut his throat. I didn't care one wit about those seventeen or the others I might have killed in combat. But, not a day goes by I don't see that boy's eyes staring at me, wanting to know why this happened to him. Don't tell me I don't understand. I understand too well. I'm also a cop. I like you, Jack. If I were in your shoes I'd probably want to do the same thing. But— it would still be vigilantism."

There was a pause, a silence. It made Brennan think Crandall may have hung up. After a few seconds the tired voice returned, "I didn't know you were a sniper."

Brennan's agitation began to evaporate, "You didn't need to. You only needed to know I was a cop. I'm team sniper and weapons specialist on a National Guard Special Forces A-Team that's been deployed twice."

"I'm sorry, Paul. I've misjudged you. But, just so you'll know, this Pyle was Special Forces."

"I heard that rumor, too, so I pulled his records. He didn't even make it through three weeks of basic training. He's a fake, a phony, a stinking wannabe." Brennan's bandaged splinted hand whirled in the air as he tried to strike at the invisible Mickey Pyle in front of him.

"That's just another reason to hate him. I need to go. I'll call back in a few days. I promise I'll turn myself in when this is over."

"Jack, I know this won't change your mind, but Sam Greggs is dead. Shot and burned out. Caruso was after both of you."

"Yeah, I'm not surprised. But the thing is Sam never had any family. He only cared about himself. Caruso enjoyed being the bully. Hurting the young, the innocent, the people you cared about more than life. That wouldn't work with Sam. He only cared about himself."

Brennan let out a deep sigh, "Jack, we have a last address on him. Let us bring him in."

"Look Paul, I'm sorry for what happened to you and I'll be eternally grateful for you saving Cindy. I feel responsible for what happened. But, I have to do this. You have a last known location, I have a known location. You know, you'd be surprised how liberating dying can be. What more can they do to me? I'm already under a death sentence with no option for appeal."

The phone fell into a sudden silence. Brennan brought up the number from his recent calls list and started to call back. After some indecisive staring he laid the phone on the bedside stand. He would dutifully report the conversation and see if they could locate the area it came from, though he was dubious it would help very much. There was a national BOLO out on Crandall and Pyle now. He wished Crandall Godspeed, pushed the nurse's call button, laid his head back on the pillow and stared at the ceiling.

CHAPTER FIFTY

New Mexico

As he drove south on route one-seventeen, Crandall began to understand the concept of Badlands. This was the High Desert he had heard so much about. It was nothing like northern Colorado where he would hunt elk. A landscape not totally barren, but uniquely formed from mounds of ancient lava flows wrinkled and folded into position before cooling, then carved by sand blown about for millions of years. Yet life adapted to this arid rocky environment and found its way into each crevice, with scrub brush and the occasional mesquite tree. Some had lost their leaves, leaving hundreds of grotesque crippled finger like branches. Hidden amongst this were the small mammals, snakes, and other animals that played the life game of predator and prey. Much like he was doing now.

He was south of the El Malpais National Monument and found himself intrigued that lava flows millions of years old still bore a strong resemblance to the fresh ones he had seen created by Kilauea in Hawaii.

Up ahead on the left appeared his destination, a hand-hewn chinked log structure that seemed a little out of place considering the many adobe style buildings he had seen. A porch ran the length of the front and wrapped around the sides, with steps in the middle. As he pulled into the dirt parking area, Crandall noticed a hand painted sign hanging from the porch railing. It simply stated, "Backcountry Supplies and Groceries." According to the internet search he made at the cyber café in Albuquerque, this was the only hiker store for about thirty miles. Dry dust bellowed into the air as he came to a stop facing the porch. There were no marked spaces, only a loose line of rocks indicating a stopping point.

Crandall put his feet on the ground and took a minute to stretch. He had been in the truck for the better part of the last twelve hours. It also gave him time to check his surroundings. There may not be any cars in the parking lot, but the police wouldn't exactly park a unit in plain sight. After stretching he rubbed his now five day growth of facial hair and continued to scan. He was beginning to look and feel a little rough. His hair was clean but unkempt and a bit longer than he was used to. The out of the way campgrounds he had stayed in the last two days had provided lukewarm showers but little else in comfort. His closest encounter with police had been a single vehicle parked in a fast food eatery when he was using the drive through and the occasional speed trap along the interstate. Crandall had decided he would not resist if caught. He was willing to go down swinging, but not with the police.

Only a single sedan and one pickup truck passed on the road. There seemed to be nothing out of place surrounding the store. Satisfied, but staying alert, he climbed the steps, crossed the porch, and stopped at the door where he noticed three peculiarities. To the right of the door was a doorbell with a sign that said, "Ring Bell After Hours." That was the first. The second was there was no sign stating the business hours. The third was a little comforting. In the middle of the door just below the glass panes was a round plaque with the Marine Corps emblem. *Friendly territory maybe.*

With no sign to indicate whether the store was open or closed Crandall turned the knob. The door eased inward to the sound of a small bell that hung on the frame and was shaken each time it was opened or closed like those in old west general stores. "Be with you in a moment," a gruff raspy invisible voice from some back room said. Crandall rubbed his left arm then leg. Both were twitching. The time between episodes was shrinking and the muscle cramps were becoming painful. He also wasn't sleeping well. He hoped it wasn't affecting his judgment.

Lawrenceville, Georgia

"I just wanted to say thank you," Cindy Fitzgerald said as she stood next to Brennan's bed. He was allowed to sit up now. Most of the monitoring devices had been turned off, though they were still checking his temperature, blood pressure, and incisions every three hours. The IV bags were gone but the catheter needles remained in place in case they needed to hook him up again. He had been cleared for discharge in the morning. The biggest problem he was having now was the itch from the tape that held the IV needles in place. You can't scratch your right arm with your right hand. The left was useless at the moment, so he resorted to using the whiskers on his chin.

Brennan looked into Cindy's sad eyes, the bandage still on her neck. She was wearing a yellow scrub top over jeans. In spite of her choice of dress and absence of makeup it was clear to him she could not hide her sensuality.

The hospital said for her to stay home as long as she needed. She told Brennan she was staying with a friend and just couldn't go home yet. But she planned to be back at work in a few days.

"You don't have to thank me, I was just—"

"Don't say you were doing your job—" she snapped—"you almost died."

Brennan continued to look into her eyes. The gentle features of her face hid the internal tenacity that stood up to Jennifer Grady and the man identified now as Will Moby. "You, too." Brennan sighed, "You've had a pretty rough time of it. How are you holding up?"

Cindy looked down and fiddled with the tissue in her hands then gripped the bed safety rail, "I'm trained to help people, not kill them." She paused and breathed in deep, "Whew, at the time I was—"

"Angry and scared," Brennan finished her sentence this time and groaned a little as he shifted his weight. "It's called survival instinct. The shrinks call it fight or flight. Mine tacks on surrender to the list. You can run, you can fight or, worse of all, you can surrender. If you hadn't pulled the trigger you might have been killed before I got there. I don't know if I would have been able to handle that. I should have seen this coming."

"No, Paul, whoever this Caruso is. He's to blame for all this."

Brennan opened his mouth to tell her about the events in Memphis, caught himself, suppressed the urge and pushed his head back against the pillow. He was unsure if she could handle it in her current emotional state. His thoughts wandered to the conversation he had with Jack Crandall. That would be withheld from her for a while longer also.

Cindy sniffed, rubbed her nose with the tissue then rested her hands on the rail again. "So. This shrink of yours. Any good? I might need to see one."

Brennan licked his dry lips, "She works for the department sometimes. Seems they want to send you to see her every time you break wind in front of a perp now days. I'm sure they already have me scheduled next week. I'll put in a good word for you, but don't call her a shrink. She's a PhD and says psychiatrists are the shrinks. Plus, my lieutenant is a psych major. I've been analyzed from every angle you can think of and they still let me carry a gun." He smiled and decided to not mention the mandatory sessions with the Army docs. Didn't want to seem like a total loon.

Cindy gripped and released the railing several times, looked up at the ceiling then back down. Her eyes were more on her fidgeting hands than him, "Uh—I hear they are going to let you go home tomorrow. I—um—was wondering—uh—you know—if you would allow me to buy you dinner." She made eye contact with him, "If you feel up to it that is."

Brennan reached over with his right hand and laid it on top of hers, "I'd be honored. But…," he held up his bandaged, immobilized left hand, "you might have to cut my meat."

Cindy let out a light laugh. She smiled. It was something Brennan had not seen from her the last couple of weeks since he met her. He decided she should do it more often. Cindy bent forward. Her lips lingered ever so slightly as she kissed Brennan on the forehead and smiled again, "I would be honored."

***

After a short nap, Brennan was watching TV. A brown haired man in coveralls was mopping the floor. As he finished up the door opened slowly and a tall, fit looking man in a suit and tie entered. The man with the mop pushed his bucket-on-wheels toward the door. As the two men passed they gave a nod of recognition.

The man in the suit approached Brennan's bed. He offered his hand, "Mr. Brennan, my name is Karl Oakley."

Brennan studied the man's face. A square jaw line, deep set green eyes, and a nose that appeared to have been broken more than once was topped off by dark, close-cropped hair. He seemed uncomfortable in his suit. There was something more to the eyes than just being deep set. Windows to the soul they say. This was a man who had seen things. Brennan offered his right hand and received a firm handshake.

"Well," Brennan began, "you don't seem to be from the hospital. I don't take you for a lawyer or doctor, so why are you here?"

Oakley smiled, "To the point. I like that. I'm here to ask if you would like to come work for your country?"

Brennan narrowed his eyes and cocked his head to one side, "I already do."

"I mean full time."

"That's what I meant. You know, 'Serve and Protect', that's what we cops do. Or is the county not part of the country?"

Again Oakley smiled, "Touché. Let's just say you have some special talents we could use."

Brennan leaned back in the bed and raised the back to a more upright position. "And what alphabet department do you work for?"

Oakley retrieved his wallet from the inside pocket of his jacket. He fished out a business card and held it out.

Brennan took the card, turned it over and studied the back, "Huh!"

CHAPTER FIFTY-ONE

New Mexico

Mickey Pyle stopped the Jeep Grand Cherokee in front of the old miner's cabin and opened the door. He waved away the dust that drifted into the vehicle, stood and reached into the back to retrieve his black long-rider coat from the rear seat. After putting it on, he smoothed it out and grabbed two packages from the front passenger seat.

The shack was a very lean structure. Three rooms, well water, a wood burning stove, and an outhouse. There was power to run the well pump and a few lights. Two kerosene lamps were kept for backup. With the latest inflow of cash it would be a short stay, unlike the year he froze his ass off after killing that state cop in Illinois. He had figured the best way not to get caught was to go somewhere out of the way and sit still for a while.

He climbed the single step. The boards creaked under his weight as he made his way to the door. The old knob had to be jiggled back and forth a few times before it would release for opening. Pyle stepped inside. The hinges gave a mighty squeak as he closed it.

Corey Gibson was heating some food on the wood burning stove that served as cook top and heat for the cabin. What dishes, eating and cooking utensils they used were stacked neatly on the sideboard next to the sink. Three wooden chairs and a card table provided all the furniture. Some fold up cots made sleeping up to four folks possible. Pyle looked up at the pitched roof with open rafters crisscrossed for support.

Pyle placed the packages on the table. He started taking his coat off. "You're going to make someone a fine wife one day, Corey."

Gibson continued to stir the pot. "I just like things neat and tidy." He lifted his head and looked at Pyle. "I hope that's the money 'cause I heard something bad today."

Pyle stopped with his long rider coat half off. "What the hell do you mean 'something bad'?"

Gibson took a spoonful of the stew he was heating and blew on it, "I was listening to the radio. The national news was updating some story from Memphis. Alex Caruso was killed."

Pyle finished removing his coat, smoothed it out and laid it across one of the chairs. "Damn, killed? You sure about that?"

Gibson tasted the stew and swallowed. "Alex Caruso, Memphis crime boss, killed. Pretty much only one of them."

"How did it happen?"

"Don't know just yet. I called my brother Ed, no answer so I left a message."

Pyle grabbed the back of the chair. "Goddamn it, I told you not to call from here. They can triangulate your location. Sometimes you can be so stupid."

"Hey, nobody knows—"

"Shut up! I don't give a shit what anybody knows or doesn't know. We'll talk about this later. Now, listen. We're getting out of here tomorrow anyway. Our compadre in Vegas is setting up a place for us. He'll have it ready when we get there. We got enough to have a really good time for a year or more."

Gibson put the spoon in the sink, "Okay, Mick, but I'm not stupid."

"Then quit acting like you are. You're one of the best guys with a blade I've ever known. But, sometimes you just don't think."

***

All he could make out at this distance through his binoculars, from beneath his carefully camouflaged ghillie suit, were two shadowy figures moving about inside the shack in dim light. Grayish smoke against the night sky rose from a stove pipe that jutted out of the south wall then turned upward at a ninety degree angle. It reminded him of that night this all started. The smoke that rose from what remained of his house. The night his granddaughter died. The night Mickey Pyle entered his life and his world fell apart, again. Crandall put his binoculars away and slowly inched backward until it was safe to remove the ghillie suit and stand.

He would try and get a better look closer to sunrise. It would be easy to take them out at five hundred meters. However, with the slim chance these weren't the guys he was looking for, he had to know for sure. For now, Crandall would turn in and hope the information the old Marine at the store gave him was correct. There was also a lot of trust placed in a man he only knew for thirty minutes.

They swapped a few war stories. The guy was with the *Dark Horse*, Third Battalion, Fifth Marine Regiment in Vietnam during the Tet Offensive in '68. He survived the *Battle of Hué*.

Crandall didn't know if the guy bought his story about being a bounty hunter searching for a bail-jumping Pyle or not. He didn't seem to care much one way or the other. It was evident he wasn't real fond of the guy. Wasn't surprised to learn Pyle was a fake wannabe. Said he had a first cousin who was Special Forces in Vietnam, *Snake Eater*, as he called him. It all made Crandall wish he had a couple of days to just sit on the porch and talk to the man. One way or the other, at least there would be no more looking over his shoulder after tomorrow.

The truck was hidden about five kilometers away. It had been a long hike after a long day. Crandall crawled into his sleeping bag and slipped his rifle inside the bag to protect it from the cold and sand. He settled onto his back and stared up at the cosmos. With no city lights and a late rising crescent moon, millions of stars covered the sky, looking like a river of lights. It was nights like this that made him feel alone, insignificant in the universe yet comforted in how it reinforced his belief all this was not an accident.

***

Jack Crandall zipped his jacket and turned up the collar against the cold wind. He rubbed his nose, then his eyes and stifled a yawn. It had been another fitful night's sleep. Clarity of thought seemed a little more difficult.

The first indications of sunrise made itself known in the distance. A cold dry air surrounded him. It stood in stark contrast to the thick fog and damp chill he left behind in Memphis. The occupants in the shack were still awake when he bedded down. He was banking on them being late sleepers, but he still had to keep his wits about him. Though it should make no difference, the cold seemed to be amplifying the disease's effect on his muscles.

He was crouched behind the Jeep, his left leg throbbed and cramped. Crandall cupped his hands together, blew a warming breath into his palms and peered inside the vehicle through the rear window in the lift gate. Other than a fair amount of plastic bags in the cargo area filled with assorted clothing, there wasn't much to provide an ID for these guys. *Poor man's designer luggage.* There were a few boxes in the back seat. Crandall decided to work his way around to the side of the Jeep shielded from the front door.

A shaking left hand tested the handle on the rear passenger side door. It was unlocked. He eased the door open and slid the closest box toward him. As he rummaged around he found his first clue, a box of .32 caliber ammunition. *David was killed with a .32,* he thought as he stared at the box.

"Hey, what the hell are you doing!" A voice shouted.

Crandall reached for his .45, but it was inside his zipped up jacket. *Damn!* He lifted his head enough to see a shadowy figure standing at the corner of the shack. He made a decision to run for it and try to reach his campsite.

He sprang away and tried to come upright while he began to run, but could not gain his balance. Each step with his left leg sent shockwaves of pain from heel to hip. After about fifteen yards he stumbled and dropped to his hands and knees. Crandall could hear footsteps closing in. He struggled to try and get to his feet and crawl away at the same time. His breathing was becoming more rapid as he strained to move. The first kick caught him in the ribs. He turned to try and grab his attacker's legs, but a second kick caught him in the same spot.

Crandall rolled over onto his side and looked up. It was the man who drove up in the Jeep. A smallish pistol was pointed at his head.

"Just who the fuck are you?" the man asked. Crandall said nothing. He realized he had found Mickey Pyle, or perhaps Mickey Pyle had found him.

CHAPTER FIFTY-TWO

New Mexico

You've got yourself into quite a fix, Crandall thought as his feet dangled several inches from the floor. All the stress of the past two weeks had increased the intensity of his episodes. The timing of them had been a little friendlier until today. He glanced upward at a rope that was hung across the largest rafter and tied to both his wrists. Crandall studied them for a bit. His pistol was lying on the small table next to his mother's Saint Michael. The rifle and ammunition he had hidden about two-hundred meters away weren't doing him much good at the moment. The pressure on the rib cage from his body weight pulling down caused a fair amount of discomfort from the kicks he received. Then there was the kick to his head when he couldn't get up fast enough.

It wasn't all bad news. The spasms in his leg had stopped, though it still felt a little weak. The left arm was still giving him a bit of trouble. A strange beast, this disease. Comes and goes. Sometimes just the arm, sometimes just the leg, sometimes both, eventually his whole body until nothing worked. When first diagnosed, Crandall planned to ride it out, enjoy what time he had left, and die in his bed at home. Now, he was wondering if he would survive the next five minutes.

Pyle stood facing him, something of a smirk on his face, "One more time, asshole, who are you? You got no ID on you for a reason so your little story about being a lost hiker is full of shit."

Crandall felt stupid. He made a big mistake. There had always been the chance he could get caught or seen, but not being able to get to his weapon was inexcusable. After all, his right arm was working fine, thank you very much. He had allowed himself to succumb to the cold, fatigue, and pain.

It was time to try a different direction. He took in a deep breath and winced, "So, you really don't know who I am. Funny, I know who you are. You're Mickey Pyle. Your lackey over there is Corey Gibson. You did some work recently for Alex Caruso." Crandall began to swing a little, front and back, then side to side to try and relieve some of the pressure.

Gibson was standing to Pyle's left, and he started to speak. "Shhhhh." Pyle hissed and held up his left hand in Gibson's face while he looked Crandall in the eyes. "So, just how did you come to know all this?"

"Yeah," Gibson interrupted. "I heard Caruso's dead."

Pyle shot Gibson a scowled glance then turned his attention back to Crandall. He pointed his finger in Crandall's face and started to speak.

Before Pyle could get his words out, Crandall tilted his head back, laughed, and looked at Gibson. Then with the best mocking tone he could muster, "Oh, I know that. I'm the guy who killed him."

Pyle balled up a fist and hit Crandall in the ribs where he kicked him earlier. Crandall sucked in his breath and grimaced. He coughed, "Phew—good right hand, but don't wear yourself out. Just ask me something."

Pyle drew his fist back again, "Why should I believe you?"

Crandall continued to swing side to side with ever so slight motions to try and keep his circulation moving. He gave a slight smile, "I know you're going to kill me. So why should I go through all the torture stuff first? I'm not that macho."

Pyle put his fist down, "Okay then. Why are you looking for us?"

Crandall stopped smiling. "For starters, you beat up my pregnant daughter-in-law. It killed the baby. You burned my house down and killed my daughter's boyfriend. Corey here cut my daughter's face up. That enough reasons for you?"

Gibson sucked in a quick breath, "You're Ted Reardon."

Crandall's mockery returned, "Ah, my reputation precedes me."

Gibson stepped forward and took a shot that hit Crandall in the ribs, "You killed my Uncle. Len Patrone."

Crandall coughed again, grimaced and cleared his throat, "Not bad. Try someplace else next time, the ribs are getting a little sore. So, you're Patrone's nephew. Cowardice runs in your family, I see."

Gibson punched him again, "What the hell does that mean?"

Pyle pulled Gibson back, "Shut the fuck up!" He looked at Crandall, "For a guy who says he's not macho, you sure like to piss people off."

Crandall flexed his knees up and down slightly, "Reflex action. You know, engage mouth before the brain. I can't seem to help myself." He turned his attention to Gibson, "Your uncle was a coward. He liked to shoot defenseless women in the head. Plus, how do you think I found you? Your brother Ed told me. Sang like the fat lady at the end of an opera."

Gibson stepped forward again. Pyle restrained him.

"Ah, let him have some fun. You see, his brother gave you guys up because he thought I'd let him live. I didn't. Oh yeah, Tony Oliveri, too."

"You're lying!" Gibson landed a solid punch to the face this time, catching the bridge of the nose and left eye. Crandall anticipated and turned his head to lessen the blow. He refused to shake his head though; *never let them see you sweat.* That didn't stop the bodily fluid that trickled from his nose onto his upper lip. He couldn't see it, but it had the odor of blood.

"Then call him. He won't answer. That's not all."

Pyle pulled a chair from the table, turned it around and sat down, crossing his arms across the back. He motioned Gibson to do the same. Gibson, instead, picked up the .45.

"Put the gun down, this is interesting," Pyle grinned.

"Yeah, Corey, cause I got the best for last." Crandall added then continued, "Your buddy here probably told you he was a big time Green Beret." Crandall turned his attention to Pyle and slowed the pace of his words with a mocking sarcastic tone, "He's just a fucking wannabe. Couldn't even handle three weeks of boot camp. Army calls it basic training. Everything he's told you is a lie."

Pyle's grin disappeared, "And, just how would you know something like that?"

"Friends in low places. Huh, you couldn't carry a Green Beret's jockstrap. But don't worry your pretty little heads. Nobody knows where I am. I wanted you guys all to myself."

Pyle chuckled, shook his head and leaned back holding onto the top of the chair back, "I suppose you got us right where you want us, and I guess that's why you carry the Saint Michael. Consider yourself an avenging angel."

"Something like that. But, I'm nooo angel," Crandall grimaced a bit with each breath.

The two men continued a staring contest, Pyle broke first, "Looks like you lose, friend. I guess it was just unlucky for you that I had to take a piss that early. We don't have indoor plumbing." Pyle turned to Gibson, "He's full of shit. I've got to go to town for a couple of hours. Come with me to the car." He shoved the chairs out of reach of Crandall, picked up his coat draped over the back of the chair, and walked toward the door. Gibson followed, carrying the pistol.

When the door closed Crandall could hear some muffled talking that faded away. Through the window he could see both men walking toward the vehicle. He looked up at the rafter again and flexed his knees some more, "Time to see if those million or so sit ups I've done were worth it."

***

"Listen up and pay attention," Pyle began as Gibson closed the door. They continued to walk toward the car. Pyle pulled his coat around tight to shield him from the wind. "I'm going to town to gas up and get some stuff for the trip. I'll scout around and see if anyone knows this Reardon asshole. I'll be back in a couple of hours. I want that bastard dead. Dig a deep hole for him so the coyotes don't find him, but don't cover him. I want to see the body before we finish burying him." He turned and pointed his finger in Gibson's face, "Got that?"

Gibson recoiled from the finger, looked around, and shivered. His longish hair tossed about in the breeze. He tucked the pistol in his waistband, stuck his hands in his pockets and hunched up his shoulders. "Sure, Mick, but can I cut on him first? Fucker killed Ed."

Pyle opened the door of the Jeep, "Yeah, whatever. Have some fun, but clean up the mess and don't take too long. The ground is starting to get hard and I want that grave done before I get back. We bury his ass and head out."

Pyle slipped behind the wheel as Gibson walked back to the shack. He cranked the car, turned around and drove off in a trail of dust. He allowed a wry laugh and spoke to his reflection in the rear view mirror, "Poor dumb bastard's digging his own grave."

***

Gibson reached the door and pushed it open while Pyle drove away. As he crossed the threshold, the door swung back hard. It pushed him to the side and he lost his balance. A rope flashed in front of his eyes. He was jerked backward as the rope closed around his neck, cutting off his air. He grabbed at the rope but something hit him in the back of his legs, forcing him down to the floor on his knees. Gibson tried to understand what was happening to him, but nothing made sense. He wheezed and fought for air while he thrashed about. Something touched the side of his head. He felt a hot breath against his ear as a voice whispered, "Next time you hang someone from the rafters don't use square knots." Gibson was jerked backwards off his knees and landed hard on his butt. He fought against the rope with both hands as he was drug across the floor. Saliva spilled out of his mouth and ran down his chin. The planks in the floor sounded and vibrated the whole shack as he pounded his feet against them trying to free himself. Small plumes of dust jumped from the floor. His vision became blurred. First the windows, then the door, then the table flashed in front of him as he was twisted about. He bent his neck back to see Crandall's face glowing with an insane, maniacal grin, "Don't die on me, I'm not finished with you yet."

CHAPTER FIFTY-THREE

New Mexico

"I hope the little shit has finished digging the hole. If not, he's going to be left to the buzzards and coyotes. I won't need to come back to this place," Pyle mumbled to the passing breeze as he exited his car. He smoothed out his coat, stuffed both hands in his pockets and strode to the shack. When he reached the door, he pushed it open and froze. His hand felt stuck to the doorknob, his legs wouldn't move. His eyes were locked on Gibson. Hung from the rafter in direct line with the door, the man's chin rested on his chest. Dried blood covered Gibson's cheeks and down the front of his shirt. A pool of dried blood stained the floor. There was a hole in Gibson's head where his left eye used to be. He looked at the table, the pistol was missing.

Pyle's right hamstring burned as if it had been set on fire. His leg was pushed forward and the front of his thigh exploded, pushing a stream of blood into the room as he collapsed. A shot echoed in his ears.

His breaths came quick and rapid, and he became tangled in his coat as he tried to pull himself inside the shack. He grimaced, whimpered and cried from the pain and effort with each inch as he reached out and clawed his way forward. When his legs cleared the opening, Pyle stretched with his arm and slapped at the door in an attempt to close it. The door came to a sudden stop just before it closed and flew back open. Pyle rolled onto his back. A shadowy man was standing in the doorway, haloed by the bright daylight behind him, a rifle in one hand. He supported himself with a long staff gripped by the other hand. Pyle threw up his hands in front of his face and turned his head, "Don't shoot—don't shoot!"

***

"I've got to admit for a guy with only one good leg, you put up a decent fight. It took a lot of work to get you tied properly.

Sorry about that knot on your forehead. But, lucky for me I missed the femoral artery or you'd be dead already," Crandall said as he kneeled next to Pyle, one knee on the ground, his hand on the man's chest. Crandall had Pyle bound and staked to the ground beside the rear driver's side wheel of the Jeep, head between the wheel and bumper. Pyle's eyes and mouth were covered with tape.

"Your friend inside was a little easier, but he was only semi-conscious when I strung him up. Oh, he was fully awake when I started cutting. He gave a full confession."

Crandall reached over and snatched the tape off Pyle's eyes. A muffled scream of pain came from behind the tape across Pyle's mouth. Crandall looked at the adhesive side of the tape. Most of one of Pyle's eyebrows was stuck to it. He tossed it aside. "Confession is good for the soul, don't you think?" Crandall asked while he checked all the bindings and knots.

Pyle shook his head back and forth and grunted through his taped mouth.

"I have an idea, blink once for no and twice for yes." Crandall said. "That's what I'm going to be doing in a year or two."

Crandall shifted to both knees and stretched across Pyle's chest to the edge of the vehicle. He bent down and peered underneath. As he straightened up he grabbed the discarded tape and pressed it low onto the fender behind the wheel well.

He turned back to Pyle. "Are you a praying man? I pray on occasion. I prayed I would find you. So, I guess sometimes prayers are answered."

Pyle twisted and strained against the ropes.

"No need to waste all that effort. I'm much better at knot tying than you guys. Maybe you should have tried the Boy Scouts. Although they'd probably have kicked you out, too."

Pyle lifted his head and grunted.

"Okay, okay," Crandall snatched the tape from Pyle's mouth. Pyle yelped and tried to spit at Crandall.

"One more time, are you a praying man?"

"Fuck you."

"I guess that's a no. Too bad." Crandall pressed the tape back in place.

Crandall struggled just a bit to stand, it reminded him he hadn't taken his meds today and he was in need of some rest.

He retrieved the kerosene lamp from the hood of the car and returned to Pyle's side. "You know I'm sure glad I saw this in your house. I was wondering how I was going to handle this." Crandall took the globe off and dropped it on the ground. He lifted his foot and smashed it with the heel of his boot. "Mazel tov." He glanced down and smiled, "Means good luck in Hebrew. You're going to need it." Crandall screwed the top off the lamp reservoir and emptied the contents on Pyle while he squirmed. A high pitched muffled scream escaped from his throat. Crandall leaned down and removed the tape again.

"What the hell are you doing? Are you insane?!" Pyle shouted as he gasped for breath.

"No more than you. You really should reconsider that praying thing. You know—forgiveness and all that." Crandall turned away. Pyle was screaming and cussing him, but he had tuned the man out. He picked up his rifle and walking stick that had been leaning against the driver's door. He hung the rifle over his shoulder with the sling. He turned back to Pyle one last time, a wicked smile on his face.

"You like movies, Mick? I do. I like science fiction. They kind of help you escape, forget your troubles for a little while. You see, there's an old Klingon proverb, 'Revenge is a dish best served cold.'" Crandall stopped smiling. "In your case I think I'll make an exception."

With the aid of his walking stick Crandall limped away. At about fifty meters he stopped. Pyle was still screaming and thrashing. He pulled the bolt back, loading a round into the chamber. With extra careful aim he put the cross hairs on the patch of tape. His left hand was shaking just a bit, but that was alright. That was his trigger hand. His right hand was steady as a rock under the fore-stock. In other circumstances he would take the shot prone. But, this was only fifty meters and he needed the angle.

The first round went through the center of the tape, dirt kicked up under the car. Nothing happened. The second round was a little higher. Liquid began pouring from the fuel tank. The third round was into the tire. The gasoline poured faster as the tire flattened.

Fuel flowed out and soaked the ground around Pyle. In the bright sunlight he could see the fumes rising into the dry air. A light odor of gasoline penetrated his nostrils. If he had placed him right, Pyle's clothes would be absorbing a good bit of the volatile liquid.

Crandall reached into his jacket pocket and pulled out a blue tipped .308 incendiary cartridge. He blew gently onto the tip and placed the round into the receiver then closed the bolt. Before placing the rifle butt against his shoulder he paused to listen to Pyle.

"No, God no, please don't."

"I guess that qualifies," he said peering through the scope. "But, I don't think it's going to help."

The incendiary round struck the fender. Sparks flew. The air ignited in a loud whoosh as the fumes flashed. Pyle screamed and bucked against his restraints. The flames engulfed first the top half of his body then worked their way down to the lower half. His convulsions peeked, began to slow then stopped after about a minute or so. The pyre continued. Then the remaining fuel reached its flash point, and the back of the Jeep erupted into a ball of flames.

Crandall stood transfixed and stared at the spectacle. After several minutes frozen in place, he dropped his rifle on the ground. "The buzzards and coyotes can fight over what's left," he mumbled to the air. His shoulders slumped. He picked up the long stick and limped off to the east toward his campsite, then on to the truck.

CHAPTER FIFTY-FOUR

Texas

THE SKY ON THE HORIZON MADE A SLOW TURN FROM BLACK TO layered shades of purple with a thin orange-ish haze where sky meets earth as the sun began its climb in the east. Jack Crandall checked the clock in the dashboard, then the odometer. After he had reached the truck, Crandall slept better and longer than he had in weeks. But now it had been just over twenty-six hours and 1,300 miles since that last sleep. The cool, still, morning air rushed in through the open window of his truck as it sped east on I-10. The mock breeze that flowed across his face rustled the salt and pepper hair just touching the top of his ears. It helped him to stay awake. He noticed in the mirror that his hair was fast becoming more salt than pepper.

A light mist that hung in the air gave ghost-like appearances to the earliest morning commuters and long haul truckers who were his only company. The occasional rattle of loose change in the ash tray, droning tires on pavement, muffled engines, and his radio were the only sounds.

He smiled. The two minute newscast at the top of the hour reported that a convenience store owner and worker in San Antonio were arrested overnight in connection with the kidnapping of Elsa Franklin. They were alleged to be part of a human sex trafficking ring.

Crandall rubbed his eyes and the bridge of his nose with his thumb and middle finger then reached for his sun glasses in the cup holder on the transmission hump. He took note of the ever increasing pile of food wrappers and coffee cups on the floorboard in front of the passenger's seat. Each layer marked his progress home. At the next rest stop he needed to clean it out. The smell of stale coffee and burgers was no longer expunged by rolling the window down.

He slid on his sunglasses then turned up the volume on the radio. Crandall found it humorous and ironic since he had just passed exit 674 for Highway 77. The local station was now playing *La Grange* by *ZZ Top*. A short drive up 77 *was* the town of La Grange. Maybe it was the sleep deprivation, but he laughed at the thought of one of his favorite rock songs being about a brothel. "*They gotta lotta nice girls, ah*", he sang along while the lyrics jumped from the speakers. He even wondered how many teenage boys from around Houston slipped up to the *Chicken Ranch* over the years. Then he thought of Caruso and all the young girls he raped and murdered over the years. His smile disappeared.

The sun was now about a quarter of the way up and started to burn the mist away while the first signs of Houston showed in the distance. *Time for a sit-down breakfast on a plate, several more cups of coffee, and a stretch of the legs,* he thought. *Denny's, Waffle House, Cracker Barrel, whichever comes first.* With one hand he removed his cap, scratched his head, replaced the cap then rubbed the six day old beard on his chin and cheek. It was more an exercise in staying awake than some annoying itch.

A few naps at the rest stops and more coffee should keep him going another twenty-four hours or so. *Mmm, I wonder if there is a legal limit for caffeine consumption. Do they have a breathalyzer test for that? Hope my kidneys and bladder hold out.* His mind drifted from one random thought to another.

Crandall pulled his sunglasses down to the tip of his nose and took a peek in the rearview mirror. The bruising around his left eye was already looking better, along with the swelling of his nose. He didn't think it was broken, but he did figure he had two cracked ribs on his left. One thing he was certain of— they sure knew how to give a first-class beating.

He could take it easy now though, and just be one of thousands of silver compact pickup trucks on the highway. It was about another eight-hundred miles to home. Crandall would have saved those eight-hundred miles had he made the return trip via I-40 out of Albuquerque, but this was more like driving in a circle. Much like his life as of late. Back in Gwinnett he would find Detective Sergeant Brennan, turn himself in then tell the Sergeant where the bodies could be found. He would also let him know Mickey Pyle was a praying man—when he had to be.

Three Weeks Later

The church van from Saint Mary's coasted to a stop in front of the Salvation Army's shelter in Lebanon, Tennessee. Father Wisniewski peered through the windshield at the clear, bright, cloudless blue skies and the contrast it offered to that night he last saw Ted Reardon disappear, swallowed by a thick fog as Ted drove away. Much happened that night and the days that followed. Blood was spilled, lives taken, lives rescued. His sister had been returned from behind the shield that had been her silence. He prayed that Ted could now be freed from his demons. Though he had no direct hand, he did facilitate the deaths. That fact had built a wall of tension between him and Father Espinoza. A wall he was unsure could be breached.

Father Espinoza exited the passenger side, opened the side door, slid it to the rear and locked it in place with a heavy metallic snap. Ramona had become the leader of the group. She stepped down first with help from Espinoza. She, in turn, helped the other young girls from the van. A cool breeze ruffled the girls' hair and they clutched their jackets close about their bodies in response to the chill.

Father Wisniewski made his way around the rear of the van from the driver's side. As he looked toward the front of the building, a man who appeared to be in his mid-forties and a woman a few years younger dressed in Salvation Army uniforms approached the group assembled by the curb.

"Major Wilson" the man said as he offered his hand first to Father Espinoza then Wisniewski. The lady accompanying Wilson also offered her hand then began conversing with the girls in Spanish.

While the Catholic Church had many acceptable shelters to take the girls, Wisniewski convinced the Memphis Police and the Parish Bishop that the Salvation Army was uniquely qualified to care for these girls and reunite them with their families. Wisniewski handed a brown letter sized envelope to Wilson that contained the girls' personal information. Father Espinoza had contacted the families shortly after their rescue. He was finally able to make that call and tell them that their daughters were safe and would be returning to Mexico soon. The call he had always wanted to make during his time in Guatemala. Everything had taken a few weeks, what with all the police interviews and such. ICE and FBI agents were brought in to gather as much information on the trafficking ring as possible from these unwitting eyewitnesses.

The two priests turned down an offer to tour the facility. Tears of sadness and joy were shared as the girls hugged each cleric. The men watched while the group made its way to the door of the shelter. When they reached the door, Ramona turned and waved then wiped more tears from her eyes.

With the two priests back in the van, Father Wisniewski reached for the key in the ignition. Espinoza reached out, grasped Wisniewski's shoulder and broke the uncomfortable silence. "Jozef, I cannot approve of what you did, but I can approve of your motives."

Wisniewski turned to his friend and clasped the man's hand. His thoughts now emerging from their melancholy, he allowed himself a smile. "For me, that is enough and it may well be my epitaph. It seems my methods do not always align themselves with church doctrine. It matters little what good came from it, the church does not need another scandal. Leaving the priesthood is for the best, though I will miss it."

As they pulled away from the curb, Father Wisniewski looked at his watch. Elsa Franklin and her parents would be landing at the San Antonio Airport shortly. He thought of the courage she showed in fighting back and protecting Carmella, not knowing help was on the other side of the door. She could have been beaten or killed. *A young girl brave beyond her years*, he thought then smiled.

CHAPTER FIFTY-FIVE

Thirty-Eight Months Later

IT'S STRANGE HOW SOME THINGS WORK OUT, TED REARDON WAS thinking when a cold blast of winter air rushed across his face. As much as he wanted to smile, his muscles no longer responded to his mental commands. John Reardon straightened the blanket on his son's lap and adjusted the headrest on the wheelchair so he could get a better look at the trees, bending and swaying in back of his house as they responded to the same cold breeze. His house was rebuilt with modifications to accommodate his deteriorating condition. Changes included a deck across the rear of the home. His father sold the house in Memphis and moved to Georgia to care for him. John also moved his beloved Margret to an assisted living facility near the home. Sadly, she died from a heart attack a year later.

The collective jurisdictions came to a compromise and quietly shelved all indictments against Ted in consideration of the medical situation. It had something to do with circumstances and sympathetic jurors. Stan Allen, Dave Maxson and Fred Hartley all received life without parole. Jennifer Grady was the curious surprise. She confessed to all the patients she killed. Then she demanded extradition to a state that insured she would be put to death. Utah stepped up first and she was now on death row, refusing to appeal. Corey Gibson had given up Leon Allred before he died. He was currently in Texas State Prison in Huntsville, Texas.

Ted was at last content. Most of Lisa's physical scars were gone or less noticeable. It was the unseen scars that took the most time. That healing process continued, though she laughed a lot more now. Mark and Andrea celebrated his recent promotion to Captain. He may have been happiest for Cindy. She was awaiting the birth of her first child. Ted had even survived a year longer than doctors predicted and everyone was gathering to celebrate his birthday, though he knew it was more because there was precious little time remaining. It was times like these the memories of Jane would preoccupy his thoughts.

Ted rolled all these thoughts and visions through his mind as his father fussed about. He heard the door open and the fall of footsteps. From the pace and lightness of it he knew it was Jozef.

"John, do you mind if I have a private moment with Ted?"

"Not at all," John said, "But, I want to warn you he's really belligerent today."

Ted laughed in his mind. That was the way he wanted it. He told his father to not pity him as time went on. His father told him not to worry about that.

Once John Reardon had left, Wisniewski stood in front of Ted and leaned backward against the railing of the deck. He held an envelope that had been opened.

"John gave me this when I arrived. Said you wrote it almost two years ago and sealed it and I was to read it in private. He doesn't know what's in it. Is that true?"

Reardon blinked twice to indicate a "Yes".

"You suspected all along?"

"Yes," he blinked.

Wisniewski put the letter in his inside jacket pocket, rubbed his hands together and placed them on the rail. "It's true. I went to see Ellison, the PI, the same night John did. I got there first. I wanted to use my priestly ways and appeal to his better nature. It seems he didn't have one. He was turning over everything to Caruso, pulled a gun, and told me to leave. I got mad, there was a struggle. It got out of control,3 and I broke his neck. I didn't mean to kill him. It was an accident."

Wisniewski sighed, took a deep breath and continued. "He didn't go right away. I listened to him die while I looked for your file. I even administered Last Rites. I cleaned off his gun and dumped it in the sewer. It was me who dropped the package with the file at John's door. I've never told Angela about this. Perhaps I should. Perhaps she knows, but is leaving it to me. Maybe I should turn myself in."

Wisniewski stepped forward and placed both hands on Reardon's shoulders. He leaned over, getting face to face. His voice began breaking while tears formed in the corner of his eyes, "I'm glad,

Ted. Glad this is finally out and someone else knows. I'm glad it's you. I should have told you sooner. All these years you have felt you were some beast from hell. But, you protected your family. It is I who went against his teachings, who trampled on all his vows, who questioned God. All in the name of hate. I deserve this burden, this guilt and whatever punishment awaits. But, I'm glad someone else knows."

Wisniewski looked down at the Saint Michael medal that hung around Ted's neck. He lifted it slightly and fingered it. "Truly you were a warrior protected. Do not worry. Saint Michael can use a man like you."

The door cracked open. Wisniewski glanced over then looked back. "I'll be inside." He smiled.

Once again footsteps faded and footsteps approached. It was his father. Ted heard him say, "Shhhhh."

"Hey, Ted, Mark and Andrea are here, so we can start your birthday party soon. But, first someone wants to say hi."

Ted Reardon felt a tap on his knee. He cast his eyes downward. A dark haired, dark eyed toddler looked up at him. Nineteen month old Margret Jane Reardon grinned and bounced up and down. "Poppy, Poppy," she squealed and giggled.

Inside, Ted Reardon was smiling.

HARMON SNIPES

HARMON SNIPES was born and raised in the 1950s and 60s in Mobile, Alabama. His father was a career police officer who rose to the rank of Captain and head of the Detective Bureau. In 1970 he was drafted into the United States Army and decided to volunteer for Special Forces.

Over the next six years he spent time on two Special Forces A-Teams which included a stint in Southeast Asia. After discharge he attended the University of South Alabama receiving a B.S. Degree in Computer Science.

He began writing in earnest in 2002 and volunteered to facilitate a writers group at the local Barnes and Noble. His time in the writers group allowed him to interface with several authors. The best advice he received about writing was from a best-selling author at a book signing who said, "write what you enjoy otherwise it's work."

Harmon has lived and worked in Norcross, Georgia for the past twenty-five years. He is married and has two children and two grandchildren. He enjoys college football, making home brewed beer and playing with his grandsons.

CPSIA information can be obtained at www.ICGtesting.com
Printed in the USA
LVOW080444060513

332403LV00004B/4/P